WINNING BID

HIGHEST BIDDER
BOOK 3

CHARLOTTE BYRD

Charlotte Byrd

BYRD BOOKS

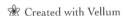 Created with Vellum

PRAISE FOR CHARLOTTE BYRD

"Twisted, gripping story full of heat, tension and action. Once again we are caught up in this phenomenal , dark passionate love story that is full of mystery, secrets, suspense and intrigue that continues to keep you on edge!" (Goodreads)

"Must read!" (Goodreads)

"Charlotte will keep you in suspense!" (Goodreads)

"Twisted love story full of power and control!" (Goodreads)

"Just WOW...no one can weave a story quite like Charlotte. This series has me enthralled, with such great story lines and characters." (Goodreads)

"Charlotte Byrd is one of the best authors I have had the pleasure of reading, she spins her storylines around believable characters, and keeps you on the edge of your seat. Five star rating does not do this book/series justice." (Goodreads)

"Suspenseful romance!" (Goodreads)

"Amazing. Scintillating. Drama times 10. Love and heartbreak. They say what you don't know can't hurt you, but that's not true in this book." (Goodreads)

"I loved this book, it is fast paced on the crime plot, and super-hot on the drama, I would say the perfect mix. This suspense will have your heart racing and your blood pumping. I am happy to recommend this thrilling and exciting book, that I just could not stop reading once I started. This story will keep you glued to the pages and you will find yourself cheering this couple on to finding their happiness. This book is filled with energy, intensity and heat. I loved this book so much. It was super easy to get swept up into and once there, I was very happy to stay." (*Goodreads*)

"BEST AUTHOR YET! Charlotte has done it again! There is a reason she is an amazing author and she continues to prove it! I was definitely not disappointed in this series!!" (*Goodreads*)

"LOVE!!! I loved this book and the whole series!!! I just wish it didn't have to end. I am definitely a fan for life!!! (*Goodreads*)

"Extremely captivating, sexy, steamy, intriguing, and intense!" (*Goodreads*)

"Addictive and impossible to put down." (*Goodreads*)

"What a magnificent story from the 1st book through book 6 it never slowed down always surprising the reader in one way or the other. Nicholas and Olive's paths crossed in a most unorthodox way and that's how their story begins it's exhilarating with that nail biting suspense that keeps you riding on the edge the whole series. You'll love it!" (*Goodreads*)

"What is Love Worth. This is a great epic ending to this series. Nicholas and Olive have a deep connection and the mystery surrounding the deaths of the people he is accused of murdering is to be read. Olive is one strong woman with deep convictions. The twists, angst, confusion is all put together to make this worthwhile read." (*Goodreads*)

"Fast-paced romantic suspense filled with twists and turns, danger, betrayal, and so much more." (*Goodreads*)

"Decadent, delicious, & dangerously addictive!" (*Goodreads*)

"Titillation so masterfully woven, no reader can resist its pull. A MUST-BUY!" (*Goodreads*)

"Captivating!" (*Goodreads*)

"Sexy, secretive, pulsating chemistry…" (*Goodreads*)

"Charlotte Byrd is a brilliant writer. I've read loads and I've laughed and cried. She writes a balanced book with brilliant characters. Well done!" (*Goodreads*) ☆☆☆☆☆

"Hot, steamy, and a great storyline." (*Goodreads*) ☆☆☆☆☆

"My oh my....Charlotte has made me a fan for life." (*Goodreads*) ☆☆☆☆☆

"Wow. Just wow. Charlotte Byrd leaves me speechless and humble... It definitely kept me on the edge of my seat. Once you pick it up, you won't put it down." (*Goodreads*) ☆☆☆☆☆

" Intrigue, lust, and great characters...what more could you ask for?!" (*Goodreads*) ☆☆☆☆☆

WANT TO BE THE FIRST TO KNOW ABOUT MY UPCOMING SALES, NEW RELEASES AND EXCLUSIVE GIVEAWAYS?

Sign up for my newsletter and get a FREE book: https://dl.bookfunnel.com/gp3o8yvmxd

Join my Facebook Group: https://www.facebook.com/groups/276340079439433/

Bonus Points: Follow me on BookBub and Goodreads!

ABOUT CHARLOTTE BYRD

Charlotte Byrd is the bestselling author of romantic suspense novels. She has sold over 2 Million books and has been translated into five languages.

She lives near Palm Springs, California with her husband, son, a toy Australian Shepherd and a Ragdoll cat. Charlotte is addicted to books and Netflix, and she loves hot weather and crystal blue water.

Write her here:

charlotte@charlotte-byrd.com

Check out her books here:

www.charlotte-byrd.com

Connect with her here:

www.tiktok.com/charlottebyrdbooks

www.facebook.com/charlottebyrdbooks

www.instagram.com/charlottebyrdbooks

Want to hear about new releases, free books and get exclusive giveaways?

Sign up for my newsletter!

Sign up for my newsletter: https://www.subscribepage.
com/byrdVIPList

Join my Facebook Group: https://www.facebook.com/
groups/276340079439433/

Bonus Points: Follow me on BookBub and Goodreads!

amazon.com/Charlotte-Byrd/e/B013MN45Q6

facebook.com/charlottebyrdbooks

tiktok.com/charlottebyrdbooks

bookbub.com/profile/charlotte-byrd

instagram.com/charlottebyrdbooks

x.com/byrdauthor

ALSO BY CHARLOTTE BYRD

All books are available at ALL major retailers! If you can't find it, please email me at charlotte@ charlotte-byrd.com

Highest Bidder Series
Highest Bidder
Bidding War
Winning Bid

Hockey Why Choose
One Pucking Night (Novella)
Kiss and Puck
Pucking Disaster
Puck Me
Puck It

Tell me Series
Tell Me to Stop
Tell Me to Go

Tell Me to Stay
Tell Me to Run
Tell Me to Fight
Tell Me to Lie

Tell Me to Stop Box Set Books 1-6

Black Series
Black Edge
Black Rules
Black Bounds
Black Contract
Black Limit

Black Edge Box Set Books 1-5

Dark Intentions Series
Dark Intentions
Dark Redemption
Dark Sins
Dark Temptations
<u>Dark Inheritance</u>

Dark Intentions Box Set Books 1-5

Tangled Series
Tangled up in Ice
Tangled up in Pain
Tangled up in Lace
Tangled up in Hate
Tangled up in Love

Tangled up in Ice Box Set Books 1-5

The Perfect Stranger Series
The Perfect Stranger
The Perfect Cover
The Perfect Lie
The Perfect Life
The Perfect Getaway

The Perfect Stranger Box Set Books 1-5

Wedlocked Trilogy
Dangerous Engagement
Lethal Wedding
Fatal Wedding

Dangerous Engagement Box Set Books 1-3

Lavish Trilogy
Lavish Lies
Lavish Betrayal
Lavish Obsession

Lavish Lies Box Set Books 1-3

Somerset Harbor
Hate Mate (Cargill Brothers 1)
Best Laid Plans (Cargill Brothers 2)
Picture Perfect (Cargill Brothers 3)
Always Never (Cargill Brothers 4)
Kiss Me Again (Macmillan Brothers 1)
Say You'll Stay (Macmillan Brothers 2)

Never Let Go (Macmillan Brothers 3)
Keep Me Close (Macmillan Brothers 4)

All the Lies Series
All the Lies
All the Secrets
All the Doubts

All the Lies Box Set Books 1-3

Not into you Duet
Not into you
Still not into you

Standalone Novels
Dressing Mr. Dalton
Debt
Offer
Unknown

ABOUT WINNING BID

He ended a life to save mine. Now the walls are closing in.

They hunt us, seeking our weaknesses. I may have to sacrifice myself to save him.

I never meant to love him.

Yet now I'm enthralled, ensnared by his every word, his every look.
The way he moves, the way he undresses me with his eyes.

I can't let go. Not when his touch sets me ablaze.

My job with his father's worst enemy is an existential threat. I'm undercover in enemy territory and I can't trust anyone.

If we can endure the gathering storm, our bond might save us.

Yet a betrayal whispers in the shadows, one that could shatter us for good.

1

JUNE

Pretend everything is normal.

That had been Anderson's advice to me. The good news was I'd had a lifetime of pretending things were normal. When I was a kid, my father used to beat the crap out of me and cheated on my mom like it was going out of style. All the while, he defrauded everyone we knew. Pretending things were normal was second nature to me for a very long time.

But the bad news was, it had been a long time since I had to pretend like that, and I was out of practice.

So, in an effort to pretend things are normal, I close the heavy blue and gold curtains in my office. I need darkness, and I need quiet. This is the only way to get it. Without darkness and quiet, I cannot think. And right now, thinking is the only way that we are going to dig ourselves out of this fucking mess. I sit at my desk and stare at my laptop. None of the words make any sense. It's not that I don't know the words. I do. I wrote them. But at the moment, my brain is too scattered for any of it to click in.

Anderson and I had spent our entire Sunday trying to come up with a game plan. Neither of us had any good ideas. Somehow, both of us being lawyers did not help. I wondered how normal people would handle it. But Monday morning came, and I had to go to work. That way, I could pretend everything was normal. Guilty people don't go to work.

Or at least that's our theory.

But sitting in my office, I can't hold still. My focus is absolute shit, and I need that to do my job. Andre Moeller hired me to find loopholes for him to be able to buy a bunch of companies, and now I can't even spell loopholes. I still don't know why he wants me on this job instead of an actual fixer, but I guess that doesn't really matter right now. All I can think about is Neil.

I've spent the last twenty-four hours shaking in my core. First, Anderson proposed Saturday night, and then Sunday morning, Neil's body washed ashore near where Anderson and Moss had dumped it.

I hadn't expected to go through all of the stages of grief about this. But somehow, I have. Not because I'm sad that he's dead. Neal deserved to die. He tried to rape me. He tried to kill me. And if Anderson hadn't interceded, I'd be dead right now. I only wish he had been better at hiding the body. As I rolled through the stages, I tried to figure out what in the hell to do.

I wanted to forget it ever happened. All of it. I wanted to pretend that Neil never existed in the first place. I've been pretty good at that since the night that he was killed. But denial isn't helping me. Denial is not a plan.

I AM SO angry about this, and I had enough anger to go around. First, Neil attacked me. That any man would put his hands on a woman that way …
Secondly, I had thought that Moss was some kind of body-burying genius. He looks like a murderer out of central casting. He's huge, with a bald head and an angry expression on his face at all times. The man reeks of murder. How is he not better at hiding a body?

And then there's the bargaining. I've never been a religious woman. But this has made me damn close to converting. If I thought that I could make a deal with God to save us from this mess, I would do it. Trouble is, I don't believe. I don't think God's making any deals with people that don't believe in him. And bargaining with people is how we got into this mess in the first place, so that's out.

A cold, sick feeling has come over me. Some might call it depression. I don't know if depression can hit quite this fast. The problem is I don't see a way out of this. Anderson beat the living shit out of Neil. He killed him. There has to be evidence on his body. If not on his body, probably some video footage of the vehicle when they dropped him off.

Anderson told me everything about that night. That he and Moss drove way out to one of the farther docks on the edge of town. Moss already had a boat there. They drove the boat out far, and then they dumped him over the side after weighing his body down. Should have been no fuss, no muss.

Unfortunately, there is a fuss.

I'd like to say that I've moved on to acceptance. But I haven't. I can't. I don't accept it. I just got engaged, and now I might be brought up on murder charges, or my future husband might be. This is not how life is supposed to go. We did nothing wrong. He saved me. Anderson is a hero. But no one will believe that now.

Until yesterday, we've been very lucky about everything. Neil had attacked me in the lobby of my apartment building. Anderson fought him off there. But it was the middle of the night, so no one was around. There is no security in that apartment building. No cameras. Moss changed the lobby by adding plants to cover up any of the damage done during the fight. He had me spray some formula on all the blood spatters and anywhere else that I thought we may have touched. I still don't know what was in that bottle. But I assume it was used to obscure any blood or fingerprints that might have been found.

He made me think that we had committed the perfect crime. I want to choke him for being wrong.

I keep clicking from the documents that I'm working on to news sites covering the story about Neil. I can't help it. It's like a compulsion. I need to know the latest, the newest information. There isn't much, at least nothing that's publicly announced. I imagine they're trying to keep the details hush-hush. The less public knowledge there is, the better chance that they have of actually getting a confession from someone. I know how this is played.

I'm not a true crime junkie, but I might become one real fast.

I know that animals in the wild tend to leave a body in the water alone. But there are always creatures that go after a decaying corpse. It's my hope that they did enough damage that they won't be able to find anything on Anderson or me. I keep thinking back to the night that Neil attacked me. People saw us together as we left the bar I worked at. Being one of the last people to see Neil alive, I know the cops are gonna come and talk to me. It's honestly surprising that they haven't yet. But just the thought of talking to the police again is enough to start me shaking.

I became a tax attorney for a reason. I love the law. I do not enjoy talking to cops. It's nothing against them specifically. But after dealing with my dad's fraud and the fallout that came from it, plus the incident at camp, I've never had a good experience with the police. I have always felt like I was going to be the one going to prison, even when I wasn't the one in trouble.

Now is different. Now, I could be in trouble.

The mishandling of a corpse gets you three years. And that's just the start of my crimes. I want to stop tallying up the years I could be in prison for all of the crimes that I was involved in, but I can't stop doing the math. Math only ends when there's an interview online with Neil's brother.

Do I click it? Is this something I really want to see?

But I can't stop myself even if I want to. I start the video.

A blonde man with red eyes chokes on his words. "Whoever did this, for whatever reason, you should know you killed a great man. My brother was going places. We were all proud of him for getting out of here and going to the city. If the murderer is watching right now, I hope you burn in hell."

I turned it off as fast as I turned it on. I feel sick. Watching that was a very, very bad idea. Obviously, his brother had no idea who he was. But I doubt most rapists go around bragging about what they do.

I sit there and shake and try to figure out how to make words again. I have a job to do. Ruminating on my past mistakes is not going to fix anything. I take a deep breath and follow it with another, trying to center myself.

No matter what happens, I know a few things.

One, I love Anderson.

Two, he loves me.

Three, we are in this together. I will not let Neil or anyone else come between us ever again.

2

ANDERSON

F uck.

I'm on the thirtieth floor of my family's corporate headquarters when all I want to do is run to a country without extradition. I've always wanted to go to the Maldives. I imagine it's nice every time of the year. But instead, I'm here to take a meeting. My father reinstated my position, and now I have to pretend that everything is normal.

It is so far from fucking normal.

Back when Dad had assigned me to work with Moss, I thought that I was being punished. But he has explained that it was more for training than for punishment. I'm of the opinion it was for both. He hated that I was with June, and he wanted to punish me for it. I have never gotten along with my old man. He uses money and power to control everyone around

18

him, but I never thought that he would use blackmail against his own son.

Until recently, I didn't know that my father was active in the Boston underworld. If he had a title, I didn't know it. But my father had powerful friends and powerful enemies. I didn't know how powerful until my assignment with Moss.

Moss is my father's wet work guy. He's also his collections guy. So when people owe him a debt, he sends Moss. When we first started, I thought that it was just going to be roughing some people up at worst. But after my first trip ended in the deaths of three people, I realized I didn't have any idea what my father was up to. That day, he made me Moss's accomplice. He collected the security footage of what happened, and he used that to blackmail me and control me. For months, I was stuck on ride-alongs with Moss. We formed an uneasy friendship over that time. That's how I got in the worst trouble of my life. Well, second worst.

The night that Neil attacked June, I called on Moss. Out of everyone I knew, he was the only one I knew who could get rid of a body. I thought that he was my savior. And for a time, he was. Not much later, when we were on another ride along, I took a bullet for the man. I didn't even think about it. There was no hesitation. I saw what was coming, and I jumped in the line of fire. It feels like a lifetime ago.

After I saved him, he swore his loyalty to me over my father. I know that Moss didn't screw this up on purpose. He wouldn't do that. This is just an honest mistake. And it's an honest mistake that may ruin my life and June's. I can't let that happen.

For the time being, I have to pretend everything is normal. That I'm not going out of my mind trying to figure out what in the hell to do. That I am just another lawyer that people pay too much money in order to take care of their problems. I have to be that guy again. I haven't been that guy in months, so Dad gave me an easy case to get my feet wet again. Some starlet who got caught with her top off. It's my job to get those pictures removed from the Internet. Five months ago, I could have done this in my sleep.

Now when I close my eyes, all I see is the bloated corpse of a guy who tried to rape the woman I love.

I have no regrets about killing that asshole. He more than had it coming. My regrets center on what happened afterward. I had been the one to talk June out of calling the police then and there. This is all my fault. That makes it my responsibility, and I have no fucking clue what to do about it.

No, wait. This is my father's fault. Had he not driven a wedge between me and June, she never would have taken Neil back to her apartment building. If my father hadn't spent months blackmailing the man he calls his heir, none of this would have happened in the first place. I want to get the revenge I swore against him for all of this. I need to make him pay. Every bad thing in my life is his fucking fault.

Though, for that matter, if Neil hadn't been a sociopath, none of this would have happened, either.

The starlet's handler waves at me from down the hall for me to join the meeting in the conference room. It's a nice corner room with pale gray carpeting and views of the city. Nothing too over the top, but with furniture nice enough to be comfortable.

I roll in, flash my smile, and charm my way through the conversation. She's less poised than I'd hoped, but I can work with her. I've already called my tech guys, so this meeting is more of a courtesy than anything else. Even still, I can hardly keep my head in the meeting. My own problems are far worse than a pair of tits sunning on a yacht going viral.

So many ifs and not enough answers. This is beyond frustrating. The air is heavy around me. Like the noose is tightening around my neck. It won't be difficult for the police to track Neil's last known location. With them flashing his stupid picture on the news, a bar patron is sure to call with a tip about that night.

Plenty of people saw June leave the bar with Neil. He walked her home. I'm sure that's on plenty of cameras between the bar and her apartment building. She will be questioned, and they won't go easy on her. I don't know what she'll do or say. I don't think she'll crack. She's harder than people give her credit. But anyone can crack under the right pressure.

I just don't see a way out of this. If—

"But I thought you could handle anything," the starlet says suddenly.

I blink at her. "What was that?"

"You said you had it handled, and then you said you don't see a way out of this. I—"

Fuck, I said that out loud. "Apologies. I need more coffee. What I meant was that the only way out of this is to take the pictures off the internet and either never go topless outdoors again or do it and accept the fact that things like this will happen, Trina. You're in the big time now. The paparazzi will not handle you with kid gloves." God, I hope she buys that.

"You're right, you're right. It was stupid. I know. I'm just tired of being hounded all the time, you know? How would you like it if everyone was looking for you everywhere you went? Tracking your every move? Hunting you down like an animal?"

I might soon find out. "That sounds like hell."

"It's exhausting. I just wanted to cut loose and relax. My manager wants me locked up forever just to keep my image clean. But I am done with that. It's time people realize I've grown up. I'm not the baby on a family sitcom anymore. Get over it."

Locked up forever? That sounds about right. "If you really want to break out of that shell, take the harder roles. You know the drill. The best way to devalue a naked picture is to put one out yourself."

"A sex tape?"

"Sure. Or something less personal. An arthouse film with tasteful nudity. Or raunchy nudity. Whatever you like. But the more people see your tits, the less those pictures are valued. If they can't make money from them — "

"They'll stop following me." She slowly nods. "I knew I could count on you, Anderson. Blake, we're doing that Grainger picture."

The aforementioned Blake smacks his head in frustration. "Well done, Anderson. I'll be sure to tell your father about how you've ruined her career."

But Trina rolled her eyes. "I'm the actress. Not you. Stop being so damned dramatic."

"I am not being dramatic … "

Their bickering goes on just long enough to set my teeth on edge. I can't believe I ever wanted to be involved in Hollywood. Even the small taste of it we get in Boston is enough to make me want to never see another movie. Or maybe that's just my foul mood.

After the meeting finally ends, I call Moss. "Hey, so I was hoping we could talk about some haddock fishing. You game?"

His muddled European accent always caught me off-guard. The man looked like a Russian bruiser, but there was an Italian lilt to his tones that bordered on French. "Of course. I am always ready for the fish."

"Ah, no fish yet. I want to discuss a trip, though. Busy?"

"Too busy for you? Never."

"You know the coffee shop on Eighth and Elm?"

He clicks his tongue. "Da. But Sal's Pizza down the road from you is better for haddock fishing trip planning."

I didn't know the place. "It's not even ten —"

"They open early for me. I am the best customer."

Ah. They're on our payroll. "Be there in fifteen?"

"See you then."

3

ANDERSON

As I pull up, it's obvious the pizza shop had not planned on opening this early. Men cart giant sacks of flour through the place, and dishes clatter loudly over a soundtrack of Italian pop. It's a standard pizza place with checkerboard floors and red accents throughout. The tables are small, and self-serve drinks come in those giant red plastic tumblers I've seen in every pizza parlor. Moss sits in the back, speaking to a short, old, white man in a stained apron.

The old man grins beneath a furry gray mustache when he sees me. He clasps my hand in his and shakes it with too much enthusiasm. "Mr. West's boy, it is a pleasure to meet you! I am Sal!"

"Nice to meet you, Sal. I'm Anderson."

"You want a pie? I make special for you."

"I'm great, but thanks."

"Okay, just a stromboli then, uh?"

I laugh. Talking to Sal is like talking to the Italian grandfather I never had. "Maybe just a soda."

"Take anything you want. If it is mine, it is yours." With that, he leaves us to our own devices, and I sit in the booth opposite Moss. "What the hell did my dad do to that guy? No one on our ride-alongs greeted us that friendly."

Moss smirks. "Your father gave him the money to buy this place."

That doesn't sound right. "Gave? He *gave* him the money? Not a loan?"

"Sal used to be like me. He did what I do for your father. Now," he gestures around us, "he retired."

"He worked for my father?"

"A long time ago."

I can't picture that little man taking down anything more than a person's pizza order. Quietly, I ask, "He ever kill—"

"More than me."

Well, shit. "I guess you never know what someone is capable of until they have to do it. How are your daughters, Moss?"

He grins broadly. The man is both terrifying and the proudest father I have ever known. "Marianna is glad you have recovered, but she misses you. She would like you to visit the house sometime."

"I might be able to make that work."

"Angela has a new girlfriend who wants to be a doctor." He pauses and crosses himself for luck on that score. "And Caterina, I fear, will be pale her whole life."

Odd thing for him to fear. "What makes you say that?"

"She is sixteen and just graduated early from the high school. She starts university in the summer semester to get a head start, where she will become astrophysicist."

"Wow."

"Da." He sighs. "She will never see the sun again with all her studies."

"Maybe through a telescope."

He chuckles and scrubs his hand over his bald head. "How are you feeling? The recovery, I mean."

"Tender today, but worth the pain. June and I were able to spend some … quality time together this weekend."

He grins and claps my shoulder hard. "Good for you! Has been very long time, no?"

"Longer than I care to admit. After that secondary stitch tear, I had to wait way too long for my liking."

"I am grateful to you, Anderson. Every day, I tell God, you take care of that man for me."

I chuckle. "I don't think that's how prayer works, Moss."

"Me and God, we have an understanding. I don't get in his way, and he doesn't get in mine. Sometimes, I mete out his justice. Such is life. I am sorry you still have pains."

I shrug. "Like you said. Such is life. I'm lucky I can feel anything at all. The doctor said if the bullet had gone an inch in any direction, I could be dead or paralyzed. So, it could be worse."

"It could be better, too." His mood turns somber. "I like that you ask about the girls. But I do not believe this is why you called meeting, Anderson."

My stomach sinks. "You've seen the news."

He nods once. "It is not good."

"Not according to the reports I've seen."

Moss leans forward. Seems that even in this place, we have to be quiet. "I did what I have always done. Deflate the body, weigh it down, sink it far offshore." He sighs. "I do not know why it did not work this time."

My stomach churns at the description of what happened that night, but my brain sticks to one part of what he said. I whisper, "Deflate the body?"

"You did not see me do it? I am quick, but —"

"I wasn't paying much attention at that point. Mostly, I was trying not to freak out."

"Ah. If you ever must do this on your own, there is a trick to it. Best to pierce both lungs and the intestines to prevent a gas build-up that makes the body rise in the water. Old boss of mine called it puncturing the pockets. Even weighed down, bodies float if you're not careful. If animals eat away the weights, the body can rise to the surface. But I am always careful. I know I did it that night. I had to clean my knife when I came home. There is no reason this should have happened."

"Good to know. Hopefully, I will never have to worry about that again." My mouth went dry, and I thought I might get sick. "So, since you did that, what do you think happened?"

"I have a theory, but you turn green, so I do not know if you want to hear it."

"Please. I just want answers."

He shrugs. "Tiger sharks come up to Boston now, even in winter. Climate change makes water warmer, so they come here. They eat almost anything. They are large enough to swallow most of a man. So, they smell meat, they eat it. It does not settle for them, they vomit." Another shrug.

"Fair play to you, you were right. I did not want to hear that." My stomach twisted harder thinking about that. Now, my mental image of Neil's bloated corpse included shark tooth marks.

"I did warn."

The only question that matters at this point. "What do we do?"

"This I do not know. Stealing his body will only make things more suspicious—"

"You think?"

"And his body is the only evidence of the incident that we know of. With luck, they will not be able to glean evidence from it. Too chewed up. Too worn. Without luck—"

"We are fucked."

He nods once. "Do you think anyone will be called in for questioning?"

"It is likely they will pull June in."

"People see her with him, da?"

"Yeah. He was hanging out at the bar she worked at. They left together that night."

He sighs through tight teeth like a hiss. "I feel we are without luck in this, Anderson."

"What do we do without luck?"

"Pray."

"I need to do something more proactive than prayer, Moss."

He sits back and smiles. "We could always call your father—"

"You knew my answer would be, 'Fuck no, before you even opened your mouth."

"Da, I did. But your father, for all his flaws, has valuable friends who may help."

I run my fingers through my hair. It goes against every instinct I have to call on my father. The man helped to get me into this mess. I cannot count on him to get me out of it. If he deigned to do so, he would just use it as another blackmail tool, only this time, he'd have something over June, too. I could never let that happen to her. It is bad enough that he manipulates me.

"If worse comes to worse, and I mean the very worst possibility, I might call on him. Unless that happens, we need to handle things ourselves as best we can. Dead silence on the matter. You and I probably shouldn't contact each other for a while, don't you think?"

He shakes his head. "We have other reasons to contact each other, Anderson. If we end communication, that is suspicious. We carry on with our days as we usually do. No more, no less. They ask questions, we know June knew him, but you two reconciled. Anything else happen? We know nothing."

Frustratingly, it is all we could do. "That is basically what June and I came up with. Glad to know we're on the same page."

He smiles and we say our farewells, and I should be comforted by the fact June and I came up with the same plan as a career criminal. Someone who knows what he's doing in this kind of circumstance.

Except that he is the same man who botched this in the first place. Maybe he's not the guy I should go to for advice on it.

4

JUNE

When someone knocks on my office door, I jump a mile. I've been jittery all morning, and sudden noises do not help. "Come."

To my not-at-all surprise, it's the guy I turned down last week. Carlos Perez. He is handsome in a slick lawyer way. His hair is too black and too perfect. His teeth are too white and straight. Every suit he wears is designer, and his shoes gleam. He is well-built and has a flirtatious way about him. If I had been single when we met, I might have taken him for a spin.

But I'm not, and he doesn't seem to care.

"Good morning, June."

"Good morning, Carlos. What can I do for you?" Please get out.

His gaze hones in on my hand. "No wonder you did

not want to see me Saturday night. You were busy getting engaged."

I smile, happy to have the *taken* label out there loud and clear. "Yes, I was."

"Congratulations. He is a lucky man."

Those words hang in the air for too long. When I met Carlos, he had been perturbed that I got the corner office. Since then, he's been trying to get under my skin. I do not like it.

"Is that all?"

"I thought perhaps you would like to know the coffee machine is up and running again, given how many times I have seen you run to it today. Something troubling you? Fiancé not letting you sleep? I can understand such an urge."

"It's Monday, Carlos. Everyone drinks more coffee on Mondays."

He lifts a shoulder and smirks. "Did I hit a nerve?"

"Is there a reason you're making a note of when I go get coffee because it sounds to me like you need a heavier workload? I'll be happy to let Andre know you're volunteering for the next case."

His mood shifts. Seems I'm the one who hit a nerve. "I am a naturally observant—"

Someone knocks on the door, and this time, it's Carlos who jumps. So much for his observation skills. Two men in suits walk in, escorted by one of the assistants from the lobby. She says, "Ms. Devlin, these officers are here to see you."

Oh my god. All the blood drains from my face, and I go boneless for all the wrong reasons.

Carlos smirks. "Seems you're busy enough for the both of us, June." He saunters out of my office.

I somehow manage to stand up and force a smile. "Officers?"

One flashes a badge. "I'm Detective Banks. This is my partner, Detective Wachowski. Homicide unit. We'd like to ask you a few questions."

I blink at them and try not to pass out. I nod at the assistant, and she scurries off, closing the door behind her. "Please take a seat. I'm happy to help in whatever way I can, gentlemen." I sit when they do and sip my water. Coffee is no longer needed. Not with this amount of adrenaline in my system. I take a deep breath but try to keep it steady.

"Do you know a Mr. Neil Johnson?"

"I did. Yes."

"Did?" His brow lifts.

"I saw the news. Just terrible what happened."

"And what do you think happened?"

I shrug. "Well, they said his body was found in the harbor. That foul play was suspected." I leave it at that.

"How would you describe your relationship with the deceased?"

Adversarial. I sigh. "I didn't really know him all that well. We met at a bar after I went through a breakup and got laid off, so I wasn't exactly in the best headspace to be meeting someone. We texted some, and then I went back to working at my old bar—"

"O'Mulligan's?"

And with that one word, I know they know way more about me than they're letting on. I am dying inside. But I roll with it. The only way through is through. "Yeah. I used to bartend there back in college, and when I got laid off, I went back to it for a while."

"Seems you've bounced back," Detective Wachowski says, glancing around my office.

"Thanks."

"Go on," Detective Banks tells me.

I clear my throat. "Anyway, one night, he shows up at O'Mulligan's, and he hangs out. It was a little strange. I mean, we'd hung out one night at another bar, and then he stays for hours when I'm too busy to talk to him?" I shrug. "I dunno. Guys are weird. But he was nice enough to offer to walk me home after my shift, so I took him up on it. Getting out of the bar late, you never know what might happen. He walked me home, and we said goodnight. I didn't hear from him after that."

Detective Wachowski pulls out his phone and reads off of it, "Several eyewitnesses said Mr. Johnson put his scarf on you and kissed you before you left the bar. Can you corroborate that?"

I laugh, shaking my head. "Wow. They have better memories than me." Those fuckers.

"Do you kiss enough men to forget the dead ones you kissed?"

Whoa, what the fuck? "I beg your pardon?"

"Seems to me the news report shoulda jogged your memory of that kiss. Don't you think?"

I sit back and try to rebuild the smile I had going a minute ago. "Tell me, Detective Wachowski, have you ever been a bartender with a killer rack and a flirty side? Because I have. Frequently. Random kissing happens. I won't apologize for having some fun with a guy, and you won't make me feel uncomfortable for forgetting about a measly drunken kiss. Slut shaming should be beneath a man of the law."

"Where is the scarf now, Ms. Devlin?" Detective Banks asks.

Oh, you want me to admit to having evidence? "I don't even remember the scarf. I have no idea where it's at now. This was months ago."

"Why didn't you text him after that kiss?" the other one asks.

"What girl does that?" I laugh as if the mere thought is absurd. "If a guy wants to talk after we've kissed, then *he* can text *me*. Let *him* prove he's interested. Let *him* stick his neck out. I am done chasing men. I do not waste my time. Life is too short."

"And did he text you?" Detective Banks asks.

I huff and give a little pout. "No. I mean, it all worked out in the end." I flash my engagement ring, which is coming in handy more times than I thought it would today. "But at the time, I was kinda bummed Neil didn't text after that. He was really cute." Saying anything nice about that monster makes me nauseous, but I hope I'm selling this. "He seemed like he liked me … wait. The news said he was in the water for a long time. Do you think that's why he didn't text me? He was dead?"

They both look at me like I've lost my mind. Detective Banks says, "It's possible. Why do you sound happy about that?"

I laugh nervously. "Well, I mean, if he was dead, then it's a little less of an ego hit that he didn't text me. I can't blame him for his bad choices if he was dead. Does that make me the asshole if his being dead is a relief?"

Banks smirks at that, but Wachowski looks appalled. He grunts, "You sure you don't know anything else?"

"I wish I knew more. He was nice enough, I guess. A little odd, but no one deserves whatever happened to him." If I can send them down the path of finding any of his other victims, then I will.

"He was odd how?" Detective Banks asks.

"Well, the night he walked me home, he said some strange stuff about women. About how he didn't like it when women were mouthy or told him what to do. I didn't know where he was going with all of that. It sounded misogynistic to me and made me uncomfortable. I mean, I think a lot of guys feel that way, but they don't say it out loud. Not Neil. He just put it out there like it was a normal thing to say to a woman. I dunno." I shrug. "He was weird."

Detective Wachowski says, "You remember a random comment like that, but not kissing the guy?"

I smile at him. "Kissing isn't a big deal, but a guy going on about opinionated women *is* a big deal. Considering most men know better than to say that kind of thing to a woman, it sticks out."

"And there's nothing else you can tell us about him?"

"All I know is he said he was a hedge fund manager, and he was from Nebraska. Oh, and he liked sci-fi novels. That's about it."

They share a look before standing. Detective Banks passes me his card. "If you remember anything else, please give us a call."

I nod and smile. "I'd be happy to. Can't have some crazy person going around attacking cute guys in the city."

5

JUNE

A s soon as the door shuts, the strength I pulled out of my ass vanishes, and I collapse to the floor. I'm not even sure where the hell that all came from. I was just … panicked. Bone-deep anxiety took over and handled the situation. But now, there's nothing holding me together. Like a puppet with my strings cut, I'm a lump of a thing now. Hot tears sting my eyes. Stress tears. Fear tears. Whatever they are, they burn like acid.

The acid Moss should have used on Neil's body.

I snort a laugh and keep crying, and I'm pretty sure I'm losing my mind. I am not cut out for a life of crime. That's why I've always kept my nose clean. Hell, even my career is based around people finding the most legal way to flout taxes. I skirt the law. I don't break it. Until now.

Now, I am a criminal who can't stop crying. I won't make it a day in the joint.

It's not even cute, girly tears. There's nothing pretty about this. Murder has ruined me. I'm on my office floor, wracked with sobs. This is a hopeless situation, and I feel like the world is ending. My chest hurts from every breath because my whole body is rigid with fear. I don't know how to stop crying.

What if they catch Anderson? That's the thing I'm most afraid of. I mean, I know for sure that I won't do well in prison. I have nice tits and a decent body, and I'm plain but pretty. I might as well change my name to "Victim" because that's what I'd be in prison. But the thought of Anderson behind bars haunts me. That's the thought that makes me want to vomit and scream right down to my very soul. He can't go to prison for this, for saving my life. It's too cruel. Life is not supposed to be this way.

I won't let that happen. If it comes down to it, I'll confess. Say I did it all. I'll take whatever is coming. But I won't let him go to prison. I won't.

And he's probably thinking the same thing about me right now.

Maybe if I confess first and beat him to it, then I can keep him safe. That way, he can't try to shoulder any blame. That could work—but are they going to believe that I beat the shit out of Neil? Me, who has no training? Me, who can hardly lift a keg, somehow beat him to death, transported his body to a boat, and lifted his weighted body over the side? No one in their right mind would believe that.

I knew I should have called the fucking cops that night.

We should have taken our chances with the law. At least then we wouldn't be in this position. We'd be on the right side of history. That night, in our panic, Anderson pointed out his father has enemies who would love to punish him by convicting his son. Also, anytime I was googled, the story about Neil would come up. I'd be tied to the man who tried to rape me for the rest of my life. Both scenarios sounded like utter hell after what I'd been through, and I couldn't accept that future.

But this one is so much worse.

An alarm jolts me from my doom spiral. I race to my phone, wiping my eyes as I go. Shit. I have to get ready for lunch with my father. It's so peculiar that he's popped up now of all times. Doesn't matter why at the moment. I have to get myself together.

Bringing out my desk mirror, I catch my reflection and cringe in horror. My eyes are red with black and pink bags beneath them. Thanks, so-called waterproof mascara. My cheeks are splotchy, too, and streaked in black. Hell, even my lips are swollen from nervously chewing on them.

The fear of my father noticing my emotional state is what allows me to stop crying. After all, he used to be the reason I cried so much as a kid.

But those times are far in the past. When Dad came last time, it was actually pleasant to have lunch with him. The man is a con artist, so I might be naïve in thinking this, but he actually seems different now. More secure. Not like a normal person is stable, but stable for him. Maybe prison did him some good.

I doubt we have that in common.

Stop thinking about your impending prison sentence, and get ready.

I shake my head free of the thought and grab the makeup remover wipes and blotting paper. After using all the removers, I'm left with a pink and puffy face. The impromptu makeover can only fix the makeup. Can't do much for the eyes. I skip the makeup there, settling on sunglasses instead. Hopefully, no one will make a big deal out of my appearance. When I'm ready, I dial up an Uber for pickup.

I grab my things and rush out the door, ignoring Carlos' beckoning. The elevator is mercifully fast, and the doors close before he's able to catch up to me. I know he hates that I got the corner office, and so he likes to annoy me, but for heaven's sake, I wish he would get a new hobby.

When I get to the lobby, my legs freeze in place. It is downpouring outside. Hoorah. So, I gear up in my galoshes and raincoat, both of which are not particularly warm, and when the Uber arrives, I launch out of the lobby for the warmth of the minivan. Dad has picked another high-end restaurant for our lunch—his treat—so I give the driver the address and try to relax.

Relaxation is not an option in any real sense of the word, but dissociating during the ride prevents me from freaking out on the driver's crazy antics. It's almost like relaxation, right?

Once at the restaurant, the driver pulls under the awning, so at least I'm semi-dry by the time I reach Dad's table by the window. We have a nice view of the harbor, or we would if rain weren't coming down in sheets out there.

My father, who I have been trying to stop calling Mitch because I am fostering a better relationship with him, looks good. His navy suit is tailored, he's clean-shaven, and he's smiling like he used to when times were easier. I can't tell if he darkened the gray at his temples, but he looks refreshed and happy, and it's disheartening to see our stark contrast.

I am falling apart while he is putting himself back together.

"Junebug!" he says by way of greeting. After a brief hug, we sit at the two-top. We order drinks, and I expect him to grill me about the sunglasses, but he doesn't. "How are you doing?"

Why? What have you heard? "Uh, fine. Didn't sleep much."

He nods knowingly. "The older you get, the more important sleep becomes. I learned that the hard way."

"Really?" It just comes out. I can't stop it. I'm too freaked out, and I've lost my filter. "Because it seemed like you used to sleep like a baby when you were conning everyone we knew out of their life savings and screwing around on Mom." Okay. It's not the nicest thing I could have said to him.

He winces, then gives a little shrug. "You're not wrong. But in prison, I learned how important sleep really is." He pauses and sips his wine. "You don't get a lot of it in there."

I'm not sure if that's his gentle way of reminding me that he's paid his debt to society, but point taken. "Sorry … like I said. I need sleep."

"No, no, Junebug. You're not wrong about what you said. I did those things. I'm ashamed of what I did back then, and there's no taking back those mistakes. They were my choices. Not yours or your mom's. It was my fault you girls had to pay for what I did, and no amount of apologizing or," he gestures around us, "fancy lunches will make up for my crimes. I know that, and that's not why I want to do these lunches with you. But I'd like to think that everyone deserves a second chance in life. Thank you for trying to give me one."

This man is a master at telling people what they want to hear. I know that. But I want to believe what he's telling me. That he means every word of it. Maybe it's the little girl in me, but god, I want to believe he is who he tells me he is now.

"Yeah, Dad. We're figuring this out together. I don't mean to harp on you about that stuff, but—"

He laughs warmly. "Junebug, you haven't harped on it at all. In fact, you've been far kinder than I deserve. You have exceeded my every expectation."

"What does that mean?"

"In the joint, you hear horror stories about the daughters of the guys in there. When a little girl's daddy goes to prison, it usually messes her up badly. I'm not going to tell you what the other guys said about their girls, but those stories are a part of why it was so hard to sleep in there." He sighs and stares out at the rain before looking me in the eyes. "Seeing you here, now, doing as well as you are, looking healthy, and now, with that fat diamond on your hand, I am in awe of you. You are flourishing in spite of me, not because of me, and I know I owe that to your mother."

I'm not sure how much more of this my heart can take. Between the need to hear that out of him for a decade and a half to his glowing assessment being only partially true, I'm dying inside for the second time today. Those are words I never expected out of him. I rasp out, "Thanks."

6

ANDERSON

By the time June gets home, I've already poured a scotch. I've gone round and round about all of this, and I'm not getting anywhere, so a scotch was in order. I smile and lift my glass to her as she walks in. "Want one?"

It's only then that I realize something is very wrong.

Her brown eyes are puffy, and the look on her pretty round face startles me. I set my drink down and go straight to her, wrapping her in my arms. "Baby, what happened?"

She shakes her head, and for a moment, she crumbles against me.

"You can tell me. You know you can."

"Let's go for a walk."

I frown at her. In all the time we've been together, we've never just gone for a walk, and it's been drizzling all day. She is freaking me out. I lift her chin with a finger to get her full attention because whatever is going on in her head must be terrible. "June, baby, talk to me. What is going on?"

There's a firmness to her now. Her jaw is tight. Her eyes shine fiercely. "I want to go with you on a walk. Can we do that or not?"

"Yeah. Let me get my coat." I don't know what the hell has gotten into her, but this seems vitally important, and she's not letting it go. I shrug on my coat and let her take the lead outside. Clearly, she has someplace in mind.

Thankfully, it stopped drizzling before we left the apartment. The air is heavy and chilled, so the walk is still uncomfortable. We end up at the little park a few blocks away, and she doesn't say a word until she dips to look under the picnic table. Once she's satisfied, she sits and gestures for me to do the same, so I do. June takes a breath to steady herself. Her voice is barely over a whisper, even though there is no one else in the park. "I think we're bugged."

"Bugged, like with a listening device?"

Her lips tighten as she nods.

"You've seen too many movies—

"Do not mock me, Anderson," her voice cracks.

"I'm not. I just think you're being a little paranoid, that's all. What has you so rattled?"

"A pair of homicide detectives came to my office today. They knew things."

"Fuck," I mutter. "What did they know?"

"That I knew Neil. That I worked at O'Mulligan's. That he kissed me and put his scarf on me as we left together," her nostrils flare as she says the words. She's on the brink of losing her shit—I can see it.

When I reach out for her hand, it's hard not to be hurt when she flinches, but I get it. She is wound tight, and I don't blame her at all. But she lets me hold her hand after a pause. Quietly, I ask, "What else did they know?"

"Isn't that enough?" she snaps.

"It's enough for them to know you two were involved. It's not enough to convict."

"Do … do you think they're listening? That the apartment is bugged? For them to know all of that … I don't know how else they'd know about O'Mulligan's."

I shrug. "It's not hard to sort that kind of stuff out, but it is hard to get a warrant to plant a bug. I don't think they're listening to us." I don't want to say what's on my mind. I really don't. But it needs to be said. "Moss thinks that if we don't talk about things, then this will eventually go away. I'm inclined to agree with him, but since he must have botched hiding Neil's body, I'm not sure if that's the right instinct."

"That's the plan? Never talk about it again?"

"For now, that's the only plan I've got. As much as I do not think this incident is enough for them to get a warrant for a bug, my father's shit is. All the stuff I've done with Moss is. So, while I don't think they'd go through the paperwork of getting a bug for one dead guy, I do think it's possible for everything else, which means, yeah. Not talking in our home sounds like a good start."

She leans to me, putting her head on my chest. "I hate this so much."

The defeated tone in her voice kills me. This is all my fault. During the fight, I was mindless. A strange Zen feeling took over as I fought Neil. I wanted him dead. I wanted to feel my fist go through his face for what he had done to her. But then I heard her voice through the violence. It was a fractured sound—Neil had tried to strangle her, and her vocal cords were bruised. But it shattered my focus completely, and I had to get to her, which meant the fight needed to stop. I worked him over to end the fight, but then he cracked his skull on a stud in the wall, and that was that. At first, I'd thought I'd knocked him out.

I wish that were all I'd done.

"I hate it, too, baby." I hate that they came to her office and that I can't stop them from doing it again. The only defense we have now is silence, and that has never been my skill. I am a talker, a professional manipulator, as one of my old law professors called it. But silence could be an attorney's asset, too. Letting a suspect talk was a good way to get an accidental confession. Not that I think she'd say the wrong thing, but I have to ask, "What did you tell them about Neil?"

"That he was just a guy I'd met at a bar. He came to my job to wait for me and walk me home. On the way home, he mentioned some weird shit about how he didn't like when a woman told him what to do, that he didn't like mouthy women. So, when we got to my place, I said goodnight, and that was it because it was strange to say misogynist shit like that out loud."

That's my fucking girl, right there. I smile at her. "Not bad, Devlin."

She quirks a crooked smile at me back. "What?"

"That's a good story, and it could lead them to look for other women he put off. Maybe even find some of his other victims ... fuck, if I wasn't in love with you before, I would be now."

Her smile goes wide, before she starts to cry. I hold her close until she stills, and it takes far longer than I'd hoped it would. She mumbles, "I can't take this."

"I am so fucking sorry, June."

"I know. I'm not asking for another apology. It's just ... I need to be able to get this out without you constantly apologizing, okay?"

I nod. "Whatever you need."

"I wish we had called the cops that night, and part of me wonders if we told them now —"

"We can't."

She sighs. "I know. I just mean, I still wonder what would happen if we did, though. If we confess to it and let other lawyers handle this … it might not be so bad."

"If I thought that even close to true, I'd do it in the blink of an eye just to stop breaking your heart. But it's not, and neither of us is naïve enough to believe that would go the way we want it."

"I know."

"Here's what we're going to do," I tell her with more confidence than I actually feel. "We are not going to speak a word about any of this in either of our apartments. Not at our offices. Not anyplace we regularly go to. If we need to talk about it or anything relating to it, we go for a walk. Deal?"

"Yeah. And definitely not on any of our phones."

I laugh and nod. "Agreed. The sun is down, and it's fucking freezing out here. Are you ready for some supper?"

"I guess so."

"You guess?"

"I haven't been hungry all day. It was a shame, too. Dad took me to Delvecchio's. I could hardly eat any of it."

My poor girl. I take her beautiful face in my hands and plant a kiss on her forehead. "I wish it wasn't so busy in your head."

"Me too."

I help her to her feet and sling my arm over her shoulders. I might not be able to protect her from the law, but I can at least protect her from the cold. She doesn't say much on the walk back, but really, what is there to say? I fucked us both, and not in the way I like.

But the closer we get to home, the more her steps slow. I ask, "What is it?"

"Just ... the thought of being spied on. After everything with ... you know, it's like I can't get away from being violated."

There is no curse dark enough for what I'm feeling right now. I gulp against a dry throat. "I know you asked me to stop apologizing—"

"Please don't."

I sigh and stare at our destination. My apartment has always felt like home until now. If she doesn't feel at home there, then it's not mine, either. But if we veer off course, now, it'll look weird if we're being watched. I swallow my guilt and anger and try to sound comforting. "I've got you, baby. Let's go home."

7

ANDERSON

ut even when we walk in, it feels ... off. Wrong. Like this is not our home, no matter how much I try to make it so. We change into our house wear — my gray sweatpants and white tee, her in yoga pants, and my old college sweatshirt.

Our usual.

Except for tonight, nothing feels usual about it. The seams on my sweatpants itch, and she takes three tries to get her wild curls into a bun. Everything is just plain off.

I dump the remaining scotch and set to work on supper. Nothing fancy, just my old standard of chicken breast, broccoli, and brown rice. It was what I ate when I was too addled to think of anything else in college, and now, it's still my go-to for that.

But it tastes like nothing tonight. Even the broccoli, which can be too strong, is bland as hell. Looking around, my apartment feels like it belongs to someone else. Like it's been invaded. The place is full of my things, yet everything seems suspicious.

The large luxury sofa that was a splurge now looks like a series of cushions perfect for hiding a wiretap. I've already been all over my end tables, the coffee table, and the lamps. Found nothing, and I'm not sure if that's a comfort or if it means I should look harder. Is that a camera in the screw of the outlet, or am I getting paranoid? Every piece looks like another place someone might have stashed something.

It's all mine, and it's all wrong.

June feels it, too. She must. She's been dead silent this whole time. It's almost as if someone stripped us of our personalities. I don't blame her for being quiet. I am, too. Both of us are so stuck in our heads that our conversation feels foreign.

I'm so close to her on the couch that I could touch her, but we are so far apart in our minds that the idea doesn't sit right with me. How fucked up is that? So, I ask, "How do you like the chicken?"

"It's fine. Did you do something different?"

"A little Dijon in the baste."

"Mm."

That's it. That's been the whole conversation for over an hour. I am going out of my mind. On any given night, we have a thousand things to say to each other. If we're being tapped right now, we have to be throwing up alarms. If we're not, this is doing our relationship no good.

I'm halfway through my meal, and June is just picking at hers, so I take her fork and plate and set them aside. She doesn't even question it. She just looks at me. I lean forward and kiss her. She stiffens up, surprised. But then she lets me kiss her for a breath. Progress. As I push my advantage, she backs off.

"I'm sorry, Anderson. It's been a rough day, and I just can't."

It is not in my nature to give up. I need June. The real June, not this weepy, cold, distant imitation of her. I need a taste of her spark. Even if only for a night. So, I decide to try something.

I let out an exaggerated sigh. "Look, I already said I'm sorry—"

"Anderson," she says my name like a warning as her eyes go wide.

"I know, I know, we said the fight was behind us —""Anderson!" She mouths, "Not here!"

"I know," I tell her firmly, trying to get her to see I haven't broken our promise. "I know you don't like to talk about our arguments once they are done, but you're not being you, and I'm definitely not feeling like me tonight."

"Argument?"

"Yes, the argument." I nod my head and try to give her a look that says, "We are talking in code." But she still looks lost. I clear my throat. "My point is, I said I was sorry for being a jackass earlier, and I am. But I feel like there's still a weirdness between us, and I'd like to make that up to you. If you'll let me."

June has the cutest furrow in her brow when she's confused, and right now, it's as deep as it's ever been. She gulps, trying to sort out what I'm talking about. "You don't need to make up anything, Anderson. You don't owe me —"

"But I do." I take her hands in mine. "I know we don't do tit-for-tat shit between us, and I never want that to change. But, baby, you nursed me back to health for months. You have put up with so much bullshit, far more than anyone should ever have to deal with in a lifetime, and we're not even married yet." I stroke her cheek, and to my relief, she tilts into my palm. "I love you more than anyone should love anyone. You have been through the absolute wringer. So, I'd like to do something nice. If you're up for it, I mean. I know you're always swamped with work, and —"

"What do you have in mind?" But she says it like she's asking if I'm high or something. June still hasn't caught on that I have a plan.

The truth is, I want to get us the fuck out of here for the night. I'd like to put all of this fuckery behind us and just go back to being Anderson and June, two crazy kids in love. Not Anderson, the Murderer, and June, the Witness. I need her. The way we connect, the love we share. I need to be reminded of what we're fighting for.

I smile to set her at ease. "Let's do something spontaneous tonight. Screw the chicken and broccoli — obviously, we're not hungry. I want to take you for a drink at the Ritz."

She laughs at first until she sees I'm serious. "What? Why?"

Because our place might be bugged and I can't breathe in here. "Because you deserve spontaneity, and they make an old-fashioned to die for. It's legendary. Come on. Our sweats are not going to pass the dress code." I stand up and extend my hand down for her.

She eyes it suspiciously but takes my hand after a beat. Once I get her to her feet, she smiles, and be still my heart, it seems genuine. "Are you sure about this?"

"Without question."

Her smile fills out a little more. "Okay. A night out sounds nice." We go to the bedroom, and as I start to dress, I watch June in profile in the bathroom. She frets over her pink eyes and pokes at her splotchy cheeks. "I can't go anywhere looking like this."

"Take your time. I'm not in a hurry." I hate lying to her, but I don't want her to feel bad about how she looks when we get there.

She nods and takes a breath before whipping out a little makeup and playing with her hair. In the mornings, she usually does all of this with the door closed, so getting to watch her from the end of the bed is novel. The open door frames her body as she works. Puffy eyes or not, she is the woman of my dreams.

Her brown curly hair gets wilder with the humidity, so lately, she's complained about it more, but I love it. The rest of June is put-together and precise, but her hair is something she can't control. It's the embodiment of her naughty bedroom side, which is one of my favorite parts of her. She can be as buttoned up as anyone, but the moment it's on, she turns into a hellcat.

She paints her eyes, trying to hide what she doesn't like. Strange to say it, but it's a relief to see stress affecting her. Not that I want that for her — not ever — but during my recovery, never once did she break down. She was there for every doctor appointment, every therapy appointment, she made me do my exercises, she washed my clothes and made my food, while she was starting a new job … all of that without a single complaint. Never once did she even bat an eye at what was needed.

At first, it was hugely admirable. But after a while, I worried she handled it too well and that she was hiding her stress from me. I'd been shot, for God's sake. If the shoe was on the other foot, I would have been a fucking basket case. Given all of that, I worried she would crack under the pressure.

If anything good can come of this, maybe June will let me in a little more. She'll let me help her. I know there are things she's never told me about her childhood. Until recently, she always clammed up fast when the topic was brought up. But with the reappearance of her father in her life, she's gotten more open about it. It's a start, but I want to be there for her always. It is tiring to be shut out of her emotional turmoil. Like she trusts me for some things and not others. I just need her to talk to me.

We have our best talks when she's out of her mind with orgasms. And we can't do that here. Not with the feds possibly watching us.

Maybe she's feeling it, too, because she puts a garter belt on and clips black thigh highs onto it. I've never seen her wear anything like that, and I've lost my train of thought. Whatever I did to deserve this woman, I'll do it again and again just to watch her strap all that on. My cock aches from the sight.

As she pulls a little black dress up her waist, a flash of the future comes to mind, or at least, what I hope is the future. I can't help but wonder what she'd look like pregnant. It's not a fantasy I often allow myself. But it's in the back of my mind now and then. Right now, though, thinking about the future keeps me grounded.

"What?"

"Hmm?" I ask.

"You're staring."

I grin, unable to lie to her about this. "Yes, I am."

She laughs and blushes, and it's lovely. "Well, stop it."

"Never gonna happen. You wear my ring, and part of the cost is me getting to look my fill.'"

She giggles and finishes dressing, then looks at me. "You're dragging your feet, mister."

"Apologies, love. Give me two minutes—"

"See? That's not fair. Guys have it so easy."

I shrug on my suitcoat. "I'll find a way to make it up to you. I promise. Oh, one more thing—"

"Another surprise?"

I smirk and nod. "Pack an overnight bag unless you want to come home in the torn version of those clothes."

She laughs again. "What?"

I close in on her, breathing her in before I pin her to the counter, my hands on either side of her hips there. "If I get you in the Ritz for the night, I'm not going easy on you, Devlin. Pack accordingly."

8

JUNE

His words send a shiver through me, and it's the best thing I've ever felt. After so much tension for a day and a half, I am ready to cut loose. I need it. Funny how a run-in with the law shifts perspective. Saturday night, I fell asleep as a newly engaged woman in the arms of her fiancée, and Sunday morning, I woke up as a criminal. It's been a rough couple of days.

But then, I knew this would happen.

Ever since my father's conviction, I have done everything I can to keep myself on the straight and narrow. I pay my taxes early, I drive below the speed limit and when I do, if someone is behind me, I get out of their way so I don't bother them, and I certainly never text and drive. Breaking the law has never appealed to me. There's no thrill in that kind of thing for me. I know the cost it entails, so the night my world came crashing down around me, I knew something like this would happen because Devlins never get away with anything for long.

Seems to me I should enjoy everything I can before I'm behind bars.

I snag a few things and throw them into Anderson's overnight bag, and as I do, I tell him, "You know, it was really shitty of you to tell me I can't find a movie actor attractive. I mean, of all the petty things you could have started a fight over, you picked that?"

"What?" It's his turn to be confused.

I smile so he knows I'm playing at his game. Hopefully. "Remember? That's how the fight started. We were watching the commercial for that new action flick, and you asked what I thought of that guy. It was the whole reason we had a blow-up, and you don't even remember it?"

Recognition brightens his crystalline blue eyes from within. He grins and rakes his fingers through his shining black hair. It's become a little shaggy since his surgery, and I like it. He chuckles, shaking his head. "Oh, right. I forgot all about it. But I remember now. The way you looked at him … I'm sorry, baby, but it gutted me."

"An 'I'm sorry' followed by a 'but' is worthless." Playing or not, that much is true.

"You're right, you're right." He holds his hands up to calm me down as if that is not the equivalent of waving a red flag at a bull. If this were a real fight, he'd be so very dead right now. But he grins at me, and it has a rakish quality that makes me want to do nasty things to him. He sheepishly says, "I will try not to get upset when I see you blatantly lusting after another man."

I press myself against him, and he holds me there. "Good."

"Just so long as you don't get upset if you see me lusting after another woman."

I smack his chest. "Oh my god, you don't learn, do you?"

"That there are separate rules for guys and girls? I think they call that a double something," he says facetiously.

"It is *not* the same thing!"

"I beg to differ."

I roll my eyes. "If a girl lusts after a guy, it's harmless. If a guy lusts after a girl, he might actually do something about it."

"Oh, because women don't have affairs?"

"With actors? Are you kidding me?"

"I see it all the time at work—"

"Because you're in entertainment law, Anderson! I mean, for fuck's sake, between the two of us, who has access to the attractive Hollywood elite? Me or you?"

He frowns. "Well, me, but—"

"And which one of us has a history of being a womanizer?"

He opens his mouth and pauses, realizing he's walked right into my trap. I grin at him, knowing I have won this round. A smirk flickers in his dangerous eyes. "Alright, Devlin, just for that, I'm going to surprise you."

I laugh, but I'm intrigued. "Haven't there been enough surprises for one night?"

"Not hardly. You ready?"

"Let's go."

The trip to the Ritz is over in a blink. Anderson clearly has more than a legendary cocktail in mind tonight, and he is as anxious as I am. The play fight weirdly got me going, and I am practically climbing the walls. However, that might also be because his car smells so deeply of him and leather, and those two scents get my brain tangled. It is all I can do to keep my hands to myself in the car. I hope this drink doesn't take too long. I need to see my man naked.

We walk into the lobby, and it's gorgeous. Golden lighting cascades from chandeliers, and the modern neutral palette is inviting, but I want to make a run for the room — oh hell. We don't have a reservation. How in the hell are we going to make this work?

I steer toward the lounge so we can figure it out, but Anderson takes my elbow and guides me to the concierge desk. I object, "We need to book a room —"

He only laughs and strolls to the desk. Being a
Monday night, there's no line. Thank goodness for
small favors. No one will see us get booted out of here.
"Good evening," he begins. I wonder what he'll say to
try and get a room. The Ritz books far in advance, so
the thought we could just walk in is ridiculous.

When the concierge looks up at him, her face
practically glows. "Mr. West, a pleasant surprise."

"Melanie, you're slipping. You should have known I'd
be here," he teases. "I booked over an hour ago online."

He did? Sneaky bastard. But I feel better knowing we
have a room booked.

But then I catch the look in Melanie's eyes. She laughs
musically while she stares at his mouth. They're so
familiar with each other, and it becomes clear they've
had a thing, and well, I hate her now. But she gives me
the once over and smiles just as sweetly at me before
turning to him. "Apologies, Mr. West, but it has been
months since we last saw you. I thought perhaps you
had taken your business elsewhere."

"Wouldn't dream of it."

"The usual?"

"Actually, is the Presidential available?"

Her blond brows lift for a moment as she goes to check
it. "For how many nights?"

"Just the one for now, but I'd like to keep the option
for tomorrow night, as well."

Oh, he would, would he? After keeping his Melanie secret, I plan to make him pay for this. He should have told me we could run into his ex. For that, I'm getting all the room service I want. Maybe I'll make her bring it.

She purrs, "Anything for you, Mr. West." She passes him a keycard, and her fingers linger just long enough to irritate me. But then her smile deepens further when she looks at me. "And anything at all for his guests."

Oh my god. She's flirting with me.

Before I can react, he says, "Have a lovely evening, Melanie."

"Don't forget—our twenty-four-hour service is available at any time. And I get off in two hours."

I bet she thinks she will.

He smiles, then takes my hand and sweeps me away to the elevator bank. He presses the button and offers no explanation of Melanie or anything else whatsoever.

"Was the drink a ploy to get me here?"

"The Ritz is notorious for taking its guests' privacy rather seriously. It's practically sacrosanct here. Particularly the upper-tier suites. They are swept for bugs regularly."

I blink up at him. "How do you even know that?"

"A side benefit of the job." He lifts a shoulder. "When we have a celebrity client under allegations or getting hounded by the paparazzi, and we need to stash them someplace safe, this is where we send them for exactly that reason."

"And is that why you're so friendly with the concierge?" I ask pointedly.

"No." He doesn't offer any explanation. Again.

As if I'm going to let this drop. It's like he doesn't know me at all. "So, is Melanie an ex?"

Anderson chuckles. "Erm, no."

"But you've slept with her."

"Is that a question?"

"Is that an evasion?"

He grins, staring at the doors as they open. "Counselor, I have never slept with her."

"Had sex, whatever. Don't wordplay your way out of this one."

"No. I have never had sex with Melanie the Concierge." He gestures for me to enter the elevator. So, I do. Once the doors close, he mutters, "However, I have watched her have sex with two other women."

"Oh my god! You could have —"

But he cuts me off with a kiss hot enough to peel paint. He backs me into the corner of the elevator, and I'm wedged there, trapped by his big body and the walls. He reaches up my dress, and I am officially scandalized that he'd do anything like this in the elevator. My blood screams in my veins as his hand slips higher up my thigh, past the top of the thigh high. His fingertips breach the edge of my underwear so methodically that he has me trembling like a leaf. When his finger slips around my clit, the elevator stops.

But it's not our floor yet.

9

JUNE

He drops my dress back into place and spins around so he's behind me now, and we look like any other normal couple. It's a good thing, too. A pair of ancient seniors walk in. We might have given them matching heart attacks.

They follow elevator convention and turn around to face the doors after giving us smiles and curt nods, so Anderson takes the opportunity to raise my dress in the back enough to slide his hand over my ass. Oh my god. I take a stiff breath in. I have to hold still, or they'll know, and he is making it impossible, the pervert.

I am marrying a pervert who likes to play in public. My stomach ties in knots, and I can't tell if I'm into this or not, but parts of me like it. A low-down throb makes my vision fuzzy.

More people walk in, but this time, Anderson doesn't stop. He merely holds still. Their view of us is mostly blocked by the little old couple. I hope.

Once they turn around, his fingers slide into my underwear again and traipse between my thighs from behind. One enters me. There's no resistance. I'm so damn wet right now. I try to shudder subtly, but he is a man of many talents, and I am too wound up. Goosebumps break out all over, and if anyone turns around, they'll see ... something. I don't even know what. My nipples pebble and press against my dress. Thank God it's black, so things are less noticeable in case someone looks.

Anderson's newly wet fingertip glides around until he skirts around the other hole. *Oh god. He's not — yes, he is.*

I can't breathe. His fingertip has entered me in a way he never has before, and it's all I can do, not to moan loud enough for everyone to hear me. I cough just to relieve some of the tension in my chest. But his fingertip is still up my ass, and I am about to squirm for him.

People file out when the door opens again, and then we're alone. But who knows for how long? Thankfully, the last floor is ours, and he releases me just in time for us to get out. The moment we're out, though, he backs me against the wall and kisses me until my toes curl. Then he snatches my hand and drags me down the hall.

Two can play at this game.

I give him a shove to the wall and pounce on him, taking his mouth for my own. He growls as I bite his bottom lip and pull back. Then he turns my back to the wall and presses himself against me. His hard cock nudges me down low, making me shiver hard again. Between kisses and bites, he murmurs, "I'm fucking you tonight. Not the other way around." Then he backs off and holds me at the small of my back, directing me to the room he clearly knows so well.

As soon as we're in, it's on. Anderson drops the bag and kneels in a flash, pushing me against the back of the door. It's still dark in the room, but I can't reach the light. Not with him dipping beneath my dress face first. I don't even care that it's dark. Not when he's in a mood like this.

Anderson unclips my thigh highs and pulls my underwear off over them. They puddle at my feet, and he slides them from my ankles, flinging them somewhere. He lifts my leg over his shoulder and opens me up to him. His tongue glides over me, and I groan, digging my head against the door. I have to hang onto something, or I'll fall, so I settle on the door handle and his head beneath my dress. As soon as I make contact with him there, he growls on my clit.

"Mm, fuck, baby, that's—"

And that is when his fingers enter the picture. While he sucks on my clit, his fingers stroke up and down me. It's such a fucking tease not to let them slide in, especially after how he touched me in the elevator. I'm not sure when the last time was that I was this wet. My knees threaten to buckle, but I know he has me. He's gotten stronger every day. I am less worried about hurting him now. Saturday night was a good trial run. Now, I'm excited to get back to the way things were.

Or to make them even better than before.

A finger enters me, pressing into my spot the way I like —right in time with his tongue on my clit. Filthy curses pour out of my lips. It's too good. This is far more pleasure than any one person has a right to, and yet, it's all mine. I grip his hair through my dress for purchase. Heat pools in my belly, and every part of me throbs. My thighs tremble from his work, and if the lights were on, I might see double.

Another finger joins the first, and I'm so fucking close. "Anderson, I need you to fuck me!"

But he says nothing. He is a man on a mission.

I whimper, wanting to come on his cock so damn bad that I'm losing my control. The second finger slides out, though, and for that disappointment, I flat-out whine. "What are you—"

That finger slides up my ass, and I lose it, erupting on his mouth, his fingers—both of them. That bonus stimulation takes my breath away, and I know anyone in the hall can hear me cry out his name. And that only turns me on more.

Only after I'm coming down does he pull back from my clit. Anderson rasps, "You taste so fucking good that I need to go again."

"What?" I chirp.

But he answers by suctioning onto me there. His fingers work me over harder, and I can't stop to breathe, much less think. My insides curl to meet his every whim, like I'm a puppet on his hand. I can't stand properly — I'm too hunched over. Need something. I don't even know. But I smack the door, shaking in frustration.

"Ander — Anderson, I can't breathe —"

"N-no-need," he mumbles on my clit. He said he wasn't going to go easy on me. He meant it.

My wetness runs down the inside of my thighs. Everything coils around his touch, begging for more while I'm trying to keep my head. I am just about boneless right now, and I don't want to fall onto him. That might actually do some damage. "Baby, I —"

But he hooks his fingers in me, and I shatter on him, coming so hard that I start to slide down the door. He props me up, though, and stops me from toppling over. And he stops me from stopping.

Anderson's gone from suck to nibble, pulsing his firm chin against my clit, and his stubble grinds into me there. I scream, "Too much!" Does he stop? No.

The man has no mercy in his bones.

I am rocking on his face, dying to come again, both for him and for me. I can't stop. This is too good, and the next orgasm might kill me, but I don't rightly care. Not now. Not when I'm climbing higher than I ever have before. I sob his name, and he keeps at me, unrelenting and determined to let everyone on our floor know what's happening right now.

Every muscle in my core locks tight, and breathing is a thing of the past. A relic of miserable times when I used to think oxygen mattered. I know better now. All I need is Anderson on me.

It starts as the crest of a rollercoaster's first hill, and the drop is a sharp pleasure that steals all thought. There is nothing left of me now. Only this climax. Only this moment. And then the next one. A third piggybacks off the second, and some muscle deep inside releases alongside my ultimate ecstasy. A breathless scream peals out of me as I gush on his face. My lungs attempt to force air back into them, and the pressure almost hurts, but nothing can take me from this bliss.

I can't recall what I was so stressed out about anymore. All I know is Anderson's mouth, Anderson's chin, Anderson's fingers. They gradually, reluctantly pull away from me, and I melt against him as he stands up to kiss me. His lips taste like I do, and I have never wanted that flavor more in my life. His strength is the only thing keeping me on my feet right now. His power. He loves me more than I knew possible, but right now, I am little more than his toy for the night.

And that is exactly what this is. His passion flows in his touch, his kiss. I feel utterly adored. Cherished beyond measure. There are no more games between us. No more lies. I am going to marry this man. I am going to give him babies. I am going to devote myself to his absolute happiness, all because he is even more devoted to mine.

Anderson West is my match, and I am his until the end of time.

His hands slide up my thighs, deftly unlatching the garter belt straps. His voice climbs low and deep, steel on gravel. "I need you on my—"

"Turn down service," some guy says behind the door as he knocks.

We both startle. There is no way I'm letting him in here right now. I feel Anderson's smirk against my neck as he projects his voice a bit. "Be right there."

10

ANDERSON

I had wondered how long we had until turn-down showed up. I wipe my mouth as clean as I'm willing to and turn on the lights while I will away my hard-on.

June's face is red, her dress is hitched up at her hip, and she's glistening. But the most notable thing is the horrified look on her pretty face. She quietly spits, "You cannot —"

But I tug her dress into place and open the door, grinning. She needs this. She's been too stressed out. A little silliness will help her unwind.

Or she'll kill me for fucking around like this. Whatever makes her happy.

A bright Englishman walks in, his uniform as crisp and pressed as if he's walked off the page of Butler's Monthly. "I am Reginald, here for your turn down service. Are there any scents you prefer? Allergies I should know of?" He doesn't give a lick of notice to our disheveled state. I'm not sure if it's because he's unobservant or if he's so accustomed to such things that it no longer fazes him.

"No allergies and I am fond of lavender. That's best for sleep, right?" I ask as if we're having a normal conversation. As if June isn't dying of embarrassment right this moment.

"Yes, sir. Many a pleasant night is had with lavender. Shall I perfume the sheets and the towels, or only the sheets?"

I smile and raise my brows to June, waiting for an answer.

But it seems her embarrassment has given way to amusement. The saucy minx says, "Everywhere. I'd like it everywhere, Reginald."

That earns a bob of his Adam's apple. "As you wish." Then he flits off for the bedroom. On his way there, he slides on her black silk panties, but the man is a pro and doesn't lose his footing or even so much as his pace.

It is all I can do not to snort a laugh, but I'm also too impressed with that move to do it. June, on the other hand, is not. She snorts a laugh and turns to collect herself, knowing that if we look at each other, we die of laughter. I know this because I'm thinking the same thing.

Only moments later, Reginald reemerges from the bedroom. This time, he manages to avoid using her panties as a skateboard. "Your service is complete. There is a full complement of our in-house spa products in your bathroom, as well as a selection of chocolates in the bedroom. If there is anything else I can do to be of assistance, please do not hesitate to reach out. You can pick up the phone and give the operator my name, and I will be here promptly. Anything else I may do for you?"

"I believe that is all. Thank you, Reginald."

"Of course. Have a pleasant evening." He leaves.

The moment the door closes, we lose it. I laugh so hard I can't breathe, and June might actually pass out if she doesn't catch a breath soon. But after we collect ourselves, I tour her around the suite, showing some of the features like the fireplace and the antique telescope. "On a clear night, you can see into that apartment there—"

She swats my shoulder playfully. "Naughty boy."

I grin and kiss her, so happy to have my girl back. Even if it's just for the night. I have missed the hell out of this woman. The past day and a half has been grueling, but having her here now is exactly what I needed.

But what does she need?

"Tell me what would make your night complete."

She bites her lower lip. "I think we were heading that direction before … "

"I like where your mind is at." Leading her to the bedroom, I ask something else on my mind as I sit on the big bed. "Tell me what you thought of the anal play."

There go those pink cheeks again. She looks down as I pull her onto my lap. "I don't know."

I've been around the block. I know that is girl speak for, "I liked it, but I am uncomfortable admitting to it." But we are getting married, and I want to be able to talk about this stuff with my wife. So, I wrap my arms around her waist and ask her, "Did it feel good or bad?"

Her voice is dry. "Good."

"There is no shameful pleasure between us. If it felt good, then it's something we should talk about so we can do it even better next time."

"Well … " she hesitates. "What did you think of it?"

"I loved it. I love any time I can find a new way to make you lose your mind."

She laughs and holds onto my neck. "You're really good at that, you know."

"Given the reception at the door, I would hope so." I rearrange her until she's straddling me. "See, I recently got engaged to this incredibly hot, sexy, wild woman, and I want to give her the best orgasms of her life. Any tips?"

She leans back and yanks her dress over her head, leaving her in her bra, garter belt, stockings, and heels. She unpins her hair, shaking it out right in front of me. If there is a better sight in the world, I don't want it. I can die happily right here, right now. She smirks and says, "I think the stuff by the door was a good start."

"Just a start, huh?"

"Mm-hmm."

"I'll have to—"

Her phone goes off in the other room, and my head falls forward in disappointment. Except I can't be too disappointed. My head fell into her cleavage.

"Sorry," she says as she climbs off my lap. "I forgot to turn it to silent." She dashes out the door, and as unpleasant as it is for her to be off of my lap, it *did* afford me the view of her ass in that get-up, and damn. Just … damn. But when she returns, the mood is dead. I can tell. Her face has that hardness she only gets when work is important.

Fuck.

"Fuck."

I frown. "That's my line."

She sighs and sits on the bed. "It's Eddie, one of the paralegals from the office. He's asking about tomorrow's Kerwin presentation, and that is making me remember that I didn't finish the slides. It's first thing in the morning, baby. I'm sorry, I—"

"I don't want to sound like a dick, but can't someone else handle this for you? Isn't that why you have paralegals?"

"Not for this. This is a big project Andre only trusts me to handle. Baby, I'm sorry—"

"Say no more. Let's um … " Shit. I don't want to make her feel worse about this, but this is not how tonight was supposed to go, and disappointed does not begin to cover how I'm feeling right now. But I fix my smile into place so she doesn't feel bad. "Let's go home so you can work on your presentation."

She doesn't jump right on the offer, and she's doing that lip-chewing thing she does when she's nervous.

Great. There's more to this. "What is it?"

"Don't be mad—"

"Every great conversation starts that way, right?"

June huffs. "I didn't expect to be able to sleep tonight, so I brought my laptop so I could do work after you fell asleep."

"I'm not sure what it says about my prowess that you thought you wouldn't sleep tonight—"

"You know how stressed out I am, Anderson. You know I don't sleep when I'm like this."

"I have never seen you like this before, baby."

Her eyes go big, and then she tries to pretend that didn't happen. "Right. Well, I'm going to—"

"Wait—when did I see you this stressed out before?"

June sighs. "I forgot that you didn't, actually."

"I don't understand."

Again, she stares down. "When you first came home … after you were shot … I stayed up the first three nights watching you sleep."

"What?"

"I couldn't fall asleep, knowing you might not wake up. But if I watched you sleep, then I knew you'd be alive in the morning." My heart breaks on those words. She huffs at herself. "I know that's not how it works. The doctors worked miracles, and you—"

I kiss her. I can't believe she did that. This whole time … I'd thought she was Super Woman, taking care of me. But I never knew how bad it affected her. She kept that from me. I break the kiss. "Never again, June."

"What? I mean, I hope you're never shot again—"

"Not that. When you're stressed out like this, you fucking tell me. We talk. We get it out in the open. We don't hide how deeply affected we are. Not from each other. You can depend on me. I need you to know that, and I need you to act like it, okay? Show me that you trust me enough to be there for you."

She leans against my shoulder. "I hear what you're saying, and under normal circumstances, sure. But baby, you were so doped out of your mind those first few days, even if I had told you, I doubt you'd remember."

I chuckle, shaking my head. She's right about that. "Okay, fine. Maybe not right then, but it's been over two months. You could have said something between now and then. Let me be here for you. Please."

"Okay." She takes a breath. "Right now, I won't be able to enjoy any of this until I get the Kerwin presentation done."

I nod. "Alright then. You put on some clothes, or I can't promise I'll let you work, and I will get comfortable and watch you work."

She kisses me, stealing my breath like a thief. "Thank you for understanding, baby."

"You got it."

11

ANDERSON

After she changes into pajamas I didn't know she brought, she gets to work, and I stay in bed next to her. It doesn't take long before the rhythm of her typing lulls me into a drifty sort of sleep. When she mumbles a curse, and I wake a little, before rolling over for more dreams of June bouncing on my lap.

They are very good dreams.

The slap of her laptop closing wakes me. But I don't let her know I'm awake. Thanks to her working with a backlit keyboard, she didn't need much light to work by, so the room is dim enough that she doesn't see me peeking through half-shut eyes. I want to watch her without her knowing I'm watching. Feels like peering behind the curtain into her mind.

June keeps her guard up — always has. Even around me.

Especially around me.

I was a dick to her when we were kids, so I had it coming. But even now, there's always a little distance between her thoughts and what she says out loud to me. I get it as much as I can. She has been through a lot of shit no one should ever experience. But I know there's more she hasn't told me about, things she keeps to herself. I doubt she's ever told anyone about all the shit she's been through. I know she loves me — that's not in question. But I wish she'd trust me more.

So, in times like this, I wait and watch June without her walls up.

Even in the dim light, I see the sweet smile on her face when she looks at me. Fuck, she's so damn beautiful that it makes my chest ache. I cannot believe this dirty angel is mine. I want to give her the world. She deserves that and more.

June bends down and plants a kiss on my cheek, and all my restraint is used up.

I loop my arm around her and pull her onto me. She squeals in surprise as I do it, and I'm hard in a flash. She giggles when I pull her legs apart, so she straddles me. "You scared the shit out of me!" But she's smiling as she says it. "I thought you were asleep!"

"You know how much I love surprising you." I thrust up at her from beneath the blanket to surprise her again.

The sweetest giggles in the world pour out of her, but she tries to sound annoyed when she says, "At least let me get my clothes off first."

"Only because it pleases me," I say as haughtily as I can.

She laughs at that, then crawls off of me to undress. I could watch that every day of my life and never tire of seeing it. Her perfect tits spring free of her top, and when she shimmies out of her pajama bottoms, my heart speeds up. June's warm brown eyes gaze hotly at me. "Enjoying the show?"

"I prefer a hands-on approach."

Her smile grows. "So do I." Then she crawls back onto the bed, pressing herself against me over the blanket as she does. When her lips are almost on mine, she pauses. "Any chance we can make this quick? I have that presentation in the morning, and —"

I pull her down to my mouth. I will eat those words and make her forget about presentations and anything else that isn't us. Her lips open to me like she's eager to forget all about that, too. I reach down and pluck at her nipples. Her moans make my balls throb for release. "No more talking about work."

"But —"

"That's it," I say with a grunt as I turn her around. She goes willingly, much to my surprise. When June has something on her mind, it's hard to dissuade her from it. If she wants to try to talk about work, then I'll steal her breath the best way I know how. "If I can't keep you focused on something else, then I'll distract you." I split her legs apart again, this time with a knee at either side of my shoulders. Fuck, the view from here. Her pussy is already wet and shining in the low light. I grab her ample hips and anchor her to my face.

For a brief moment, she tenses up, but then she melts against me as I taste her. She gasps, "Oh god!"

Being that she's upside-down over me, I use my chin on her clit, hoping I'm not too stubbly for her there. But she sounds like she loves it. I take long, sweeping licks of her pussy until I bury my tongue in her and drink from the source. She tastes so damn good I could weep.

Her wet mouth swallows my cock down, and I groan into her. Been a long time since I've done it this way, but fuck I've missed it. She goes after my cock like this might be her last chance to taste one. The angle must be off for her because she uses a fist around the base to keep my shaft covered. Her grip is tight.

I tip my head back. "Loosen the hand a little."

She does, and it's exquisite. Like wet velvet come to devour me.

I return to her pussy and dive in face first. I cannot get enough of her, and she's dripping down my neck. June rocks against my face and her body tenses in the good way. I know she's close, but I want to change this up before that happens. Reaching beneath the pillows, I grab the bottle of lube I stashed in there while she got her pajamas on. I slick my fingers up and glide them around her ass until they dip into her there.

She comes up off my dick. Her hot breaths fall on the head, making me twitch. "Oh my god, what are you … oh … "

"Feel good, baby?"

"Yeah, I just … fuck," she mutters before going back to my cock.

Now, it's not only her core that tenses, but her pussy, too. She pulses on my tongue. Her breaths are ragged around my cock, and when she comes, I worry I might drown. But I'd do it for her. Anything for her pleasure.

She tries to roll off of me, but I follow her and end up on top. I turn to face her and let her taste herself on my tongue. "See? You taste amazing."

Her sultry eyes send a jolt of heat through me. She pulls me down for another kiss, lapping herself up off my tongue. I hoist her legs over my shoulders and fold her in half before sliding myself into her pussy. Her shocked moans tell me it's good, but when she gasps for breath, she tightly growls, "Yeah, baby, just like that!"

I've got her trapped beneath me. No more work talk. No more thoughts of the horrors of her day. Just me and her and this moment, pumping into her, connecting us like nothing else ever could. Sweat drips down my back while I pound into her. Fuck, this is everything. *She* is everything. When she comes again, her scream must carry into the hall because I've lost my hearing. Temporarily or not, it's worth it. The woman of my dreams is squirming on my cock, better than any fantasy I've ever—no. There is one more thing.

I gentle her legs down and pull out, rolling her onto her side before she can even speak. I slide into her from behind and hook her thigh over my hip in the same fluid motion. Once in place, I start up with her clit as I fuck her slower from behind on our sides.

She babbles incoherently, shuddering against me as she rolls herself back for my length. It's too good. If I don't switch it up now, I'll lose it. But then she clenches on me again, and I force my body to obey. Not yet. Not until she's done.

June's shriek is music to my ears. I keep at her until she tries to pull away. Only then do I let up on her clit. I pull out and aim for her ass. Without a word, I slide around there, waiting for her permission or her objection. She squirms against me, and I can't tell which that is.

I growl in her ear, "You have five seconds before my cock is in your ass, baby."

She whimpers, "Mm, yes."

Thank god. I slide in, just the tip at first. But she tenses up. I tell her, "Breathe and let yourself relax. I'm not going to shove in. I don't want to hurt you. I want to make you come apart the right way."

She bobs her head, and I hear a big breath flow out of her perfect lips. "Okay."

Gradually, I work my way in, back and forth just a half inch at a time. By her reactions from before, I don't think she's ever done this, and I want to make her crave it, so I reach around and start in on her clit again. A tremble courses through her, and I almost slide back out. But I get back in a second later, and she starts to roll back to meet me not long after. She likes it. Fuck, yes.

June pants, "Why does this feel so good?"

"Because it's you and me, baby. You and me. I will always make you feel good if you let me."

She murmurs more prayers than I can count, and in between them are curses that would make a sailor blush. Her head digs back against my shoulder as she shakes. A voice so hoarse I can hardly hear it rasps, "Close!"

"That's my girl. Come with my cock buried in your ass." I add a finger into her pussy, keeping my palm on her clit. I'm fucking her pussy and her ass together, and I've never felt so electric in my life. Her ass is so tight and all mine. Every part of me is wrapped up in her pleasure. It's too much. Heat broils me from the inside. I'm ready to pop, but then she lets out a guttural, primal thing from her very soul, and I vow to keep going. She rocks so hard against me that I'm convinced I'll bruise her ass with my hip bones. Something sears me from the inside out, and I can't keep going. This is too fucking good. "You're gonna make me come—"

"Yes!" she bellows.

I pull out, shooting on her back and marking her as mine.

-

12

JUNE

Who turned the lights on? Anderson is still in bed, and I didn't do it. Maybe turndown service? But why would—"

Oh shit. It's morning!

"Anderson, wake up! We overslept!" I jump out of bed, not waiting for him to respond. On my way to the shower, I hear him mumble into the pillow, but I can't stop now. I have the Kerwin presentation in less than an hour.

Never have I scrubbed a debauched night off my body so fast. But even as I rub the soap all over, I can't stop thinking about last night. Not the presentation work. Anderson. The way he touched me in places I've never let anyone else explore…hell, I'm getting distracted. *Focus, June.*

Promising my body to revisit what we did is the only way for me to get out of the shower without jumping his bones. I'm still tender from last night, but I am so game for that again. It was earth-shattering, and I want more.

I throw on the pantsuit I had packed last night as Anderson manages to sit up in bed. "Good morning. I am sorry to fly out of here, but—"

"It's fine, baby," he says with a sleepy smile. "I have to get going, too. But I have a little more leeway on when I walk into the office than you do."

I nod once, then bend over for a kiss. He grabs me and pulls me onto his lap for a better kiss, one that swipes any thought I had of work and replaces them with thoughts of last night. I growl in his mouth, annoyed that I have to pull away. "One of us has to be a responsible adult."

He grins. "Yeah, I know. I wasn't going to let it go anywhere."

"Then why are you hard?"

His grip tightens. "That's entirely your fault, missy. You look too sexy in that pantsuit. And out of it. And in your floppy pajamas, and your—"

I giggle. "Thank you, but I have to get going."

"Alright, alright." With reservations, he relinquishes his hold on my hip. "I know you have to run. Sorry."

"We can continue this conversation tonight. Or maybe this afternoon if I can get out of there early."

He grins. "Deal."

With that, I bolt out of the most expensive hotel room I have ever stayed in and onto the street. My office isn't far, and thankfully, it's not raining today. Just freaking freezing. But I'll take that over icy rain or snow.

Once I get to work, I grab a coffee on my way to my office. It's then that I realize Anderson let me sleep for an hour last night. One solitary hour. The initial jolt of adrenaline from when I realized we'd overslept is gone, but the coffee hits way too hard and too fast, and I have the shakes in minutes that feel like seconds.

I get to the conference room, and most of the people are already inside, including my boss, Andre Moeller. He's a strange man, and I cannot figure him out. Andre was friendly with Elliot West—Anderson's dad—a long time ago, but they had a falling out after a debt wasn't paid, and in response, Andre kidnapped me. Once that got settled, he offered me a job, and because Elliot had me blackballed out of my industry otherwise, I took it out of desperation. In his own way, Andre has been nothing but respectful to me. But the man is a sociopath, and I cannot afford to forget that. Who else has someone kidnapped?

He smiles when he sees me enter the room, and there is always something unsettling about his smiles. It's like watching a shark smile right as they close in on you. Not so much a smile as opening their mouth a bit wider to swallow you whole.

Andre is a white man in his fifties with brown hair, neatly trimmed and silver-sided. He has a medium build, which makes you want to underestimate him.

But looking into his green eyes tells you that would be your final mistake. "June, by the spring in your step, I assume you're here to dazzle us. By all means, get started."

"I thought the others would be —"

"Now."

Okey dokey. I smile and nod, then get jacked into the system for the big screen on the far wall. The conference rooms are almost all the same, except this one. It's the room Andre uses exclusively, so it has the best over-padded chairs, espresso station, electronics, and views. Even though I have the caffeine shakes, I eye the espresso station longingly before I begin.

Apparently, an hour of sleep after a night of filthy sex was exactly what I needed because I sailed through the presentation. When the latecomers showed up, I didn't stutter. My data was on-point, my voice clear, and for once, I actually enjoyed presenting my work to Andre. Fielding his questions was a breeze. I felt less like a bug under his magnifying glass, and more like the professional that I am. It's been a long time since I've felt gratified in my career.

Before everything went to shit at my former employer, I'd begun to hate my job because I was busy catering to the rich and famous and helping them avoid their rightful tax burden. Everything annoyed me and I was counting the years until retirement. After Elliot tore my career apart and left it in shreds, I hated that being a tax attorney left me with so few options outside of my field, but right now, I'm almost grateful for his foolishness because it got me here to this moment.

Andre grins at the end of things. "So, I'll be able to purchase all of them if I'm following you."

I nod. "Every last share will be yours, Andre. All you have to do is place the order. The other shareholders are looking forward to the change, and those who object, well, they don't have a leg to stand on."

He claps once, startling everyone else, but then they nervously clap with him, and the mood in the room shifts. "June, I knew you had it in you. You doubted yourself, but I knew. I told myself, there is a woman with a fire in her that would burn down cities for me if I let her. This is big. Huge, really. And you'll be by my side for all of it. We will remake Boston in my image. The Moeller name will echo—"

His phone rings, and he interrupts himself to take it but says, "Tell Marla to get champagne for everyone. We're celebrating."

I smile, happy he is so happy and also glad he got a call because I sense that little speech of his could have gone on forever. I start for the door to tell the EA in the vestibule to grab the champagne.

Moeller cuts himself off again and says, "Not you, June. You don't do those kinds of errands anymore. Harrison, go tell Marla."

Harrison is one of his partners, and now *he's* the one made to do errands Andre sees as beneath me? Is he getting ousted? He winces a bit before being made into Andre's errand boy. But once the champagne is poured, everyone is more relaxed. Even Harrison.

I cannot believe how easily the presentation came to me. I'm sure it helps that I was able to tell Andre what he wanted to hear, but still, I'm pretty proud of that. Everyone mixes into different clusters of chatting suits, and a few congratulate me on my work, but when Andre comes to me, I'm less nervous than usual.

Sure, it wouldn't shock me to see him push a partner out of a window one day, but today, I've made him happy, so I have no reason to think something is up.

"You saved me, June. My hero."

I laugh and sip, unsure quite what to say. I'm glad to have the crystal flute in hand. It gives me something to stall with. "I'm just happy to help, Andre."

"You have earned my trust, and I admit, there are few who have it. Certainly not this lot," he says dismissively as he looks around. No one is paying attention to us—not outwardly. But I'm sure each of them heard that, and it's a little awkward for me. Some of these people are my direct colleagues. He continues, "As the purchases go through, I'll want you as my right hand on the deals."

"Of course."

"Pity about your fiancé."

I should be used to Andre's wild subject changes by

now, but I'm not, especially when he hits Anderson territory. "Pity?"

He takes my hand, examining my ring. Still smiling, but less so around his eyes now. "He has exquisite taste." He looks into my eyes. "In rings, I mean." He does not mean rings.

I've always wondered if Andre's flattery is interest, and I still can't quite tell. Some men just like to speak flirtatiously to keep a woman off her game. But he has no reason to do that now. So, I go with a neutral response. "Anderson picked well."

"Truly, he did." His lips twitch. "I hope he does not mind when you'll be working late at the office. We'll practically be on top of each other until this is done."

I gulp the champagne, wishing it was whiskey. "He knows what my work entails. It'll be fine."

Andre closes the gap between us, almost in kissing distance, and I could not be less comfortable. But I don't step back. If this is some kind of power play, I'm not giving in. His voice is quieter now. "I require a picture from my office, and I'd like you to get it for me while I handle some things here. It's on a silver digital frame, one of those that changes the images every minute. Right on my desk. You can't miss it."

"Sure," I almost frown. I fetch his personal things now? Weird. Maybe that's a step up from ordering champagne, I can't tell. "But I don't have access—"

He passes me his guest keycard. "Now you do. Thank you in advance." With that, he strolls to annoy Harrison.

When it comes to Andre Moeller, I never know what to expect. But today has gone better than it has any right to, so I zip out with the keycard and go to his office. It's huge and extravagant, just as I expected for someone of his stature. But I'm not here to stare, so I head straight for his desk and grab the picture frame. It's the only one there, so that makes it easier.

But as I grab it, a word catches my eye on some papers on his desk. "E. West."

I shouldn't snoop. I know this. But when it comes to Anderson's family, I don't have boundaries. Quickly, I flick through the paperwork, and as I do, my stomach sinks. No, no, no, please, no.

Every company Andre has had me set up for him to take over is linked to Elliot West. He is the majority shareholder, or sometimes, the silent partner, or set up in one arrangement or another, and ... he's going to lose everything but West Media. If he loses all his other holdings, how long is it before Andre comes for that, too? How long before his shareholders lose their faith in Elliot? For that matter, how long before the West family is a relic from a bygone era?

I'm gonna be sick.

I've been working to tear the West family apart this whole time. What have I done?

13

ANDERSON

"..." So the question becomes, who gave her the idea to do the Grainger picture?" Dad asks, while he already knows the answer.

There are times I hate being a West. Staring at my father is one of them. He looks like me but thirty years older. It is disconcerting to know my blue eyes, black hair, and strong jaw come from him. I like seeing the gray in his hair these days. It makes me feel less connected to him, given my hair remains black. But if I had my druthers, I wouldn't be connected to my father at all.

Sure, we've become a little closer since I got shot. The old man worries about me in his own way. I can't say how much of that is from him or from Mom, though. I have never doubted her love for me. She never gave me a reason to doubt her. His love, on the other hand, has been in question since the day I was born.

None of that matters now, though. I still want to destroy Elliot West for everything he's done to June. And to me.

"We both know it was my idea, Dad. Why are you drawing this out?"

With his elbows on his massive desk, he steeples his fingers and huffs. I've never enjoyed being the target of his ire, but being the source of his irritation? No one does it better than me. But right now, I have too many things on my mind to enjoy getting his goat.

For one, the police harassing June. Two, being at my office feels like being a sitting duck, and I don't like it. So, three, dragging things out with Dad means I don't have to be in my office. The police would never barge in here. Aside from the fact Dad has a lot of powerful friends, enough of them know to steer clear of him.

I really wish that fear translated to me, but I doubt that it does.

He snarls, "Because, Anderson, that was my attempt to gracefully encourage you to explain yourself. In what reality is it a good idea for a teen actress to show her breasts? Maybe more, actually, given Grainger's reputation. His excuse for arthouse is little more than pornography."

"You mean, why is it a good idea to devalue her topless paparazzi pics? Aren't you the one who taught me that move?"

He remains unconvinced. "It is the right call—"

"See?"

"For an *adult* actress. Trina Malark is practically a child! We do not engage in that kind of thing, and we certainly do not encourage others to do so!"

"She is nineteen —"

"Exactly!"

I laugh, shaking my head at him. "If she can be tried as an adult, she's not a child."

"I am not speaking in legalities, Anderson. I am speaking in morals."

My second laugh explodes out of me. "Are you fucking kidding me with this shit? Since when do you, Elliot West, give a shit about morals?"

"All that money spent on a proper education and still you pepper your sentences with curse words like some drunken bar patron," he mumbles to himself.

"Because you're such a saint?"

"We both know I am not, but I save my spicier language for when it is appropriate."

I smile, sitting back. "You a fan of that family show Trina was on?"

For once in my life, I see my father taken aback. It's refreshing to see him on the shocked side of the equation. In fact, I'm practically giddy over it.

But his stunned expression vanishes in a flash. "We

both know I do not watch television. Who has time for that nonsense?"

"So, if I text Mom right now and ask about it, she won't confirm that you—"

"Do not pester your mother with such things. She does not have time for your nonsense today."

That doesn't sound good. "She okay?"

"Fine, fine. Kitty has her annual doctor appointments today. All routine, nothing to worry over. But she's too busy to entertain you." He lets out an exasperated huff. I can't tell if it's for me or something else. "Fine. I liked Trina's show. Are you happy?"

"I really am." The thought of my father watching some family sitcom tickles me. The man, who has had countless people killed and beaten down, has a soft spot for the world's most generic show. "Who'd have thought Elliot West—"

He cuts me off with a flick of his hand. "Enough."

"Is that why we rep for her?"

"No. We were hired to do a job. Her father, Abe, is a friend. He is none too pleased about my son recommending his daughter get naked on camera for money."

"Ah. So, here's the real answer. Your pride's been bruised, and now you're trying to save face with a friend."

He leans over the desk, glowering. "Trina is a child, Anderson. I watched her grow up on that show. She's not doing the Grainger film. Period."

"This has nothing to do with your pride, does it? Is it because it grosses you out?"

"Get her to quit the film. That's an order." He resumes his normal position now that he's laid down an order.

As endlessly amusing as I find this situation, I do not want to renege on my advice. It looks weak. "She'll think I don't know what I'm doing—"

"Lie to the girl, Anderson. It doesn't matter how you get her out of it. Just get her out of it. Tell her you heard the film is going to tank. Stir a rumor about Grainger himself. I don't care how you do it. Just see it done."

"Fine." I shrug a shoulder. Now that's over, I have other business to attend. Mostly to figure out what the hell I have to do to get the police off our backs. I give a tight smile, unsure what I'll tell Trina about the Grainger film, but I'm pretty sure I could tell her anything, and she'd do it. She trusts me. "I'll take care of it."

But as I stand up to leave, he shakes his head. "We're not done."

"There's more?"

"Sit."

That can't be good. I struggle not to keep standing just to annoy him. His office chairs are lacking in the comfort department. In fact, everything in his office is. It's all cold, hard surfaces, gray-on-gray. One of the first things I'll change about his office, if I ever take the mantle of CEO like he wants.

But I sit down to make whatever else he has to go over easier. "What is it?"

He checks his phone, looking pleased, before he glances at me. "While I am certain you had your reasons for killing Neil Johnson, they are immaterial to me. What I need you to do is to clean up your mess. As such, I have hired Otto Pym."

My face feels cold. Makes sense. All the blood has rushed away from it. With three simple sentences, Dad told me everything I needed to know. He knows I've killed someone. He doesn't know why and doesn't care. And he's hired the sharkiest lawyer in this hemisphere to handle it.

I'm not sure when I stopped blinking, but my eyes are dry. So is my throat. I don't even know what to say, and the only thing that comes out of my mouth is, "What?"

He smiles like the cat who caught the canary. "You seem to think you can keep me in the dark about your life. It would be funny if it didn't prove to me how ill-prepared you are to live life without my help."

"I didn't—"

"Now, now. I thought we were past lying to one another. Tell me what June told the police."

So, he knows about that, too … just not what she said. Does he have a spy at Andre's office? That would track. I imagine he has spies in the confessional at the Cathedral of the Holy Cross.

"She didn't give them anything—"

"What did she say?"

"She made it seem like she was a ditzy bartender who flirts with everyone and that Neil was one of them. That we were on a break then and she was looking for some comfort. But when he went off about women telling him what to do, she sent him home for the night."

He eyes me carefully like he's trying to suss out whether I'm lying. But finally, his gaze settles. "Was that your plan or hers?"

"Hers. We couldn't figure anything out, so she came up with it on the fly."

"Smart. You have a good one there, son." He pauses, almost as though he might retract that statement. "What did Neil actually do?"

Should I tell him? Is there harm in that? "He attacked June."

Points to my father, he looks repulsed. I guess there are things that are beneath him, after all. "And you took him out, but instead of calling the police, you called Moss."

Moss. That has to be how he knows. But Moss wouldn't betray me. At least, I don't think he would.

"Given my martial arts background, I thought it best the police stayed out of it."

"I'd hardly call a few state championships a background, but at the moment, people panic … " He takes a breath. "Which is why you're not ready for this office yet. If you were, you would not have panicked. You would have called the police and let them handle things. You fucked this up, Anderson. It's a good thing I called Otto. You need a man of his skill. Do whatever he tells you to do, without question, and he will save your life."

A comforting thought. But, then again, I'd thought the same about Moss.

"The police wish to speak to you. Otto will be with you. Don't fuck this up."

-

14

JUNE

I should tell Anderson. But each time I start to text him, my hands shake. He's going to hate me. Even if he doesn't, do we really need this kind of stress right now? With the police sniffing around, the collapse of his family's fortune and legacy isn't something he needs to deal with at the moment.

So, by keeping it to myself, I'm protecting him. Aren't I?

Okay, I'm protecting myself. I know I am. It would be foolish to think I'm doing anything else by keeping this from him.

Instead of calling him about Andre, I use voice-to-text to tell him to meet me at home tonight instead of the hotel. I'd rather be there, where we know not to talk about legal issues. That way, if I clam up, he won't try to dig into things. I can be evasive without him getting upset.

I can get away with keeping this secret for at least one more day and give myself enough time to come up with a way to tell my fiancé, "Hey, I accidentally helped destroy your family." Though, I'm not sure one more day will help with that.

After I delivered the picture frame to Andre, I made up an excuse and went to my office for a few hours before texting Anderson about going home. I've been in here ever since, trying to figure out how to calm the hell down before meeting up with him. Pacing in heels is not my idea of fun, so I'm barefoot in my office with the curtains drawn and the lights down low to help me clear my head. Thankfully, my carpet is plush.

How in the hell am I going to get out of any of this?

I'm an accomplice to the improper disposing of a body. I am also an accomplice to hostile takeovers of the Wests' companies. For fuck's sake, I'd like to be in trouble for something I did on purpose for once in my life. Instead, I'm just an accomplice.

I laugh once and sharply at myself. The truth is, I'd prefer never to be a criminal and to never be in trouble. Keeping my nose clean was how I got places in the world. It was how I kept my scholarships for schools my family could not afford and how I kept my grades up once I got there. I did not screw up. I did not fall for scams or make poor choices. When I was younger, I was the friend whose friends' parents used as an example of a good kid. They used to complain that at home, they'd hear, "Why can't you be more like June?"

Pretty sure those days are over now. No one wants a kid in the kind of trouble I'm in.

Okay, what to do … If I come clean with the police, there will be legal fallout all over the place, mostly in the form of Anderson facing serious prison time while I have short prison time. So, that is not an option. If I come clean with Anderson, he has every right to break up with me. I'm supposed to be smarter than this. I should have seen this shit coming. He will be so fucking disappointed in me. Almost as much as I am.

I should have known Andre was up to some shit when he hired me. He wants to use me to twist the knife. To hurt the West family that much more when he scoops up half their revenue. Hell, that was his move with me the first time when he kidnapped me. He'd done it just to prove a point to Elliot. That point being that no one on his side of their equation was untouchable.

How in the hell didn't I see Andre's devilry before now?

And if I tell Anderson any of it, he will break up with me. The thought makes my chest tight. I force deep breaths, and it hurts. My ribs are too tight. No, it's the bra. I unhook it, leaving my blouse undone in the back. Okay, I can take deep breaths now, but am I even worthy of them? I've fucked everything up.

I groan at myself and fall onto my couch. It's far more comfortable than it looks, and it's long enough for me to stretch out on. But being still feels like going backward. Somehow, pacing feels like I'm doing something useful.

I sit up and debate more pacing. But the truth is, I'm just spinning my wheels, and I know it. Something has to give. Anderson kept bringing up me trusting him lately, and he's right. I need to depend on him more. I can't handle this all myself. If I could just tell Anderson about Andre's scheme without worrying he'd dump me, then I would tell him about this.

But if I do that, then that's one more thing on his shoulders. I know he says he's fine about his brush with mortality, but he was shot and almost died, and now, he's worried about the whole Neil thing. He doesn't need another huge worry stacked onto him. It's just not fair, and I—"

Someone knocks at my door, and I damn near leap out of my skin. I hook my bra together and tuck my blouse back in. "Come in."

In walks Carlos, looking like a million bucks in his designer suit. But for once, he isn't smiling. At least, not with his mouth. His eyes, on the other hand, practically dance in his well-formed skull. Unlike every other time he's come into my office, he closes the door behind him.

It feels like a threat.

I stand up, not willing to deal with him sitting down unless he is, too. "Carlos, what can I do for you?"

It's then that his trademark smile slashes across his face. "June, June, June. Devlin, soon to be West, correct?"

I have never told him who I'm marrying, and I do not like that he knows so much. Though, to be fair, when you're involved with the Wests, it's almost like everyone knows your business before you do. "I'll be keeping my name. What makes you ask?"

Unbidden, he strolls to my guest chair and plops down before fiddling with the arm of the chair. "This office needs a refresh, don't you think?"

"Considering I decorated it less than three months ago, no. I don't." I walk to my desk, but I don't sit. I'd hate for him to mistake us as on equal footing. Instead, I lean on the edge with my hip and fold my arms to glare down at him.

"It is nice enough, I suppose," he says, glancing around. "But it will be so much nicer once I've put my mark on it."

I huff a laugh at him. "And what makes you think you'll have the chance?"

"Fate."

"Are you here for a real reason or simply because you're bored, because I'm sure Andre would love to know — "

"I'm sure there are many things Andre would love to know, June." He smirks up at me. "Don't you?"

What the fuck does he know? He can't possibly know anything about Neil, right?

But instead of giving him the satisfaction of seeing me panic, I smile down at him. I will not give Carlos what he wants. Let the police drag me away in chains, but I will *never* let Carlos see me upset. Every time he opens his mouth, I want to punch his perfect teeth.

Calmly, I tell him, "Andre is a curious man. I bet you're right. Why don't you bother him with whatever is on your mind instead of bothering me?"

"He's out for the rest of the day, sadly." He picks at invisible lint on the chair arm. "Seems he's too excited with his new protégé to sit still. He said something about taking his yacht out for the afternoon. Which means the rest of us are left with little more to do than to amuse ourselves."

"Well. As amusing as you think you are, I have work to do. Don't let the door hit you on the way out."

"Do you truly feel dismissing me is your best course of action, June? For all you know, it could be the worst mistake of your life."

Credit to Carlos, he is good at saying cryptic shit to make me curious. But I have enough on my plate to deal with. Whatever he's getting at—telling Andre about Neil, telling Anderson about Andre, talking to the police about something he thinks he knows—it's like a hidden gun. No point in getting upset about it until I know for certain it's there or until he shoots. I don't have time to deal with anything less.

"I've made a lot of worst mistakes in my life, but you know what happens every single time, Carlos?" I step closer to him and look up into his eyes. "I win. So think carefully about coming into my office and threatening me with your smoke and mirrors. The worst mistake you can make is underestimating me. Now go." I turn around and flick my hand dismissively toward the door as I walk to my chair. "I have actual business to attend to, something I'm sure you're not familiar with since Andre doesn't like you."

That earns his arched brow as I put my feet up on my desk and lean back. Petulantly, he asks, "What do you mean Andre doesn't like me?"

"A slip of the tongue," I lie. "Nothing for you to worry about. Yet."

He recovers his smooth exterior by smiling like a used car salesman. "I suppose we'll see. After all, legal issues don't ever really disappear, do they?"

After he closes the door behind him, I hold my head in my hands. What the fuck was that?

15

JUNE

I did it. I managed to keep my mouth shut for a whole day about anything serious. Me and Anderson had a nice night at home, complete with snuggling and talking about day before bed. We pretended to be a normal couple, and not just for whoever might be listening, but also for ourselves. It was a luxury, and we both know it, but like the hotel room, we needed the artifice of that.

Today, though, I'm back in the line of fire. Or at least, that's what it feels like when I see Mitch. Dad. Whatever, I've decided to call him now.

It's still strange to think of him as Dad, even though I do. After he totally upended our lives when I was a kid, Mitch was what I had relegated him to. But he's making an effort to fix his life, and that includes a relationship with me, evidently. How can I crap on that?

Experience, my bitter inner monologue says. But I'm trying to get at least one thing right in my life, and if that ends up being my relationship with my father, then so be it.

He's taken me to another fancy lunch — Dock 814, this time. It's a seafood joint on the water, and each time Dad takes me somewhere nice, it is still a strange thing for my brain to wrap around. When I was a kid, we weren't even middle class. He was too busy spending his ill-gotten gains on his mistresses instead of me and Mom, so it was a childhood of boxed macaroni and cheese and basic cable only on the months we could afford it. Sitting here with Dad is surreal.

Over oysters, he asks, "So, how is engagement treating you?"

"Good, thanks. Honestly, things between me and Anderson have never been better." Because I'm keeping things from him.

"Glad to hear it. He better keep treating my daughter like the prize she is."

"Oh, now you're protective of me?"

He smiles but frowns at the same time. Happy, wide lips but a line in his brow. "What's that supposed to mean?"

"Remember the time you had me steal Mrs. Flanagan's apples?"

He laughs. "That old bat was just letting them rot. It wasn't right."

"Yeah, and you made me go get them because you knew she wouldn't shoot a kid."

"You know you were never in any danger. She would have never—"

"I was seven!" I say with a laugh. "All I knew was what you and Mom always said about her. That she was crazy and armed. I mean, I know now, but at the time ... " I shake my head, still smiling at the memory. "At the time, I was sure I'd get shot for a backpack full of fruit."

"They were really good apples if I recall. Might have been worth it."

I laugh and smack his hand. "You jerk."

He grins. "And you were never shot, so I think we came out ahead on that score."

"Nuh-uh. When she found me and dragged me into her house, I damn near peed myself."

"Aw, poor kid. I never meant for you to get caught."

I shrug. "Well, I did. But I never told you about what happened after that."

He thinks for a moment. "I don't think so. What happened?"

When I think about it, I can still smell the inside of that crazy woman's house. She was a hoarder, so there were stacks of newspapers lining the walls, and some of them had gone to rot. "She showed me her shotgun—"

"No!"

I nod. "And she showed me that she had no ammo for it. Just that she liked to wave it around to scare people off. She asked if I was hungry, and I said yes because I was, but looking back on it, I think she meant *going* hungry. She said I couldn't steal again, but if I was hungry, then I was welcome to come get a couple of apples for myself whenever."

"That mean woman did that for you?"

"Yeah. And I'm pretty sure she's the one who started dropping off those anonymous bags of groceries that showed up sometimes."

He smiles and lets out a sad sigh. "Well, hell. I've been thinking about her all wrong this whole time. Guess you can't judge a book—"

"She's still the same woman who pointed a shotgun at children to scare them, so don't go getting the warm and fuzzies for her just yet."

"Eh, still. She tried to help my family when I should have been doing exactly that. I can't hate her anymore."

It makes me incredibly happy whenever he says things like that. It shouldn't, and I know that. Acknowledging his failures counts as doing the bare minimum. But not long ago, he didn't even do that, so I see it as big progress for him. And what can I say? He's my dad. I want to see him do better.

If he can get redemption, maybe there's hope for me, too.

"Okay, sure. Old Mrs. Flanagan gets a little redemption for helping us. Do you remember her Christmas decorations?"

He laughs. "That sad string of red lights around her railing that made it look like she was either running a winter brothel or beckoning the devil to her door? Yep. Hard to forget it. Every time she came out to yell at people in her winter coat and bathrobe and curlers, she was underlit in red and looked like the crotchetiest demon this side of hell."

"But it *was* festive," I say, laughing.

"Certainly put Mr. Bryson in the holiday spirit. That codger was her best-paying customer."

I roll my eyes. "Dad, she wasn't running a brothel."

"I guess it's not a brothel when it's just one sex worker." He shrugs and gobbles an oyster.

"You don't ... she wasn't ... no."

Slowly, he nods. "You didn't know?"

"She was a thousand years old!"

He laughs. "She was somewhere in her seventies."

"A seventy-something sex worker? You're pulling my chain."

"I wish. But Mr. Bryson was more than happy to brag

about what she could do when she took out her dentures and—"

I plug my ears. "La, la, la, I do not need to hear that. You are ruining my childhood."

He laughs, and we order post-lunch cocktails. Once the server leaves, he says, "I'm glad you said ruin*ing* your childhood."

"What do you mean?"

"That means I didn't ruin it back then."

Oof. My heart. "No, Dad. You didn't. I mean, I definitely had to grow up way too fast, and there are things I'm still … processing. But I had good times as a kid."

"Mixed in with the bad."

I nod. "Pretty sure that's a fitting description of most people's childhoods, though. I imagine yours was a mixed bag, too." He never talks about his youth, and one day, I'd like the story.

"I suppose you're right. Everyone has a childhood with ups and downs." Our drinks come, and we sip in contemplative silence for a few minutes. It is not the awkward silence we used to have, though. Progress. Dad asks, "How are things at work?"

"I killed my presentation this week on one hour of sleep, so I have that going for me."

"That's my kid. Devlins do well under pressure."

Good thing, too. "Guess so."

"And your boss is Andre Moeller, right?"

"Yeah, why?"

"I was hoping you could introduce me to him."

Fuck. There go all the warm feelings and all the happy thoughts of my father just wanting to be my dad again. He's been buttering me up this whole time, and it feels like betrayal. I grit my jaw. "Is that what all of this has been about? Getting in good with me to connect with Andre—"

"What? No!" He looks offended, and I'm not sure if I'm happy about that. "June, we are family. I just thought since you work for the guy, you could do me a favor. But if that's too much to ask, if it's so soon in our reconciliation that you think it's not on the up and up, then forget about it. I have loved getting to reconnect with you, and no multimillion-dollar business deal is worth jeopardizing my relationship with you. So, just forget I asked, okay?"

Crap. Crap, crap, crap. This is the trouble with my father. I can never get a solid read on the guy. "What deal are you talking about?"

"Don't worry about it. This is my problem. Not yours. Dessert?"

"Dad, if there's a problem, then let me help you. Are you having trouble at work?"

He shrugs. "It's not a big deal. I just need to land a big account, and Andre Moeller's law firm would be perfect for that. We'd handle the digital marketing and … " He shakes his head. "Never mind. We are not here for business. You are my daughter, and I never should have asked."

I should let this go. I know it. But he's my dad, and if I can help him, I feel like I should. Still, I need more details. "How did you even get a job there, anyway? Given your record and all that."

He leans in and quietly admits, "I *may* have changed my name and fudged my job history—"

"Dad!"

"But only because I knew I could do the work. And I've been there for years, so I was right about that. Besides, no one checks that kind of thing. They just want to know what you can do for them."

I sigh at myself as well as out loud. "Give me a little time, and I'll see what I can do."

"Thanks, Junebug."

What's one more infraction on my formerly spotless record?

16

ANDERSON

I didn't tell June about Dad knowing yet. I could have told her we needed to go for a walk last night so we could talk, but fuck, she shouldn't have to have this on her. She already takes on too much as it is—I cannot let her know Dad knows about Neil. It'll stress her out even more to know I have to speak to the police.

So, I'll keep it to myself.

Besides, Dad got me Otto Pym. With him in our corner, this is as good as over. I'll let him handle things, and when it's settled down, I'll tell her all about it.

Still, I'm pissed that Dad knows anything about this. That means there's a leak among me, June, and Moss, and I know for fucking certain it was not June, which means I cannot trust Moss as much as I thought I could. Admittedly, that stings. Maybe I am naïve, but I didn't doubt Moss before. He had my back. Or, so I thought.

On the drive to Otto's, my mind races faster than my car. Even with Otto there, I'm not invincible. This could go sideways in a million different directions, and any of them could end up with me in the slammer. That's why we have to meet up first, so we can discuss strategy.

Even innocent people need a strategy when speaking to the police. The job of the police is to make the public feel safer. Sometimes, that means catching the bad guy. Sometimes, that means finding someone to blame, no matter the cost. Innocent people go to prison all the time.

And since I'm not innocent, I need one hell of a strategy.

Otto's office is nothing like what I expected. It's a stump of a building near the outskirts of town. I double-checked the address, but I've got it right. The building looks more industrial than office. It's small, white, and has just a few windows. Nothing high-end about it. This man bills millions of dollars annually. I cannot figure it out.

But I park in front and walk in to find myself in the petite lobby of his office. There's an office manager at her sparse desk. There is not even a filing cabinet in sight. Just two chairs and her. "Mr. West?"

"Yes."

She gestures to one of two doors in the place. "He's expecting you."

I walk in to find a grizzled veteran of the law world behind his desk. The legend, Otto Pym. Gray-haired and grumpy. His voice is gravel in a blender. "Sit. Close the door. Let's talk."

I follow his instructions and find his guest chairs are only slightly more comfortable than Dad's. The office is white and brown, and none of it is designed to match. His desk looks like a discount number from a big box store. How is this Otto Pym?

"Elliot's kid, right?"

I nod. "Otto Pym?" I just need to hear him say it because I'm skeptical.

"That's me. I understand you've gotten yourself into some trouble."

"Forgive me, but you have a reputation for handling some of the highest-profile cases in Boston and New York, and this is your office?"

He laughs, his belly bouncing beneath his shirt. He presses his intercom button. "Gladys, I owe you a steak dinner. You were right. This one is under five minutes."

"Told you."

"The hell?" I ask.

He releases the button. "You're a West. Do you even know how to park your own car, or has a world of valet drivers made that impossible?"

"I'm not here to be belittled for my wealth. I'm here to—"

"Save your ass. Yeah, I know." He pulls an orange out of his drawer and starts peeling it. "And now, you're wondering how I have my rep if this is how I work, right? I'll tell you. It's because I don't take shit from no one. I require absolute transparency from my clients because that is how I save you. I don't bullshit you. You don't bullshit me. We bullshit anyone outside of us, and we do it together."

That's more like it. But still, this office? Those clothes? I know he makes more money than this. But that's none of my business really. If he gets me out of trouble, what do I care what he does with his money?

"Alright then. How do we get started?"

"What happened with you and the dead guy?"

"How do I know there aren't recording devices in—"

"Get out."

I blink. "Excuse me?"

"Clearly, you don't care about saving your own skin, and you don't trust your father to provide the lawyer you need. So, we're done here." He eats a section of orange like he didn't just fire a client. This is just a regular day for him.

"Do you handle all your clients like this?"

"You're not my client. Your father is. Stop wasting my

time. You talk, or you leave. But this doesn't work if you don't trust that I am the man of my reputation."

"We fought. He died."

"Details, sonny boy."

I blow out an irritated breath. "He attacked the woman I love. I didn't lay a hand on him until he put one on her."

"So, let me fill in the blanks for you," he says, devouring another section. "You saw the two of them on a date. You didn't like it. You stalked them, saw him getting friendly, and you attacked him. That about sum it up?"

I slam my hands on the desk. "We're done here."

"Quite a temper on you, kid. Sit down."

"Fuck you! I'm out!" I turn for the door.

"See, that's the difference between me and the cops. When I question you like they probably will, you can leave. When it's them, you can't. So I suggest you get your pampered ass comfortable with being handled like an adult for once in your life."

My jaw grits as the wheels turn in my head. I turn around and snarl, "That was a fucking test?"

"Yeah. You failed. Lucky for you, I grade on a curve." He stands up, setting his orange down on a napkin. Instead of the trousers to match the top half of his suit, he's in boxers from the waist down. "It's not all sunshine and roses in a police station, Mr.

West. They're not gonna blow smoke up your skirt. It'll be rude and brutal because they think you're a murderer, and they wanna catch someone for that. Since you happen to actually be the guy who did the job, they're gonna be extra rough on you because they don't have any other leads, according to my sources."

"You have sources in the BPD?"

He looks at me like I sprouted a fourth head. "In every department. This isn't amateur hour."

He's annoyingly right about everything, and I'm not sure if I'm more bothered by that or by the fact that I feel like I've been verbally sparred into a corner. I take a breath to simmer down. "Fine. I apologize for being rude. If you'll still have me as a client, I would be grateful for your help."

His caterpillar brows shoot up his forehead. "All that West money bought you some nice manners. Sit. Catch." He tosses me an orange. "They're fresh from my sister's grove in Florida. You'll like it."

What the hell? So, I peel my orange, too. "Okay. What do I do?"

"After you killed Neil —"

"In self-defense."

"What did you do then?"

I sigh, staring at my orange. "I called my father's associate who helps with ... other business. He has experience in what I needed, and he helped me get rid of the body."

"Full service, that guy. Would this be Moss?"

I nearly drop the orange. "Yeah, how—"

"We go back. So, you called Moss, and what happened?"

"He came, and after he rolled the body in a tarp and took it to his van, he had June spray the hallway down while we cleaned things up and put some potted plants around the area to cover up the damage. Then drove out to the docks and went to his boat. He weighted the body down, and we dumped it."

He nods, chewing on his fruit and thinking. "Sounds like Moss' work. Except this time, he fucked up somehow."

"Maybe. Or maybe the body got tangled in a fishing net or something. I don't know."

"Alright, here's what I'm going to do. I will reach out to the detectives on the case and ask for a meeting with them directly. We'll feign cooperation. They love that. You will make a list of anyone who can corroborate your alibi—"

"I don't have one."

"Get creative. Then—"

"What about June? They've already tracked her down as a person of interest."

He takes a breath, hesitating. That is never a good sign. "I am your lawyer. Not hers."

"We keep her safe. This doesn't work otherwise."

"Your father paid for your freedom, Anderson. Only yours."

Of course, he fucking did. But if given what she told the cops, and if I create a good enough alibi, then we're both in the clear. I nod and bite into my orange. He was right about it. Best I've ever had. Hopefully, the same is true of him.

We wrap up the meeting, and as I leave the odd man's office, I feel better and worse. Better because I have the best on my team. Worse because the legal shitstorm is only just beginning.

17

ANDERSON

Every interrogation room looks alike. I haven't been in many of them—most of my client's troubles are not of the legal variety. But each one smells like sweat and fear. They have a rudimentary set of chairs and tables. Sometimes, there's the big mirror that you know is one-way, sometimes there isn't one. No clocks. If you're lucky, there's a window for natural light, but when interrogating a suspect, it's best practice to keep a suspect off their game, and that means no window. The passage of time is psychologically grounding, so with no window and no clock, a suspect loses that grounding.

This room has no window, a one-way mirror, and the chairs give my Dad's office chairs a run for their money in the uncomfortableness department. It's the room they use for serious suspects, I'd imagine.

Considering their focus is a murder, it seems appropriate I was brought here.

Doesn't make it any more palatable, though.

Otto says, "Remember what we talked about, Anderson."

"I know."

"I know, you know, but lawyers make the worst clients. You're used to doing the talking. Now's the time to keep your mouth shut."

"I know."

"If they ask you a question, you look at me. I'll nod if you're to answer."

I huff. "I. Know."

"Then you also know why I'm drilling this into you, so you can take the attitude down a notch. Belligerence doesn't win you friends. Not with the cops, not with me."

"Apologies, Otto."

"Don't worry about my feelings, Anderson. Just keep yours in check."

Two men walk in. Suits, not uniforms. One has a file folder in his hands. They sit across from us. The file folder guy begins, "Thank you for coming in peacefully, Mr. West. I am Detective Banks. This is my partner, Detective Wachowski. Understand, this conversation is being recorded."

I shrug.

"We'd like to begin by asking some questions regarding Neil Johnson. Are you aware he is deceased?"

It's a benign enough question, but still, I look to Pym. I want him to know I'll play by his rules for now. He nods, so I respond, "Yes."

"How did you come about that knowledge?"

I killed him.

Pym nods. "I saw it on TV."

Wachowski sits back. "Why are you checking in with Pym before you answer? Nervous?"

"Out of line, Wachowski," Pym snaps. "You're homicide detectives, which means you think this is a murder, and you're looking at him like you want his dick for lunch. Why the hell wouldn't he be nervous?"

The detective glares at Pym but says nothing in response.

Banks says, "We understand your girlfriend knew the deceased, as well. In fact, we've narrowed down his time of death to the last night she saw him. That's a little suspicious, don't you think?"

Trap. I don't even bother looking at Pym. He grouses, "Are you going to keep up with this rookie shit because we both have better places to be."

Banks taps his finger on the table, thinking. "Mr. West, what do you think of your girlfriend kissing the deceased in front of her place of work? Are you into some kind of polyamory thing or something?"

Just trying to rile me up. I glance at Pym, who nods. I keep my voice level and aloof. "We are not polyamorous. She kissed him while we were not together."

"Interesting," Wachowski says. "June is a firecracker, so I get why you're not enough man for her. You're smart. You know it, too. Makes sense why you'd follow her. I mean, who wants to get cheated on, am I right?"

"Beating around this particular bush will get you nowhere, Wachowski," Pym says. "Ms. Devlin is not a cheater. Mr. Anderson is not a murderer. You have nothing on them, or you would have arrested them by now. This is amateur hour, and I'm bored, so either cut to the chase, or we walk."

"The thing about that is we do have something. Or things, rather," Banks says. He opens his file folder but doesn't show us what's in it. He's looking at something in there. "On the night in question, a man matching your description was seen at the docks where Mr. Johnson's body was found."

His words are ice in my veins, but Pym laughs. "A tall white guy with black hair was seen at the docks at night? Stop the presses."

"We have witnesses that put you near Ms. Devlin's building the night of the crime," Wachowski says.

"I'd love to speak to these so-called witnesses," Pym sneers.

Really wishing I had his confidence right about now. I shrug and act bored. "Your witnesses are obviously mistaken."

"Maybe they are," Banks says as he leans forward, "but cameras rarely lie."

Fuck, fuck, fuck. Maintaining a cool exterior is getting harder by the second. If I was caught on camera doing anything outside of my alibi, I am fucked. But I'm not giving them an inch. They might have more than they're letting on, but they might not.

One thing that always stuck out to me in law school was the fact that cops are allowed to lie to you. Didn't seem fair to me then, and it's certainly not now. I don't want to go to trial, but that's the only place they're not allowed to lie to you. Doesn't mean they don't do it, but at least they're less likely to lie in a courtroom.

I glance to Pym to keep up the question-and-answer status quo. But he's the one who responds. "Was that a question, Detective? Or are you just spit balling ideas for your next empty accusation?"

Banks smiles. "I like you, Pym. I always have. But I need you to understand just how much trouble your client is in right now. We have a mountain of evidence that puts him at the scene of the crime, and if this goes to trial, it won't go the way you want it to."

"And you're telling me this as a favor?" Pym scoffs. "No, you're saying it to make Mr. West nervous because that's all you have. Scare tactics. If—"

"You should be scared," Wachowski says directly to me. "Prison is mean to pretty boys, especially the rich ones. You rich fucks always think you can do whatever you want, don't you? This was cold-blooded murder out of jealousy because your girl is a slut. You—"

"Watch your fucking mouth," I snap.

But the detective only smirks. "Why? You gonna throw me in the bay, too?"

"Enough," Pym interjects. "Unless you have something concrete, my client has nothing to say to you." His gentle reminder to keep my mouth shut.

I'm embarrassed that I needed that reminder, but this guy bugs me, and I'm about to go to fucking prison if I'm not careful. Sweat pours down my back, and it's not warm in here. It's me. Feels like a noose is tightening. I still have no clue what evidence they have against me, but they're making it sound like they got me on camera someplace. Yes, they can lie to me during interrogation, but how far would they keep that lie going?

"We have plenty of evidence against your client, Pym," Banks says coolly. "But we gave you the chance to talk to us like men and set the record straight. Mr. West, how about you do that? Tell us where you were on the night in question—the truth this time—and we'll make sure the prosecutors go easy on you. We just want some cooperation so we can put this case to bed. Mr. Johnson's family deserves some closure."

I glance at Pym, and he nods. "I already gave you my statement." Our agreed upon response if they came at me like this.

Banks sighs, then nods to Wachowski, who barks, "That joke of a statement has more holes in it than I-93. We have you, pretty boy. Witnesses, cameras, fingerprints, DNA. It's gonna be fucking sweet to see your privileged ass behind bars, and on a murder charge, it'll be decades before you breathe the free air again." He laughs. "Just imagine June, all lonely and brokenhearted that her man is in prison … she won't be lonely for long, will she? A slut like her—"

I want to lunge across the table and punch the detective, but Pym speaks up, "You paint a pretty picture. A shame you won't be able to see it, Wachowski. We both know if you had any of that, Mr. West would be behind bars right now. So cut the bullshit."

The detectives sit back in unison before Wachowski says, "When you're gone, maybe I'll call June myself."

I snort a laugh at the thought. "Not sure your pride could take it."

"What's that supposed to mean?"

"She'd laugh in your face, and I don't think your ego would ever recover."

"So that's what it was, wasn't it?" Banks asks. He sounds like he thinks he's onto something. Too much confidence in his voice, but he's trying to sound soothing. "Seeing her with him that night—your pride took a hit you couldn't recover from, right? I mean, I get it. Seeing your woman with another man ... that's gotta hurt. Can't even imagine how bad. It's understandable, Mr. West. We're all human. People make mistakes. Sometimes, those mistakes go too far. Things get out of control fast in a bad situation. My partner thinks this was a premeditated thing, but I don't think so. This was a crime of passion, if ever there was one. Juries understand these things. So do prosecutors and judges. You don't have to live with the guilt forever. You're a good man, so I know this is eating at you. If you sign a confession, this will all go a lot easier on you."

Pym told me not to be belligerent, but right now, it feels like that's the only thing I have going for me. They've got me in a corner, don't they? If this were a dog-and-pony show, they would have given up by now, right? Fuck, I don't know. All I know is I need to get out of here before I say something incriminating. I can't breathe in this damn room, and the vultures are circling.

I bark, "If I had something to confess, I'd fucking do it by now just to be done with the two of you. In fact ... " I stand up. "I'm not under arrest, so I'm walking out that door. Pym's right. You've got nothing on me. I'm out." I stomp to the door, trying to project righteous indignation instead of culpability.

18

ANDERSON

As soon as Otto's car door shuts, he snarls, "What the fuck was that?"

I huff and stare out the passenger window. The problem is, I don't have an answer. Not a good one, anyway. The truth is, I panicked. In the past year, I've dealt with everything from my father freezing my assets to getting shot and almost dying, but this was a different kind of stress. The guy who shot me was at the end of his rope. He was armed and out of his mind, and so I was shot.

What happened with those cops in the interrogation room was planned and intentional. It was a completely different feeling from facing a man with a gun but no less potentially world-ending. They wanted to tear me apart mentally until I confessed or said the wrong thing. Those assholes were out to get me like it was personal.

"I'm gonna need an answer, Anderson."

I shrug. "I don't have one."

Otto's black driving gloves gleam in the cloudy afternoon light as he grips the steering wheel in anger. But then his shoulders slide back, resigned. "Fine. What would you tell a client who did that in there?"

I grumble, "That running off like that makes you look guilty."

"Glad I don't have to be the one to tell you." He sighs, staring out the windshield. "But in fairness to you, I should have known more about what they were coming with. My guys inside can't get close to this investigation, or they woulda told me."

"You need better guys inside."

He shrugs. "Neither here nor there at the moment."

"I'm not ... I don't do criminal law, but I don't think that went well."

"It isn't good. They have something, or they wouldn't be so confident. I've dealt with Banks before. His partner's a piece of work, but Banks is usually decent. I've never seen him so adamant, which means—"

"They have something."

Otto nods. "Not enough, though. That's what today was about. They wanted to trip you up and get you to say the wrong thing while they recorded it. That, plus whatever they have, would be enough, or at least, that's what they're thinking."

Outside, my jaw firms and my gaze hardens on the police officers going in and out of the building. Inside, it feels like being swallowed by cold mud. It's funny — before I killed someone, I would have thought being a lawyer in this situation would be an asset, but as it turns out, it's not. My education only makes me think I should be able to worm my way out of this, and when I can't see the light at the end of the tunnel, I end up more frustrated than before.

"I want to see their evidence, Otto. I need to know what I'm up against."

"The only legit way to do that is if this goes to trial. That's what discovery is for. But I don't get the feeling that's what you mean."

I try to collect my thoughts. Recently, every illegal thing I've done has gone sideways, so I'm not sure about any of this. "Think about it — if they were blowing smoke about everything they said they had, then all they really have is a body. That body was in the water for a long time, so how much evidence can they really glean from it? I'd venture to say none. I think they got some witnesses, put two and two together, and that's all they have. Otherwise, they'd have me locked up, right?"

"Bet your life on it?"

A twinge of panic tells me no. "I want to see their evidence. Somehow. And I'm not talking to them again, Otto. That was bullshit in there. If they want to talk, they can arrest me. If they want anything else, they can get warrants. We are done being nice about this."

Otto takes a deep breath and sits back. "You know that's what they want, right?"

"How's that?"

"If they can't get you to confess, their next step is to piss you off and make you do something stupid, so they have probable cause. Banks tried to softball you in there, but Wachowski was going for cause. He knows their next steps are warrants and knocking down your door. If you change your mind about talking, tell them you'll only speak to Wachowski—"

"The fuck for?"

He smirks. "Because that hothead is going to get a bad wake-up call one day, and I'd love it if you were the one to do it."

"I don't understand."

"Banks has pulled Wachowski's sac outta the fire too many times. He has a rep for playing just outside the law to get confessions, evidence, whatever. I have no proof, but I know he's planted evidence. My sources inside don't like the guy. They don't trust him, and for police, trust is everything. They want him gone almost as much as you do."

"So, why the hell would I want to talk to him instead of Banks?"

"Because Wachowski is the one most likely to fuck the case up. He's volatile. He doesn't think through things. You can use that to your advantage if the time comes. As much as they'd like to piss you off into doing something stupid, it would be just as easy for you to do the same to him."

I nod, thinking about how to use that. "If the time comes, I'll consider it."

"Aside from all of that, what aren't you telling me about June?"

"What do you mean by that?"

His lips lock tight in a straight line as his brow arches. "I'm not an idiot, Anderson. You're a good guy. Protective. You'd do anything for the woman you love, right?"

"Of course."

"Including cover for her when she murders someone."

I laugh sharply. "Wait—you think that's what happened? Are you shitting me?"

"Wouldn't be the first time I've seen it."

"She … she didn't do it." I force a breath out, trying to erase the memories of that awful night. But it doesn't help. Nothing helps except time. But now, with the cops breathing down our necks, it keeps coming back up like bad sushi. "He had her by the neck. He was choking her out. Whether he wanted to kill her before he raped her, I don't know. Not sure he cared if she was alive for that or not. She had these bruises on her throat for days after … every time I saw them, I saw the light slip from her eyes the way it did that night. When I tackled him, I thought she was dead. That I was too late."

His lip curls in disgust. "The world's better off without the creep."

"Yeah."

"But that doesn't change the fact that June was involved in his death, even if peripherally. She will remain a person of interest, as will you, after the show you put on in there. Problem is, had you called me that night when it all went down, I coulda gotten you out, looking like a hero. Now … " He sighs, shaking his head.

"Now, what?"

"The BPD is out for blood. They won't be happy until they have it."

"Why are they acting like Neil was one of their own? He was a hedge fund manager—"

"At Bryce-Connolly, yeah, I know. Problem is, Connolly is a big donor to a lot of city, county, and state charities, including police associations. I wouldn't put it past him to pressure them on this, kid. He's protective of his public image. He likes his name in the headlines for positive press only, but now his name is tied to a murder victim. That means someone's nuts are in the fire, and they won't stop until this is solved."

My head falls into my hands. "This just keeps getting better and better."

"You hit the lotto with this one. Only it's the lotto in reverse."

I want to scream. Or punch. Or just go to town on something breakable. This is too much. It's all fucking too much. "What do we do now?"

He blows out a deep breath. "You're not gonna like it."

"I don't like any of this. How will your idea be any different?"

"There were three people involved in this incident. Neil, you, and June. One of you is dead. The other isn't my client. If it comes down to it, you know I'll pin this on her."

"The fuck you will!"

"Calm down. All I have to do is get in front of a jury, make them think it *could* have been her, and there's your reasonable doubt. It's not enough to make the police go after her, but it's enough to get you off. Isn't that the goal?"

"Not at her expense! If you so much as point a finger her way, the police will reopen the investigation and go after her. You can't do that!"

He picks at his driving gloves. "I think you'll find I can do whatever I need to in order to secure the well-being of my client, and when it's my client's life or June's, I'm picking my client every time."

"Stop fucking with your gloves and look at me. I want your full attention because I do not believe I've made myself clear." I wait until he gives an annoyed grunt and stops with his damn gloves. "If it were to ever be a choice between mine or June's freedom, she is the priority. Always. Fuck my father, fuck anyone who says differently. I love her too damn much to see her behind bars ever. So no more talk about pinning this shit on her. If worse comes to worse, I'll take my punishment. But she stays the fuck out of this."

Otto looks tired. "You're making a mistake."

"It's my mistake to make." And it wasn't a mistake, but I wasn't going to argue with him.

He mumbles something under his breath, then puts the car in drive. "You think you're noble for choosing her over yourself. You're wrong. You made the right call that night—obviously. But this? How many square feet is your fancy apartment?"

That was an abrupt change of topic. "Around fifteen hundred square feet. Why?"

"Massachusetts prison cells run about thirty-five square feet. So the next time you're in your bathroom, imagine what half of that would be like for the rest of your life, then tell me if you're willing to throw yourself on your sword for her."

I glare at him. "Yes. I am."

"Damn kids."

19

JUNE

I'm just minding my own business when Anderson walks in with a look on his face so scary that I would have sworn he'd been in another fatal fight. I leap to my feet and rush to his side. "Baby, what's—"

But he grabs me in a bear hug that he clearly needs more than my words. So, I hold on until his body goes … well, not limp exactly, but slightly less tense. He kisses the top of my head, then goes straight to the scotch.

"What is going on? Did somebody die?"

That makes him blink at me. "What? No."

"The way you looked when you walked in, I wasn't sure. Tell me what's going on now. I don't think I can take another surprise."

He sighs and sets the scotch down. "I spoke to the police today."

My book falls from my hands, and I don't bother to pick it up. "You did what?"

"Yeah. With Otto Pym—"

"Otto 'The Blade' Pym?" A shiver shoots down my back.

"He's not as scary as the rumors would have you believe."

"I'll take your word for it. How—your dad, right? He hired him?"

Anderson nods. "And Otto is worried."

Fuck. The Blade is nothing if not confident. "Worried why, specifically?"

"Connolly, of Bryce-Connolly, does not like the bad press that's coming out over this, and he has connections at every level of law enforcement."

I can't wrap my head around that. "Neil was a new hedge fund manager. Why would Connolly care about that?"

"Doesn't matter. Since no one local knew Neil, the only connection people make in the news is that he worked there, so their name is tainted, and Connolly thinks it's bad press. Pym says he's likely a part of the reason this is getting so much attention. Connolly wants this solved, so they're going to come down hard on anyone associated with the case."

I snatch his scotch and knock it back before pouring him a new one. This is too much. I can't keep taking more shit, and I can't avoid it, either. It's all I can do to keep breathing, and my legs are going boneless. "I can't … I just can't … what do we do?"

His head tips back in frustration before he drinks his scotch. "In a perfect world, we'd just run away. Leave it all behind. No forwarding addresses … just ghost everyone."

"In your perfect world, we're fugitives?"

He lifts a shoulder and smirks. "Think about it, and tell me it doesn't have a certain appeal."

I huff a laugh. It's absurd. We're adults. We can't just run away from home.

But…

Admittedly, it sounds amazing. Still not an option, though. "It's a nice fantasy, but we live in the real world, and in the real world, we are fucked."

"We are not fucked. We —"

"If Otto Pym is nervous, then we are fucked with a capital F." And now, I hear it in my voice. The fear.

Anderson takes my hands and presses them to his chest before kissing my palms. "Baby, I love you."

I don't know why, but hearing that now brings tears to my eyes. "I love you too, but that doesn't —"

He kisses me.

I push him away. "We need to talk!"

"I don't want to talk. I don't want to think. I just want you."

"You're being ridiculous! We have to talk about this and face things like adults. And what are we doing talking about this *here*?"

"If you want to go for a walk, then we can, but it's raining, and it's icy, and it's not as if I'm going to say anything I didn't say in the interrogation room, so relax."

I laugh in his face. "Relax? Did you really just say that to me? The police have questioned us both about a possible homicide, and you want me to relax?"

He takes a deep breath and stares into my eyes. "June. Nothing gets solved by panicking, right?"

"Because panicking is optional to you? It's not to me. Panicking is pretty much my go-to response when the police are sniffing around."

"Not your first rodeo?" He arches a brow at me.

"No." I can barely get the word out. The feeling of drowning and that hand dragging me under ... God, it comes back so fast.

"What—"

"Now is not the time." I put enough steel in my voice that he only nods in response. "What are we going to do?"

"We've both spoken to the police. Now's the time when we wait to see what comes of that. If they're smart, they'll see we had nothing to do with anything." He mouths, "Bugs." Then he continues, "I'm sure they will keep an eye on us in one way or another, and that's fine. We have nothing to hide. I think our best course of action is to do what we'd normally do."

The thought of going to work tomorrow is almost as unfathomable as prison. I'm too boggled, too messy. Go there and pretend to be an adult? I've run out of my capacity for pretending. It's just gone.

"I don't think I can do that. I'm too freaked out. Normal? You mean go to work? Friends? Family? Anderson, I am out of fucks. I have no more fucks to give. The police took them all. How am I supposed to operate like this?"

"There's option b."

"Whatever it is, yes."

"We take a few days off and find a cabin in the woods to renew ourselves."

I laugh. Hard and loud. "Are you insane? We're persons of interest in a murder investigation. We are lawyers. We know what that looks like!"

He strolls up to me, putting his hands on my hips. Anderson's smile makes me want to smack him for being so chill about this. "You're right. I do know what it looks like. It looks like two people, stressed out, going for a little rest and relaxation. We will call everyone important, tell them we're sick, and head up north for a little while. We've never done a road trip. It'll be fun."

"You're insane."

"About you."

I roll my eyes, but I can't stop myself from smiling. "You're better than that. Try again."

He grins. "Baby, it's not like we're heading to someplace without extradition. I was thinking about Vermont. No one told us not to leave town or the state or anything like that. We're not under arrest, and given the circumstances, I think we deserve a chance to enjoy something before this shitshow gets any worse, don't you?"

He's right about that, at least. Some time away does sound nice, especially out of the city. But the implications are terrible. "And how do we explain this to the police?"

"Why would we? We're not in their custody. We don't owe them explanations about our leisure time, and even if we did, what are we doing wrong?"

In all fairness, he's got me there. "I'm just … I'm just scared, baby."

"I know." He kisses my forehead. "And all the noise in that big brain of yours isn't going to get better here and now. But some time away might be just the thing you need to quiet that down."

I lean my head on his chest. It feels so good to let him hold me right now. He's my rock. "So, when you brought up the fact that I keep stuff to myself … is that what inspired this idea?"

"Might be."

He's trying to be there for me. I should let him. I take a deep breath of him. His scent always puts me at ease. But I also steal the rest of his scotch again. "Let's do it."

"Is that you or the scotch talking?"

"Please. The scotch is good, but it's not that good. You're right. We need a damn break, and if the world won't give us one, then by God, we will take one."

He smiles, his face finally relaxing. "You mean that?"

"I do. When do you want to—"

"How about now?"

"Seriously?"

"Can't think of a better time. Can you?"

He's right. I shrug. "It's like a four-hour drive to Vermont from here. Are you sure you're up for that?"

"Absolutely. Let's pack some bags and get the hell out of Dodge."

"I'm feeling more relaxed already." I pad to the bedroom and grab the luggage.

"Just one thing you have to do before we go."

"What's that?"

"Promise me you're not bringing your laptop."

I laugh, shaking my head. "Not an ice cream cone's chance in hell am I bringing my laptop."

He smacks my ass, then works on his own luggage. From the decision to walking out the door takes fifteen minutes, and even though every lawyer instinct in me screams this is a mistake, it's one I want to make.

-

20

JUNE

"I can't believe we're doing this."

"You said we needed to get away." Changing his mind? What the hell? "Why do you sound like you're backing out now?"

He shakes his head, smiling. "I'm not. I just mean, I'm surprised I was able to talk you into this."

"Oh." I sit back against the passenger seat and stretch. "Well, I mean. I guess I get that. I have been a little intense."

"Not you, baby. This situation has been intense. It's not every day you get called into questioning for a homicide."

"Thankfully." As the miles pass by, I wonder what people would think. Well, not people. A jury. I'm not sure what to think of it myself. But Anderson was right. We need a break. I can't think straight in the city.

God, he looked handsome in profile. Or any other angle. Maybe my hormones are getting the best of me, but with the idea of relaxing comes the hormones. My sex drive has definitely been on the fritz. Stress, I guess. That shit really is a killer.

"Baby, why don't you go to sleep? We've already called everybody that we need to call to let them know that we're sick, and there's nothing else for you to worry about right now. I've got this."

"That's not fair to you. I should stay up to keep you awake."

He just smiles. "I'm not worried about what's fair to me. I want to see you bright and chipper when we get there."

"I know you said Vermont, but where specifically are we going?"

"I booked an Airbnb for us. It's a little cabin in the woods."

I groan happily at the thought. "That really does sound perfect. Okay, I guess I could use the nap." I was right. The moment I close my eyes, I'm out. The next thing I know, he's shaking my thigh. "Hmm? What?"

"We're here."

I glance out the window. Moonlight glitters on the snow. Trees stand like sentries to guard the A-frame log cabin. It's a little place tucked in the middle of the woods with no visible neighbors anywhere. A deck wraps around, and I can see the hot tub from here. Perfect for just the two of us.

"Wow."

"I hoped you'd like it."

"I didn't bring a bathing suit."

He grins. "Neither did I. Come on." Anderson bolts out of the car and around to the back for our luggage.

As soon as the door opens, I'm hit with a blast of frosty air. I'm not sure I'm getting naked for the hot tub in this. But looking at my handsome fiancé, it might be worth it. I've never had sex in a hot tub.

Once I'm out of the car, the cold really hits. I dash through the snow, straight to the front door, right behind him. My teeth chatter as I rattle, "Hurry, hurry, hurry."

He laughs while he gets the door open. Thankfully, the code worked. He turns on the lights after I've run in. It is a beautiful cabin inside. Walking in, we're in the living room, where there's an enormous tan stone fireplace and a few loveseats. A small but efficient kitchen sits off to the right. And to the left, a master bedroom that takes my breath away.

The first thing that catches my eye is the enormous A-frame-shaped windows. They have a view deep into the forest. Then there's the bedroom's fireplace. It looms near the foot of the bed, perfect for keeping our feet warm. Plush navy blue throws sit across the bed on crisp white sheets.

"It's perfect here, baby," I gush.

"I hoped you'd like it." He sets our luggage near the dresser. "How about we unpack, and then we'll bundle up; I will get us some wine and start a fire in the fire pit outside."

"That sounds perfect. Thank you."

The firepit is on the deck and lined by comfy loungers. Once we're settled in at the fire, I feel the knots of tension begin to release. It's a good start to our little vacation.

Anderson says, "This is living."

"I could not agree more."

"You know, I'd always thought that I might retire to the Maldives or someplace tropical like that, but I could get used to this."

"You think about retirement?"

"Of course. Don't you?"

I sip my wine and sort of laugh. "It used to be all I thought about. That was what got me through my days at my old firm."

"I get that. But if you hated it so much, why did you stay?"

"You know how it goes. You start making good money,

and then you don't ever want to stop." I pause. "Wait, maybe you don't know how that goes."

He laughs. "Not really, but I understand the idea of it. It's hard to imagine going backward once you're used to a certain level of wealth."

"Exactly." Even with our completely different socioeconomic backgrounds, it's nice that we have some common ground. "So you're slated to become CEO at West Media, but you still think about retirement? And I get the impression that your dad would never even consider retirement if you weren't around. Why is retirement on your mind when it would never cross his?"

"Once I'm in the CEO seat, I plan on doing things very differently than he does. He always works too hard. And he uses work to avoid the family. I'm never going to do that. Honestly, I can't imagine not racing to come home to you every night."

That might be the sweetest thing he's ever said to me. He's *so* getting rewarded for that one. "I know what you mean. Like I'll never understand the people who text on their phone on their whole commute home. It slows them down. I always want to ask them, don't you want to get home? Why would you rather sit in traffic and text versus being home? But I assume that those people are going home to something that they don't want to go home to. And I can't imagine that being the case with you ever. I always want to come home to you. You're what makes it home."

He warmly smiles, and I think I've touched him. "That's very good to hear. So, what about kids? We haven't had a chance to talk about any of that in any real way."

"I'd like a few, I think. But also, the thought of being pregnant scares the bejesus out of me."

He laughs. "It would scare the bejesus out of me too."

"And what if you don't like my post-baby body?"

"Not possible."

I smirk at him. "Well, now you sound naive. There are plenty of guys who are not happy with their wives' post-baby bodies."

"They're assholes."

It makes me giggle. "Well, that much is true."

He takes my foot into his lap and starts massaging it. I could melt right there. "Sweetheart, if you grow me babies, I will love every inch of that body. Possibly even more than I do now."

I can't figure out why this conversation is turning me on, but it is. "You really think a baby won't change things between us? Sexual things, I mean."

"If anything, I think it would just make you sexier."

"Do you have one of those MILF fetishes?"

He laughs, shaking his head. "The only MILF that I want is you, once you've had plenty of time to recover from carrying my child. It's not about a mother's body or anything like that. It's about this intrinsic, cosmic connection that we would have. June, it's not just a physical thing. It's never just been a physical thing between us. It's *us*. And creating new life together ... I can't think of anything better."

He has this look on his face that makes me swoon. I don't know if he's getting better at saying all the right things or if I'm just happier to hear them now that I'm relaxing. It might be the foot massage.

Just then, my phone rings. "Sorry. Thought I turned this off." It's my dad. I have no urge to talk to him right now. The only person I want to give my attention to is Anderson. So I text him back and let him know that I'm sick with laryngitis—hence why I didn't answer the phone—and that I'll need a few days to myself.

Thankfully, his response is quick. "OK, Junebug. Just checking in for our next lunch. Feel better soon."

With that out of the way, I turn my phone off and my focus on the man I'm going to spend the rest of my life with. His brows lift in question, and with the fire lighting his face, somehow, he's even more gorgeous than usual. "Everything okay?"

"Just Dad. He wanted to know about our next lunch." I shrug. "No big deal. How many kids do you want?"

He gets this faraway look as he stares into the fire. "As many as you want to have."

"What does that mean?"

"When I'm CEO, I'll have the means to support as large a family as we want to have, and I've always liked the idea of having a big family. Growing up, it was just me and Cole, and he's … different from me, so it was a little like growing up with a stranger. I don't want that for my kids."

That sounds like he wants a lot. I gulp my wine down. "Throw a number on that for me."

He grins. "Maybe … seven or eight—"

"What?" Damn. I almost spilled my wine. How is there no air outside?

"We can negotiate a number. I don't want to put your body through hell, and I love the idea of adopting if that puts your mind at ease." He takes my other foot to work on. "Thoughts on adoption?"

"I kind of love the idea, truthfully. I mean, I would like some of my own, too, but I especially like the idea of adopting some older kids. The ones people usually ignore because most people want babies." I sigh. "It just feels like the right thing to do, and I don't mean a moral obligation, but it feels right in my heart. Like I'm supposed to do that."

"I didn't know I could love you more. But here we are."

"You're up for adopting older kids, too?"

He nods. "I think it's a great idea."

21

JUNE

As cozy as things are out here, I need to lie down. "Do you think we could go inside. I'd like to stretch out."

"I think ... " He gets up and adjusts the loungers so they lay down flat. "Better?"

"That's perfect."

"Not yet." He jogs into the cabin and returns with a few blankets and pillows, before scooting his lounger next to mine, and we create a makeshift bed. After he gets in on his side, he takes a deep breath, sighs, and says, "Now it's perfect. Look up."

Above us, the sky shimmers in stars framed by bare treetops. "I forgot what the sky really looks like. You don't get this kind of view in Boston. Too much light pollution."

He laces his fingers with mine. "Right here, right now, it feels like our problems are so small. Across the galaxy, worlds are forming and dying, stars are burning their last bit of fuel. And who knows what kinds of problems aliens have— "

I BURST OUT LAUGHING. "ALIENS?"

He grins at me. "What? I can't have theories?"

"Dazzle me with your theory, sir."

"I'm not saying I buy into the whole little green men thing or farmers getting probed or whatever. But I think it's either bold or egotistical to think we are the only remotely intelligent lifeforms who exist. So, yeah, sometimes, I think about what aliens could be out there and what their lives could be like. You don't ever think about that kind of thing?"

I shrug. "Most of the time, I'm thinking about how I'm going to pay my bills."

"And that is why I need you in my life. You keep me grounded."

"I know you're not 'Go to Mars' rich, but if you had the chance, would you?"

He laughs. "In your hypothetical scenario, it would greatly depend on my family situation at the time. If I didn't have one, sure. I'd be all for it. But if I had a family, no. I'm not going to take those kinds of risks when I have children." He takes a beat. "And when I'm CEO, I'm ending all of West Media's illegal activities. No more crime. No more people getting shot at under my watch. It'll piss off some people, I'm sure. But I'm not putting me, you, or our kids in danger." He says it with such a tone that I'm compelled to ask follow-ups.

"Are you mad at your dad for that? I don't mean how he blackmailed you into working with Moss because, duh, of course, you're mad about that. But I mean before all this crap started."

His mood shifts as he nods. "As far as I'm concerned, it is only dumb luck that has kept me, Mom, and Cole safe all these years. The fact that Andre kidnapped you … " He huffs out a steamy breath. "It is a miracle that never happened to Dad's family over the years, considering all the shit he's up to. He has kept us in perpetual danger since before I was born. I will not be doing that to my kids or my wife."

"Huh." I stare up at the stars.

"What?"

"It's just … I never thought about it before, but I guess it makes sense that our kids could be in danger from all of that. We will have to button up whatever Elliot has going on before we can actually think about children."

He nods. "I know it's the job of every generation to clean up the mess from the one before, but I feel I have more to clean up than most. And I don't even know the extent of Dad's crimes, so it'll take time. But it will be worth it when I hold my child."

I smile at him. Can't help it. "You're really into this idea, aren't you?"

"If I had my druthers, you'd be pregnant already."

"Oh really?"

Another nod. "But I'm not going to be reckless like him. I'm going to do it right and ensure my family's safety before they come into the world."

I give his hand a squeeze. "*We* will ensure their safety. You're not alone in this."

He rolls onto his side, smiling. "And I won't forget that." He kisses me. Just a peck, but it's nice.

Except, "Your lips are freezing. We should get you back inside—"

"No. A little longer out here."

"Okay, but if you get sick and ruin our vacation, you'll owe me a new one."

He smiles. "Deal."

We lie back and watch the stars in silence for a while. It's such a relief not to hear anyone or anything but ourselves and the forest. No airplanes, no cars, no people. No cops. It's funny how the stressors of the day slip away into nothingness when you can let them.

"See that constellation there? The five bright stars, kind of makes a pentagon?" I ask.

"Yeah, I think so."

"According to ancient Greeks, that's Auriga. He was said to be a great charioteer and the inventor of the four-horse chariot, the quadriga."

He slowly turns his head and stares at me for a minute before teasing me, "Nerd!"

"What? I can't have layers?"

He laughs. "I mean, yeah, but I had no idea you're into astrology."

"Astronomy. Astrology is zodiac stuff. And it's less astronomy and more history, really. When you look into the constellations of different cultures, you can learn about them. What they thought was worthy of commemorating shows you their values."

"So, astro-anthropology."

"I guess so."

He settles back down. "Where'd you learn about Auriga?"

I take a breath. "Summer camp got me started learning about them, but I kept at it long after. You know how every kid goes really hard into some niche subject? Mine was that. What was yours?"

"Frogs."

I laugh, but he doesn't. "You're serious?"

"When I was a boy, I found a planter with a ton of these goopy little balls in it. I scooped them up and carried them in to ask Mom what the seeds were. She was grossed out, so of course, that made me like them more. Mom told me they were frog eggs, and she said to put them back where I got them, and I told her where I'd found them, which made her worry."

"How come?"

"She knew the eggs would dry out, and the babies would die. So, we collected the rest and looked up how to make a terrarium to keep them safe. We spent a summer with those things, learning about them and taking care of them. I loved it."

Thinking of a young Anderson doing something so scientific warms my heart. I want to do that with our kids. "So you saved them?"

"Every last one. We released them when they were old enough, but before then, we had the best time with the froglets."

"God, I want that. Not goopy egg things being brought to me but exploring the world with our kids. That sounds amazing. Also, it's nice to know I'm not the only nerd here."

He laughs and kisses my forehead. "Yeah, well. It was a lot of fun. I always liked the idea that you could start your life as one thing and end up as something else entirely. That kind of metamorphosis is inspirational."

"When you were a kid, you wanted to be someone else?"

"Sometimes. I wanted to be a kid with a dad who liked him."

My heart pinches at that. "Your dad likes you—"

"He likes what I can do for him, June. I'm not under any delusions that it's more than that."

"I don't know if I think that's true. He was shaken when you were shot—"

He laughs bitterly. "Pretty sure a good parent should show they care about you in all the years *before* you get shot."

Well, he has me there. "I mean, I'm not the guy's biggest fan, but I think he cares in his own way. Whatever that might be."

He shrugs. "Whether he does or not, I didn't feel it when I was a kid. I wanted to be someone else, someplace else, for my whole childhood, other than when I spent time with Mom. We had some decent nannies, but it's not the same thing."

"No, it's not." On that topic, "And depending on just how big our family gets, I could see having one, but I'd prefer to raise our kids ourselves."

"Would you consider quitting your job to do that?"

I nod. "I'll never be CEO of some multi-million dollar corporation, so since you'd be the breadwinner, I'd happily be the stay-at-home parent. I don't see a reason not to do that. Do you?"

He blows out a breath like he's been holding it forever. "Thank fuck."

"What?"

"I know you're a strong, independent woman and all of that, so I worried you'd want to farm our kids out to a fleet of nannies."

"Every study I've ever read on the matter talks about positive outcomes for kids who have at least one parent home, even with nannies around. If I'm bringing new life into the world, I want it to have the best chance for health and happiness possible."

His breath hitches before he rolls to face me again. "Speaking of health and happiness—"

"You're not sick, are you? I don't think I can take some other catastrophic—"

"No, I'm fine as far as I know. Nothing like that."

And now, I can breathe. "Okay, what is it?"

"Given how my dad is about you and the fact you're just starting to build a relationship with your father, I'm guessing the giant wedding my mom wants is not exactly your thing."

Oh, just wedding stuff. I chuckle. "You know something? I just keep thinking about how I want to be married to you. The wedding is one day in our lives. It's the marriage that matters to me."

"So, you don't care about having a day where you can be doted on like a princess?"

I laugh at the thought. "Hell no. I know every girl is supposed to plan that stuff since they were little, have dresses picked out in their mind, or whatever, but I've been kind of dreading that. Being the center of attention when all I'm doing is some imitation of what's been done for hundreds of years ... it strikes me as weird. Not to mention, the whole white dress thing is just tacky to me since it's supposed to represent virginity, and then there's the whole 'giving the bride away' thing, like I'm chattel ... it's all just a bit Handmaid's Tale for my liking."

"Then how about we elope?"

I look to see if he's joking. "Your family would kill you."

He shrugs. "I've been dead before."

I punch his shoulder, earning a wince out of him. "Don't ever say that."

"When I was shot, I was pretty sure I was going to die. Is that better?"

"No, and yes."

He smiles. "My point is, my family probably won't kill me since they're glad I survived, and I don't think yours will go after you. We can hit a courthouse, go to Vegas, whatever you want. But I don't care about a wedding, either. I just want to be married to you."

It sounds so romantic. But I don't want him saying this just to make me happy. "No dreams of some gala wedding for you?"

"Not at all. I've only ever dreamed of my wife. Will you marry me? Far, far away from everyone we know?"

A smile pries my lips open. "Yes."

22

JUNE

I love that he wants to elope. I thought marrying Anderson West would mean a big, formal nightmare. But now that we're here and disconnected from everyone else in a world where no one else's opinion matters, I think it's easier to think about just us. Not the stress of our everyday lives. Not the expectations of far too many people. Us. Making our wedding be about just us is even better.

I roll onto my side, then crawl over to him, straddling him. The delight in his eyes lifts my heart. He asks, "What are you doing?"

"Showing you how happy I am that we're eloping." I lean down for a kiss, and even though his lips start out cold, they warm up fast. He grips my ass over my blanket, pulling me closer. It makes me feel so wanted when he does that. And then I feel the proof. He's hardening up beneath me. The moment I start to grind against him, he breaks the kiss.

"It is too damn cold out here for that."

"I don't want to stop."

"Who said anything about stopping?" Anderson sits up and scoots off the lounger, picking me up with him. For a brief moment, he stares into my eyes. I don't know what he's going to do next, but the air is electric between us. The fire crackles, tossing amber light upward. He growls, "Clothes. Off. Now."

He sets me down, and I tear at my clothes and his, and he does the same until we're both stripped to the skin and then he's on me. The cold doesn't even register as his mouth slides down my throat to my breasts, his tongue dancing against my nipples while I grab the back of his head, urging him on. Liquid heat builds in my core as everything tightens and loosens at the same time. My moans echo on the hardwood walls and floor.

Maybe it's the fresh mountain air, being on vacation, or simply existing in this safe bubble away from the horrors of our lives, but my body is on another level right now. Everything is heightened. His touch sends sparks through me, charging me up. When he reaches between my thighs, I almost come undone.

Anderson presses his lips to my earlobe and whispers, "Baby, I can't believe how wet you are for me."

He's right — I am soaked right now. "You do this to me."

I feel him smirk against my cheek. "Good girl." Then he pushes me onto the loungers, face up. He grabs my ankles, splitting them apart, and then I notice the cold air. Fuck, I notice it. It's all I can do not to slam my thighs shut. But then he gives me a reason not to. He lays between my legs, kissing me all over. Everywhere but *there*. "The whole drive here, I've been thinking about this. Remembering how you taste. The feel of you against my mouth. It's a fucking miracle I didn't wreck the car."

I giggle, but then his mouth is on me. Tongue, painting me all over before his lips get in on the action. I roll myself against his face, wanton and carefree. There are no thoughts in my head anymore. Not when he eats me like I might be his last meal.

One hand feathers through his hair for grip, while the other loops over my shoulder to grab the edge of the lounger. The firepit gives off just enough heat to not worry about frostbitten nipples, but only just. The combination of a cold upper body and a sizzling hot lower body makes for an interesting time of it as I ride against his face. And then it hits like a bomb, and I am gone, utterly obliterated by the pleasure deep inside.

I'm still coming when Anderson mounts me.

I cry out, my voice echoing through the dark forest. Like two wild animals, we rut outside, snarling and groaning and mewling and clawing. He pounds into me as if his life depends on it. I cock myself up at him to take him as much as he's taking me. Wet smacking sounds fall between our grunts. Abruptly, he curls down onto me and clutches me close. He gasps, "Fuck!

You keep doing that, and this will be over before it should be."

Okay. I'm a little proud of that. But I figure I can do some of the work. "Turn over."

He rolls us onto his back, so I'm on top. At this angle, the lounger no longer keeps my back warm, which is very encouraging to move faster. But I love this angle, too. When I look down at him from here, he's staring up at me like I'm a goddess.

His hands glide up my sides and hook over to my breasts, warming them. "You're so damn beautiful."

I lean against his palms and work my hips back and forth, side to side. His cock hits delicious parts of me that way. But then his hands slide down to my ass, holding me tight there. He grinds me against him at his pace, not mine. It's like I'm his personal sex toy, and I love it.

He groans, jutting himself deeper into me. "Fuck, you feel amazing."

I want to say it back to him, but I am lost in the sensations in my body. Can't help it. He's gonna make me come. I need something to hold onto, or I might float away. My nails dig into Anderson's muscled chest, and he hisses steam from the pain but doesn't try to move me. I bear down on his cock, and it shoots me over the edge. This is no gentle push. It's more like I've just gone over the hill at the top of a roller coaster.

My body vibrates and burns and coils, I am helpless to it, out of control on his body, and just as I think I can't take anymore, he sits up and kisses me, devouring every sound, every inkling of a thought. He bounces me on his cock and forces me to come again.

This time, the pleasure washes away my bones. I go limp on his lap, my head resting on his shoulder while I struggle to catch my breath. Somehow, even in this frosty weather, I've worked up a sweat, and when the wind breezes by, I shudder in his arms.

He wraps a blanket around me and holds me to him. He strokes down my back. When I've calmed down, he pulls the blanket away, making me whimper. But then he rolls us over once more. At least I have the lounger to keep my back warm now.

Nope. Thought too soon. Anderson pulls out and flips me onto my stomach before working himself into me from behind. He curls his arms beneath my shoulders, effectively locking me onto his cock. When he lays on my back, something inside of me unwinds. I'd thought we were rutting beasts before, but now, we're in the right position for it. He bites the nape of my neck like a wolf who won the right to mate, and then he stops holding back.

Anderson fucks me so hard and so fast it's almost as if someone is applauding us. His hips bounce against my ass like he's spanking me with his body. Being outside must be working for him, too. Every stroke stokes my fire, and I'm heating up from the inside. His teeth in my skin, the rough canvas rubbing my nipples, and the way his cock hits my spot all has me gripping the edge of the lounger again. My body tenses from my impending orgasm. I just need something unbreakable to hold onto, or I'll lose myself.

He releases my skin, then licks where he bit me. He growls in my ear, "You're gonna come for me again." He punctuates every syllable with another thrust, and I'm trembling all over. Just one more, please, one more —"

"Right now," he demands, and my body gives in to him, opening the floodgates of my pleasure and making me scream out the last of my breath. He roars behind me, coming deep inside with a mighty final thrust.

Anderson collapses onto my back, gasping like a strangled man. His puffing breaths move my hair into my eyes, so I brush it away. He pants, "Didn't … didn't think about … clean up out here."

"Same," I manage to utter.

Gently, he slips out of me and quickly pulls the blanket over us. I pull myself onto his chest, and he holds me tight. As his breaths slow, he quietly admits, "Gets harder to hold back when I think about getting you pregnant."

That's news to me. "Oh?"

He stares up into the sky. "Maybe it's being out here in the wilderness or something, but that was different, wasn't it? More … "

"Primal?" I nod. "Yeah."

"Is that okay—"

"It was hot. But I'm surprised the thought of getting me pregnant gets you going."

He smiles and nods. "Funny. When you're young, it's the most terrifying thing in the world to think about that. But ... " He sighs. "I'm ready to be a dad, and there's just something animalistic about the whole process that appeals to me on a deeper level."

"I get that, I think. If things were different, I'd ... I'm ready to be a mom. Once the craziness has settled."

He draws me close for a kiss. "Once the craziness has settled."

Suddenly, I am dying to settle the craziness.

23

ANDERSON

I t has been a long day but a good one. And an odd one. I'd never been much for the outdoors. Urban outdoors is different than rural outdoors, it seems. I'd grown up enjoying the urban outdoors for short stints, enough time to know I wanted to go back inside. But this was something else. When it came to June, the outdoors only increased my hunger for her.

She leaves to tidy herself, so I lay on my back, still staring at the stars. The fact she knows constellations and how they relate to the people and culture ... there are multitudes in that woman, and I've scratched only the surface. I intend to plumb her depths for decades to come.

For a long time, I'd thought of myself as the luckiest man alive. Born into the right family, gifted with good genetics, and driven to succeed. When it all started to fall apart, I fell into the trap of self-pity. It was easy. Things with June went south, as did things with my finances and career, thanks to my father. I killed a man to defend her. And then I got shot. If I hadn't felt at least a little sorry for myself, I might have been delusional. But now, at this quiet cabin in the woods, I've come to realize how lucky I am.

I have the greatest woman in the world at my side.

The rest of it matters, but none of it compares to her. Whatever comes of the murder investigation or my father's ire for June, we will weather it together. Part of me hopes he gets pissed about us eloping. If he throws a fit over that, then Mom will see him for the petulant, abusive child he is. But she's forgiven him more than anyone ever should, so I doubt it will make a dent in her opinion of him. Besides, I'm not doing it to piss him off—that's just a side benefit. I will elope with June so we can start our life together without the interference of everyone else. It'll be intimate and just for us.

Just thinking about it, I have the urge to drive to the nearest airport, jet to Vegas, and do it. Is there any real reason not to?

But then June walks out of the cabin, wearing only a blanket and a smile, and there's my reason. She lays next to me, cuddling against my shoulder again and setting off something warm in my chest. There's only one better feeling than this. She murmurs, "You got cold again."

"Then warm me up." I turn and kiss her. Must have taken her by surprise—she's a little stiff at first. But then she melts against me, letting out those sweet moans that seem to have a direct line to my cock. As I kiss her, I wonder what's on her mind. Is she thinking about elopement or the stars or something else completely? Sometimes, I think I'll never truly know her, and that only spurs me to try harder. Dig deeper.

I move over her, relishing the sensation of her soft body beneath me. She lets out a gasp and breaks our kiss. "You're hard again? Already?"

"You do this to me, baby."

She leans up and bites my lower lip for that, and we're back to kissing like teenagers in the backseat. The feel of my shaft straining on her warm thigh and the look in her brown eyes is seared into my brain.

My balls are a low throb that tries to steal focus. If I don't get some relief, I will go out of my mind. I murmur into her ear, "I need to be inside of you."

"Mm, fuck yes," she whispers with that filthy mouth of hers. Her eyes light up, anticipating pleasure. But I love surprising her with something new. The fun we had in the hotel was one thing. Out here, though, we have a whole world to experiment with, and I'm not going to waste that. She thinks she knows, but she has no idea.

I cup my hand over her pussy, soft and wet for me. She sharply inhales — my hand is cold but quickly warms up against her as I dip my fingers deep. She grips my shoulders and writhes on my touch. Two fingers in and my thumb on her clit, and she's bucking on me, trying to force her climax already. Oh, my poor, sweet girl is going to be so disappointed.

Briefly.

Just as she crests, her body goes tense, and that's when I pull my hand away. Her whimpers are such intoxicating things I am *this close* to giving her what she wants. But not now. Not tonight. Tonight, I'm getting what I want.

I scoop my hands beneath her with one thigh on either side of my waist as I pick her up. Once we're standing, I don't thrust home. She's grinding on me, trying to take me inside of her as I walk out onto the snow barefoot. The cold has become background noise. I hardly notice it. Not with her on me. She whimpers, "What are you doing?"

But I don't answer. I'm a man on a mission, and when I find the right tree, I go straight for it. Smooth enough not to hurt her, wide enough to take it. When I brace her back on the tree, she gasps and shouts, "Cold!" But I thrust home, burying myself deep into her pussy, and the cold is forgotten. She screams in delight or in confusion, I'm not sure which. June looks baffled by this turn of events but also elated. Once I'm sure she's not going to slide on the bark too much, I begin.

Short thrusts, long thrusts, rapid, slow, whatever I feel like at the moment. I'm keeping off-rhythm to draw it out. Savoring the moment is all I want. The hot, wet glide of my cock through her folds is heaven, and I don't want to stop. Not ever.

She peppers me with kisses and curses, reaching back to brace on the tree with one hand and clawing my shoulder and neck with the other. Her hair goes wild with every thrust, dark brown curls unbound. Snarls pour up from her throat, and in this position, she can't do anything to stop me from making her come. She can't get tense or fight it. Her body is mine.

This time, when she crests close to her orgasm, I unleash myself on that pussy.

Her screams echo on the trees as she gushes on me, her body milking mine again and again. Her wetness pours down my shaft, and I let out a prideful growl. I did this to her. I made her lose control. And I'm not stopping.

I bounce her on my cock, memorizing the feel of her, the look on her face, the yearning. She can't catch her breath. The faint light from the cabin shows her pink cheeks and puffing lips. But instead of slowing down, I press myself to those lips, devouring her cries. Every one of those sounds belongs to me. I earned them.

Her body tries to tense again, so I hammer into her harder, faster. This is why I do so much cardio. To give her the fucking she deserves.

But my balls threaten to bring the fun to an end. She's so tight and so sweet that it's hard to resist. Then her pealing cry erupts from her perfect mouth as she comes, and I'm so fucking proud I got two out of her like this that I join her, pumping myself into her. I want to fill her up with me, and for a fleeting moment, there's that thought again. The only one I have when we're like this.

I want to see her belly swell with my child.

It's a strange and primitive thing, this thought. Equal parts marking my territory and connecting us eternally. Fuck, I want that with her. I crave that forever bond with June, and I will have it one day. But not now.

As we pant in the dark, frigid forest, I slide out of her. She takes a moment to find her words. "That ... cold. So cold—"

I scoop her up in my arms and carry her back into the cabin this time, and she races into the bathroom. When she comes out, I wrap her in blankets and spoon her on the thick, shaggy rug in front of the fireplace. As she turns around, some bark abrasions are visible on her back, but it's nothing too worrisome. Once her teeth stop chattering, I stroke up and down her arm, confident my cold hand won't make things worse. "Was that okay?"

A small laugh burbles out of her. "Is that a serious question?"

"Yes."

"That was ... Anderson, I'm not sure if there are words for that."

"In a good way?"

She nods.

"I was worried I might have hurt your back or—"

"Oh, it did. But I kinda liked it."

"A little edge of pain to spice things up?"

Another nod. June isn't terribly shy about what she likes in the bedroom if it's something standard. But when it comes to anything remotely kinky, she's a church mouse. That's okay. We have all the time in the world to help her with that.

We lay by the fire a bit longer, and her snores come fast. It's the most peaceful I've heard her in a long time, and I am glad I could do that for her. My girl needs some peace in her life. I carry her to bed, and when my eyes close, I dream of her lips all night long. The perfect ending to a perfect night.

24

JUNE

There is something about waking up in Anderson's arms that sets my heart at ease. Warm sunlight pokes at the edges of the dark gray curtain, beaming a laser onto his naked hip. When I look down, I realize I've stolen nearly all the blankets. That's his fault. If he hadn't carried me to the tree, I might have let him have some blanket.

If he hadn't carried me to the tree, though, I wouldn't have had the most amazing orgasm of my life.

Seriously, that was incredible. He said it last night — that added touch of pain spiced things up. It felt as though my whole body was coming, from the bottom of my feet up to the ends of my hair. Even my fingernails had their own orgasms. I have never experienced anything like it.

I want to again. And again, and again …

Oh, boy, he might have made an addict out of me. Well, if I keep jumping on his dick, he has only himself to blame. But for now, cuddles.

I bury my face against his chest, lingering in the shallow valley between his square pecs. He's on his side, so that makes it easier. This close to him, I get a hint of his natural scent and let it permeate my lungs. If I had only one thing to smell for the rest of my life, I'd pray it was this.

And not a penitentiary cell at a women's correctional facility.

I know we said we were putting a pin in all of that, and last night, that flimsy idea held out long enough for crazy good sex, but mornings are always filled with dread, aren't they? The dread of what the day might bring…I try to squash my anxiety and worries by pretending they don't exist. That it's just us here. That there isn't a world outside the cabin's walls. I take several deep breaths of Anderson and can almost fool myself into believing it. I have this weird urge to roll around on him, so I smell like him, too. But when his arm tightens on my back, I know he's waking up, so I don't have much time for that.

Anderson kisses the top of my head and lets out a muffled, "Good morning," that sounds more like, "G'emorn."

"Good morning," I purr up at him, wondering what other surprises he has in store for me.

But then his stomach snarls like a mangy beast. It's so loud that he starts laughing. "Well, that is not how I intended to start the day."

"Normally, it's me who has the growly stomach. Are you okay?"

"Fine, I think. But last night burned a lot of calories, and my body is telling me all about it. I am famished."

I frowned. "Is there a diner or something nearby?"

"Uh, the Airbnb people said they'd stock the fridge for us, so hopefully, there is something in there."

I got an idea. "You stay here, and I will bring you breakfast in bed."

He smiles. "June, you don't have to do that. I am capable of—"

"I know you are. But baby, you've been cooking most of our meals for a couple of months now. Let me cook for you."

His smile grew as he put his hands behind his head. "Alright then. Don't think anyone has ever brought me breakfast in bed, so I am looking forward to this."

I beam at him. "Then you keep your pretty little ass right there, and I will hop to it." I jump out of bed.

He laughs. "If either of us has a pretty little ass, it's you."

I drag my pajama bottoms up a bit slower than normal

to give him a show. "Can't we both have them? You have a phenomenal butt."

"Well, thank you. I work hard on my ass—it's the engine that powers fucking."

"Then you've done spectacular work, sir, because last night … " I shudder thinking about it, and blood rushes to my cheeks. "I better go get that breakfast started—"

"No way. What about last night?"

I lick my lips and take a fortifying breath. "Best. Ever. And I am going because if I don't go now, I am jumping you."

"No objections here—"

"Nope, breakfast!" I announce as I flee the room. If he's going to give me anything like last night, he will need his strength.

I putter around the kitchen, looking for ingredients. Thankfully, the owners actually did stock it for us. Breakfast, lunch, and dinner ingredients. Color me impressed.

I dig up a buttermilk pancake recipe on my phone because, to my shock, they included buttermilk in their grocery haul. I hope whoever owns this place has a spot in the Florida Keys or Hawaii because I'd like to rent from them again, and I am craving the tropics after all of this cold. Not that I minded it much last night.

I crack an egg into the bowl and just as I start to stir, someone knocks on the front door, and I almost whack the bowl off the counter in surprise. Did that really just happen? I look up and see a shadow at the door. It's wooden with a frosted glass pine tree in the middle of it, so I can't see who is there, but they're big.

Anderson pops out of the bedroom with his lounge pants on, frowning with his eyes on the door. "The fuck?"

"Who knows we're here?"

"Just the owners. Did you tell anyone —"

"Of course not. You?"

He shakes his head as he walks to the door.

But I don't want an intrusion on our perfect escape. If he opens that door, the illusion of freedom is ruined. I hiss, "Don't open it! They could be dangerous, and there's no one out here to go to for help."

"It's probably just the owner. Maybe they forgot something." But all the same, he grabs a fireplace poker on his way. He tucks it behind his back as he cracks open the door. "You?"

Fuck. It's someone we know.

He sets the poker aside, so at least I know they're not dangerous. But when Anderson opens the door wider, I see I am dead wrong.

Moss darkens our doorstep. Such a short, insignificant word to describe such a hulking, substantial man. He's white, and I'd guess of Russian descent, but I don't know. Sometimes when he speaks, his accent is Russian, sometimes it's Italian, sometimes it's something else. I'm not sure if it's an affectation or if that's truly how he talks. Maybe it's so he can be an international man of mystery. I'd never ask.

The man scares the panties off me.

He's huge. Not just tall, but actually huge. Somewhere near six and a half feet with the biggest hands I have ever seen. Bald, but like today, he often wears a skull cap. His black overcoat could be a tent for me. He is heavy, both with muscle and a layer of fat, good for long winters or the energy needed for his work. Given that his work includes fighting, killing, and disposing of bodies, he needs all the energy he can get.

During Anderson's convalescence, Moss came to the apartment with relative frequency, so it's not like I'm not familiar with the man. He's always been nothing but polite and kind to me. I have no personal reason to fear him. But there is something at his edges that sends a lick of frisson through me.

I know Anderson trusts the guy, and I trust Anderson, so I should extend that to Moss. But I can't. Something about him puts me on edge. Maybe it's knowing he's killed countless people. For now, I try to comfort myself with the knowledge that, even though he's a murderer, he's on our side, and that might come in handy before the end of this.

But I also don't want a living, breathing reminder of our troubles in our downtime.

"Come in," Anderson says, and I can't fault him for that, but I want to.

Moss smiles big and friendly at me. "Good morning, June." Today, it's Italian with a hint of Russian.

"Good morning, Moss. Coffee?"

"Erm, I do not intend to stay long, but thank you." He takes off his skullcap like he's a polite man from the fifties instead of a gangster from now. He's done the same thing each time he came into our home. Moss is many things, and one of them is odd.

Anderson closes the door. "How did you find us? No one knows where we are."

Moss smiles like Anderson is an adorable child who asked why mommy was kissing Santa Claus. "It is sweet that you think this is possible. But no. If you pay with credit card, you can be found."

Anderson closes his eyes and sighs at himself. "Right. So, I know this isn't a social call—"

"Da," Moss mutters with a heavy Russian accent. The guy is all over the place this morning.

"Have a seat—"

But he shakes his head, a solemn look coming over him. Oh hell. What now?

"Okay, then out with it."

"I wished to tell you in person this. According to my people inside the BPD, there may be a video of you attacking the haddock."

I blink. "Wait, the haddock?"

For a moment, Anderson doesn't speak. He looks like someone punched the air out of him. But then he finds his words, quiet though they may be. "Moss' code word for Neil."

I reel on Moss. "But you said there were no security cameras in my building!"

"The conversations have pointed to a neighbor with a phone who recorded it. But understand, these conversations were overheard, with bits missing. I know nothing for certain, including how much was potentially recorded."

Anderson leans against the wall, then slumps down it until he's on the floor. Then he just sits there, staring off into space.

If he had yelled, or cried, or cursed, I would be less worried. But I've never seen him like this. I don't know what comes next. For any of us.

25

ANDERSON

G one. All of it. Hope. Peace. My fantasy of a future with June. It's all just empty air. My body went weak with the news, and I feel deflated somehow. Hollow.

They have me dead to rights. I'm ruined. My life, my career, my wife—

A cupped hand under my chin forces me to look up. It's her. My former bride-to-be. I won't drag her down with me. I can't. She snaps her fingers in front of my face. "Baby, baby, I need you here with me, okay?"

Gently, I shake myself free of her hand. "Oh, I'm here. I'm fucked, but I'm here."

"You can't go all catatonic on me. We need to think—"

"I'm not catatonic. It's just... this is a lot."

She squats in front of me. "I am going to make you breakfast—"

I laugh. "You think I can eat right now?"

"You think I care if you think you can eat right now? I am going to make you breakfast, and you're going to shove it down your throat. whether you like it or not, and that will give us the strength to figure out what the fuck we do now. But you're not going to think with a clear head until you've eaten and gotten some coffee in you, so march to the dinette table and sit your pretty little ass down, and I will bring you food. Go." She points angrily at the table.

Well, shit. "Alright, alright," I climb up off the floor and go to the table as she stomps to the kitchen.

Moss' eyes go wide. "You are right. She is perfect for you."

June is still in a snit, but it's impossible not to catch the curl of her lips as she smirks a little. Moss joins me at the table while she works in the kitchen. I am in awe of her. How she can function right now is so far beyond me that I'm speechless.

For her sake, I try to form sentences. "What, uh, what did your spy tell you?"

"That Wachowski spoke to someone on the phone, and what I have already said is what she heard. She was uncertain about the context, and that keeps her safe for now. My informant is good. Solid. She has never steered me wrong before."

"Banks and Wachowski all but said they had video," I

mutter, stomach twisting in on itself. "But until now, I could tell myself it wasn't true."

Moss takes a breath. "Could be that he is feeding her information."

I frown up at him. "You mean he knew she was listening?"

He shrugs his huge shoulders. "Could be. But I would not bet my life on it if I were you. Wachowski has … a reputation. He plays games. Tries to make people act outside their best interest to trip them up. He could have been lying to make her report this—"

"And see if I go on the lam?"

"Da."

I blow out a breath, trying to clear my head. But it's still muddy. "Fuck."

"Da."

June projects from the kitchen, "It seems to me there are two paths in front of us. One where we flee the country and spend the rest of our days running from the law, and one where we face whatever this is. What do you want to do?"

"Well, I don't want to go to prison—"

"Duh."

"And I want to spend the rest of my days with you. Come what may."

She smiles up at me before pouring batter onto a skillet. "Good."

"The problem is, I don't know what that requires. If we flee, obviously, it's to someplace without extradition, and that means passports, which are back in Boston, and fleeing is its own set of big problems. I'll never see my family again. My friends … my home country. Not any of it. We'll have to create a whole new life, new identities, new everything. I'm a lawyer in the US. I don't have marketable skills outside of that, so I have no idea what I'd do to support us."

Moss lifts a shoulder. "New identity? I can help. New job? That, too."

"Thanks, but I feel like I shouldn't even be going down this rabbit hole when I haven't heard from Pym yet. He has informants in the BPD, too, and I would think if Wachowski is pulling some stunt, he'd be feeding them information, too, right? So, Pym should be calling. But he hasn't. It doesn't make sense."

"Not to mention," June begins, "I don't want to raise children on the lam in some foreign country where I don't know anyone, don't speak the language, etcetera. I wanted to raise our kids here. I want them to have a normal life. What kind of life would they have if we're looking over our shoulders all the time?"

Moss shrugs. "It is not so bad to raise children this way. My girls are thriving."

We both stare at him for a solid minute before I ask, "You're on the lam?"

"Is a matter of opinion. And jurisdiction. But I am wanted man in many places, and I raise my girls happy and healthy anyway. Children do not need to know the troubles of their parents. They need shelter, food, and love. Anything else is bonus."

She sighs as she delivers a stack of pancakes, butter, and real maple syrup. "Point is, I want our kids to have normal, and Moss, forgive me, but I am not cool enough about murder charges to be able to give my kids normal under those circumstances."

If the pancakes didn't look picture-perfect and steamy, I wouldn't have touched them. But they are, so after an unhealthy amount of butter and syrup, I dive into them. After the first bite, I once again find myself marveling at the woman I want to marry. "You can make these ... like, anytime?"

"Well, yeah."

"I'm gonna get so fat."

She snorts a laugh and makes two more plates, bringing one to Moss and one for herself. To my surprise, he does not object. In fact, he engulfs his stack with the same gusto I do. It's a surprise, considering every time I offered him a meal at our place, he refused it. Maybe he's a little afraid of June. I kinda hope so. I like the thought of her scaring the big bad thug.

After a few moments of silent eating, June asks, "Have you considered calling the Blade to see if he knows anything yet?"

"Calling seems like a bad idea. My phone could be tapped."

But Moss shakes his head. "Is unlikely. Getting a warrant for that is a big headache. Most will not do it."

"What about a tap in an apartment?" June asks.

"Less paperwork, but also usually too much for them to try. You are both lawyers. How you not know this?"

I shake my head. "I'm a corporate lawyer, she's a tax attorney. We went through some criminal law classes, but *de jure* is what we learned. The letter of the law. Not how it actually functions day to day. *De facto* is what matters here. It's one thing for us to know the steps for a cop to obtain a warrant, but the odds of whether or not they'll do it is another thing entirely."

She goes on, "So, since it's a pain in the ass, then they probably haven't planted a bug in our place?"

He thinks for a moment, then shakes his head. "Getting information from a person is much easier than the work that goes into planting a bug because judges do not like giving their approval to such things. Convincing judges is trouble for police. Physical evidence is far easier to come by. Confessions are even easier. Anderson, you did not confess to anything?"

I shook my head. "And I'm not about to."

"Then what they need is physical evidence. If they have video of the brawl or of us handling the haddock, then ... you are proper fucked. But if they have video of the attack followed by the brawl ... "

"Mitigating circumstances," June mutters. "We need to know if that video exists and, if so, how much it saw. If they recorded that piece of shit attacking me, then we can argue fighting back was justified."

Moss nods along, but I'm not sure. "The only way to find out what's on the video is the hard way. We go back, we face the music, and let the chips fall where they may. I'm not sure I'm ready to do that." Going back sounds like the exact opposite of what we should be doing.

June takes my hand in hers. "Like we do everything else. Together."

Moss smiles at us. "I will do what I can to help. Whatever you choose."

"Thank you. How are your pancakes?"

"Best I ever have. Thank you." He finishes his stack before either of us.

She smiles. "These aren't special, guys. One day, I'll make some sourdough pancakes, and you'll see how good they can really be."

One day, she says. As if we aren't going to prison forever. I'd like to think she's right, but all of this makes me feel like the noose is tightening, and I can't escape it. Did I cheat death when I was shot only to end up in prison? I don't want to believe that's my fate. I'd like to believe fate let me live for a reason. I just wish I knew what the hell it was.

-

26

JUNE

The car ride back to Boston is tense. Not a mile goes by that I don't want to take him up on the offer of fleeing. But I can't give up on the dream of a normal life for us and our kids. Not yet.

We cross the border into Massachusetts, and I'm half-convinced that the police are going to pop out from the next billboard to swarm us. Nothing happens, though. I know this isn't a movie, but when you think about running from the law, everything gets grandiose.

Anderson gives my hand a squeeze. "Holding up?"

"I'm here. You?"

"In my mind, I'm in the Maldives."

I smile at him. "That sounds nice."

"No extradition there, you know."

"I googled non-extradition countries in the bathroom earlier, so yeah, I know. Pretty far from Boston."

The muscle on the side of his neck that pops out when he's stressed has been popped out since he figured out it was Moss at the door. Poor thing. "That's the idea. Far from Boston. You're sure you want to go back?"

No. Yes. Maybe. "I'd like to know what we're facing before we figure out if we want to give up on our lives here. But if things feel off in any way, we'll bounce. Okay?"

It's the same thing we decided to do in Vermont. But it bears repeating.

He nods. "I know, I know. And even though Moss says it's not likely that we're bugged, I think we should keep acting as if we are. Any important conversations happen in the park. Agreed?"

"Agreed. No sense in taking unnecessary risks when we have options." Just another half an hour before Boston. Feels like every minute ratchets up the tension in us both. But I have to trust that everything is going to be okay. We will have our normal life at some point. It's just going to take a lot of work and some patience. But we will get there.

Anderson is a West, and that means, despite his father's enemies, he also has his father's friends in high places who can help us. We have Otto Pym helping us, and there is no better defense attorney on the East Coast. I'm still amazed he was available for us on such short notice. There's Moss, who, no matter my personal feelings about the man, is someone I like having in my corner. It's like owning a rowdy pit bull who likes you and only you. We are not without resources.

And, break glass in case of emergency, I have Andre Moeller. He might be my boss and some kind of an underworld criminal, but that only means he, too, has resources that might come in handy. I don't want to have to lean on him. But he *did* kidnap me, so the guy kind of owes me. Plus, he likes me, as he's brought up time and time again. I don't want to lean on him — he's a sociopath — but if it means saving me and Anderson, I'll do it.

Walking into our apartment does not feel like coming home. I don't get that sense of relief I used to when I walked into my apartment. It's more like the calm before the storm. Since we called everyone and said we were sick, it would be weird if we just bounced back in a day, so we agreed to spend the rest of the day at home, eating too much Chinese food and enjoying a sick day. It's as relaxing as it could be, which isn't saying much.

I keep waiting for the other shoe to fall. A call or a text from the detectives, or god forbid, a hearty knock at the door. Although, at this point, I've been tense for so long, I could almost believe it would be a relief for them to contact us. Sort of letting the steam out of the pressure cooker.

When night comes, neither of us initiates sex.

In the morning, we get ready and go to work like it's any other day. Back to pretending life is normal and we didn't kill a guy and improperly dispose of his body, and the police are not circling like buzzards.

As soon as I get into my office, things feel fishy. I get strange looks from the paralegals on my way to my office, and I want to stop and ask why, but if I do that, isn't that an admission of guilt? Doesn't it make me look suspicious if I'm asking why everyone is looking at me suspiciously?

Maybe I'm overthinking it.

I get into my office, close the door, drop the curtains, and keep the lights low. When I get my laptop open, there are over a hundred new emails. I'm glad I have everything shut down and dark, because I could use some peace and quiet while I pretend to work. And it will be pretending because now that I'm back, I have zero concentration. I just keep waiting for another paralegal to knock and announce I have detectives here to see—

Knock, knock.

Oh my hell, seriously? Already? I haven't even gotten my coffee. I wonder how prison coffee is. Oh god, is there prison coffee?

I clear my throat. "Come in."

But it's not the police. It's Carlos. Of fucking course, it's Carlos. He saunters in, all swagger, no couth.

"Good morning. I heard you were unwell, but you look fine to me."

That's either an accusation or a flirtation, and I don't care which it is. "What do you want, Carlos?"

"I thought I made that clear the first day you arrived." He peers down my blouse for a moment. "Your office."

I roll my eyes. "Why are you here now?"

"So testy—"

"Carlos, I have a sinus headache from being sick. Can you just get on with it?"

He winces in false sincerity. "My apologies. I did not realize you were not up for our usual repartee. Andre wants to see you in his office. Now."

"Why didn't he just shoot me an email?"

"I would never be so bold as to assume I understand how his mind works."

"Fine. Thanks. Message received."

He smiles curtly, then leaves, and I'm grateful for the silence, but I better get moving. Never a good idea to leave a sociopath waiting.

As I pass by the breakroom, I give a longing sigh toward the coffee machine before the elevator whisks me up to the top floor. It's funny how I have been able to block out what happened in Andre's office the other day. With all the discussions of running away from home and what that might entail, I couldn't bear to mention that Andre is scheming to upend West Media. It didn't seem relevant to fleeing for our lives. Not even irrelevant—it felt small and meaningless, truthfully. But now that I'm going back to his office, it feels like that should have been the first thing out of my mouth the moment I saw Anderson.

Before I can knock, I hear, "Come on in, Junebug."

What the hairy fuck?

I throw the door open, and there, I find Andre sitting across from my father. It is all I can do to not shout at the man. My father, not Andre. Although, at the moment, I'm not sure who needs yelling at. They're both all smiles as if they've been having a grand old time. It makes me want to rip them apart. No one should be having a good time right now. Not when my life is on the line.

But I clench my teeth and force a smile. "Dad, I didn't know you were acquainted with Andre."

He smiles, and I know that smile. It's as fake as my own. "You don't remember the introduction email you sent for me?"

With that one sentence, I know precisely what's going on. Somehow, he sent an email, made it look as if I'd sent it, and gotten the introduction that he wanted. If I say anything right now, he'll never forgive me, even though I'm not the one who needs forgiveness. I could ruin whatever deal he's got going, and all I have to do is open my mouth and speak the truth. The truth has always been the one thing my father is afraid of. He must really trust me to think I won't fuck him over for this.

But right now, I have enough of my own shit to deal with. I don't want to deal with his, too, whatever that is. So, I suck it up. "Right, sorry. It must have been the fever that made me forget. I'm still catching up."

"Well, don't let me stop you," Dad says as he gets up. He shakes Andre's hand. "Good seeing you again. We'll have to do it on my yacht next time."

Andre smiles and nods. "Splendid idea. I'll bring the champagne and the," he stops himself to look at me before meeting Dad's eyes again, "entertainment."

Women. He means women. Probably sex workers, by the tone in his voice.

Dad chuckles. "Deal. This weekend?"

"I can kill a few things off my calendar. Saturday it is." Anyone else would have said, "Clear my calendar." Not Andre. He wouldn't say something so mundane as that. Or he actually meant to kill some things off his calendar in the literal sense. I was not dumb enough to ask.

"Sounds good. See you then."

"Uh, Dad, can you hang back for a moment?"

"Junebug, I need to run —"

"Hang back," snaps out of me. But then I lose my tone. "Please? I need to talk to you."

"Oh, of course. I'll meet you at your office."

"Great." He leaves, and I turn to Andre. "How can I help you?"

"Your father is quite a character."

I smile. "He really, really is."

"Did you know he saved a child from a burning building?"

No. Because he didn't. "I may have heard the tale a time or twenty."

He chuckles. "Or that he used to be a track star in college?"

My father never went to college. But I smile. "He's had an interesting life."

"Indeed. I understand the two of you had been estranged for a time. Why is that?"

None of your business. "Family is complicated." I give a shrug, hoping he leaves it at that.

"Too true. My own father and I stopped speaking the moment I had him committed against his will. The old bastard never forgave me for that. It is as you said, family is complicated."

I gulp. "Since we're sharing, why commit someone against their will?"

"He was getting ... troublesome. I don't like trouble, June. You are level-headed like me, so I value your opinion. Is your father trouble?"

More than you know. How do I say this without saying it? "He's boisterous and likes to stretch the truth. Sometimes, that gets him in trouble. But he's not malicious."

"Ah, Sounds like most of my friends. Very good. That is all." He turns to his laptop, dismissing me.

Good, because I have a father to tear into.

27

JUNE

When I get to my office, he's there, standing outside. "Junebug—"

"Not a word," I order and barge past him, ushering him in. Once he's inside, I shut my door as quietly as my anger will allow. "What the fuck is going on?"

"Thanks for not letting my little impropriety slip—"

"A little impropriety? Is that what you call forging an email introduction?"

He gives me that, "Aw shucks," look that has gotten him out of and into trouble more times than I can count. "You were sick, and what kind of father bothers his sick daughter just for an email? That's downright cruel. Monstrous. How could I possibly do such a thing to you?"

"Of course," I gripe as I start to pace my office. "The old make-it-sound-like-you-did-me-a-favor, instead of making it sound like what it was. You're a real piece of work, you know that?"

"I've been told."

"How long?"

His brows draw down. "How long what?"

"How long have you been planning this?"

"Planning? What are you talking about, Junebug?"

"Don't call me that!" I snarl in his face. "That nickname is reserved for use by the man who I call Dad. You're not him anymore, Mitch! You're the bastard who pretended to give a shit about his daughter long enough to use her to get to Andre. So tell me, Mitch, how long have you been planning this? Weeks? Months? Or did you see an opportunity and jump on it last minute, the way you used to jump on women?"

His facade shakes, and lines form on his face in hurt. I might have actually struck him with that one. There's no guile in his tone when he says, "June, I didn't use you."

I'd love to believe that. It would mean the past month of lunches with Dad haven't been built on bullshit and that he really was trying to turn his life around. But I've been hurt by him too many times to be suckered in now. "Yes, you did. How did you even make the email look right? Andre isn't dumb enough to open something from an account he doesn't recognize — wait." It's falling into place. The tech firm he works for is full of guys who could have done it. "Did you have one of your coworkers break into my email?"

He swallows, "Now, June, you're upset —"

"Don't tell me what I am! Tell me the truth!"

"I had a friend make some arrangements, so it looked legit —"

I laugh, shaking my head as he rambles on.

"But I only did it so I didn't have to bother you, honey. You know me. I left a life of crime behind me. I'm trying to do the right thing these days, and I'm not always going to get it right, but I'm still trying. You make it sound like I did something wrong by not bothering you."

I close my eyes because I can't even look at him right now. "So, what you're saying is, you broke the law to avoid annoying your daughter. That's your excuse for this?"

"There's a law about that?"

"Yes!"

"Well, I apologize."

I laugh. The sincerity in his voice is genuinely funny to me. "You apologize and poof? Nothing's wrong? Is that how you think this works?"

"What can I do to make it up to you?"

"Oh, so now it's my responsibility to come up with your penance?"

"I don't mean it that way—"

"You could have cost me my job, Dad! Do you get that? You still could!"

He sighs. "Come on. You know I'd never do anything to put you in jeopardy."

Another laugh pops right out of me. "Do I know that? Because I seem to remember a childhood where you did exactly that, over and over, ruining any chance I ever fucking had at a normal life."

His lines and wrinkles deepen, and for once, I can see the years on him. I can't tell if it's sadness or guilt that coats his voice, but whatever it is, he's good at making it sound like I should feel bad for him. "You're right about that. I'd like to say I'm a different man now, but I'm still the man who did those things, and I thought you'd started to forgive me for them. But I guess I'm wrong about that, huh?"

"If I thought that any of this was sincere, then yeah, I would have forgiven the shit you pulled back then. The abuse, the selfishness, the way you acted like me and Mom weren't shit to you. But you hijacked my email and went behind my back to meet my boss, which means you're up to something, and it will ruin my career. So, no, *Mitch*, I don't forgive you. I don't accept that you're some new man because all I see in front of me is the same bastard who broke my mother's heart and is setting up to do the same to his daughter."

"What do you think I'm up to, June? Tell me that. Aside from befriending your boss, the only other thing you seem to be hung up on is the email part of things, and I've apologized for that, so really, this is on you."

"Befriending him? At lunch, you told me you had a multimillion-dollar business proposition for him." I smirk up at Mitch. "So, which is it? Friends or business?"

"Now you sound like your mother."

I shake my head, smiling. "You were always one hell of a gas lighter, and I see that hasn't changed, either."

"You know something? You could stand to do more to ingratiate yourself with Andre. Your father befriending him will go a long way for your career. It's called networking, June. Something you can't easily do from your high horse."

"Oh, so not only did you do me a favor by hijacking my email, but now you're helping my career? What, out of the goodness of your heart?"

"Friends go into business with each other all the time. I don't know why you're making such a federal case out of it."

My fingers ball into fists as I count to ten. It doesn't really help. It just leaves me with two fists and ten more seconds of anger. "What business are you getting into with Andre?"

"I didn't say I was getting into business with Andre. I just said I could help you with your career by befriending him. You are so paranoid—"

"Don't." The word comes out hard like steel. He says this to me now? After all the years, I heard him call Mom paranoid when she confronted him about another pair of panties in his car, or another bill that showed up marked "Past due," or any number of people who stopped her in the supermarket and asked what he was doing with their money. He told her she was paranoid, that he had things under control, and to stop snooping around. That shit was not going to cut it with me.

"Whatever you're doing with Andre, it ends now. You two are not friends. You'll never be friends. You'll never be business associates, either. Andre Moeller is my boss. I do not want my personal life and my professional life to cross. Ever. I am drawing this line in the sand. If you cross it, we are done. For good. Forever. I have never asked you for a thing in my life, but I am asking you for this. Prove to me that you want me in your life by giving me this."

His jaw clenches. "I want you to think about what you're saying, June. You're telling me you think so little of me that you can't trust me not to screw things up for you here. Do you understand how hurtful that is?"

"If you can't do one simple thing for me, then I guess we're done."

"You are a grown woman. Ultimatums do not become you."

I laugh. "You are a grown man. Bullshit does not become—oh wait. Maybe it does."

He sighs, shaking his head at me. He looks defeated, but I know better. There is nothing that puts him down for long. With a heavy tone, he says, "I am so sorry for everything I did that's made you become this cynical. I did a number on you, and I am sorry, kiddo."

His apology is as hollow as I feel right now. "We're done here. You can go."

His lips smash into a flat line of disappointment, then he pats my shoulder. "I'll give you a couple of days to think about what you said. You're still getting better from your cold, and I'm sure that's playing a part in how you're being right now. All that attitude. Maybe give me a call this weekend when you've got your head on straight."

I shrug his hand off. "Thought you had a playdate with Andre."

"Not if it costs me you." Then he walks out.

Whatever strength I had is gone when the door closes. It's easy to be stubborn and angry when we're face to face, but now I'm just a girl who wishes she had a normal dad. I crumble onto my couch. I'm on the verge of tears, somewhere between sadness, regret, and pure anger. I know for a fact he didn't want to meet with Andre for shits and giggles. He already let slip that he's got to land some big account for his firm and that he wants Andre. My father is a liar, a cheat, and a criminal. What the fuck was I thinking by letting him back into my life?

I try some deep breathing to relax, but it's no use. I feel like a firework with a smoldering fuse. All I need is someone else to fan the flame.

28

ANDERSON

I kick the lower drawer in my desk. Pretty sure I dented it this time. My office is nice, or rather, it *was* nice. But with me destroying the furniture, my office will be thrashed in no time.

I'd spoken with Otto briefly this morning. He had no new news for me. But I didn't believe him. I didn't believe any of it. Otto is a practiced liar—it comes with the territory. I should trust him. He's the best at what he does. Dad hires only the best. He'd told me I was getting paranoid and that he was handling things. To trust the process.

Even still, I just have a feeling. I want more reassurances, and I'm not getting them.

I hate making actual phone calls, and this is humiliating. I shouldn't have to hunt my lawyer down. I'm not up against a traffic ticket, for fuck's sake.

When I get his voicemail for the fifth time, I want to punch something. But first, I leave another message.

The words snarl out of me. "Otto, this is Anderson West. Again. I've heard some disturbing rumors about new evidence, and I need you to call me immediately." Not for the first time, I wish I had a handset so I could slam the phone down and have it matter.

If I had another way to find out about the video, then I could forgo this embarrassment. But Moss' people don't have direct access to it. Otto is the only legitimate way for me to find out about the evidence without drawing more attention to myself. If I go to the police myself, then it looks suspicious. Because it is.

I have no way around Otto. And he's not returning my calls.

I try to give him the benefit of the doubt. He could be in trial. He has other clients. But this is a murder case. Surely, that takes up more of his time than anything else. The man carries three phones. Perhaps he lost this one.

I'm being too generous. He's Otto Pym. The Blade. You don't get that nickname without being able to multitask.

Drumming my fingers on my desk isn't getting anything done, and it's not as if I can work like this. Not when I'm convinced the police are going to knock at any moment. If they have a video of the fight, it'll be sooner rather than later. But if I bail on work again, that's suspicious activity.

Think, dammit.

The first thing I do is test my desk drawer. Yeah, I dented it good. When I pull it out, the mechanism sort of scrapes on itself. Hoorah. I'll have to get maintenance or a handy man in here to fix it. One more thing on my to-do list. Just what I've always wanted. But this drawer is important. It's where I keep the whiskey. So, I definitely need to get this fixed.

My mind runs on with what I'm supposed to do about Otto. I don't know. Am I being obsessive? Yes. Should I be? Also yes. Murder charges don't sort themselves out.

Not that I've been charged yet. I'm a *person of interest*. But it's coming. I can feel it.

Dad might know what's going on with Otto. He *did* hire him, after all. But asking Dad for information is like asking a snake not to bite you. It'll happen. You just don't know when.

When the time came to make an excuse about being out, it was easy enough. His secretary, Margaret, had gotten a well-timed cold. I hope she's doing well. She's older than sliced bread. I don't know what Dad will do if Margaret retires or dies. God forbid the cold takes her out. He'd be lost without her. He likes things the way Margaret does them, so he's too stubborn to hire a temp to sit in as a replacement, which means his door is unguarded.

When I walk to his office, it's eerie to see her desk empty. She sits right outside his door, the rabid guard dog who fixes his coffee. The woman is like a grandmother to me, and I have nothing but respect and admiration for her. But her absence *does* make this easier.

Just before I knock, I hear voices. One voice in particular catches my ear. Dad is meeting with Otto.

No wonder he didn't take my call. Is anyone else in there? I listen in to find out. No sense in going in there without knowing what I'm dealing with.

My lawyer's gruff voice carries well through the door. "… could be worse. Could be a *double* homicide."

Dad laughs. "I didn't hire to you to play Devil's Advocate, Pym. I hired you because the Devil himself is what he's up against." He pauses. "My boy against a murder charge. It's surreal. He's still green. How in the hell did he get himself into this mess?"

"Moss should have taught him better by now. Pounding a man to death in public? Jesus Christ, he should have known better."

There'd better not be anyone else inside. Fuck, I cannot believe they're discussing the case among them. Yes, Dad hired him, but confidentiality makes their discussion beyond inappropriate. Otto could be disbarred for this. My blood boils as their conversation goes on.

Dad says, "Moss is clearly getting soft. I like the guy, but you're right. Anderson should have known better. Still can't believe he wants to marry that whore."

My fists clench.

"The boy swears they weren't together when the incident happened —"

A loud slam echoes in his office. Dad snaps, "Bullshit! They were together, I promise you. He's embarrassed she was cheating on him, and he lost his temper when he saw them together. That's all this is! His whore of a girlfriend couldn't keep her legs closed, and now my boy is up on a fucking murder charge!"

Just as I'm about to storm in, Otto's laugh sends a shiver up my spine. He says, "Well, that's why we're pinning this on her."

The fuck.

When Dad speaks, I can just picture the sneer on his face. "It's no more than the bitch deserves. You know, I invited her into my house several times, and she sits there and eats my food, making polite conversation, and all the while, all I can think is, who the hell else is she fucking behind Anderson's back? When she went to the bathroom, did she go snooping around here? It's maddening."

Is he fucking kidding with this shit? What in the fuck? But I have to think. This is Dad. He thinks the worst about everyone. No matter how much I want to run in there and pummel his face into a pulp for saying that, I have to be careful. For one, he's paying for my lawyer and it's his connection that got me Otto in the first place. And two, if I beat the shit out of the old man now, all my careful planning to destroy him will go out the window.

I have to keep a lid on my rage. For now. Most importantly, I need to find out what the fuck Otto meant about pinning this on June. If he can still do that, then how would he account for a video of me in the fight?

He laughs bitterly. "I told you. After she got kidnapped, you should have installed cameras in your place. You were the target. They took her to get to you."

"I'm not living on camera, Pym. Even closed circuit systems can be tampered with, and I'm not giving anyone that kind of access. No one is invading my privacy."

Someone shifts in their seat. "Maybe not, but you could put cameras in strategic places—your den, for instance. Or just over the doors. Not enough to tell anything, but enough to know where someone went."

"That's not a terrible idea." Dad pauses for a beat. "How are you going to put this on June?"

"You'd be surprised how many juries don't like women. It's easier than you think. Especially when she's been cheating … " He laughs. "That's enough for most people to convict her of whatever's in front of them. Give me a cheating woman, and I'll give you a free man."

Oh, hell no.

-

29

ANDERSON

I throw the door open. "What the fuck are you two doing?"

It's nice to see them both so startled for once. They both act like captains of their own industries, so it's good to see them taken off guard. Dad is the first to speak. "Anderson, a classy entrance as always. Come in, We were just discussing things."

Otto's voice is even gruffer in person. Though that might be because I scared the shit out of him. "Anderson, good to see you."

"Is it? Because from where I'm standing, you shouldn't be happy to see me at all. If you were happy to see me, you would have been taking my calls."

"You understand as well as anybody that we all have meetings to attend."

Something inside of me snaps. "And this meeting? Why wasn't I invited? Since it's about me, I mean."

"Close the door," my father orders.

"And why should I do that? Seems you're happy to discuss my business with anybody."

"Now, Anderson." The tone in his voice brokers no debate.

I slam it shut, largely because I don't want this getting around. "Happy?"

"I've been happier. Sit."

Otto says, "Perhaps I should leave this to the two of you. This seems to be a family discussion."

I point directly at him. "You're not going anywhere. This is on you as much as it's on him. I heard what the both of you were saying. You're both just as wrong."

"About?" Dad asks.

"Every single fucking thing that came out of both of your mouths."

Dad flicks his hand dismissively at Otto. "You can go. I'd like to handle this personally."

I glare at Dad, but Otto leaves. Interesting that The Blade is more afraid of my father than my father is of him. I've never learned the depths of my father's foothold in the underworld of Boston, but seeing Otto Pym flee from him like that is enough to tell the story.

But right now, that means fuckall to me. "You're not pinning this on June. Period. And keep the filth in your mind off of her. If I ever hear you call her those words again, I'm going to cut you off at the knees."

It's never very comforting when a threat like that is met with a smile. "My boy, you act as if you've heard things that you haven't been thinking."

"Excuse me?"

"Surely you're not naive enough to honestly believe her story."

"June is going to be my wife. I saw what I saw. I don't care what you believe. You're gonna keep that filth out of your mind when you think of June. You will never say those things about her again. And if—"

He laughed. The bastard laughed. "June Devlin will never be my daughter-in-law."

"What makes you think you have any control over who I choose to marry?"

"Let me tell you a few things about this girl that you love so very much that you're willing to threaten your father over her."

It's my turn to laugh. "As if you know a fucking thing about that woman."

"Then you should be open to hearing what I have to say. What do you have to fear? If you think that it's not true, so be it. But I will say my piece before you walk out that door again."

"Out with it."

Dad sat back, steepling his fingers over his lap. "June works for Andre Moeller. This you know correct?"

"Yes. What of it?"

"Are you aware that Andre intends to unseat me?"

I frown. Where is he going with this? "Unseat you from what?"

"Everything."

"I don't understand."

"Country clubs, charity boards, you name it. He intends to oust me from everything that belongs to me. Seats on boards of other companies and from the chair I sit as I speak."

That makes no sense. "That's ridiculous. This is West Media. It's only West Media if a West is in the CEO seat."

"Come now, you don't believe that. Plenty of companies are run by people whose names are not on the door."

"But a West has always been the CEO of West Media. It goes through our family line. Everyone knows that."

Dad takes a stiff breath and runs his fingers through his hair. The man must be shaken to show so much emotion. "Things change, Anderson. And Andre is looking to accelerate that change. With June's help."

That earns a laugh. "What in the fuck are you talking about?"

"Your little wife-to-be has decided that she's going to help Andre unseat me from everywhere I belong. What do you have to say in her defense now?"

"You are out of your mind if you think that's true."

He brushes a piece of invisible lint from his sleeve. "And if you didn't believe that the possibility is real, you wouldn't look so nervous right now."

"You're mistaking my aggravation for nervousness. It's not the same thing."

"So you say." I can't read the expression on his face. Contemplative. Furious. For Elliott West, they are one and the same. "The trouble, my dear boy, is that I have proof. You should know by now that I know everything that happens in my companies. That includes what happens when someone is sniffing around them and asking for documents. Such as what June was doing for the past few weeks."

"You're out of your mind, old man."

He smiles. "That's the sort of accusation you make when you know you've lost." He dials up something on his laptop, then turns it around to face me. On screen, I see June. She's making copies of documentation, furtively glancing around. I can't see what it is until she closes a Manila folder over it. But there's the Branson and Associates logo. One of the companies my dad is on the board of. Then, the picture changes. She's sitting in an office with someone I don't know.

"Am I supposed to know what's happening here?"

"Oh, right. The sound." He clicks a button, and I can hear everything.

"You're sure those are the files Andre wanted?" she asks.

The woman nods. "Everything on the board, including their nastier proclivities. You've got your work cut out for you."

June smiles and shrugs. "Just following orders." She gets up and leaves.

I'm not sure what to think. "Am I supposed to believe that was something nefarious?"

"That was for the Wilco Casino. I am on that board. If she was not up to something nefarious, then why is she collecting information on everything that I have my fingers in?"

I don't want to admit that he had a point. June and my father have been adversaries since before we got together. This does not look good. "I'm sure there's a perfectly logical explanation for this." But even as the words come out of my mouth, I'm having a hard time believing them. I had woken up feeling like I was standing just over quicksand, and now, there's no solid ground. What in the hell is June up to?

"Lucky for us, I am not as naive as you are. I also retain spies in my enemies' quarters. This ... issue has not gone unnoticed. June is known to be associated with us, and thus, when she goes around asking questions and prying into things she ought not, it weakens us in the eyes of our enemies. Given your precarious legal situation, do you think we can afford to look weak right now?"

My stomach flips at the thought. None of this makes any sense. My voice goes hoarse. "Of course not."

"Your woman is a traitor, and she is using you to destroy me. I don't know for how long this has been going on. Perhaps she took the job with Andre innocently enough. Though I doubt it. Considering he had kidnapped her and allegedly terrified her, I have to think that she took the job knowing that there was something else going on, A deeper game. Or perhaps during the alleged kidnapping, he turned her against us. Who can say, other than them?"

This is wrong. I know that it's wrong. There is no way that she has been playing spy since then. "She's not ... that's not who she is."

"I'm sure plenty of people would love to believe that the person that they love is being genuine with them. That's how a honey trap works."

"No way. No fucking way."

"Think about it, Anderson. The woman that you've had a crush on for years just happens to be at a sex auction the night that you're there? And she somehow falls head over heels in love with you in a matter of, what? Days? Weeks? Then, somehow, she gets kidnapped from one of the most secure buildings in all of Boston. But she's returned to you unharmed. You two play your little dating game. She breaks up with you. And the night that you happen to be following her, she happens to be attacked by an investment banker. As if investment bankers aren't the perfect people to have on the inside of a bank."

I'm shaking. I'm so angry. "What are you saying?"

"Neil had access to all kinds of information. What better way to cut an asset loose than to have it taken out by your enemy? Certainly makes it easier to pin the murder on you when she tricked you into doing it."

I slam my fist on his desk. It's either going there or his face. "I fucking saw what I fucking saw. He attacked her."

"And if you thought you were fighting for your life, wouldn't you attack the person threatening you?"

"It wasn't like that. It was pervy and sexual and gross."

Dad lifts his shoulder. "Perhaps those were the sex games that they played. You'll never know now. Tell me, Anderson, does she like it rough?"

She does, but that's not the point. "That's immaterial."

He laughs. "I believe a jury will say otherwise, as will a judge. Son, face reality. She has played you from day one. I don't know how long this plan has been in action. It truly could have started at any point. Andre plays the long game. And June has been his best tool. I need you to understand that. You are in danger from this woman. This company is in danger from this woman."

I don't want to believe anything he says. The picture he paints is too ugly. But. I also know this kind of thing happens in corporate life. But I just can't … fuck, I can't breathe. "What are you saying?"

"I'm saying that you are never to see that woman again. Kick her out of your home today. Go no-contact because I don't trust you to not fall for her bullshit again. Do it for yourself. For your family. For this company. Show me you're not a traitor, too."

"I'm no fucking traitor."

"Prove your loyalty. Be done with her. Save yourself. Before it's too late."

30

ANDERSON

"**M**eet me at the Chamberlain Museum at six."

That is all I put in the text. It's where we reconnected after so many years apart. Where I bought a night with June. The night that started my downfall, according to my father. But even with the evidence stacked against her, I can't help but think of it as the night I finally found what I was made for.

Her.

I pull up early, unsure of what I'm going to say. The building is all classic architecture and stately landscape, and every flourish is lost on me because I am still shaking. In anger. In fear.

He can't be right. Can he?

He made a compelling case in his office, but I can't help but think he's wrong. I feel it in my gut. My twisting, nauseated gut. Have I even eaten today? I don't think so. I'd skipped breakfast because of worrying about the cops and lunch for the same reason. Now this. I know I need to eat to keep up my strength and make good choices, but the thought of putting food in my mouth sends another wave of nausea through me. It's not happening anytime soon.

Not until I know the truth. I need to hear it directly from June.

If, by some horrid miracle, she is a spy, then she won't come out and say it when I confront her. I'm not dumb enough to think she would do that. Not after months together. If she could fool me for this long, there's no telling how she'll react to a confrontation.

Hell, if Dad's right, she might try to kill me. All it would take is for her to admit she's been honey-trapping me this whole time. I am pretty sure the shock would be enough to kill me.

How can this be happening? How can I doubt her like this? But after what he showed me in his office, how can I not?

It feels like I've been on a roller coaster for the entire day, and all I want is to get off and lay down so the world stops spinning. I lean on my car—something I never do so I can preserve the paint job—and gulp as much fresh air as possible. It's still cold, even though winter is gradually loosening it's hold on Boston. A slow process, as always. But the crisp air helps to clear my head, as much as it can be at a time like this.

The museum closed at four, thankfully, so no one is around. Just me in an adjacent parking lot, listening to a mild breeze wash through the barren trees. It's dark already, and I'm looking forward to summer when the days grow long. Assuming I'm not in prison and/or single, it'll be nice to spend the days with June. Maybe I can get her in a bikini at a beach somewhere. One of those retro numbers to hug her hips and tits just right. She has an inner bombshell she keeps under wraps, but I plan to unwrap her, layer by layer.

Again, assuming she's not a fucking spy.

And I don't go to prison.

When did my life get this fucking complicated? Oh right. My last night at this museum. That was one hell of a dull event until I found out about the auction, or rather, until I found out June was going to be in that auction. From that moment on, my life has been nothing but insane. Both good and bad in equal measure.

A car pulls up with a ride-share light on the dash. I forgot she doesn't drive much. Hell, she walks to work, so it's no wonder she had to get a ride share. My mind has been elsewhere all day. It's a miracle I know my damn name right now.

She gets out, and my heart pinches at the sight of her. The driver leaves us. June's black trench coat hugs her ample curves, making her even sexier because it makes me wonder if she's wearing anything underneath. Of course, she is—it's fucking cold out. I can see her black tights, too. But in my mind, she's naked under that thing. For that matter, in my mind, she's almost always naked. Son of a bitch, I am hooked on this woman. But the question remains. Am I looking at the love of my life, or am I looking at the woman sent from hell to ruin me? Only time will tell.

Her boots make the hottest clicking sound as she strolls to me with a worried expression on her perfect face, hands tucked in her pockets. Her bag dangles on her shoulder — she came from the office. She smiles up at me, and I crush my mouth on hers. Before I know anything for certain, I need one more kiss to build a dream on.

When we pull apart, she looks confused or stunned. "Baby, what's wrong?"

If she's a spy, I have to play this close to the vest. Be smart. Be tricky. Trip her up. Lie if I have to. Anything to get the truth out of her. Whatever it takes. My family, my freedom, everything is at stake. I have to be as ruthless as she is. What can I say to interrogate her while keeping in mind this could all be some terrible mistake? She could be innocent. It's June. Of course, she's innocent. How could she not be?

No. I have to play this right. No benefit of the doubt. Not now. Say something brilliant that will get a confession. Do it now before you lose the nerve.

"Are you a spy?" Well, that wasn't particularly stealthy of me.

At first, she just blinks at me. Then she lets out a gasp of a laugh. "What?"

"It's a simple question, June."

"Um, I don't think it is. What the hell are you talking about? Why are we here, of all places? What is going on? Baby, forgive me, but you look like shit right now, and you're scaring me."

I huff a laugh. I've been scared all day. Only seems fair —

"And what are you talking about spies for? How can you even ask me something like that? Are you high?" She sounds like herself. It's either the complete truth, or she's the best actress I've ever seen.

In law school, they teach you about how people act when they're guilty. Some people fall into the trap of buying into the whole body language thing, but I never did. Body language is often culturally based, so what's a tell in one country is perfectly innocent in another. But one thing most liars do is obfuscate and turn the questions around onto the asker.

Like she is now.

I have to harden my heart to her to say what I need to say. No mercy. "June, are you using me to help destroy my father?"

Her eyes dip down for the briefest moment. A flash of shame.

My heart sinks. This can't be ... oh my fuck. No. I can't breathe. I can't think. Everything, all these months together ... it's been a goddamned lie. I grit my teeth to stop it from raging out before she can answer. As sick as I've felt all day, it's nothing compared to now. My heart is shredding on her every breath.

June worries her bottom lip. "It's not like that—"

"What is it like?" I snarl.

She looks frightened, and I hate that. I don't ever want her to be frightened of me, but fuck. Fuck, fuck, fuck. She takes a breath, and it's labored, like she can't breathe right, either. "I didn't know—"

"Didn't know what?" I shout.

"I wanted to tell you everything," she blurts, "but with the cops sniffing around, it was never the right time—"

I take her upper arms in my hands to steal her attention. "Start fucking talking before I lose my fucking mind!"

Tears trickle down her cheeks, sparkling in the parking lot lights. The sight would have broken my heart if it weren't shattered already. She sobs, "Andre ... he's trying to take over everything your father has ever touched."

There it is. A confession. Sort of.

"What did you do?"

She gulps. "I helped. I didn't mean to. I thought he wanted to buy some companies. That's not out of the ordinary. But until right before we left for Vermont, I didn't know they were companies your dad is involved in. It looked like legitimate-ish purchases—"

"Then why are you gathering dirt on the board members?"

Her eyes widen. "How did you know—"

"My father has spies everywhere, June. You know that!"

She takes several breaths, close to hyperventilating. "I was gathering dirt to make it easier for Andre to buy the companies. I swear, I thought the whole thing was just business! I didn't know it was about your dad! I had no idea! Please, baby, you have to believe me!"

I have to ask it. I don't want to. But I have to. "Did you trick me into killing Neil?"

Her jaw goes slack in shock. Only half a word comes out. "Wha?"

"Did you? Was he some other mark you had to get rid of—"

She shoves me off of her. Her voice sizzles in rage. "How fucking dare you?"

"Just tell me!"

For a moment, we glare at each other. But then her face softens into a look of abject pity, even though she is the one in tears. "What did your father do to you? How could you ever even … I know this is him. All of this. I didn't go into the project for Andre for the purpose of destroying your father, but right now, I wish I had. He has you so fucking twisted up that I don't know who you are."

One last terrible question. "Has this been the plan all along? From the night of the auction? Use me to get to Elliot?"

She laughs so angrily that I know I'll hear that sound in hell. "Are you actually asking me that?"

"Answer the question, June. I need to hear you say it."

"I shouldn't dignify that question with an answer. This conversation should have never had to happen. You should have more fucking faith in me than this, you asshole!"

I whisper the only word I have left in my heart. "Please."

"No! Are you happy now? No, I didn't go into the auction to get to Elliot! No, I didn't trick you into killing Neil! No, I didn't do anything you've accused me of on purpose! Andre is using me to get the information he wants, and I think he's doing it to rub salt in the wound once he buys those companies because it's the only thing that makes any sense—why else would he hire me, right? It can't be because I'm a fucking excellent lawyer," she throws her hands up in a violent shrug, "No, of course, it has to be to piss off Elliot just that little bit more by using someone close to his family, because Andre is almost as big of an asshole as you are, and—"

I grab her face and kiss her. It's messy and unwelcome, and I don't fucking care. She's so indignant about this that I know it wasn't her. She's not a spy. She's the woman I love, and I have said possibly the worst things I could ever say to her, and all I want to do is make up for that, but she pushes me off of her.

"The fuck was that? Do you have any idea how furious I am with you right now?"

"I will spend the rest of my life making this up to you, June. I'll swear it in blood if you like. Today has been one of the worst days of my life, and I am at my breaking point. I am so fucking sorry for what I said. But I had to hear it from you. Dad's evidence—"

"What evidence?"

"Footage of you in different places with materials he thought you shouldn't have. And then he spun a tale that sounded like a textbook honey trap, and with the footage ... it all lined up in the worst possible way. I have hated myself since the moment I started to believe him, and I will keep hating myself for a lot longer for actually saying those things to you. Baby, I am so fucking sorry."

Tears are chased by others down her face. Her nose goes pink. Her voice crackles. "We're supposed to be a team—"

I wrap her up in my arms, and to my surprise, she lets me. In fact, she clutches onto me tightly, like she needs this closeness as much as I do. We stand there in the cold night, just holding each other for the longest time.

I am the world's worst fiancé, and if she wants to call it off, I can't blame her. This is all my doing. Every bit.

But when we finally look at each other, I know this isn't over. She chirps out, "I am hanging by a thread right now. More hugs." Then she holds her arms up for another hug, and I am ecstatic she wants another. Only then do I feel the warmth of her body. I think I've been numb for hours.

I murmur, "Do you hate me?"

She counters, "Do you hate me?"

The thought feels foreign. "Absolutely not."

"But I snotted on your expensive coat."

I laugh and bring her face to mine. "You can snot on whatever you want."

She giggles. "How is it that feels like romance after this conversation?"

I laugh again and kiss her. It's like the iceberg in my heart is finally starting to melt.

31

JUNE

"So why meet here?" I ask between nose blows. Thankfully, he keeps quality tissues in his fancy car. I'm still reeling from what he said. Those questions. How fucking dare he. But I also know the hold that Elliot has on him. It's hard not to stay angry right now, and for the moment, I am. But he's also the man that I love. So, for the moment, I don't know what to do other than ask inane questions.

"In case you were a spy, I wanted to come back to the scene of the crime. The first crime, I mean. Me buying a night with you. It's a strange thing that this building holds a special place in my heart. It brought you back to me."

I laugh at the craziness of that. "Guess that's true."

Anderson looks like he's aged five years today. He's paler than he should be. And my poor baby has bags under his eyes. I don't know how I can think of him as *my poor baby* when he's pissed me off so much tonight. Maybe that's the trick about love. It fools you into thinking things that you shouldn't. I don't know where we stand right now.

How could he have thought those things about me?

But I know how. It's his father, Elliot. That man has put Anderson in harm's way countless times. He's betrayed his trust. He's lied. He's nearly gotten killed. And yet, Anderson keeps going back for more. It's a textbook abusive relationship with a bit of mob flavoring. And he doesn't know how to get out of it. And at this point, I don't know how to get him out of it.

I don't know how much of a future we can have together with Elliot in our lives. But I'm not willing to give up Anderson just because of him. I won't let that bastard win.

"I'm not … we're not okay right now. But I'm also not going anywhere just yet. Okay?"

He nods. "You're sure you don't hate me?"

"I'm not sure of a lot of things, but I am sure of that. I don't hate you, Anderson. I'm angry. And hurt. But more than anything, I feel bad for you. Your father is a monster. If I hate anyone, it's him. I know that he did this to you."

But he shakes his head. "I made my own choice about coming here and saying those things to you."

It's almost like he's trying to get me to hate him. Like he thinks that's what he deserves. "Yes, you're an adult who made his own choices. You fucked up. But that doesn't change the fact that your father is the one who laid the groundwork for this. And I don't mean just today. I mean your entire life."

Anderson looks at me with awe in his eyes. "I don't deserve your pity, June. Whatever kindness you think that you should bestow on me, I don't deserve it."

"If we got what we deserved, we'd be fucked."

He laughs, and it warms my heart. "I imagine you're right about that."

"So what now?"

"I'm not sure. Dad has really put his foot down about this. He firmly believes you're a traitor. And to prove my loyalty to him, myself, and the family, he wants me to ghost you."

The thought sends my jaw clenching. "And what do you want to do?"

"I want to prove him wrong and make him eat crow. The problem is, I don't know how to do that. He thinks he has solid, incontrovertible evidence against you. And it is hard to convince Elliott West of anything that he doesn't want to believe."

I shrug. "That makes this easy then."

"What's that?"

"All we have to do is break into the office and steal evidence that I didn't know what was going on."

He laughs for a moment. But then he sees my serious face. "Please tell me you're joking."

"I am not in a joking mood."

"June, we have somehow managed to get over on the law a lot. We have broken ... at this point, I've lost track of how many laws. Breaking into your office is not going to be easy, and there's going to be a lot of evidence that we broke in. Key logs, witnesses and that's to say nothing of video footage. I'm not sure how you plan to get around that. But I don't really want to go to jail over something that mundane, do you?"

"Obviously not. But after working for Andre for a few months, there are certain things that I know. For one, he doesn't have cameras on his floors in the building. He prefers to be able to come and go as he wants and not let anybody know. So that's not really much of an issue. Key logs could be a problem. But I can also lie and say that I forgot something that I needed to grab. So shouldn't be that much of an issue. Witnesses? At this time of night, we're probably talking about cleaning staff and only the most dedicated lawyers and paralegals who might still be in the building—"

"Wait, you're talking about going there now?"

I nod. "What better time to clear my name with your father than now?"

His eyes go wide, and his mouth opens and closes a few times, like a fish. "You're serious?"

"I don't want your father to have any excuses to hate me any more than he already does. He's back to giving you ultimatums about us, and I don't plan to let that stand, do you?"

Anderson takes a breath while staring at the ground. "No. But there has to be another way."

"What other way? Either we find evidence and rub his nose in it. Or he makes life incredibly difficult for both of us. Those are the choices in front of us right now. Neither is good. But short of leaving the country, there is nothing else we can do." I rest my hands on his chest and look up at him. "And to be honest, as much as I love the idea of leaving the country and never coming back, I also relish the idea of making Elliott West eat his words. If I go to prison, I would love to have that memory for the rest of my life."

He smiles down at me. "That shouldn't be as hot as it sounds, but. It is."

I giggle and pull him down for a kiss. Strange to think of how things started with us. In school, he had been the bane of my existence. Now, I can't get enough of the feel of his mouth on me. Our fleeting kiss turns into a full makeout session. His hand snakes into my trench coat, cupping my breast to elicit a moan out of me. Regretfully, I push him back.

"As much as I like where you're headed with that, we

have things to do, and we are in a public place with, I'm sure, plenty of cameras."

He grins with the devil in his eyes. "Are you sure you're not punishing me a little bit too?"

"How so?"

"Getting me going like that and then telling me to stop."

I roll my eyes at him. "Come on, we have an office building to break into."

As I start to walk around the car, he has my hand still. And he hasn't taken a step. "What evidence?"

"What are you talking about?"

"You said you want to break into the office building and get evidence that you didn't know anything. But what evidence would that even be?"

I smile. "See, I'm more clever than you think. I've spent weeks on this project for Andre. Don't you think that if I had seen your father's name attached to any of the companies, it would have been a red flag for me?"

"So you truly had no idea."

"None. I imagine a lot of your father's involvement has shell corporations between him and the actual companies."

He huffs a laugh. "That's not possible. He's on their boards. Board members have to be listed publicly, right?"

It sucks, but he has a point. "Then the only reason that I haven't seen him on their board member listings is he's using a pseudonym."

"Is that even possible? I don't do tax law."

"Possible? Yes. Legal? No. But it is commonly done. It's a way for investors and whoever else to protect themselves. By keeping those pseudonyms in place, it prevents people from complaining about things like conflict of interest. Sort of one of those things that people do all the time but nobody talks about. If the IRS got wind of it, of course, he'd be screwed."

"And you gathered dirt on a pseudonym?"

God, but he's innocent. "The best way to have a solid pseudonym in a corporation is to make sure that they have an online presence. And that's not difficult to fake. I just wish I knew which of the board members was his pseudonym. Hell, since I didn't see too many commonalities between the boards, it's probably more than one."

Anderson's jaw grits tight. "Which means that he knew that you didn't know that he's on those boards."

Slowly, I nod. "Whether or not he believes I'm a traitor is one thing. But setting you up to believe that I am? That was on purpose."

"And the only way that we prove this is by breaking into Andre's office, isn't it?"

"Yep."

"Shit. You have access?"

"I do. He gave me his spare key card to his office a while ago, and he never asked for it back."

Anderson pauses. "Wait, so how did you figure out this was going on?"

"Over the hundreds of documents that I have procured for Andre for this project, there was one with your father's name on it. Some company where he's the majority shareholder, and he couldn't hide it. I knew from that point on that Andre was up to something terrible."

"Why did you assume the worst over one company?"

"For one, he's been making big moves about buying a bunch of companies all together at the same time. So they had to have something in common. And two, it's Andre, the bastard who kidnapped me to upset your father. It wasn't that hard to put together. The man is a sociopath."

"Yeah, on that. Why in the hell did you agree to go work for him?"

It's a valid question. "I thought he was in my corner. And I thought that maybe having a sociopath in my corner wasn't the worst thing. Not to mention the fact that your father got me blackballed from every other company in town. It was either switch to a new industry, or move. Or take the job with Andre. I knew that taking a job with Andre would piss your father off, and that was honestly a big bonus."

He smirks at that. "Fair enough. Let's go steal some documents."

32

JUNE

As we pull into the parking garage, I go over the plan again. "Right? So if somebody finds us in his office, what do we say?"

"That you forgot some documents, and you're here to make sure that you don't screw up a big presentation."

"And if they find us making copies of those documents?"

"Same thing. You say that it's not unusual for lawyers and paralegals to be there late, right?"

I nod. "But it is pretty late now, and it's gonna be kind of weird to explain that. Do you think that this is a bad idea?"

"Considering when we were in the hotel that one paralegal texted you in the middle of the night and he was still at the office, I think it'll be fine. I imagine everybody here knows that Andre doesn't accept any excuses for screw-ups. This is just a natural consequence of that."

I blow out a breath of relief. "All right. We can do this." Just as I unbuckle my belt, he grabs my hand. "What?"

"Are we sure we can do this? Is this the best way to go about things?"

Is he asking that *now*? "If you can think of a better plan, tell me before we go in there."

Anderson stares ahead. Silence falls in the car as he thinks. If this man can pull a better plan out of his ass before we get out of the car, great. I don't exactly see another way out of this. Doing anything against Andre could be a death sentence. But he shakes his head. "I've got nothing."

"Okay, then let's do this."

We get out of the car and go into the building. Pretending everything is normal used to be second nature to me. But right now, it feels like hell.

If we take this evidence to Elliot, then he will know what Andre is up to, and he can act to stop it. If he stops Andre from making these purchases, then my boss will know that he has a mole. Given my closeness with the family, I'm the most likely suspect.

So, right now, I may be setting myself up. I don't want to be in Andre's crosshairs. But I don't have much of a choice. I have to earn Anderson's trust back. He says he believes me. But proof is much more convincing.

And I don't want to leave any room for a shadow of a doubt.

We get on the elevator and go up to Andre's floor. Using the key card that he gave me, I have access to everywhere. All Executive rooms. His office. Anywhere. Now, I just have to hope that that's where he's storing the documents.

It's after eight so most of the lights are off, and we use our phones for light. Anderson quietly notes, "Snazzy office."

"Andre likes nice things."

"No wonder he hired you."

"Flatterer."

He caresses my ass as we go down the hall. "Nothing like a little danger to get the blood flowing."

"Are you serious? You're turned on right now?"

"June, we may be facing some serious consequences soon, so anytime I'm around you, I'm turned on. No point in wasting opportunities."

I hiss at him, "This is not an opportunity. We are here for good reason."

"And?"

"And stop touching my butt," I whisper.

He snickers, but his hand drops away.

We have been extraordinarily lucky so far. No maintenance crews, no cleaning crew. I'm not sure if they come later or what because the office is always immaculate. When we reach Andre's door, I have to steady myself. This is it. No going back now. If we're caught, we have to use our cover story and hope that it is convincing.

I really don't want to have to use the cover story.

First, I knock. No answer. I slash the key card, and the door opens. We dash inside and quietly close the door. Anderson reaches for the light, but I stop him. "No. Keep using your phone."

"Why?"

"In case he has eyes on the office externally, I don't want to have to worry about it."

"June, it's weird enough that we've been using our phones this whole time, but if we keep using our phones, it's going to look like we have something to hide. You're a lawyer who came back for documents. That's all this is, remember?" He has a point.

"Okay, yeah, you're right. Let's turn on the lights. Make this look legitimate." So I click them on. Everything is as I saw it before, with the exception that there is no convenient pile of documents on his desk. "Well, I can't say I'm very surprised that he put them away someplace, but I am disappointed because that makes this more complicated."

"You know, it's sort of amazing that in this digital day and age, he would have anything in writing. The practice of law is still remarkably old-fashioned."

I narrow my gaze at him on my way to Andre's desk. "That's brilliant. Help me look in these files." But when I pull the drawer, it's locked. "Well, shit."

"Got a Bobby pin?"

"You can pick locks?"

He shrugs. "Well, no, but that's what they always do on TV."

I skim my hands around Andre's desk. "If I were a key, where would I be?"

"Do you really think that he'd be keeping such important files in his office?"

"Where else?"

"His house. That's where my dad keeps his."

But I shake my head, still skimming my hands around. "No, Andre likes to keep things compartmentalized. This is business stuff, so I think that business stays here." Then I feel a latch. I give it a pull, and all the drawers open. "Are you fucking kidding me? That's not secure."

"Maybe he loses his keys a lot and needs a backup system. Who cares? Start looking."

"Not yet." I point my phone at Andre's organizational setup and start clicking.

"What are you doing?"

"I want to be able to pack everything back in the way that he had it."

"Oh. Good idea."

After I get enough pictures, we dig through the files and find them right off the bat. "This is it right here. All the shit that I gathered for him. He wanted everything in original hard copy and no other copies made."

"Makes sense. If it's not digital, it's harder to find. Where's the copy room on this floor?"

"I'm not taking that chance. I downloaded a document scanner on the way here." And with that, I whip out my phone and scan all the documents, front and back. I'm not taking any chances that Elliot could whine about the documents not being real. Afterward, I photograph them on Andre's desk. I will give him no excuse to say that we lied about this.

I tell Anderson, "All right, that's everything. Let's pack this up and go." We tuck away everything just as we found it according to the pictures I took before. In some ways, this has felt almost too easy. Our luck has never held out for this long. Before I open the door, I click off the light. "How soon do you think Andre will know? That it was me, I mean."

"He may never know." But by his tone, I can tell he doesn't believe that either. For now, I'll let the pleasant fiction slide. We might be lying to ourselves, but I'll take it.

Just as I turn the door lever, we hear a sound in the hall. Squeaky wheels.

I whisper, "Cleaning crew."

"Do they come in here?"

I don't bother to answer. The squeaking is too close. I grab his hand and race to the nearest door. There are three off of Andre's office. One is to his private bathroom, but I don't know what the other two are. Fearing the crew may be here to also clean the bathroom, I pick one of the other doors. It happens to be a utility closet.

Anderson closes the door behind us, and silently, we listen. The office light clicks on, shining around the doorframe. But it's not enough light for us to see much inside the closet. After a minute, I realize whoever it is isn't snooping around. We hear the wheels squeak, and then they go silent for a minute, like the person is cleaning. They're not looking for us. They're just doing their job.

I whisper, "We'll wait a few minutes and then go out there."

"I guess we kind of blew the whole 'hey, we're just innocently here for forgotten documents' thing when we decided to hide."

I snort a laugh. It was a stupid move on my part, but

instinct took over. It couldn't be helped. Still, I can laugh at myself for it. "You think?"

"We are not cut out for a life of crime."

I shake my head, smiling. The utility closet is bigger than I had expected. Maybe ten by ten. There're all sorts of equipment in here, and I can't see them because I refuse to turn on the light. But when I flash my phone over them, it's mostly wooden boxes and miscellaneous storage. Odd that Andre would have this kind of storage attached to his office. He's so meticulous … "

Maybe there's more in here than meets the eye. But no matter how curious I am, I'm not here to explore. Besides, exploring makes noise that we cannot afford, so I leave the crates alone and concentrate on listening for the cleaning crew to leave. I leave my phone on a shelf so we can kind of see, and it doesn't shine around the doorframe for them to spot us.

Anderson murmurs in my ear, "Well, if we're going to get caught, then maybe we should get caught for a different reason."

"What are you talking about—"

He presses me against the cabinet and kisses me, stealing my breath away. A shiver rushes through me, forcing out a gasp. Parting my lips, I let him in. I know this is stupid. We're as likely to get caught making too much noise as we are for being in the wrong place, but after everything we've been through, I need this. I need him.

Alarm bells go off in my mind as I reach for him over his pants. He lets out a hiss of need, grinding into my hand while we kiss harder. He's already a rock for me. I can't tell if it's a fear boner or if he's feeling as needy as I am. The heat in my body is impossible to ignore.

Anderson unties my trench coat belt and unbuttons my blouse, leaving me exposed. He growls in my ear, "This is one of my favorite bras."

"The lace?"

"The front clip." He unhooks it, and my breasts spring free. His mouth is on my nipples, nibbling and teasing me. I can't believe we're doing this here and now, and part of me is into it. The fear. The rush. We've faced countless dangers together. This one is entirely different. This is a danger we're choosing.

That cleaning crew could walk in here at any moment. Better make them count.

33

JUNE

Anderson kisses down my stomach, slowly lowering to a kneel. I shudder when I feel his hand ride up my inner thigh. His heat scorches my skin through my tights. This is too far and not far enough at the same time. He's such a fucking tease. I run my fingers through his hair, and he raises my skirt.

Wait — is he not teasing me? This isn't right. I whisper, "What are you thinking?"

An unfair question. Hell, I'm pretty sure I've completely stopped thinking.

But he doesn't answer. Instead, he rips apart my tights at the crotch, all the way to the waistband. I gasp, but before I can even speak, his fingers trace my anatomy over my underwear. Sensation trembles through me. Only then does he look up. "Palm over your mouth. Now."

I follow his order, and feeling compelled only makes it hotter. Wrong. Against my grain. But hotter.

Anderson lifts my leg over his shoulder, scoots my soaking underwear out of the way, and tastes me. The moment his tongue brushes against my clit, it's all I can do not to cry out. As he licks me, I'm sure we're going to get caught. We're going to get caught, and we'll end up in pervert jail, I just know it. This is how it ends. With a bang *and* a whimper.

I curse under my breath before I hiss at him, "Baby, we can't do this. They'll hear me! Have you lost your mind?"

With a wet, sucking sound, he pulls his mouth off of me. The loss of sensation is so abrupt it's almost painful. My body wants more, but my mind is demanding we stop. I didn't know he could growl and whisper at the same time, but he manages. "We will get caught only if you keep talking. Be a good girl and stay quiet. You're interrupting my meal. That's rude." Then he latches on again.

I obey, but it's a struggle. It's not in my nature to go along with things. I'm a fighter. I like to argue. This is all his fault. If he wasn't so good at this, I might be able to stay quiet. Can't, though.

But it doesn't matter. I can't stop, either. This feeling, this rush, it's addictive. My desire for Anderson is overriding my will to stay safe, and I'm not even sure how much I care. I keep pushing my hips at him, silently begging for more even when I know better.

Maybe that's why I can't stay quiet—the danger of this is getting me off.

I don't recognize this side of myself. I've never been a thrill seeker. The most excitement I usually like is eating chocolate pudding with barbecue potato chips. Odd snacks can't hold a candle to what is happening inside of me now.

His tongue circles my clit, while I wriggle and press against him for more pressure. Electric tingles dance through my body. The heat swells inside my belly, threatening to drown me in its tide. This is so naughty it borders on a felony, and I don't care because I'm about to come harder than I ever—

The squeaking gets close.

We freeze in place. I'm teetering on the edge, and I want to cry. If that cleaner ruins this orgasm, I will mourn the loss of it for the rest of my life.

But then the cart rolls away, and his finger enters me. I bite my fist to stop from shouting. I'm so tense that I'm tighter than usual, and the intrusion makes me shake against the shelving unit behind me. One shelf digs into the middle of my back, while another supports my ass, and another stops my head from tipping backward. Anderson's mouth stays on my clit as his fingertip brushes against my G-spot, and I whimper for more. My body goes molten as he works me over, and it's impossible to stop now. I'm at the precipice of something glorious and devastating, and there is no going back. When it hits, I bear down on my fist to stop from screaming in sheer ecstasy. I don't even feel myself biting as waves of heat and bliss course through me. A hazy mind eraser of an orgasm.

I'm still twitching and gasping as I tap his head to tell him I'm done.

But apparently, he is not. He doesn't stop, not even as I try to pull back. Anderson is too hungry for me to stop. I can't believe he isn't done yet—I've come. What else could he possibly want from this?

But he goes after me with some new sense of purpose, even more vigorously than before. I'm too sensitive to stay quiet for long, and a moan escapes me. Not even that stops him. Guess he's stopped worrying about getting caught. But I am. We have to stop. I dig my nails into his scalp, but that only spurs him on. This isn't the sweet favor a nice guy does for a woman. This is primal, rough, and utter perfection. A sexual mauling.

It's like he can't get enough of my pussy.

His free arm hooks around my ass to pull me against him even tighter, and I'm pulled off balance, but that doesn't matter. He has me trapped against him. I'm not going anywhere. I am helpless to do anything but stand here and take it. He's forcing me to ride his face.

I brace on the other shelves as he brings me close again. Now, without my hand covering my mouth, I'm worried I'll draw the cleaning crew's attention. I turn my head sharply, biting my trench coat shoulder. But then I hiss down at him, "Baby, you're done! It's too much!"

But he still doesn't stop. A throaty, proud chuckle echoes in his core. He knows exactly what he's doing to me. I'm so mad and so turned on that I can't try to stop him. I want this, too.

I open my mouth wide to quiet down my gasps—if I keep my lips tight, they're only going to get louder. Sounds like I'm doing Lamaze in here. Maybe we should stop—

But then Anderson spreads me wider and adds a second finger. I shudder out the words in a breath, "Oh my fuck!" It's so much. Almost too much. I'm going to come on him again. This is gonna get loud, and there's no stopping me now.

That second finger slides out, thank god. He must have sensed that it was too far. The man reads my body better than anyone ever has, and I'm grateful for it. But then that wet second finger searches around. No, he wouldn't. Not here. Not now. But then it enters my ass. Every nerve fires through me, and I can't breathe.

I peep into my shoulder, biting the rough material in hopes it kills the sound. With a finger in my pussy and one in my ass, and his mouth on my clit, I'm ready to explode again. But then he slows down, drawing out my pleasure and making it delicious agony. His rapid rhythm slows to a painful crawl, and I'm about to beg him for more when I hear the squeaking nearby again.

All it will take is for them to open the door, and this goes from bad to deadly. So why am I about to come?

But I can't even bring myself to worry about that right now. After a taste of sex on the edge, how are we supposed to go back to normal life? Vanilla sex is ruined now. The sharp pulse of danger makes me worry I'll need this to get off every time. Normal sex will never be enough again. It can't compete. How could it? Once you've flown first class, coach is never good enough.

Right now, I feel like I'm standing on the airplane's wing. Or that I'm freefalling. Except here, I can't scream.

The moment the squeaking slips away, Anderson speeds up again, forcing me to come on his fingers, his lips, his tongue. This pleasure, this high, is more than one body is meant for. It's so much that I'm almost numb from it. Nothing else matters but this ride. Fast, ragged breaths steam over the shoulder of my trench coat as I go boneless against him. Holding me up doesn't deter him. He keeps at me, working me into another right after my second climax. His fingers reach some deeper spot in me, and I can't keep bracing myself up anymore. I need my hands to cover my mouth because he's making me scream. There's no holding back anymore. I shatter on him, feeling every cell come apart in burning pleasure.

Only then does he slow down for real this time. Gradually, his grip on my bits loosens. He kisses his way up my body, and I taste myself on his tongue. I need it. The taste of myself makes me want more. I suck his tongue into my mouth, and he groans. It's a heady sound that makes me want to earn more of them.

As he leans against me, his erection presses against my belly. He pulses against my belly, and a precum wets my stomach as we kiss. I wish I could do something about it. Maybe just a taste of him … but my lizard brain triggers my alert system. We have to get the hell out of here, and I know it.

I give a little push and whisper, "Can you hear them?"

He huffs. "Who?"

"The cleaners."

He runs his fingers through his hair and steals another glance at my tits, then huffs again before going to the door to listen. As he strains to hear, I straighten out my clothes and hair, clip my bra, and button back up. Nothing to be done about the tights, so I shrug them down into my boots as best I can. When he turns around, he says, "I can't hear anything. What are you doing?"

I should think that is obvious. "Getting ready for our great escape."

He smirks. "We're not going anywhere."

34

ANDERSON

"Please tell me you're kidding," she whispers.

But I'm not. "Honestly, what is Andre going to do if we are discovered in his utility closet being naughty? He gave you the key card to his office. If he didn't think you'd use it, he's a fool."

"Anderson, please! We have to go when we can. If we're caught—"

"Then we'll be punished," I tell her as I step close enough to breathe her in. "We've come this far. What's a little further?"

Her eyes scan over my face like she's still waiting for me to crack a smile and tell her this is all a joke.

Instead, I brush my lips over hers and kiss my way up her jawline to her earlobe. I exhale hot breath on her there, earning a shiver. "You're a bad girl for getting dressed. I will have to punish you."

"We can't do this. As much as I would love to, it's wrong. This is my boss' office."

I lick up her neck. She lets out a moan like a good girl. "That's why you want to do it. Because it's wrong. The thought of getting away with something like this turns you on, right?"

She breathes the faintest version of the word, "Yes."

"Besides, it's not like you're the only one with needs. Getting you off has made me rock hard."

"Still, I don't think it's a good idea."

"The best ideas are the worst ones. Get on your knees for me."

Her breaths come harder now as she kneels before me. When she looks up, there is so much lust in her eyes it's hard not to come in my pants like a horny twenty-year-old at his first Spring Break sighting of a girl flashing her tits. As she reaches for my zipper, I tell her, "No. Not yet. Show me your tits."

June sits back and slowly unbuttons her blouse. When she unclips her bra, her breasts burst forward.

I will never get tired of that. "Now you can unzip me."

She unbuttons my fly, jerks the zipper down all the way, and reaches into my trousers for my cock. I've been straining against my trousers for what felt like hours. Now I'm free, and much more relaxed. Probably shouldn't be, though, considering we could be found at any moment, but truthfully, the thought turns me on.

Andre has been a thorn in my family's side for a long time. That piece of shit kidnapped June, and now he's trying to take over my family's businesses. Getting caught fucking in his utility closet would be hilarious. Seems only right.

The moment her lips breathe over the head of my cock, it is everything I can do not to yank her to her feet and fuck her. She's had me on edge since I felt her come around my fingers. Not to mention the danger of it all. What I wouldn't give to see Andre's face once he finds out about us here.

She's being such a little tease. "Are you going to just lick me like a lollipop? I thought you were worried about getting caught."

She smirks up at me and then sucks me down into her throat. A stiff breath goes in as I grab the shelves to brace on. Fuck, she is too good at that. I can't believe I'm getting to marry this woman. She sucks cock like she was born to do it. It's second only to how she gets when she rides me. The woman is a hellcat.

My sac tightens. But I push it back. Not now, body. I have plans.

I reach down for her tits, flicking my fingers on her nipples. Each time she shudders and moans around my cock, and that sensation travels up my shaft, lighting me up like a fucking Christmas tree. I'm holding on, but I can't fight this forever. She's too good.

June's tongue wraps around the head of my cock, and she shuttles back and forth down my length. I've never felt anything like it. Part of me thinks it would be kinder to have an open relationship. Someone this talented should be shared.

But I will end any man who touches her. She is mine.

When she reaches up for my balls, a new burst of pleasure courses through me, bringing me right to the edge. But this is not how I'm going to come. I have bigger plans in mind for that.

I flick her nipples a little harder than I had been. It's the fastest way to get her attention when she's this into her work. She whimpers and looks up. "On your feet."

"But you haven't—"

"No shit. On your feet."

She stands, but her gait is wobbly when I walk her to the steamer trunk in the back of the utility closet. It's next to some dusty crates and the only thing that looks personal here. I imagine Andre keeps his soul inside the steamer trunk in some Dorian Gray gambit to live forever. He's twisted enough to try anything, I imagine.

With June standing in front of me, I lift her hair and kiss the back of her neck before I bite her there. Hard. She squeaks and melts against me as I bend her over the steamer trunk. Slowly, I lift her skirt out of my way and lower her panties. God, this ass will be the death of me. I want to give her a proper spanking, but alas, that would make too much noise.

Maybe when we get home. Where we have lube to do things right …

No. Stay focused.

I rub my hand over her soaked pussy from behind, and she backs against my palm. "Needy girl. Trying for your pleasure again before I've had mine." I swat her there. It's a love tap, nothing more, but she inhales like I surprised her.

Good.

I stroke her labia with my cockhead, taking my time with it and savoring every honeyed fold. Fucking June is utter bliss, but the part right before is something to be enjoyed. She makes the saddest little sound when I don't thrust home. "Are you going to be a good girl, love, and take my cock?"

"Please," she gasps.

I shove forward in one go. Fucking perfect fit. She must be biting her hand because her groan is muffled. Mine is not. I try to keep it contained, but this is forbidden fruit and I can't help myself. When I start in on her, I'm merciless. Our bodies smack together loud enough that I'm surprised security hasn't run in yet, thinking to stop a fistfight.

After her tongue has driven me to the edge, I worry this will be fast, and I'm not a man to leave a lady in a lurch, so I reach around her hip for her clit. She shakes her head and murmurs, "I'll scream."

I don't stop. "So?"

"They'll hear!"

"I don't fucking care," I hiss, still pounding her, still playing with her. I need her to come like I need air.

"Ander … oh god," she whispers.

Then I feel it. Her pussy pulses on me. She bucks against me while she comes with both hands over her mouth as she tries to swallow her scream. That's all it takes. I growl and erupt, pulling out to come on the steamer trunk.

You're welcome, Andre.

Slowly, June turns around, panting. "I can't believe you did that."

"Which part?"

"All of it. The cleaners—"

"Look at the door, June."

She leans over. "What about it?"

"No more light means the cleaners left."

"Wait—you knew they weren't in there, and you made me think we would get caught … ?"

I smirk down at her as she rights her clothing. "I did. And you came so fucking hard I thought you might rip my dick off with your pussy."

It's still dark inside, but I'm sure she's blushing. "Well, what do you plan to do about your mess on the trunk?"

"Not a damn thing."

"Anderson —"

"Let's get out of here."

She blows out a breath, glancing at what I'd done. "Yeah. You know what? Fuck Andre." She leans up for a kiss. "But if you ever again make me think we're going to get caught fucking, and you know better, I'm cutting you off."

I laugh. "It's a deal." I'm a lawyer. Every deal is negotiable.

35

JUNE

When we finally make it home, all the tension drains as he closes the door. I press my face to his shirt, breathing him in before I kiss him. "That was—"

"Terrible of me?" he asks, smirking.

"Something like that."

He wraps his arms around me. "Don't pretend you didn't love it."

Just then, my stomach growls at us, and my head falls against his chest to hide my face from the embarrassment. "Um, I think I need to eat."

"Chinese?"

"You want to cook?"

"Hell no. I want delivery."

"Oh, thank god." I nod vigorously. "I need dumplings with a side of dumplings."

"On it," he says, pulling out his phone to order. When he chooses from the healthy menu, I wonder if I should get something better for me than dumplings. Before I tell him to change mine to chicken and broccoli, he adds half a dozen egg rolls and chicken wings. I glance up at him with maybe a little judgment in my eyes, to which he responds, "I worked hard today. I earned it."

"No argument here."

We change into our jammies and settle on the couch while waiting for the delivery. To my surprise, he takes my feet onto his lap and rubs them. It should not feel as good as it does. His thumb coasts up my arch, and my eyes flutter back in my head as I moan.

Anderson teases, "Bet you were making that face in the utility closet."

"Yeah, maybe."

"So, about that—"

"More rubbing, less talking."

He snorts a laugh and digs in, causing me to groan. "Did you enjoy the anal play again, or were you too tense for it? You seemed … tighter. All over."

My face heats up. I'm still not sure about that stuff. "It was good. Just, given the circumstances, I wasn't exactly prepared for that. And next time, actual lube."

"So, you want a next time?"

"I'm not opposed to it."

The fire in his eyes sends a shock straight to my girlie bits. "Good."

I want him. Damn him for pulling that trickery in the closet, but I almost don't care. I want to jump him. "You know we can't do that kind of thing again, right?"

"I don't intend to break into Andre's closet again if that's what you're saying."

"No. I mean, well, we're definitely not doing that again, but also, the whole *fear of getting caught* thing isn't my kink."

"No?" he asks with a smirk. "Then what is?"

"You know what I like." Why am I not comfortable with saying it out loud? I've never been shy about what I want in bed, but with Anderson, it's like the stakes are raised. He's the man I'm spending the rest of my life with. I should be able to tell him anything, but if I tell him and he thinks I'm gross for it, then where does that leave us?

"Tell me, June. Tell me your filthy private thoughts. I'm all ears."

I'd been nervous in the closet—butterflies in my stomach, that kind of thing—but this is different. This means more. Still, I try to be brave. I take a deep breath and start, "Well, um, I like it when—"

Delivery knocks on the door.

"Hold that thought." He sets my feet aside and gets the delivery, and soon, Chinese food smells waft through the apartment. That smell tears through my fear to call to my stomach. I'm on my feet following him like he's the pied piper of Hamlin, and I'm helpless to his tune. We eat straight out of the containers. "Hey, if you wanted egg rolls, you could have said so."

Half an egg roll hanging out of my mouth, I shrug sheepishly and devour the thing. "Next time, you get some of mine."

He grins at me. "Agreed. So you were telling me something naughty ... "

"I was stalling, actually."

"Great, then now we're past the stalling. Go ahead."

With a smile, I snap, "You pushy asshole."

"I pushed into your —"

"Stop right there." I dust egg roll crumbs from my fingers. "Rule number one — I am not up to discussing things that graphically. We can do them, but talking about them will take me some time. Okay?"

He ponders this for a beat. "Agreed."

"Two — I will tell you what you want to know, but I must do it at my own pace. Pushing me on it sends me mentally spiraling, and neither of us wants that because I'll shut down the way I did the night at the diner."

His face darkens. "Then let's not do that. I will respect that boundary if you don't want to talk about things. But I need you to know how much it turns me on to talk dirty with you, not just at you. That's something I need from you, June. It makes me feel closer to you like we can talk about any filthy thing with each other. I want that kind of relationship with my wife."

"It's just that … I worry you'll think I'm messed up or something, and we're engaged, so if you think I'm disgusting—"

He drops his food and chucks my chin with a crooked finger to make me look into his eyes. "Nothing you could say would make me think of you that way. You are my soul mate, my confidant, my passion. You are everything to me. Never think you are less than that."

But I jerk my chin away. "Are you joking right now?"

"Fuck no. Why do you ask?"

"After what you said to me in the parking lot—"

He blows out a breath and looks away. "I was fucked up, and I fucked up, and I'm sorry for all of that. I wish you hadn't seen me like that. You should never have to see me at my worst."

That won't do. I take his hands in mine, but still, he stares off. "Look at me, Anderson."

Reluctantly, he does.

"A year ago, I might have agreed with you on that. But I'm coming to see that a real relationship means you see the other person at their worst, and you still love them. Yes, what you said to me in the parking lot was fucking awful, and if you start saying something like that on the regular, I don't know where that will leave us. But I refuse to hold your worst moments over your head because that was only a moment in time. It wasn't who you are."

"But that shit ... those thoughts ... I should have kept them to myself."

"How could you?" I shake my head at him. "And if you had, where would that have left us? You'd still think I was some spy for Andre or something, and your dad would still have his hooks in your mind. As much as I hated you for saying those things, I am glad you did because we were able to get them out in the open and deal with them. We are a team, and teammates fight. But they're still a team."

"So, when something shitty comes up, you want me to talk to you about it?"

"Always. Just maybe next time, remember we're on the same team."

Anderson closes his eyes, sighing. Then he pulls me in close for a bear hug. "I have no idea what I did to deserve you."

"Understand me — I'm still mad about that shit. But I also love you, and we're in this together, no matter what."

"Know what I'd like to do now?"

"Something dirty, I imagine."

He laughs and kisses the top of my head before breaking our hug. "I want to look through the documents we stole."

"Oh. Well, can't say I'm not a little disappointed."

"I promise to do dastardly things to you after."

"You've got yourself a deal." I send the documents to his printer so we have hard copies, and while we finish up our very late supper, we go over them. Seeing it all laid out, I feel like a fool. I should have seen this coming. "Dammit, I was so fucking naïve this whole time."

"You were doing your job, baby, you didn't know."

I gulp. "You're sure you believe that now?"

He sighs. "Yes. I know you didn't do this intentionally, and I will make sure my father knows that, too. Admittedly, a part of me has been wondering about this ..."

"What do you mean?"

"He knew he covered his tracks well enough to keep from anyone knowing he was involved in these companies. He knew his aliases were top-notch. But then he blames you for being a spy for Andre, which means either he thinks you are so good that you'd see through aliases that the federal government doesn't and therefore I should break up with you, or he thinks I'd be so angered by the accusation itself that I'd break

up with you. I think he's banking on how I used
to be."

"I don't understand."

As Anderson flicks through the documents, he says, "I
used to be a hothead. I was angry all the time. Bitter.
Things are different for me now, thank you for that,
and if he's still counting on me to be off-kilter, maybe
we can use his underestimation of me to our
advantage."

"I like that idea."

"And you must stop beating yourself up about not
seeing this coming. We've been a little distracted by the
haddock."

I snort a laugh. We're back in our place, and I'm trying
not to say things we shouldn't in case we are wire-
tapped, but I shake my head. "There has to be a better
metaphor."

"Well, I mean, when someone sleeps with the fishes—"

I press my finger to his lips. "We'll figure out another
term. In the meantime, we need to figure out a plan."

36

JUNE

L ooking up at the big building, I feel a little intimidated. "You're sure about this?"

"As sure as I can be about anything," Anderson says. He'd set up this meeting, saying Dana Horowitz was like an aunt to him as a child. Dana is one of the best. That's probably why she and Pym don't get along."

"But you said she and your mom had a falling out. Why was that?"

He laughs under his breath as he opens the lobby door for me. We stroll to the building directory before going to the elevators. "The summer when I was thirteen, Mom thought Dana had a thing for Dad, but she couldn't say anything outright without proof. By that point, they'd been friends for years, so saying something out of pocket would have been an embarrassment. She waited, invited her to the big Fourth of July thing they do yearly, and the trap was set."

"Huh?"

"Mom thinks Dad looks great in swim trunks," he cringes as he says, "and I don't wanna talk about it. Summer means they're off like rabbits and is, therefore, the season I need the most therapy."

I giggle at him. "Go on."

"Dana's there, and Dad shows off, pulling some big jump on the diving board. Mom is distracted, but Dana sees it. She also sees he's not coming back up from under the water. She dives in, pulling him out. Turns out he'd cracked his head on the pool bottom. Dana does rescue breathing, which Mom sees at a distance, and she storms out there, assuming they're making out. She screams at Dana—not listening to anyone who is trying to tell her what's happening—but then the ambulances arrive and cart Dad off. He recovered just fine, but their friendship never did."

"Oh, god. Your mom had to be humiliated. And poor Dana."

He sighs as we enter the elevator. "Yeah. She's a great lady. I still get birthday cards from her, but I haven't seen her in a few years."

"And she's a defense attorney who Pym doesn't like?"

"I don't know all the details, but I doubt he likes anyone who is in the same line of work as he is, especially not one with her reputation. She threatens to outshine him. And anyone Pym doesn't like is good by me because he is on my shit list right now."

"Because he wants to use me as a scapegoat?"

Anderson squeezes my hand. "No one is using you for a scapegoat, June. I won't allow it."

That is as reassuring as I can ask for. The doors open into another lobby for her law office. It's posh, with gold and silver accents and streamlined pale wood décor. Pretty, but not overpowering. The attendant seats us in the waiting area, and I can't help but tap my foot impatiently.

Anderson plants his hand on my knee. "It's going to be okay."

"We only got this short-notice appointment because you know her. If she can't fix this, then who will? How many other high-powered defense attorneys do you keep in your back pocket?"

"More than most. Remember who my family is."

"Okay, yeah, but that's good and bad, and I'm just freaking out—"

"Breathe," he says calmly as he takes my hands. "And please stop destroying yourself."

"What?"

"You were picking at your cuticles again."

I look down, and there's a bit of blood at the corner of my thumbnail. "What the hell?"

He tips his head to the side. "You didn't know you do that?"

"No, I just thought … I thought I had crummy cuticles."

He smiles. "Your whole life you never noticed you pick at your cuticles when you're nervous? And no one else pointed it out?"

I shrug. "No one pays attention to me like you do."

"That doesn't seem possible, but I'm glad for it. I like keeping you all to myself."

Aw. The big lug. Just as I start to speak, a handsome assistant fetches us. "Ms. Horowitz is ready for you now." He leads us to her office, and I am as nervous as possible. What if Anderson has overestimated her? What if she's secretly on the take and working for his father? What if she won't take our case?

What if I'm so full of anxiety that I actually explode and ruin her pretty office?

As the tall wooden door opens, I gulp. Inside, the place is even nicer than the lobby area but carries the same color palette. But I can't take any of it in because the woman behind the desk is something else, and when she stands, I am in awe. I don't usually get taken in by someone's attractiveness. Having tended bar, I became used to seeing all kinds of people. Pretty, ugly, in between, none of it fazes me. But Dana Horowitz breaks my brain.

She has long, dark, wavy hair with a stylishly gray streak at her forehead and sparkling green eyes. Her red dress is business chic-meets-the runway, all polished modern lines that hug her ample curves. Her rich olive skin is perfect. Not a blemish or a line out of place.

In my mind, I can hear that old Sesame Street song, "One of These Things is Not Like the Other." I have never felt like Anderson and I match on any level. We are so different from each other. But now I stand before a woman who I reckon is out of *his* league, and I am staggered by her presence.

Until she smiles. It's warm, inviting, and a little crooked, like God had to give her an imperfection to keep people from hating her. She swings around her desk on impossibly high heels and locks me into a hug. "You must be June. I am so happy to meet you!"

"Uh, you too."

She holds me at arm's length. "Well, you two sit, and we will figure out what the fuck is going on." Then she tools back around her desk and pops her intercom on. "Mujo, coffee, and lunch." She turns her attention to us. "First of all, June, please call me Dana. As much as I'd love to hear how you two met, Andy tells me you're in a heap of trouble with a short time frame, so that will have to wait until we can make a social call. I've done some digging myself, but I'd like you two to tell me what is going on in your own words."

As much as that sounds like a good plan, I still worry about telling anyone about what we've done. Unfortunately, I'm too tense to hang onto her calling him *Andy*. I begin with, "How much do you know about Andre Moeller?"

A curl of disgust reshapes her lips before she can shake it off. "He is a man with his fingers in many, many pies all over the world. Some legal, some questionable, some that would get him the death penalty, if the rumors are to be believed—"

"They are," I cut in.

She raises the most exquisitely formed brow in existence. "All this to say, I have a history with Andre. Not a pleasant one."

"May I inquire as to the nature of this history? It's important."

"The bastard cheats at poker," she hisses with seriousness.

I almost laugh. "*That's* why you don't like him?"

"Not entirely, but it would be enough for me to loathe him. I don't take much seriously in life, but poker is sacrosanct."

"Understood." Not really. "Okay, so a few months back, Andre kidnapped me to annoy Elliot West."

Her brow dances higher on her face as she turns to Anderson. "Andy, you said this was a break-in situation, not a kidnapping."

"Oh, there's more to it than I'd like to admit. June, please go on."

"Right, well, Andre did that and returned me once he was done annoying Elliot. He treated me … okay, I guess. No violence—well, not much. After that, Elliot and I had a falling out of sorts, and he had me professionally blackballed. I lost my job, where I'd been since law school. Couldn't get hired anywhere. Then Andre offered me a job, paying me way too much money for what he wanted done. I didn't have much of a choice, so I took the job."

She tips her head to the side a little. "From the man who kidnapped you?"

"It wasn't personal. His goons only took me because I was on the street when they were around. If anyone else associated with Elliot had been an easy target, they would have taken them instead. So yeah, while I was totally freaked out at first, I didn't have a lot of choices at the time."

Anderson added, "And she knew taking a job with Andre would piss off my dad."

That earned a smirk from her. "Well, that makes it all better, I suppose."

"Right, well, that's where this gets ugly." I pass her a folder with the hard copies of the documents we printed. "This is a series of documents from companies Andre wants to buy and take over. Some are legal documents, some are affidavits from people who the board members have pissed off—"

"This is the sort of kill file you put together when you're looking to win a fight," she says, perusing them.

We nod. Anderson says, "And my father is involved with these companies." He points at a few of the names on various documents. "These are some of the aliases he uses to keep his name out of things."

Dana glances up at him. "Andre is looking to oust your father from over a dozen different companies."

"Yes, and he made June an unwitting accomplice by having her dig up the dirt."

"I didn't know Elliot was involved, thanks to his aliases. But now he's trying to say I've been spying for Andre this whole time. He's trying to make Anderson hate me—"

"Why does Elliot have such a grudge against you?"

I sigh. "There's a lot to it, but it all boils down to the fact that I would not be a good move for Anderson's political career."

He laughs. "You still think that's it?"

"Well … yes. Why else?"

"Baby, it's because you have a big mouth."

I laugh hard. "Excuse me?"

"You think for yourself. You voice your opinions. When he says something, you don't just go with it. You push back if he's wrong, and you do it politely, which pisses him off even more because if you were rude about it, then he could point to that and make you seem like a terrible person. He *has* to try this hard to stand a fighting chance against you. Otherwise, he can't control me."

Dana grins. "I knew I liked you. Alright, so where does the break-in play into this?"

"That's how we obtained the documents—well, that and breaking into his desk drawer," I explain. Most of that is stuff I got for him, but some of it—the parts confirming Elliot's involvement—were in his office. The only way to get them was to break in."

"And you did that how? Any evidence left behind?"

My face heats up at the thought of Anderson's DNA left on the steamer trunk. "Um, I used the keycard he gave me."

"So, a key log, if his security keeps one, which I imagine they do. You're not getting out of this with your job intact, but you knew that when you decided to use the key card." She sits back, thinking. "And you had no idea about Elliot's involvement … If I didn't know how much those two hate each other, I'd almost say they coordinated to set you up to take the fall for this."

"They're both setting me up in their own ways. Elliot is telling Anderson I'm why Andre is about to buy them out, and Andre used me to twist the knife about these purchases just that little bit more." I grip the arms of my chair to stop from shouting. "I am so fucking sick of men using me that I could choke on it."

Slowly, she nods. "And that's where they are fucking up. They're both using you, June, you're right about that. But you can use them right back. Let them know what it feels like."

"How?"

"Well, first of all, to CYA, you two must negotiate immunity from the illegal break-in. Sure, you could say he gave you the keycard and, therefore, you had legal access, but breaking into his desk takes that shell of an excuse away. The only way to get immunity is to offer or threaten. You don't have much to offer Andre, so you have to go with threatening him to get your immunity, and that is where things get interesting because what he's doing is so much more illegal than what you did."

"You mean blackmail?" Anderson asks.

She nods. "He's looking to blackmail board members, specifically Elliot, with his illegal activities, or at the very least, make him seem suspicious enough to be ousted. By using an illegal strategy, he's made himself vulnerable to basically the same thing. Not to mention the fact he fucking kidnapped June. Use that. Use all of it to back him into a corner."

All this time, I hadn't thought to use my own kidnapping against him that way. I just figured a man like him would get away with it. But if he's afraid of it being used against him, then why the hell not try?

Dana produces a folder of her own. "Like I said, I did some digging since you brought up Andre, and his shenanigans go back decades. I found all kinds of fun, *exploitable* details he would not enjoy becoming public." She passes him the folder. "Have fun, kids."

37

ANDERSON

When I walk into Andre's office the next day, I wouldn't exactly call it fun. It would be more like playing with fire. It could be interesting, but it could also burn my face off. I'll need luck, skill, and all the information we've obtained to pull this off.

Since this meeting wasn't scheduled, I walk in using June's keycard. Andre is getting a blowjob from his assistant. I pull up an innocent enough smile. "Am I interrupting something?"

She stands, wiping her mouth, while he buttons back up. "I'll get security."

"No need, Esmeralda. Close the door behind you when you leave."

She nods and doesn't make eye contact as she passes by me. The door latches shut, and he smiles. It's as unsettling as June told me. He smiles the way

298

predators smile. All teeth and intent. It's funny. The man who has been trying to ruin my family looks so *normal*. Average. Just another middle-aged white guy. Except for the smile.

So easy to underestimate.

"Anderson West. I assume you've come here for a reason. Would it have anything to do with that key card in your hand? Or the fact that it was used to get into my office the other night?"

"Yes."

I may have surprised him. His brows lift just a little. "Color me intrigued. Take a seat."

I sit on the edge of his desk instead of a chair. "You look very comfortable there, Andre. Pity you won't be in that seat for much longer."

"And pray tell, what does that mean?"

"Only that you could probably use a vacation. Never hurts to get out of town."

"And what would I find in a vacation?"

"You've been a busy, busy boy. I think you work too hard. A vacation would be good for the soul, presuming you have one."

He sits back. But his body is just as stiff as if he had been sitting straight up. It's an oddity. Is he unwell? Andre says, "Are you implying I'm soulless? I'm flattered."

"You know, I remember when you were still friends with my parents. Back before you had your falling out together. You weren't always like this."

"People change. Given your circumstances, you should know that better than most. Tell me, Anderson. How is June?"

I'm tempted to yell at him to keep my woman's name out of his mouth. But I don't give him the satisfaction. "Delightful as always."

"So get on with whatever this is about."

"No appreciation for flair? I suppose I shouldn't be too surprised by that. June said when you kidnapped her, all of the flair belonged to your goons."

His smile shifts. He's almost eager to say what's on his mind. "You should know something, Anderson. I have technology in this room that interferes with microphones. So, if you aim to get a confession recorded, you will be sorely disappointed."

"Neat trick. But I'm not looking for a confession. I know what you've done, and I don't need you to confess to them. I'm looking to work out a deal."

"I imagine you are. Breaking and entering is quite the crime."

"So is kidnapping."

"True." He smiles, pointing at me for a moment. His voice and finger drop. "But considering June's less-than-stellar reputation, I don't think anyone will take her word over mine. The goons, as you called them, will be impossible to locate. When people are buried under another country's soil in unmarked graves, it isn't easy to find them. So you see, my dear boy, you have no evidence against me."

Considering he just roundaboutly confessed to killing the people who kidnapped June, I'm not exactly loving my chances. But this is our only chance, and I'm taking it. "He said/she said cases are notoriously difficult to prosecute. You have a good point."

He gives a slight nod. "So then, what is this deal you're interested in?"

"Well, you see, kidnapping is not the only crime I'm aware of. That's on your rap sheet."

"Do tell. I'm all ears." His smirk makes me want to punch him in the teeth.

"Well, like I said, kidnapping is a good one." I hold up the folder that I brought in with me. "So is illegal gambling."

Andre laughs. "Who doesn't bet on the ponies?"

Time to use Dana's material. Reading her killfile on Andre Moeller was like taking a nightmare trip through a sociopath's wet dreams. I needed a shower afterward and still didn't feel clean. I won't until I leave his office and this is finished.

"Ponies? Is that what you call the people pumped so full of fentanyl they can't feel when you and your friends whip them into running through your hedge maze for your amusement?"

The fucker doesn't even flinch. "That's an interesting allegation. You have a colorful imagination. I should hire you for my entertainment division."

"Thanks, but I'm very happy at West Media." I pull out three affidavits and set them on his desk in front of him. "It has come to my attention that you intend to use this as some leverage to buy out my father's holdings and positions. Is that true?"

"Elliott West has been involved in several high-profile problems in Boston. The only thing that keeps him safe is his name and his money. It's not my fault if he's decided to fuck things up for himself."

"While that is true, the problem here is that none of these affidavits are real. The signatures on these affidavits have been falsified. Each person whose name was falsified here is interested in ensuring that these are not used against Elliott West." When his smile starts to crack, mine widens. "See, Andre, the smart thing would have been to use dead people. You know, the person who can't take back an affidavit or say their signature was falsified."

"What is this?" At least he sounds annoyed.

"See, the thing about taking over other companies or buying them out or any of those things you're interested in is that it can't be predicated on fraud. If it is. Then not only are you liable for those purchases and having fucked up with the boards, but also The Federal Trade Commission will get involved. The IRS would get involved. All kinds of people would be interested in finding out what you've been up to. I could be wrong, but I don't think you'd like that."

Andre's jaw sets. I believe I've made him angry. It almost makes me laugh. In the time that he's silent, I'm nearly convinced that he's doing the math on whether or not he would get away with murdering me now. He snaps, "And this deal you were looking for, what is it?"

"You will not press charges against June or me for the break-in. That is water under the bridge. Furthermore, you will not touch any company my father has his fingers on — not ever."

"And if I were to give you what you wanted … ?"

"The evidence that I have against you will be locked away. You'll get your key card back. Of course, I'll keep a copy because you never know when that might come in handy, but you can have the original."

He growls, "I want the evidence."

"Not happening."

"I will not take a deal where I am not in control of the evidence."

I shrug. "Then I guess this discussion is over."

"I will prosecute."

Smiling, I looked down my nose at him. "Press charges and your whole world will end. Fraud, kidnapping, extortion. And that's the minor stuff. In this folder is some unsavory nastiness I didn't have the imagination to conjure. I never would have thought of using spiked clothes pins on *those* parts of the human body."

That makes him flinch. Finally. "You can't prove anything."

"You're right. *I* can't. But pictures are worth a thousand words—and maybe a thousand years in prison, given all the charges you could face. You're a smart man, Andre. I'm shocked you were dumb enough to take trophies. Even if you were to press charges against us, I'm pretty sure June and I will be out of the big house long before you."

The glistening sweat on his brow makes all of this stress worth it. "How do I know you won't use the evidence against me?"

"Well, like any other deal, this one requires a little bit of faith on both our parts. I don't exactly savor the thought of spending any time in prison. And if June were ever to find her way behind bars, I might lose my mind. So you have that over us. We have this folder over you. If I or June is ever brought up on charges, this kill file will be automatically released to the press and law enforcement. Considering what you've been doing overseas, Interpol would also be extremely interested in what I know. So, I would say that you have a vested interest in ensuring I am never brought up on charges. And neither is June."

"All this to save your father's failing empire? What a loyal boy you are."

I laugh. "Coming after my father is the same as coming after my inheritance. Loyalty has nothing to do with it."

"You're more ruthless than I thought. You've done something today that few men ever have."

"What's that? Impressed you?"

"Pissed me off." He sips his water. "But I do appreciate ruthlessness. Even when it's aimed at me. You have a bargain."

"I thought I might." I pull out another document from the folder. "This agreement stipulates that neither one of us will go forward with the information that we have. Obviously, it's not legally binding. But given our circumstances aren't exactly legal, there are detailed notes about how the other will be destroyed if one of us fails to live up to the deal. Sign it."

Like anyone with a mind for the law, he takes time to read the document. But then he signs it, passing the signature page to me along with his pen. I sign as well. Andre shakes his head, smiling. "What I wouldn't give to be twenty years younger right about now."

June mentioned that he goes off on side tangents in the weirdest ways, but I still didn't see that one coming. "Oh? Why is that?"

"I would have loved to have gone head to head against you instead of your father. *You*, I find interesting."

"Do yourself a favor and don't find me at all. That would be a costly mistake."

He smiles at my threat. "Be seeing you, Anderson West."

I take the contract and leave, knowing Andre Moeller won't be a problem again. At least for now.

38

JUNE

When Anderson comes home, he has a few shopping bags with him and a big smile. "Hi honey, I'm home."

I roll my eyes and kiss him. "What's all that?"

"I felt like celebrating because Andre signed our mutually assured destruction contract."

All the tension that had animated my body flows out of me. It's so sudden that I wobble on my feet. "And you couldn't text me? I've been waiting here for hours—"

He cuts me off with another kiss. "Considering that we are blackmailing one of the most high-profile people in the city, I decided that texting might be a little dangerous. And I wanted to see your face when I told you, so that's why I didn't call."

"Okay, well, I'm thrilled, and I'm curious to know what's in your bags."

"I require wine. This calls for a celebration."

"Screw the wine. I want prosecco."

He grins. "Perfect."

While I crack open a bottle, he stows his purchases. Some are food, while others get taken into the bedroom. Maybe clothes? Maybe he has a gift for me he wants to hide? I won't be one of those nosy wives who always dig into their spouse's business, but I *am* curious.

When he returns in his lounge pants and tee, I see the man I fell in love with all those months ago. He's a bit more relaxed than he's been since we figured out Andre's bullshit. "Thank god I thought about Dana."

"No shit. I like her a lot. She's sharp, and given the rift between her and your folks, I don't think she's secretly in cahoots with your dad."

He chuckles. "No, not at all. It's funny to think Mom was worried about her and Dad."

"Why is that?"

"You didn't pick up on the look her assistant gave her when we walked in?"

I shake my head.

"Dana has a thing for younger men. Always has."

My insides clench. "You're not about to tell me she was your first, are you?"

He laughs. "Fuck no! It's like I said before—I think of her as an aunt. The only reason I know that is she was caught with two of the pool boys at the country club. Don't make that face—they were in their twenties at the time. The point is, she would have never touched my dad. It's a pity Mom never understood that, or they'd probably still be friends."

I sigh, thinking about his mom. She never struck me as particularly jealous, but I'd never seen her in a position to be jealous, either. "Maybe one day they'll bury the hatchet."

"Perhaps." He clinks his glass to mine. "One problem down. One to go."

"Don't mention the other one right now. I am trying to calm down."

"Agreed." He smiles at me, studying my lips for a moment. "You've been a fucking trooper through this, June. Thank you."

A laugh chirps out of me. "You're thanking me for what?"

"After all the shit I said to you ... accused you of ... and now, you've lost your job."

"Trying to calm down, remember?"

He pulls me in for a kiss, and I taste the prosecco on his lips. "I know. I'm just telling you why it is. I appreciate you. You have sacrificed so much to be with me, and that is more than worthy of my gratitude."

"Well, I love you, and I'm willing to make sacrifices for you. I know you'd do the same for me. Hell, you may end up sacrificing your freedom for me, so," I shrug, "that's just what we do for each other."

His face goes pensive—the line in his brow forms. "It really has been one thing after another for us, hasn't it?"

I giggle, feeling the prosecco's warmth bubble through me on my empty stomach. I was so nervous all day that I couldn't eat much. "Since we re-met, things have been turvy-topsy."

"I think the phrase is topsy-turvy."

"That's how fucked up it's been. Even that's backward for us."

He smirks, but it dies fast. "You know Andre will want revenge."

"Oh, I'm aware. He's not the kind of man to let this slide."

"But we'll handle it together. Like we handle everything else."

I've been tense all day, so my mind bounces from topic to topic rapidly. I'm sure my father's deal with Andre will fall through after this. The poor baby. I almost roll my eyes at myself for worrying about him. He certainly didn't worry about me when he was working with Andre for a deal. I take a nervous breath. "Did you tell your dad yet?"

"No. Let him sweat it out. We fixed this. He's safe now, so he can wait."

Slowly, I nod. "Still sucks that I'm out of work again, but I'll take that over being Andre's stooge any day."

Anderson loops his arm with mine, and he guides me to the couch to sit there instead of our breakfast bar in the kitchen. "I will take care of you, June. It's literally the least I can do after all you've done for me."

"Thank you, but you know how I feel about that."

He smiles. "What I mean is, until you get your feet under you, I've got you. Just like you said—you sacrificed for me, and I am happy to do the same for you."

"Thanks." But I still feel weird about sharing money before we're married for some reason.

"You look like you're thinking too hard again."

It makes me laugh. "Stop being a hyper-observant weirdo."

"Never. Not when it comes to you."

"Yes, I'm thinking too much again. Happy?"

"How about I help you shut down that big brain of yours, and we celebrate properly?"

I'm not sure what he means by that. "You want to go out?"

"Not even a little." He digs into his pocket and produces the biggest sapphire I've ever seen. At first, it steals the show, but then I realize it's attached to a glass butt plug.

A big one.

"Are you out of your mind?" But even as my mind says the words, my body warms up from the inside, telling me she's on board.

"You can take it. I know you can. You've taken my cock. I know you can take this little thing, and I think you'd look fucking hot as hell with that jewel right there, flashing at me."

I bite my lip, trying to restrain myself for some reason. But that reason is quickly dissolving into nothing. "I don't know—"

"If it hurts or you want to stop for any reason, then say 'Sapphire,' and I will remove it, and we do whatever you want to instead. I promise."

"Even if what I want to do is watch some super scary movie?"

He smirks. "Yes. I will watch whatever fucked up horror movie you have in mind. But you'll have to rock me to sleep tonight."

I snort a laugh at the thought. "Oh, I'm sure the man who faced down Andre today is scared of a little ghost and some gore."

He holds up the butt plug, and the fake sapphire glints in the light. Admittedly, it *is* pretty. Somehow, it takes all the focus in the room. "So, are you game?"

Okay, now it's my turn to be scared. I gulp audibly. "Um—"

Anderson kisses me, but it's more like he's devouring my mouth. His hand runs up and down my body until it slips beneath my tee shirt. His thumbs graze over my nipples, and I jump from the stimulation. It verges on too much, and he stays right there, making me squirm.

I peel my mouth from his. "I'm still not sure about this."

"Honestly, baby, I just want you. Toy, no toy, I don't fucking care. I want to bury myself in you until I feel you milk my cock as you come. I want to earn your screams. And tomorrow, I want to see you step wide because I made your tight little pussy sore."

How is this handsome man, this pillar of society, such a filthy boy?

I wrap my legs around his waist and pull him on top of me, reveling in the weight of him on me. He crushes me into the couch, and his kisses are demanding and hungry. His hard cock presses on me through our clothes, rubbing my clit as he dry humps against me. I grind up against him like that, sending pleasure through me. This is getting me so damn wet. But fuck, I ache for more.

I want this. All of this.

"You really want to put that thing up my ass?"

He swallows. "Yes."

"Let's try it."

A new hunger invades his handsome face. He rears back, grabs my legs, and flips me over onto my stomach before he scoops me up at my waist and pushes me over the padded arm of the couch. When he yanks down my yoga pants, he bites my ass cheek just enough to hurt. I yelp, and he murmurs, "Sorry, love, couldn't be helped. I need to mark this ass and make it mine."

This is going to be a night to remember.

39

JUNE

I don't know quite what to expect. Anal sex was one thing. But it wasn't like I was on display for him with some strange object up my ass. This feels like a strange idea.

Yet, I can't deny how hot it gets me.

Bent over the couch arm, I'm waiting to feel more contact between us. When I get it, it's not what I expect. Anderson's finger is slick against me there, running in circles until he hits his target. It's odd. But also tantalizing.

"Why so much lube?"

"The more I use, the better it will be for you."

"Oh. Okay."

And then I feel it. Warmth comes over me there. "Is it one of those warming gels?"

"Mm, hmm. You like?"

My voice shakes. "I ... I think so."

"I'm switching to the toy. Like I said, if you don't like it or want to stop for any reason, say 'Sapphire.'"

I bob my head and clutch onto the couch arm.

"Relax, baby. When you feel me press, exhale, okay?"

"Okay."

The hardness of the toy is the first thing I notice. It's not cold—he must have kept it warm in his pocket. But it's hard and unforgiving. Nothing like his fingers or cock. It has a flared base, thank god, because I've heard all about people doing anal play and getting things stuck. The flared base is supposed to prevent that. I hope it works because I do not need to add the world's most embarrassing trip to the ER to my night.

When the toy penetrates me there, the stretch is a whole different experience from anything we've done. It forces me to open to it in a way that is non-negotiable. I almost panic and tell him to stop, but then ... then something else kicks in. The urge to please him? No. This isn't about him. This is about me. About what I want.

And I want to see if I can do this.

It's not only the newness of the sensation or the unexpected pleasure I'm getting from this experiment. It's the challenge of it. Can I do this? Can I take it? To my surprise, I can.

"Almost there," he assures me.

"Keep going." I almost don't recognize the voice that came out of me to demand that. It's like this challenge is changing some fundamental part of myself, and I like it.

The gradual stretch opens me up almost too much right before the toy slides up to the hilt inside of me. He takes a deep, appreciative breath. "Fuck, June, you're practically dripping."

He's right. My hips are slightly canted to the right, and I feel it on my right inner thigh. I've never been aroused like this before, and it's making me feel daring. I give my ass a little wiggle. "What are you gonna do about that?"

The growl he looses sends a shiver straight up my spine. He shifts around on the couch, and I ready myself to feel him impale me on his cock, but then he shoves my yoga pants all the way down and tightly forces his head face-up between my thighs, using the pants as some kind of a pillow or brace. Anderson grabs my hips and presses me down an inch to his mouth.

I'm trapped and helpless against him. The couch holds me in place. My yoga pants cling to keep my knees together, but Anderson has pried a space open for his head, making the pants tighter like binding. I'm absolutely certain he couldn't hear me if he tried—his ears are suctioned to my inner thighs. And I have the prettiest butt plug stuffed in my ass.

I might not be bound in the traditional sense, but I am utterly stuck here with nowhere to go and a tongue deliriously ravishing my pussy. A girl could get used to this.

He suckles on my clit, knowing what that does to me. I thought I was aching for his cock before, but it was nothing compared to this. As much as I'd like to switch things up and bounce on his dick for a while, he can't hear me, and I can't pull away. I'm stuck like this until he changes things, and knowing that I'm helpless to his whims only turns me on more.

His tongue should be insured for a million or more. It's worth every penny on the planet. Pleasure ratchets up in my belly as he drinks me down. If he keeps this up, I might drown him. I'm kinda glad he can't hear me right now because the sounds coming out of me are choked and beastly. Not the sexy gasping sounds I normally make. This is something straight out of the primal part of my soul because he's being such an animal.

The plug only makes things better. I almost regret every other time I've been eaten out because I wasn't wearing a plug then. It's like all those nerve endings have been waiting for exactly this and are finally happy. It's making me pant like a dog in heat, and I grip the couch arm as my climax hits.

This is like nothing I've ever felt. It's world-ending.

My head tosses back when I scream out my ecstasy, only to then feel every muscle lock tight, sending my head forward as my whole body curls in on itself.

Muscles thrash in my skin while heat and bliss tear through me. I am at his mercy as one orgasm triggers another. He grips my hips tighter, locking his strong arms around my ass to keep me in place. He growls on my clit, and that forces me to come again, only this time, I can't stop from grinding against his tongue for more. I need it. More pressure there, more of his attention, more of his love. All of it.

I want everything!

I hump down onto his face, gliding back and forth. His nose sweeps against my clit, while his tongue dips into me. His day's stubble burns my delicate skin, and I don't fucking care. I need it all! Every sensation. The pleasure, the pain. It's not enough. It could never be enough because none of it is his cock.

"Anderson, fuck me!" I order.

But his sounds are garbled by my bits.

With regret, I lift up as much as I can so I can hear him. "Baby, I need you to fuck me!"

Instead, he turns us ninety degrees, giving me the back of the couch to hang onto. It forces me to sit up more on his face, which must give him more support because then he slides a finger into my pussy. Oh fuck!

I grab the back of the couch, bracing for dear life as he finger-bangs me while still mauling my clit. He strokes my G-spot to sparks, and I can't stop or slow down. He's forcing me to come on him again. It radiates from my belly, washing over every inch of my skin like a cool breeze on a sizzling hot day.

And then it feels like that sizzling hot day is inside of me.

I screech it out, heat escaping my lungs as I burst from the pleasure. It's too much for my body to contain. Too good and hot and excruciatingly perfect. I can't take much more of this, and I want to take it all. I want to weather whatever Anderson wants to give me. For him and for me. This man has taken me to the brink of madness time and time again, and I'd take it all over again if it meant I got to keep him. To be his forever.

To be in this moment forever.

When it's finally over, I have no words. No strength. There is nothing left of the woman I was. Only this weakened jelly form, half bent over the back of the couch. Anderson carefully removes himself from me without hurting me or, by some miracle, himself. He must have grabbed a towel or used his shirt, because by the time he shows up in front of my face, his is relatively dry again. He kneels in front of me with such a boldly smug grin on his face that I'm sure he's about to say something in Assholese.

"Are you in there?"

All I can do is try to laugh and gently shake my head. Words ... well, they feel optional at this point.

"I'll get you some water. And a straw."

I don't mind the view from this angle. Mostly, I get to watch his butt in his lounge pants, and that's always a good show. I'm going to have to get him to take me to the gym and show me what he does to have such an exquisite rear.

When he turns, I have a view of his erection, stretching the front of his lounge pants, and damn, that makes my mouth water. I'm sure he could fuck my face at this angle. And right now, I'd beg him to if I had any saliva left in my mouth. Because he's the best man ever, he feeds me the straw, not expecting me to be able to lift my head.

Unfortunately, drinking with my head almost upside down means the water goes out my nose instead of down my throat.

Choking shoots a little life into my body, but only a little. I'm able to sit up on my own, and I drink half the water once I can breathe again. Once that's done, though, I'm a limp noodle. Anderson puts his arm around my shoulders, trying to help me sit up. He nuzzles against my ear and murmurs, "That was so much fun, and we're just getting started."

40

JUNE

"Just getting started?" Oh yeah. He hasn't come yet. Where is my head? I can't think clearly. When he scoots closer to me, the couch sinks in his direction, and I feel why I can't think clearly. The plug. It's still in place.

Anderson nuzzles against the shell of my ear. He growls in my ear, "I have plans for that body of yours. Can you walk?"

A rush of heat flushes through me, residuals from what we just did and from what his primordial growl promises. But I'm still weak from his mouth all over me. "I ... I don't think I can."

"Well, then." He stands up, then bends, scooping beneath me to carry me. Every bouncing step makes the plug shift inside of me, and it stirs up all kinds of feelings. Trepidation, lust, the need to see how far I can push myself tonight.

But I'm still wrung out from all those orgasms, and I laugh. "Anderson, watch your step!"

"Oh?" His tone is so cocky like he knows I'll do whatever he wants. "I think you like it. The feel of the toy up your ass. Especially when I do this." He bounces the next step extra hard, forcing a shudder through me. "Fuck, you're so hot when you're like this."

"Like what?" I pant.

"Wound up. Ready for whatever I want."

His words turn me on so hard, but I'm drained, and I don't have anything left to give him. So, I try to change the topic. "Why are you carrying me to bed?"

"I told you, baby. I have plans." He kicks the door closed behind him once we're inside, then carefully lays me on the bed. He makes sure the pillows are under me right, fussing like a nurse for a moment. Anderson's gaze isn't on me—it's on the bed and the pillows.

I don't want to disappoint him, but I have to be honest. "Baby, I'm wiped out from that. I don't have the energy for more."

He leans down, his lips a fraction of an inch from mine, as he stares into my eyes. "All you have to do is lay there and let me do all the work."

What kind of woman would I be if I turned that offer down from a ridiculously sexy man? "Um, okay."

He has me face up on the bed, so I get to watch him consider where to begin on me. He's methodical, studying my body almost clinically. "Where to begin … "

I tease, "And here I thought you had a plan."

"Mouthy girls get spankings."

"Don't threaten me with a good time." I say it as a joke, but seeing the look in his eyes, maybe I shouldn't have.

Or maybe I should have said that months ago.

Another growl lodges in his chest. "You don't know what you've started."

"Show me." Why am I talking trash like I can take it? But that urge to push myself is still inside me, no matter how tired I am.

Anderson props me up and steals my shirt, letting the material tickle my arms as he pulls it away. Then he pinches the waistband on my leggings and peels them from my body with such slowness that I'm sure he's doing it to make me crazier, as though I need the help. I'm exposed head to toe for him, and his appreciative gaze leaves heat in its wake.

Then it's his turn. With his expression locked on me, he slowly removes what's left of his clothes—no more lounge pants. His cock is hard and proud, and the head shines with precum. He must have loved what we did on the couch. He's not normally like that.

Anderson picks up my right ankle and kisses the top of my foot before trailing kisses up my inner calf and thigh. Before he gets anywhere good, he pulls the same move on the other leg but slower. Like he's telling me, this is only the beginning.

He peppers my upper thighs with more kisses before blazing a path with his lips over my stomach and my ribs, avoiding my breasts and up my sternum. He branches out over my collarbones and down my arms, paying special attention to my fingertips, one at a time. I cannot figure him out tonight. He's so unlike himself. But I also kind of like it.

When he licks up my throat, I can't help but exhale a deep sigh. As much as he's keeping me on some unknown edge, this has also been the world's most intimate massage, and each sensation is a new bit of bliss. And then he's face to face with me. "I love you, June."

"I love you, too, baby."

He smiles sweetly. "I need you to know that."

"Of course I do. What's on your mind?"

"This." Abruptly, he gets off of me and flips me over onto my stomach. He yanks my hips up so I'm face down and ass up, and he spreads me open before he presses on the jeweled end of the plug. I hiss out a breath—it's so intense, and I'm a little sore. He'd lulled me into a false sense of sweetness, and now, he's ripped that away. He's not the gentle lover he was a moment ago.

This is someone else.

I'm not sure what he's up to until he brushes over my pussy with the broad head of his cock. It feels so intense and delicious. But then he pulls back, and I can't feel him anymore. *Oh, fuck, is he —*

Anderson grabs my hips and slams all the way into me, making me squeal into the pillows. It's so fucking intense! Painful, yes, but the pleasure is almost too much as he bears down on me. But then he starts to fuck me, and I can't hardly stand it. Our bodies smack together, and each time, a wave of pleasure cascades through my pelvis. I'm already on the edge from what we'd done before, and with the plug still in me, I'm losing control.

It's. So. Tight.

It's never felt like this before. He's big compared to most guys, and some nights, he's almost too big. But now? Now, it's like being fucked by a soda can because the plug has tightened me up. I don't know how much more of this I can take.

And it *is* fucking. No one could mistake this for making love.

I'm just so full. Every spot is tended, from my G-spot to whatever the hell else is in there, and when he reaches around for my clit, I grip the sheets and lose it. I screech, "Fuck!" as the orgasm begins.

He buries himself as deep as he can go, riding the

squeeze of my body on him. "You feel so fucking good when you come, baby!"

I can't even respond — I'm lost inside of myself, inside this shimmering, inescapable pleasure he gave me. When it finally starts to subside, he rears back and wiggles the plug, sending me tumbling into another orgasm. Each muscle has squeezed tight. I can't breathe, but who the hell cares? I have no words, and I must scream.

When I can finally inhale again, it sounds like a reverse scream when my lungs fill up. He hammers into me even more, and every thrust collides against the plug, making one orgasm into multiple. I can't even count them — they're like echoes in a cave. I don't think you can turn inside out from climaxing too much, but he's forcing me to try.

As one orgasm strikes another, I realize things are going black in my vision. I have to make myself breathe, and it's a struggle. I turn my head for air and try to tap out, slapping the bed so he'll see. He taunts me, "Need a break?"

I whisper, "Yeah!"

But he grabs that hand and pulls it into the small of my back. "You can take it." He pops himself against me harder, deeper, faster until his cock swells inside me. Just as I'm ready to pull away from him — not that I really could — his body goes rigid behind me. He jerks forward, as deep as he can go, as he roars out his orgasm, pouring himself into my body. All that heat melts me inside to soothe my ache.

Anderson collapses onto my back, half kissing, half huffing breaths against my sweaty skin. But when he lost himself on top of me, he pressed the plug in even more.

I whimper, "Plug!"

Quickly—well, as quick as he could after all of that—he rolls off of me. "Sorry."

"S'kay," I gasp, also trying to catch my breath.

After a minute of panting in the relative dark, he asks, "You okay?"

I need a minute to make actual words. "Think so."

He laces his fingers with mine. "You are a goddess."

I laugh, which weirdly moves the plug. "Your goddess wants to clean up."

"Not yet." He rubs my ass for a moment first, then smacks me there. "Okay. Now you can go."

41

ANDERSON

Over coffee the next day, I text Dana before returning to our conversation. "And you liked it?"

When June blushes, she is so fucking sexy. "Yeah, I think so."

"You sound unsure. What didn't you like?"

"It was just a surprise, that's all."

"The plug, you mean?"

She nods, then turns away. "I didn't. I never knew. I just—"

"It's okay to say that you liked it. I want to know all the things that I can do to please you. No matter how unusual or deviant they might be."

"Call them, um … "she starts. It's hard for her to look

me in the eyes when she says it. "Do you think maybe we could try a little bondage one day?"

Oh, if she's not careful, she's gonna make this table rise another eight inches. I swallow, trying not to sound too eager. "I think I can make that work."

"I mean, is that something that you're into, or are you thinking of it more like a favor to me?"

I huff a laugh. "Anything I get to do to please you is a favor to both of us. Whatever you want to try, June, I am up for it. And besides, I think you'd look rather sexy in a pair of shiny handcuffs."

Her eyes widen. "I was thinking maybe those pink fuzzy ones. They seem safer."

I can picture it now. I am not getting out of here today without fucking this woman. "Whatever you want."

A moment later, Dana texts me back. "I'll look into the video rumor."

It had been on my mind for a while now, of course. The only thing that really puts it out of my mind is fucking June. Or thinking of fucking June. Really, the moment she's naked in my mind, all of the noise disappears.

When she's naked in real life, the world goes away.

But for now, I have to stay focused. Moss wouldn't have brought any of this to my attention unless it had the potential for fallout. If only we knew —

"I just so happen to have a pair of those pink fuzzy handcuffs. They're stored in my underwear drawer."

And just like that, I have no more thoughts in my head. "Let's go see what you look like in pink. Last one to the bedroom loses."

She grins and squeals before I race her to the bedroom. I bar the doorway so she loses. But I make sure she wins, too.

Hours later, June is asleep, and I check my phone on the kitchen island again. There's a text from Dana. "They're bluffing. Call me."

For fuck's sake, please let this be the news I need to hear. "Dana, what's going on?"

"It was all bullshit. I had my people on the force dig into it for me. They found out the rumor of the video was so that they could pressure you and June into a confession. They've got nothing."

I can't believe it. "You're sure? A lot of important lives hang in the balance here — "

"Anderson, come on. You know me. I wouldn't tell you it was bullshit if I didn't know for sure it was bullshit." She sounds very offended.

"I know. I'm sorry. This has been one of the most stressful things in my life, and I'm … I'm not sure that I want to believe that it's going the way I need it to go. I can't have hope and have it taken away from me again."

"Honey, I know. But I promise you, I'm not giving you false hope. This is real. They have nothing on you. All they have is a bloated corpse and a lot of suspicion. A murder case that does not make."

I blow out a breath that I didn't know I was holding. It still feels too good to be true. "So when we're questioned again —"

"You have every right to tell them to fuck right off. You're in the clear, my boy. Don't make the mistake of accidentally confessing anything. Not even so much as speeding to get there. Anything that you confess to can give them probable cause, and that will definitely amp up their investigation on you. This is the very definition of giving them an inch, and they will take a mile. Give them nothing, and you'll get nothing."

"One thing I don't understand. How is it that Moss' people had it so wrong?"

She sighs. "It seems to me that the cops know who to tell that rumor to. Moss' people are compromised. I don't know if they truly believe that the video exists or if they are plants to feed him false information. Either way, they can't be trusted. He needs new people." She pauses. "He's not getting mine."

I chuckle. "Fair enough. Dana, thank you so much for your help on this."

"Anytime, Anderson. Hope to see you around more often."

"I'd like that." Visitation will be much easier since I won't be behind bars. Now, to handle the rest of it.

By the time the detectives actually call me, I've been expecting them. I don't even speed on the drive in. Like Dana said, I will give them no excuses. Inside the police station, they're all smiles. But behind their eyes, something else lurks.

Confidence.

Give me an interrogation room, Banks carries a folder in one hand and pulls out my chair for me with the other. "Take a seat, Mr. West."

"Why, thank you." The three of us sit like civilized people. Banks and Wachowski on one side, me on the other. Their interrogation room looks like any that I've seen on TV. Whoever stands behind the one-way mirror is about to get one hell of a show.

Banks sets the folder on the table. "I'm glad you could make this meeting."

I chuckle. "Well, you are the police. I don't think I have much of a choice."

"You have all kinds of choices, Mr. West," Wachowski says in that nasal voice of his. "A man with your kind of money? I'm beginning to see you think you can do anything you want."

"Pray tell what that's supposed to mean?"

He leans forward, dipping his chin down like he's

conspiring with me. His voice lowers. "Come on. We both know what went down that night."

"What night is that?"

When he sees I'm not playing the same game he is, he sits back and hisses between his teeth. I've always enjoyed disappointing my father, but I think I enjoy disappointing Wachowski even more. "Cut the crap, West. We know it was you."

"Oh? You know what was me?"

He stands up and throws his chair across the room. "Stop fucking around! We know you killed him! We have all the proof we need!"

I sit back and smile. "I'd love to see it."

"See what?" Banks asks.

"Your proof, of course. I would assume you have more than just a bloated corpse. Maybe some fingerprints? Or DNA? Or even a video?" I can't say that I know about their little lie, but I can certainly intimate it.

Wachowski slams his fists on the table. "Are you asking for a video just to piss us off? Or are you asking because it's some kind of a sick fetish for you to watch yourself beat a man to death?"

And right then, I know for certain they don't have it. If they did, Wachowski would rub my nose in it.

So I calmly tell them, "I am merely asking for the proof you claim to have. Seems to me that if you don't have any, then I'm free to go. In fact, since you don't have any, I'd be happy to sue for harassment, as you have pulled me in here on more than one occasion with no kind of evidence, harassed my fiancée at her place of business—"

"Listen, Mr. West," Banks begins. "None of us need to speak to our lawyers to make this go away. All we need is some cooperation from you." He does his level best to make it sound like such a simple thing.

"What cooperation is that, Detective Banks?" But I know what he wants. He wants a confession.

He opens the folder. There on a slab is Neil's swollen corpse. The sight of it turns my stomach. "Not a pretty picture, huh?"

"Rather nauseating, actually. But I don't know what it has to do with me."

"A fresh corpse always looks better. Could almost believe that they're still alive." He pauses for dramatic effect. "Whoever dumped him into the Bay must have thought that he was dead. But he wasn't. At least not according to the coroner's report."

I know the police are allowed to lie during an interrogation. In fact, the only place they're not allowed to lie is on the stand, which isn't to say that that doesn't still happen there, too. So, sitting here across from Detective Banks, I know that he's lying to me. His skull was bashed. He had no pulse. He wasn't breathing. June confirmed it. I confirmed it. And Moss, our expert on making dead bodies, confirmed it.

Yet the thought of Neil having survived until we dumped him overboard still makes me sicker.

"That sounds horrifying."

"It is. The stuff of nightmares, really." He fans out a few more pictures. I know he's trying to get a rise out of me. "Can't imagine what that was like for the guy. That's why I'm determined to get whoever did this. I need to be able to give his family some closure."

"I can certainly see why."

He meets my gaze. "I had a wife once, Mr. West. But this job makes relationships hard. I wasn't always there for her. When I found out about her affair, I went a little crazy. Spent way too much time at the gun range. Bought a new sports car. All that shit. I understand it is hard to deal with a woman who's cheating on you. Guys like us, we don't get a lot of sympathy on that. But I get it."

I'm impressed. They're still trying. Even without evidence. "Detective Banks, I'm not sure what you think you and I have in common, but I am certain that you're wrong."

"Your girl got a little action on the side. That could make any man crazy. Juries are very understanding about that kind of thing."

"My statement is not going to change. I had nothing to do with any of this. And now that I'm here and you two have been wasting my time for close to an hour, I know for certain that you have nothing on me. I'm sure that stings, but that's not my problem." I stand up. "My problem is a pair of detectives who won't let this go."

"Why the hell should we?" Wachowski barks. "You rich boys always think you can get away with murder."

I shrug. "Maybe you can clear this up for me. Am I a rich boy who thinks he can get away with murder? Or am I a sympathetic man who got cheated on? Which is it? Maybe you two can make up your mind before you bother me again. In the meantime, I'm leaving because you don't have enough to hold me here. Have a nice day." I stroll out of there, breathing a sigh of relief. The fresh air smells like freedom.

42

ANDERSON

My first instinct is to go home and tell June the good news. But there are more pressing matters. Moss' people on the force are compromised.

We text to meet up at the pizza parlor. Instead of sitting in the restaurant part of things, the owner gives us his office. "You take all the time you need," he says before leaving us there with a closed door.

Moss looks tired. "Is it as we feared?"

"Well, if it was, I probably wouldn't be out." I shake my head at him. "They don't have shit."

"You are certain?"

"I had another person look into it for me. Their people are good. I dare say better than yours. There's no video."

He growls under his breath. "My people are the best."

"Maybe usually, but not this time. I'm not sure if they knew and they lied to you, or if they were lied to. Whatever the case, you can't trust them. They're giving you bad information."

He sighs deeply, cursing in Italian under his breath. "Should have seen this coming. I should have known. Anderson, I am so sorry."

I could tell him that it's not his fault. These are people that he trusted. People who had helped him before. I imagine he had helped them, too. I know how hard it is when somebody that you should be able to trust lets you down. But if I tell him that he's no longer on the hook, then he will deny it.

Above all else, Moss knows he's responsible for this. Had he done a better job with the body, this wouldn't be happening. It's his people who fed us the wrong information. If I were an underworld boss, like my father, there would be serious consequences.

But I am not my father. "I know you're sorry, Moss. But what I need you to be is better."

He nods respectfully. "I will do everything in my power to be that."

"Their lack of a video is a win, but this case isn't going away. While I was in questioning, I threatened to sue them for harassment. Hopefully, that will keep them at bay for a while. Make them hesitate to bother us again.

But I'm not sure it will work forever. Those detectives are like a dog with a bone."

"Should they meet an end like the haddock?"

"What? No! No more haddock. From here on out."

He sits back and takes a breath. I can't tell if he is relieved or disappointed. "Your father's lawyer is a piece of work."

"You heard from Pym?"

"No. I only watch him for few days. He makes threats, but I never see him carry through."

I shrug. "His reputation precedes him. Most people are happy to do what he wants."

"Yet you see other lawyer."

"Pym wanted to hang June out to dry over this. So I needed somebody in her corner."

"Despicable." He spits on the floor. "When men blame women for their troubles, that is when they are no longer men."

"I could not agree more."

"The evidence they do have. It's not much." He rubs his hand over his bald head. "My people may be compromised, but they can get their hands on evidence. Or maybe evidence lockup has fire." He's still trying to make it up to me.

"I appreciate the offer. But I think I'd rather take my chances with where we stand now."

He nods. "As you wish, boss."

"Their forensics lab is going to have to really earn their paycheck this year if they think they can build a case on a soggy body."

"It is unlikely. But not impossible."

"What do you mean by that?"

Moss says, "With enough supposition and a little bit of evidence, I have seen people convicted for murder with less. Though, that was in Europe."

I'd studied enough case law to know what I was up against. "Well, here we have more burden of proof on the prosecution. As much as I hate to admit it, I will use every bit of privilege that I can to keep my ass out of jail."

"There is no shame in this. It is no different when I do my job. Some say it is dishonorable to use poison." He shrugs his giant shoulders. "I say to be a great killer, you must use whatever you have available. Poison. Fire. Sniping. Anything. Whatever gets the job done. That is what I do."

Icy spiders dance up my spine. I know he killed people. I'd seen him do it. But those methods … then again, who am I to judge? I had killed a man, and in the heat of the moment, I would have used anything to end that bastard.

He tried to assault June. He would have killed her, too. If it came down to it, I would have killed him with anything I had.

"You're right about that. Any tool in the toolbox."

He nods. "The world is an ugly place for men like us. But we sleep well knowing we protect those we love."

"Indeed." I sip my soda and think. "For now, we should lay low. Keep these meetings to a minimum. As things stand, you and I don't have much in the way of official business, so being seen together is suspicious."

"We don't exactly travel in the same social circle, eh?"

"Not yet."

"This means … "

"When the organization is under my control, Moss, I want you by my side. I trust you."

The brute is silent for a moment. "It is not a good idea."

"Why not?"

"I fail you on this. I could fail again."

But I shake my head at him. "You know better now. You learn from this mistake, and that's that. I know you'll never let this happen again. That's what makes me trust you."

I watch as the gears turn in his mind. It would be a mistake to think of Moss as simple or dumb. The man has been in his line of work for decades. He knows how this world works better than I do. He knows the players. Their men. He is an invaluable resource. And a silent one right now.

So I tell him, "When I get you in that position of power, you will be paid as such. This I guarantee you. So yes, for now, we are not in the same social set. But we will be."

He takes a breath, surprised by what I said. "You believe in me that much?"

"And more."

His voice goes hoarse with emotion. "Thank you, boss."

I am fairly certain my father never paid him that kind of respect before. He looks struck. I smile at him, unsure what to say next. "I should be getting back. You should, too. I need to let June know about everything."

"You tell me first?"

"The sooner you stop trusting your people on the inside, the better for all of us."

"Agreed." As we part ways, he says, "This is good news. I do not like losing assets, but it is good news."

"Losing assets?" I don't like the way that sounds.

"They could have gotten you in prison. They are no longer assets."

"Moss, you're not going to hurt them."

His lips tightened. There's a coldness in his eyes. "If you say not to, I don't."

"I'm saying not to. We don't know if those people deceived you on purpose. It could have been a completely innocent mistake. If those detectives fed them false information, that was all they had to go on. That's not their fault. And we don't punish innocent people."

"As you say." But the frostiness doesn't leave him.

"I'm serious, Moss. Don't lay a hand on their heads." That might not be specific enough. "No harm is to come to them. Not from you, not from anyone you know. No one connected to us will harm them. I want them protected."

He sighs, defeated. "Very well."

"If we're going to do things better than my father, then we need to start now. I won't keep doing things the way that he would do them."

"Your father, he makes a lot of money. Not all his schemes are bad ones."

"I don't care. I'm not him. Things will be different when I am in control."

"Yes, boss."

I am mostly certain that Moss will not hurt those people when I leave. But dealing with him is sort of like dealing with a tiger on a leash. One wrong move and things could become very bad, very fast.

But I can't focus on that now. For now, I get to tell June the good news. I didn't want to tell her when

Dana told me. If this shit went sideways, I didn't want her to be disappointed. But when I come home and find her there with expectation on her pretty face. I tell her, "There's no video."

"What?"

"There's no video. I found out from Dana, and I confronted the detectives. They don't have anything. All that they have is Neil's corpse. No video of the attack. No physical evidence of us being there. Otherwise, I'd be in jail right now."

"Oh my God." Her knees go loose, and I catch her before she falls.

"Are you okay?"

She laughs at herself. "I think I almost fainted. Like some weak Southern Belle or something. That's embarrassing."

I smile and kiss her. "Nothing to be embarrassed about. Not ever. Not with me."

She stands on her own two feet and hugs me. "So, does this mean we're out of the woods?"

"Not yet. There's still the matter of a dead body to be dealt with. But for now, the focus is less on us. I threatened to sue them for harassment for both of us, and they didn't like that much."

She laughs. "Of course, they didn't. The last lawyer you walked in there with was Otto Pym."

"He does tend to scare the panties off of cops."

"We should celebrate."

"I have been working on some ideas to incorporate those fuzzy cuffs again."

She grins. "Oh?"

"Race you to the bedroom."

43

JUNE

Now that the cops are no longer breathing down our necks, things settle down a little bit. It's nice to not constantly look over my shoulder. Part of me kept thinking one of the detectives would just show up someplace I was. But with no video, no harassment.

Now is the time to focus on me. And in the realm of me, things are a little sideways. I have no job. I haven't seen my friends in a long while. And my father has struck a friendship with the man who kidnapped me.

Not that he knew that last part before they became friends. But still.

I've always known my father was opportunist. He's a con artist. It's in their blood. But using me to make contact with somebody that he can use was a little bit beyond my scope. It's awkward to admit I didn't see it coming. That trick with having one of his work buddies fake my e-mail? That was genius.

And now I have to yell at him for being a genius.

I arrange to meet him at my old apartment. It was his mother-in-law's place, so he knows the address. There's no way I'm meeting him at our place. I don't want him to be familiar with where I live. A shameful state of affairs for a father and daughter, but it's true. I have no doubt that if he thought he could get money from Anderson, he'd figure away. He used me for contact with Andre. Why wouldn't he do the same with my fiancé?

It's been quite a while since I've been back. The air inside smells a little stale, so I opened up the windows. It's raining again. And cold. Winter in Boston. But at least the air is fresh.

I tidy up the place just to make sure that everything is in order. Not that I'm worried about impressing my father, but I still want the place to be neat when he shows up. I also pack another bag of clothes. I've been running out of things at our place.

I don't know when I stopped thinking of it as Anderson's place and started thinking of it as ours. But I'm glad for it.

Dad shows up, looking dapper as ever. He smiles as he moseys around. "Your granny would be happy with how you've kept the place."

"Thanks. Want a drink?"

"I'll take a bottle of water if you've got one."

"Coming right up." I dash to the kitchen.

He says, "Given our last conversation, I wasn't exactly expecting an invitation."

"Well, there are things that we need to talk about," I tell him as I walk in with the waters. One for him and one for me. As much as I'd like alcohol for this conversation, I don't think it's a great idea.

"So what is it you'd like to talk about, Junebug?"

"How much of what Andre had me doing for him was your doing?"

That earns a frown. "I'm not sure what you mean."

"He had me looking into the properties owned by Elliott West. He wanted to buy up those properties out from under him." I look him in the eye. "He wanted to ruin the man."

"And what about all of that makes you think I had anything to do with it?"

If he had given me a flat-out denial, I would have thought it was a lie. Asking questions? He didn't know about it. Good. "Just checking."

"I don't imagine that's all that's on your mind."

"Not hardly." I shift in my seat, uncomfortable right now. I've never liked confronting my father. But if we're going to have any kind of a relationship, I have to be able to do that. "I need you to tell me why it is that you want Andre's account."

"I already told you. I need to land a big account."

"Why him? There are hundreds of other CEOs in Boston, and even more in Manhattan, that you could have easily gone for. But you pursued Andre. Viciously, I might add, considering you used me to do it."

It's subtle, but I see his fingers twitch. Dad never twitches.

"So Andre used you against the father of your boyfriend?"

"He did."

"And that makes him a bad guy ... " He strokes his chin.

"Where are you going with this?"

For a moment, he hems and haws. But then he admits, "I may not have been entirely forthcoming about my connections to Andre Moeller."

"No shit. So tell me what you're up to."

"Well, it's not completely on the up and up, and I don't want to get you tangled up in it. Let's just say if things go the way that I want them to, he'll be real angry. And since he's a bad guy, that's a good thing, right?"

I frown at him. "Dad, just tell me what's going on. For once in your life, be straight with me."

He smirks a little. "Well, it is kind of a genius plan, and I haven't been able to talk to anybody about it, so that would be nice."

"Go on."

"One of the more interesting facets of life that I've discovered since being outside of prison is the amount of interesting things you can do with a computer."

"You mean like faking my e-mail?"

His smirk grows into a full smile. "I mean digital fraud."

"Yeah, the e-mail—"

But he shakes his head. "That was small potatoes compared to what I'm talking about. Back at HQ, we've got these real smart guys. And smart girls. They know all about those advanced algorithms and bots and a bunch of other stuff that they yammer on about that I don't understand. And some of them came to me with an idea."

Oh hell. "What idea?"

"Now don't go getting an attitude. This has a very high success rate."

He must have said that to himself about every scam he'd run until now. It's funny. I'm pretty sure the first con that any con man pulls is on themselves to convince themselves their crazy plans will work. "Just tell me."

"Alright, see, what I do is, I sell Andre on a big advertising push online. And I mean big. We're talking in the millions. And my tech friends, they generate a bunch of false traffic using their algorithms and bots and whatever so that it looks like the website is getting an inordinate amount of hits. It inflates the web traffic. All the ad views go way up. His advertisers, marketers, they don't know what's going on other than it's working."

I don't quite follow him. "And that makes *you* money?"

"Well, sure. I come off looking like a marketing genius. More importantly, because of the way that we set up the contract, we get a cut every single time somebody clicks. Even if we made that somebody up."

Yeah, that's fraud. "That's one hell of a gamble."

"It gets better. Andre, being Andre, is happy to recommend me to any of his friends who might need some online marketing help. I get in good with his friends. I get their accounts. Soon, a little project getting us a few million is a big project getting us tens of millions of dollars, maybe more." He grins. "Now my little techie friends there, they know all about digital marketing platforms and networks and all that good stuff. They do the back end. I take care of the front end."

"You're the salesman."

He nods. "I do what comes naturally. I make friends."

"And use them to steal from them."

"Now, now, I'm not stealing from Andre. Though given how he's treated you, I don't think you could really be mad at me for that. Mostly we're stealing from the advertisers."

"I can't believe you still have your job."

He laughs. "Of course I do. I'm in sales. The first thing you ever sell is yourself."

In the grand scheme of things, it doesn't really matter. Dad is Dad. If he's breathing, he's scheming. I am genuinely unsure what to do with that. I can't trust him. But I know it. With him being close to Andre, maybe I can use that if I need to.

"Granny always said you were a real piece of work."

He laughs hard. "That woman always hated me. Even before I gave her a reason to."

"Sometimes you just know when somebody's up to no good."

"Ah, now, Junebug, you're going to hurt my feelings."

"Is that even possible?"

His laughter fades away. He looks me in the eyes. "It is. You did a good job of it last time we spoke."

"Was I wrong?"

"It's good to see you." A swift dodge as ever.

I'd like to be able to say that it's good to see him too. I'm just not sure. "So this whole time you were trying to get to know me was actually you trying to get in good with Andre, right?"

"I'm a networker. Things for me are never that black or white. The world is full of grey."

His words struck a nerve. "You're right about that, Dad."

44

JUNE

So I don't have a job. Who needs a career anyway?

I do. Damn it.

Maybe I shouldn't be getting my self-esteem from my job. Maybe I should have a better sense of my intrinsic self-worth. But the fact of the matter is, I like having a job. I like being respected by my colleagues. I like feeling valued at my place of employment. I enjoy impressing clients.

So, sitting at home and taking care of the small apartment isn't quite enough for me.

It would be one thing if we had kids to take care of. But sitting around, surrounded by these four walls— four admittedly beautiful walls in an amazing apartment building—but still, it's not … it's not the same as having a job. Or even a hobby.

Somehow I have managed to read almost every book on my TBR list, a task social media would have me believe is impossible. I've started hitting the gym in the apartment building twice a day. I've even watched some of the cooking shows that Anderson was hooked on during his recuperation, but I still can't get sucked into them. That is firmly a *him* thing.

Maybe I'm going stir-crazy. Or just crazy, crazy. I'm not sure.

Weirdly enough, I've started to come to grips with who my father is. And the fact that he's defrauding Andre is kind of funny, given what that sociopathic bastard has put me through. I wouldn't exactly call it closure, but it might be closure-adjacent. Whatever it is, it feels like that chapter of my life is complete.

Given that it's complete, what the hell else can I do with my time?

I was already short on options when I went to work for Andre in the first place. Elliott West had gone scorched earth on me before then, and it seems pointless now to try and find work when I'm on everyone's blacklist. It's funny. Thanks to my soon-to-be father-in-law, I can't get a job and must depend on his son more, which is antithetical to what he wants.

Well, he did that to himself.

I don't depend on Anderson just financially. Every day, when he comes home, I feel like one of those new moms who's excited to talk to an actual adult. He walks in, and I take his coat and hang it on the rack. "How was your day, sweetie?"

"Fine, thanks. No new news from the cops, so that's always good."

"Glad to hear it. Ready for dinner?"

"Oh, who did we order from this time?"

I give him a mock scowl. "No one. I actually made dinner. I can cook, you know."

He smiles at that. "Then I look forward to trying your dinner. What did you make?"

"Nothing fancy. Just pork schnitzel, homemade applesauce, and coleslaw."

His lips part in a gasp. But then his brow furrows. "You made applesauce?"

"The store had some Braeburns that smelled really good. Didn't make sense to buy premade." I trot off to the kitchen. "I also picked up a bottle of Riesling to go with the German-themed dinner. You hungry?"

"I'm pretty sure my stomach has an erection right now, so yes."

I snort a laugh. "What?"

"That meal sounds amazing. I was wondering why the apartment smelled so good."

"Don't get too excited, I haven't made schnitzel since I was a girl."

"How come I'm getting it now? What's the special occasion?"

I shake my head. "Nothing all that special, really. Talking to my dad the other day made me think about Granny. Pork schnitzel was one of her favorite things to make." I portion out our plates and get us set up on the kitchen island-slash-breakfast bar while he changes into his lounge pants and a tee shirt. "I know we normally eat in front of the TV, but you kind of need a fork and knife for this. Oh, the bread." I duck to the oven to get it out.

"You made bread?"

"Well, we got you that stand mixer when you were doing all of that cooking, and it hadn't been used in a while, so I figured I'd give it a shot."

After I slice the bread and bring over the butter, he looks at me funny.

"Why are you looking at me like that?"

"First of all, that smells and looks amazing. Secondly, we really need to get you a job, don't we?"

I laugh, but it's only to hold back the tears. I'm so relieved that he understands. "Yeah."

He pulls me onto his lap, wrapping me in his big, muscular arms. "I am sorry that my father fucked you over so bad. We will make this right."

"That sounds great and all, but I don't understand how. Your father hates me. He keeps trying to make you break up with me." I shrug. "I don't think that there's any way we can fix that."

"First of all, we should eat. Once we have full stomachs, we can have full brains and come up with a plan."

"Is that your polite way of telling me to get off of your lap so you can eat?"

"Baby, it just looks so good, and I'm afraid I'm going to start drooling on you."

I giggle and go to my chair, and we dig in. "There's sauerkraut if you want some. I never got a taste for it, but I figured it goes with the meal if you like it."

"I prefer my fermented cabbage kimchi style. I like the spice."

I'm not sure how to say what I want to say. "You're right about me needing something to do during the day. I would prefer to be able to contribute to the household one way or another."

"You're cooking and cleaning. I can't ask for more than that."

"You know what I mean. Either financially. Or domestically."

"I just said—"

"I was thinking more domestically."

His brow drops. "You lost me."

"For all intents and purposes, the case is over. We can start living our lives now. It's not out of the realm of possibilities for us to consider having a child. We've talked about it before."

He smiles, but it's tentative. "I absolutely love where your head's at."

"But?"

"No, *but*. That said—"

"Fancy *but*."

He smirks. "Yes, fancy *but*. I think things are still too up in the air at the moment."

"I had a feeling you'd say that. And you're right. But it is on my mind."

"Mine too. It's a big part of why I want all of this behind us." He takes my hand in his. "I am overwhelmingly thrilled that I get to start a family with you. If I could start that tonight, I would. But I don't think we're in a good situation for it just yet. Soon. As soon as possible."

"I'd like that."

He gives my hand a squeeze, and we go back to eating. "Are we good?"

"Why wouldn't we be?"

"That's a touchy subject. I was hoping that I handled it to your satisfaction."

I smile warmly at him. "I'm touched that you're trying to be sensitive. But I'm good. You handled it just right."

He breathes a sigh of relief. "I never would have pegged you for baby fever."

"I wouldn't say I have baby fever."

He grins. "Says the woman who was looking at baby clothes last night."

I laugh at him. "So you knew this was coming?

"Or you could just call it intuition."

"Nope, you already let the cat out of the bag. Now I know my fiancé spies on my computer."

"You were sitting right next to me. I was looking down your shirt. I happened to glance at the screen —"

I giggle. "I'm not mad, Anderson. I think it's funny. Wait, you were looking down my shirt?"

"Well, I was trying to, but you were wearing one of those high-collar crewneck T-shirts. Don't be surprised if those things disappear out of your laundry. It's impossible to check out your tits in them."

"Don't you dare! They're very comfortable."

"We will see."

After supper, we go to the living room for our usual routine of scrolling online while watching TV. But he pulls me against him, so I have to lay my head on his shoulder. He kisses the top of my head and murmurs, "I really am glad you're thinking about babies. I hope I didn't make you think otherwise."

"I'm fine. You don't have to try to make me feel better about not thinking it's the right time —"

"Maybe I'm not." He sighs. "Pretty sure I'm trying to convince myself of it."

I sit up to look at him. "Really?"

He nods. "I've wanted to start a family with you for a long time, baby. If things were different, I'd have already made it happen."

"Right, well, the cops —"

"It's not entirely about them." He rakes his fingers through his lush, dark hair. "It's my father."

"How so?"

"You're right about him. He doesn't see you the way that I do. I think it's time we change that."

I laugh. That asshole has hated me from day one. Changing his mind about me would be impossible by now. "How do you propose we do that?"

"A little work, a little luck, and a PowerPoint presentation."

"You can't be serious."

He smiles. "I'm not." Then he pulls me close again, and I nuzzle into him. "It'll be the raw documents."

"Please tell me you're joking."

"When it comes to dealing with my father, I do not joke."

I exhale worry and inhale potential trauma. This should be fun.

"I t won't be that bad," he swears as we ride the elevator up to his father's floor. "Think of him like a judge you need to impress who maybe doesn't like you."

"Judge, jury, and executioner, you mean."

"You're being dramatic."

I cock a brow at him, and that shuts him up. "Given your father's illustrious reputation in certain circles, am I really?"

We had agreed not to speak about his father's illegal underworld dealings inside the building unless Elliot brought it up first. We didn't know who knew what or what rooms could have been bugged, so it seemed prudent. But when I said what I said, he knew what I meant.

"Well, he did kill your career, so you're entitled to your opinion."

"Gee, thanks for your permission."

Anderson sighs at me. "You know what I mean."

"And you know what I mean."

Things had been like this since he suggested we meet with Elliot. I love Anderson with my whole heart and soul. I love him more than myself, truly. So, the painful hold he allows his father to have over him absolutely kills me. It's beyond unhealthy. It's straight-up abusive. From what he's told me, it always has been.

Elliot West is a cold, distant man who treats people like objects instead of human beings. I felt that way before I learned he was some kind of mafia don, and learning that has not improved my opinion of him. I've always been the kind of person to give the benefit of the doubt, but when someone fucks me over, I will cling to my grudge until it no longer serves to remind me who they are.

But I am not sure about this particular grudge. Does it serve me any longer?

Yes, he was an absentee father to Anderson and his brother Cole. But, given what he does, maybe that made sense to him. If he had been warm and kind to his sons, his enemies might have used them against him. Or he probably thinks being icy to his sons helps them in some toxic masculinity sort of way.

Should I even try to give the benefit of the doubt to a man who has ordered people to be murdered? Probably not. But, since he is going to be my father-in-law one day, I need to make peace with him. If for no other reason than he is going to be my children's grandfather, who also happens to be loaded.

College is expensive, and sometimes, we have to do what we have to do.

I almost shake my head at myself for thinking that. Here I am, giving him shit for thinking of people as tools, and I am doing the same thing. But at least I've never ordered the murder of another human being. I'm still morally ahead of him for now.

But if he keeps pissing me off, that might change.

Anderson waves his hand in front of my face. "You in there?" The elevators doors are open. I'm not sure how long they've been open.

"Yeah," I tell him, smiling brightly. "Let's do this."

He leads me through the floor. It's not much of a maze, but I'm glad I have a guide. The place is beautiful, with all high-end furniture and flattering lighting on warm wooden surfaces. But I don't let the beauty fool me. We are here for one reason and one reason only.

Change the mind of an underworld boss.

When I told myself I needed a hobby, this was not what I had in mind.

We stroll hand in hand toward an old woman at a desk. She smiles at Anderson, gives me the once over, and then smiles when she sees our hands joined. "Laddie, you get yourself in some trouble here, eh?"

He grins down at her. "Margaret, this is June Devlin, my fiancée."

"Oh, blessed be," she says in her Irish accent. "Your father is the one in trouble, then, for not telling me."

"He's a private man when it comes to family. You know that."

"Aye, but he's still in trouble. No shortbread for him this week—"

Anderson gives a teasing gasp, clutching at his chest. "No, not the shortbread!"

She snickers at his acting. "Maybe just one because you're being kind about it. Go on in, laddie. He's ready for you."

"Thank you, Margaret."

I try to get a word in edgewise. "Nice to meet you."

"Oh, you too, dear." During the entire interaction, the woman never stopped typing.

Anderson opens the big dark door behind Margaret's desk. "After you."

"Coward."

He smirks, and I walk past him into a room better suited to hang meat in than to be an office. It's got an office temperature technically, but the whole room is so cold I worry about frostbite. Everything is hard and gray. The huge view, the furniture, the walls, all of it. Nothing looks comfortable. No warmth anywhere.

Of course, this is where Elliot West works. The man is allergic to humanity.

But that assessment didn't track with the woman outside. She clearly has a history with Anderson — there is too much affection between them for that to be based on anything but a long-term relationship. Which means she's worked for Elliot for that time ... how could he want to hire someone like her?

The man is an oddity who is staring at me as I enter his office. It's like being stared at by a snake. There's nothing behind the eyes. "Hello, June. Anderson. Take a seat." He gestures to the pair of guest chairs in front of his desk.

Anderson warned me they are terrible to sit on, so when I find my seat worse than he told me, it's a surprise. Like sitting on pricy cardboard, but without all the support.

"Thank you for meeting with us, Dad—"

Elliot holds a hand up to silence him. To my surprise, it works. Anderson really must want him to like me. His father says, "I agreed to this meeting because you said you want to enlighten me about some facts I do not have regarding June. Given my last directive to you was to dismiss her from your life, I am curious to see what it is you think you could possibly tell me that would dissuade me from having her accosted by security, seeing as you did not mention she would be in attendance."

"You didn't tell him I was coming?"

Anderson smiles. "Thought it would be a nice surprise for him."

I almost laugh at that. I would if I weren't also pissed off.

Elliot sighs disdainfully. "My son has a taste for dramatics that he gets from his mother. But since you did not know he was springing you on me, I'll hold off on calling security. For now."

"First of all, Dad, you need to know that no matter what comes of this meeting, I am with June. Period. She is my partner, and one day, she will be my wife. I love her. We are together. That is not up for debate or discussion. We aren't here to ask your permission to be together. We are here to mend fences, if possible. That is the scope of this meeting."

The elder West sits back regarding his son. "Funny you think to lay down the law in my office when I could easily have security remove you both. Considering the situation, I'd think you're practically begging me to do so."

"Why security, Elliot?"

"You know very well why, June. You're a spy. From the sound of things, you've either seduced my son into denial or convinced him to join you—"

"That's where you're wrong," Anderson says, standing. He passes his father the folder with the documents. "I'm no more a spy than June is. These are from Andre Moeller's office. We broke in there — sort of — and stole them."

"Do tell how you *sort of* break into an office, son."

"We had the key."

Elliot grunts at that and peruses the documents. "And I am supposed to see — wait." He studies one further. "These are in my aliases."

I nod. "That's right, sir."

Anderson says, "She didn't know. Not about any of it. You put your alias on the documents, and there was no way for June to know any of this was tied to you."

"I had no idea any of this was going on." I sigh at myself. "Andre used me. On more than one occasion. The first time, kidnapping me to make you feel weak. Now this, using me to ruin you. A way to rub salt in the wound that someone close to you had been the one to help him." I can hardly control the tone of my voice, I'm so angry when I speak. "He has been nothing but a thorn in my side from the moment I met him — "

"Then why did you go to work for him after your kidnapping if it was a true kidnapping?" he rumbles.

I snap, "To piss you off."

He blinks in surprise. Then he laughs sharply. "Is that right?"

"You hurt me. You hurt Anderson. I wanted a way to hurt you back. But I never dreamed he'd use me like this. It wasn't even on my radar—I thought just working for him would be enough to piss you off. It's hard to admit it, but I never saw this coming."

Elliot takes a deep breath, looking from me to Anderson and then the papers again. "And you two are together, no matter what comes of this, as he said?"

I bob my head as Anderson takes my hand. "You may not like me, Elliot. Hell, you may hate me. That's up to you. But that doesn't change how I feel about Anderson. I love him. Always. Come rain or come shine. I cannot wait to be his wife and start that part of our lives together. He's my person, and I am his."

The smile on Anderson's face makes me go all warm and fuzzy inside.

"I see," Elliot says flatly. "If—"

"No, I don't think you do," I cut him off. "Like I said, you can hate me forever. But I am dedicated to making this right and making some sort of relationship with you work. If that's pointless, fine. I don't care. But I want our kids to have a good relationship with you and Kitty."

He shifts in his seat. I'm pretty sure he is uncomfortable with my honesty, and I kind of love that. "Fine, fine. I'll consider what you've both said. You may go."

46

ANDERSON

It makes no sense, but as we leave Dad's office, somehow, my bones feel lighter. In fact, it's easier to stand straight, even though I've always had good posture. Miraculously, the world looks … different. Brighter. Better.

Is this what relief feels like?

"Why are you smiling like that?" June asks as we get into my car.

Didn't know I was, but when I look in the mirror, she's right. I'm practically grinning. "I think … I think I feel good."

She chuckles. "Why wouldn't you?"

"No, I mean … " It takes me a moment to put together the words. In some ways, it makes no sense for me to care this much, but I do. Perhaps we all have that inner child, always seeking their parents' approval of their partner. "Having cleared your name and the air with Dad, I feel good. Like, really, inexplicably good. Like I'm not weighed down anymore."

"Was I really such a burden?"

I laugh, shaking my head. "I don't mean it like that, baby. He knows everything now. Whatever he decides to do with that knowledge, it's on him. If he writes me out of the will, if he opens his arms to you, it's his choice. He has all the facts, and if he uses them to be cruel, there's nothing I can say or do to change that, but also, if he does, then Mom and Cole will judge him harshly for it. I think that's what's always been missing from my family."

"Their judgment?"

"Consequences for his actions." I start the car and pull out of the space to get us on the road, taking my time with everything. Now that I'm unburdened, the tension is gone from my neck and shoulders, and I have to adjust my seat and mirror positioning to make up for the change.

I had no idea how much this stress had affected me until it was gone.

I explain, "Dad has always been able to do whatever he wanted and expected us to fall in line. The times we didn't, *we* were the ones in trouble. Now that he has no excuses to be such an asshat to you and me, if he doesn't straighten up, I feel confident they will tell him all about it."

"If—"

"More importantly," I interrupt to save her from saying something wrong, "he likes you."

She laughs bitterly. "What?"

"He does. He won't say it now, and he may never say the words out loud, but he does. Otherwise, he would have had security escort us out. Don't expect an apology … ever. But he would have made his feelings known if he still held that grudge against you."

She licks her lips, deep in thought. "So, you're practically giddy because your father did not have us taken away by security?"

"Yes."

"You have a shockingly low bar for what makes a positive interaction with your father."

I snort a laugh. "Are you kidding? That was the best meeting I've ever had with the man."

"Then let me reiterate what I just said."

"This is good news, June. Be positive. We should celebrate. Stop trying to snatch defeat from the jaws of victory."

"You cannot think that was a positive meeting—"

"It was!"

She face palms. "Okay, then tell me you're not planning to parent our own children that way."

"Oh, hell no."

"Thank god!" she says, laughing.

I smirk and drive us toward a nice pub I like on this side of town. "There will be no passive-aggressive shit, no jumping through hoops for our approval, no arbitrary punishments, none of that. The bar is in hell for my father, but I plan to hold myself to a far higher standard. And you."

She gives my thigh a squeeze. "Same."

"We won't be perfect. I'm not naïve enough to think so. No parents are perfect. But my folks have given me a pretty good road map of how not to be."

"Your dad, sure, but I love your mom."

It warms me to hear that. "So do I, but she's not perfect, either."

"How so?"

"She enables Dad's bullshit. Always has. Sometimes, she tries to rein him in, but it never amounts to much. He's too dominant for her to manage. I wish she had more influence over him, but she doesn't."

June counters, "On the other hand, imagine how bad he'd be without her around to rein him in. I have a feeling Kitty polishes his sharper edges."

The thought of Dad without Mom around is a bleak one. "For the love of Boston, I hope he dies before she does. The world does not need him in it without her around."

"Hard agree," she says, nodding.

I park just outside of Clair's. "Thought we could get a drink to celebrate if you're up for it."

"Sounds good."

Clair's is a black façade-fronted hole-in-the-wall of a pub, complete with hardwood floors, green interior walls, and a copper tile ceiling. It smells like old beer and spilled whiskey, and the fireplace in the back corner is always burning in winter. The furniture is worn from too many butts and elbows. The server catches our order as we take off our scarves.

In short, it's lovely.

I ask June, "So, how many?"

She gives me a confused brow. "Well, I thought I'd start with *one* single-malt—"

"No, sorry." I'm in too good of a mood to stay on track, apparently. "How many kids do you want?"

June's surprised laugh makes me smile. "I don't know. I've never been pregnant before, and I don't know how my body will handle it. If it goes badly … I don't want to say a number."

"But if it goes well?"

A shy smile creeps over her lips. "I'm not sure. I kind of love the idea of having four or five of our own. Maybe more."

The hesitation in her tone reminds me of when we talk about sex. She's too worried about my opinion to say what she really wants. So, I call her on it. "Did you say four or five because you thought a higher number would freak me out?"

Her smirk sends me. What did I ever do to deserve seeing that expression on her perfect face? She admits, "Maybe."

"How many do you actually want?"

"I don't—"

"June!"

She huffs. "At least six. I think."

Wow, holy shit. But I keep my expression placid—

"See?" she asks, pointing at me. That's why I didn't want to say it! You look horrified!"

I laugh, too excited to do much else. "I'm not, actually. The thought of … " I take a breath to keep my erection from tearing through my trousers. "The thought of seeing you, swollen with my child inside of you … " My mouth is dry. Is it hot in here?

The server delivers our drinks, and I slug mine back in one go, ordering another. When she leaves, I lean in and quietly tell June, "If we weren't in a place I love, I'd take you to that bathroom and get you pregnant right here, right now."

June's cheeks flush pink. "I thought it was too soon for that kind of thing."

"It is. It really is. And I have to keep reminding myself of that, or I will do something inadvisable. I have to think about this strategically, or I'll lose my mind trying to knock you up. I'll never let you out of the bed. So, it's a good thing my second drink is almost here." The server delivers the next one, and I take my time with it. Her cheeks have darkened by the time I'm sipping. "What is it?"

Her words are almost a whisper. "The thought of being tied to the bed for you to use whenever you feel like, it … "

A growl escapes me before I can catch it. My throat is completely dry, but now I'm worried about making a wet spot on my trousers. "Saying things like that when we are too far from home to do anything about them is cruel, young lady."

She nibbles her bottom lip as she half-smirks, and I'm going to have to punish her for that later. But I'm certain she'll enjoy it. "Guess we'll have to negotiate all of that when we get home."

If she keeps this up, I will drag her to the bathroom, regardless of wanting to come back to Clair's. I have to switch gears. "Erm, so our wedding—

She laughs. "That was one hell of a non sequitur."

"Entirely your own fault. I have to change topics, or we will jump to the baby-making right now." I rake my fingers through my hair, desperate for any change in stimulus. My cock is still aching for her attention. "Are you still up for eloping?"

Her head bobs enthusiastically. "I want our wedding day to be about us. Given your father's side work, I don't want it to become a day of business deals between him and our guests, and I suspect that's how it would be. I have no desire to have my father walk me down the aisle—we're only barely back on speaking terms, and I never dreamed of that in the first place. My mom will probably be bummed, but it's not like she's a big part of my life, so really, the only person I'm worried about disappointing is your mom, but you don't seem too worried about that."

I shake my head, grateful for talking about our parents. Thinking of them kills my boner. "She won't like it, but given our situation, I think she'll understand. Besides, I'm not getting married to make them happy. I'm doing it because I want to marry you. The truth is, I wasn't sure I'd ever marry—"

"Why?"

Time for a little truth, I guess. "June, I have been in love with you since we met. I know I didn't show it, but I was. Before we started seeing each other, I figured I'd never get married because no one else could live up to the fantasy of you in my head. The thought of marrying someone else didn't feel fair—like I'd be setting them up for failure. I certainly didn't want to have kids with someone else." Tears glisten in her eyes, and it sends a rush of panic through me, so I take her hand in mine. "Did I say something wrong?"

But she smiles and wipes a tear away. "No. You said a lot of things right."

That must have been relief I felt earlier, because I feel it again now. I give her hand a gentle squeeze before sitting properly. "You're it for me. Now and always."

"You are, too, you know."

"Good to know."

"Courthouse good for you?"

I nod. "Just need to make it official, right?"

"Yeah." She pauses nervously. "Soon?"

"Yes."

47

JUNE

For what I hope is the very last time in my life, I slept in and woke up alone. I'm lazing in bed, smiling to myself. It's silly. But after deciding that today would be the day we get married, Anderson and I decided to spend the night apart.

So I'm actually in my very own bed alone for the first time in months. Part of me missed it. Getting to stretch out is a luxury of sorts. But trying to fall asleep without him next to me last night was hell. Burying myself next to him in the sheets to absorb his warmth at night has become a vital part of my nighttime routine. I'm spoiled.

And tonight, I will get to go to sleep next to my husband.

When I sit up looking around at my old apartment, it feels incomplete without him. Not that we spent all that much time here together. Technically, this was Granny's old apartment. It always felt that way. Sort of like I was just caretaking for the place, even though I lived here for years. But it never felt like mine.

His apartment has become *our* apartment, but I want to find a place for the two of us. A place that we pick out together. I'm so excited to start our new life as a married couple. But today, being the last morning of my alleged freedom, I've decided to take my time getting ready.

We aren't inviting any of our friends or our family to the ceremony. Hell, who would come on a Thursday anyway? They all have work. But it's kind of perfect that way—I feel a little less guilty for not inviting anyone. Today will be just another day for everyone else. And for me, it'll be the most important day of our life, and we have it all to ourselves.

I crawl from the bed and head for the shower. My old stuff is in here. Shampoo, conditioner, soap, all that. I never bothered to cart it over to our place. Strange to see that the bottles are dusty.

As I wash my hair, I miss feeling his fingers do it for me. Anderson is startlingly good at washing my hair. But that's a part of why we decided to spend last night apart. When he washed my hair, our shower turned into something else. Without fail.

We had booked an appointment at the courthouse for four online. No chance of being on time if he had washed my hair.

Once out of the shower, the real work begins. I'm not hiring a stylist for this. That sort of defeats the purpose of keeping things as *just us*. Plus, it would feel like cheating since he isn't doing anything overtly special to be prettier today.

Like he needs it. I roll my eyes at the thought, which makes me have to start over on my mascara.

It is so weird to think of Anderson as mine. He's just too handsome. Way out of my league. He always has been. I have no idea how we ended up together when I think about it. Hopefully, we'll be married fifty years before he figures that out. Pretty sure they don't grant divorces after that long. Marital law was never my thing in college, so I might have that wrong.

I consider a classic red lip that would look great in pictures, but I want to be able to kiss my husband without worrying about him wearing it too, so I opt for a nude gloss instead. In fact, I've kept my whole look simple.

My frizzy brown hair has somehow decided to cooperate with the smoothing products I grabbed on my way here, and my curls are doing that pretty, fresh-out-of-bed thing I'd always wished they would do. I'd splurged on the pricy stuff, and apparently, that has paid off.

On my way home last night, I picked out a dress in a boutique window. It's nothing fancy. In fact, it is pointedly minimal. A white satin A-line dress with long sleeves and a sweetheart neckline that looks demure but has a scandalous slit up the thigh. There's something about it that makes me think if it were red or black, a Bond villainess would wear this dress. Classic, yet modern. Sexy, yet naughty. I fell for the thing the moment I saw it.

I have a pair of nude heels to not distract from the dress, and once everything is on, the butterflies go double time in my stomach. Eating feels like it's out of the question. How does anyone do this when they're expecting everyone they know to show up? My nerves are bad enough, and it'll just be us.

But when I check my look in the mirror, I'm stunned. This isn't me. This is the me I always want to be, but never bother to put the time into becoming. I look like someone who belongs on Anderson's arm, and I'm so excited to see him I could vomit.

Okay, maybe I'm not the classy gal he deserves, but I'm the one he chose.

My stomach roils, and I realize I have to eat, so I take the dress off and throw my pajamas back on. It was too soon to be dressed and ready anyway, but I was too excited and got ahead of myself. Plus, now I know what it'll look like when the time comes, which is a relief. I had tried the dress on at the boutique, but without the right undergarments, it looked wrong.

Padding out to my kitchen, I remember I haven't been here in a while. What the hell do I have for food that won't give me botulism? As it turns out, not much. Every dairy product is far past its prime, so when I —

Ice cream.

Immediately, I throw open the freezer and dig out my stash of ice creams. Vanilla, chocolate, mint chocolate chip, and rocky road are all here to rescue me. "Hello, boys," I purr as I pull them out. They had been my boyfriends between breakups for so very long. I'd missed them. Anderson doesn't usually keep sweets in the house, save for his weird marshmallow protein bars he considers acceptable candy bars.

I have to work on that man.

Scooping out a healthy dollop of each makes for an oddly colored bowl of heaven that is tied together only when I drizzle chocolate syrup over the mounds. The first bite is mind-blowing utter bliss, and digging my way through the bowl as I Netflix up a horror movie brings back too many good memories.

And bad ones.

This was what I used to do when I was single and bored. Or taken and bored. In fact, it was pretty much my nightly routine unless I had someplace to be. Ice cream and horror movies go well together, but after so many years of doing it out of habit, it made me numb to the world around me. Which may have been the point.

I was so unhappy with my old life, but I'd talked myself into believing it was serviceable because I wasn't hurting anyone, and no one was hurting me. As if that's the standard of a good life.

Holy crap, was I depressed back then?

I set the half-empty bowl aside and turned the TV off. It was like my old life didn't sit right with me anymore. It no longer fit who I was. The ice cream tasted good, and the horror movie was entertaining, but I wasn't their target audience anymore.

I like the healthy food we eat at home. Okay, I hate protein bars, but if I need something sweet, I usually eat fruit, and I feel better for it. Anderson is a big baby when it comes to horror movies, but that's probably because his real life has been horrific enough that it's not entertaining for him and having lived with him, I get it. Seeing people shot on screen is very different after having dealt with my fiancé's gunshot wound and recovery for months. My suspension of disbelief is another casualty of that incident.

Thanks to Anderson, I've changed. A lot. And I'm okay with that. In fact, I love it.

We've made each other better in so many ways. Aside from my own changes, he smiles more now than when we got together. It's unguarded these days, as though he couldn't fully smile back then, or he'd risk someone's judgment.

Likely his father's.

And that's another thing that's changed. At least, according to Anderson. I still don't know if I believe his father likes me now, but, in the grand scheme of things, it doesn't matter.

Today, I am marrying Anderson West, and there is not a damn thing anyone can do to stop me.

48

ANDERSON

I've always had an appreciation for a black-on-black suit, but today, even that does not feel formal enough for our casual ceremony. In fact, nothing feels good enough for marrying June. God knows I'm not.

I still cannot believe she wants to marry me. It's like a dream. Hopefully, nothing turns it into a nightmare.

Without her at my side last night, that was all I had. One after another. Embarrassingly, I woke up cuddled on her pillow after I'd pulled it next to me as a poor imitation of her. It was the first thing I fixed this morning. Didn't want her coming home thinking I'd had my way with her pillow in her stead.

I made coffee, and as I stirred the dark liquid, I fell back into the memory of those nightmares. My father, showing up at the courthouse to stop us from getting married, so I could marry the daughter of one of his associates instead. Some enemy of his, spraying June's white dress red with bullets as she said, "I do." Or, my favorite one—the judge telling us he wouldn't marry us as a favor to my father because he revoked his approval of June.

No need for a Freudian interpretation of my dreams. I feared my father ruining my future happiness with June, one way or another. Probably because he had tried so often to do precisely that.

In the light of day, I knew those things were highly unlikely to happen. But that didn't do much to shake the nightmares from replaying in my mind.

So, I hit the gym to work out my nervous energy. Since the apartment building has a decent one, I don't have to travel far to sweat it out. Cranking up the tunes to the grungiest punk music always helped clear my mind when I lifted or ran on the treadmill, so that is the plan. But after two hours of brutalizing my body, I remember I have wedding night duties to perform. I slow the treadmill to a stop and wipe everything down before I leave.

The blonde who flirts with me walks in. I only notice because, despite my apartment building being full, the gym is empty in the middle of a Thursday. She saunters my way, smiling.

Crap.

"Haven't seen you in a while, Anderson."

"Been busy."

"Too busy to spot me?"

The last time she asked for a spot, she made sure to arch her back unnecessarily as she benched just to flash me more cleavage. I feel bad for the girl. She is very pretty—like a Swedish bikini model. Surely, there are other guys out there for her.

I smile apologetically. "Yeah, sorry. If I don't get cleaned up, I'll be late to my own wedding, and that's no way to start a marriage. Excuse me."

Her bright blue eyes widen. "You're getting married?"

"This afternoon."

"Oh my god!" She giggles and clutches onto me for a hug. Apparently, she doesn't notice me not hugging her back. "Congratulations!"

"Erm, thanks."

She leans back, looking up at me. "My wife and I would love to have you and the missus over for supper sometime."

My brain reset. "Your wife?"

"Yeah. Viv is always on me about how I don't invite people over." She shrugs awkwardly. "But it's hard to make friends as an adult. You know what I mean?"

"I thought … I would have sworn you hit on me. You gave me your number, and—"

She grins bashfully. "Okay, well yeah, I did. At first. But then Viv and I got back together. All's well that ends well, right? We got married two months ago. Never been happier. You'll love married life."

I chuckle, unsure what to say to all of that. "Can't wait—"

"Oh my goodness, I'm just delaying you. Go get married. Don't let me keep you."

I slowly nod, still wrapping my head around all of that, as I walk into our place. Do I even know the blonde's name? I should learn it. She was distracting enough that I forgot my nightmares for a little while. I owe her for that alone.

I hit the shower, style my hair, and get dressed. I look good, but something still feels missing. It's June. Has to be. Looking at myself in the full-length mirror, I realize I'm standing to the side of the view because I usually stand there with her.

I am so addicted to that woman.

When I get to the courthouse, I breathlessly search the crowd for her, and somehow, when I see her, she takes away the little breath that I have.

June Devlin is utterly stunning.

My heart stutters in my chest at the sight of her, and it's all I can do not to get choked up. When she meets me, I can't hold back the hoarseness in my voice. "You look incredible."

She smiles shyly. "I know."

I laugh, cutting the tension. She giggles, too. But that fades away when I whisper in her ear, "I cannot wait to tear that beautiful dress off of you."

She gasps, faking a shock. "Mr. West, don't you dare! I love this dress!"

"I love how fragile it looks. Perfect for ripping with my teeth."

"You're so bad!"

"And I'm all yours."

She sighs happily. "No backing out, then?"

"Hell no. You?"

She shakes her head, still smiling. "You'll have to pry me off of you if you want to be free of me."

I'm still not sure if she knows how much it means to me when she says things like that.

We wait in the courthouse chapel's anteroom alongside a few other nervous couples. Some wear street clothes, while others are dressed up like us. It's interesting to see what other people are wearing or how they're treating today. I'm surprised to see an elderly couple looking just as nervous as the rest of us. But it's clear they're here to get married, too—they keep giggling at each other and making silly faces to entertain one another. I hope me and June are like them at that age.

This is nothing like the weddings my cousins threw. Big ornate affairs that were more business and performance than romance. I'd hated each and every one of them. So synthetic. It was fine for them — they liked the artifice and having the family's focus on them like that. But it made me uncomfortable to think that was what would be expected of me. To put on a show like some kind of trained animal … just no. In my opinion, a wedding should be for the people getting married. Not everyone else.

One couple in the anteroom seems to not even like each other, but the moment they're called, their lovey-dovey side comes out.

June whispers, "Green card?"

"Unsure. Maybe."

She laces her fingers with mine. "Did you write your vows?"

"Shit. I knew there was something I forgot to do —"

"Anderson!"

I smirk and shake my head. "That's what you get for even asking such a thing, young lady."

She smirks up at me. "Oh, be that way."

"Did you write yours?"

"I am not justifying that question with a response."

I tip my head against hers. "So you forgot, huh?"

She laughs and girl-punches my shoulder. "Just for that, I'm going with the bog standard vows. Nothing fancy. Nothing personal."

"Liar."

They call us, and I thought I'd be more nervous than I am. There's a little of that, but with no Elliot West in sight, what is there to be nervous about? I'm marrying the best person I've ever known.

We face each other in front of a judge in a dressed-up hearing room. There are fake flowers in big vases on either side of him and a few flags lining the walls. Not even a window. It's perfect.

He gets to the part where he asks about vows, and I let her go first. Her nervousness has been rolling off of her in waves, and I figure if she goes first, she'll feel better. June's voice is so pretty when she's emotional. "Last night, I tried to come up with something profound or significant to us. Something personal. But I couldn't, and it took me until this morning to know why. I didn't have you with me. Last night was one of the worst nights of sleep of my life—"

I can't help but laugh and nod.

She smiles and continues, "Because I need you with me. Always. Maybe it's co-dependent or whatever, but you're my person, Anderson West. You make my life better. You make me better. It's like the world is in focus when you're in it, and I want you by my side for every step of life. I promise to love you, to cherish you, and to be your partner in crime from now until forever."

I doubt the judge knows that last part to be absolutely

literal. She gives my hands a squeeze. The judge says, "And now, the groom."

I take a breath to steady myself. "Right now feels like a dream I don't want to wake up from."

Her smile absolutely glows at that.

"That's what life is with you, June. All the hardships we've faced, all the challenges, and the good times, too. None of them feel real because I get to experience them with you, the woman of my dreams. The first breath I ever took was when I saw your face because I finally found my purpose. My first moment of happiness was the first time I made you laugh. Give me your bad hair days, your spilled coffee days, your stubbed toes days, your rotten days at the office. I want to be the one who makes those days better for you the way you do for me."

A shining tear dances down her cheek.

"June Devlin, I am madly, irreversibly in love with you and everything you are and will be. Every day, for the rest of our lives, I will give you all of me. I am yours. Now and always."

I know the judge says something, but I hardly hear him. All I know is her. This woman is my world, and now, the world knows it, too.

"… may kiss the bride."

I'm on her before he can finish the sentence. My wife's lips are soft and sweet, and I want to have my way with her right here and now. A sound like rain catches my ear. No—clapping. It's only then that I remember there are other people in the room. I'd forgotten all about the courtroom witness and the judge.

"Congratulations to the happy couple," the judge says, trying to collect our attention.

We break the kiss, and once the paperwork is complete, we bolt out of there, eager to get home. But my sadistic side has other ideas. That bastard.

On the courthouse steps, I tell her, "Let's go to supper."

"Really? I thought you wanted to get home."

"I do. But I want to take my wife out more."

She beams at that. "I like hearing you call me that, husband."

There is something so erotic about hearing her call me husband. "A quick supper."

She giggles. "Sounds good."

49

JUNE

When Anderson pulls up to Copeland's, it's all I can do not to laugh. This is never going to happen. "What are you thinking? You sneak a look at their reservation list, and we pretend to be another couple to get in?"

"Now, why would I need to do that?"

"It's *Copeland's*! There's a six-week waiting list that you get on only if you know someone. Or bury a body for the Copelands."

He smirks at me and pulls into the valet line.

"Come on. I'm not up for pretending to be other people on my wedding day. I'd be happier getting Chinese from our favorite delivery place than trying to scam our way in here."

But he pulls forward when the valet motions to him.

"Anderson —"

The other valet opens my door. Shit. I guess he's feeling adventurous. Or he's playing some weird version of Chicken with me that I don't understand yet. No matter what else is true, life as Mrs. Anderson West will never be dull.

I step out, and Anderson comes around to my side of the car to take my hand and lead me into the grand old restaurant. One of Boston's original businesses, Copeland's, feels like it's a step outside of time. Wooden floors that must have been refinished a hundred times by now shine under warmly lit chandeliers, heavy with crystal from more than a century ago. The decor is stark — white, black, espresso — and the rest of the lighting is ancient sconces that have been preserved. Despite the stuffy surroundings, though, the live music is jazzy and at ease, playing at just the perfect volume to allow for conversation.

I absorb as much of it as I can right now because we are about to be booted at any moment. I meant what I said in the car — I am not pretending to be someone else on my wedding day. Today, I am officially Mrs. Anderson West, no matter how badly I have always wanted to eat here.

Though I'm not sure if I'll actually change my name. I guess that depends on what the future brings. I'm professionally known as June Devlin. But considering my professional reputation is utter garbage thanks to my father-in-law, it might do me some good to change my last name. Hell, it would probably piss Elliot off to share his last name with me. That's reason enough alone.

We walk up to the tuxedoed maître d, and Anderson gives him a nod. "Gibbs, good to see you."

"Mr. West, Ms. Copeland sends her regards and with them, her finest table. This way." He leads us through the place.

I'm left gathering myself for a quick moment before I struggle to keep up. The table is in a corner by the window with a view of the harbor. We're seated and given menus to peruse for only a moment before our server takes our drink orders. I hadn't thought about how this dress would look when seated, and the slit makes it expose my thigh almost too high, which I kind of like.

Once we finally have a second to breathe, I blink at my husband. "You know the Copelands?"

He shrugs, eyeing his menu. "Gretta Copeland and my mother go way back. I texted her when we got in the car, so she set this up."

The matriarch of the Copelands? Oh my god. "I thought she was a myth."

He laughs. "Hardly. I still remember that old woman's claw pinching my ear when she caught me spying on her granddaughter."

"You did what?" That might have come out a little too loud for our surroundings.

"Cindy is our age. We were nine or ten at the time and getting ready to jump in her pool." He gives a guilty smile. "I was a curious boy, so … "

"You've been naughty since birth, haven't you?"

His laugh is handsome. I'm so lucky. He nods once. "Perhaps I have been."

"And Gretta Copeland caught you? I'm amazed you lived to tell the tale."

"Admittedly, so am I. Gretta Copeland is a delightful menace. Cured me of spying on girls, I can say that much."

"Well, good. You little pervert."

He laughs. "I was curious. It's natural. You can't tell me you never did anything like that when you were a kid."

"I was not a peeping tom when I was a kid. Maybe it's a boy thing. Hell, is there a girl equivalent of a peeping tom?"

"I don't think there is."

"Wait, you said she is a *delightful* menace. She's delightful, how?"

He leans close. "She makes the world's best chocolate chip cookies. They serve them here, allegedly the same recipe, but it's not. She swears it is, but then she gives you this look like you know she's lying. That woman is an enigma."

"Maybe I'll have to make you my chocolate chip cookies and see if I come close."

"You've made them."

I cast an innocent look at my husband. "I made you my mom's recipe. Not mine."

"Oh, devious. Then, by all means, we will go home right now and —"

"Hell no! I am not leaving until I've had their roast and Yorkshire pudding. You could not drag me out of here right now. Oh, and the walnut crème brule."

"As you wish, wife."

Why is hearing him call me *wife* so hot?

Our drinks arrive, and sipping my martini while looking out on the harbor makes me take stock of the day. It's not the wedding I pictured. He's not the husband I imagined. Nothing is what I thought I'd get.

It's so much better.

Even though I'd never dreamed about my wedding day as a girl, I wondered about what kind of man I'd end up with. Married or not. Given my own father and his abusive relationship with my mom, I didn't understand how a relationship could be a good thing. All the women on TV were pretty and married to slobs. They weren't abusive unless they were on one of the expensive channels, but for the most part, no one on TV sold me on the idea of a husband.

Boyfriends were always cute, though. I was pretty sold on the idea of boyfriends forever.

But Anderson did a good job of changing my mind about that. It is startling to even think about, and for the moment, it is all I can think about. "We're married."

"Is that what all the hubbub at the courthouse was about?"

I roll my eyes. "I'm just saying it's ... well, for now, it's surreal."

"How so?"

I laugh, still trying to figure out the words for it. "Married. Me. Who'd have thought it?"

"Me. Every moment of every day that we weren't married."

"Seriously?"

"June, I meant what I said." He toys with the rings on my finger before he speaks again. I love my wedding set. I keep toying with it, too. It feels like pieces of my hand that I've been missing until now. He declares, "You are my everything. I have waited a very long time for this day."

I sigh, smiling at him. "If you keep looking at me like that, you're going to get me pregnant with just your eyes."

He laughs. "I'm pretty sure that's not how it works."

"Or, we could be naughty and go into the bathroom here—"

"June, Anderson," Kitty says out of nowhere as she comes to our table. Elliot is next to her, and my libido takes a nosedive into hell. "How good to see you!" She hugs each of us in turn while Elliot gives his version of a warm glance.

Out of instinct, I subtly drop my left hand beneath the table. Telling his parents about our wedding is not something I want to cover right now.

Anderson's face tightens the way it does when he's stressed out. "Mom, I didn't know you and Dad were coming to dinner here tonight." Every word in that sentence rings with the tone of, "For fuck's sake, we have to start checking these things because I did not want to see them today."

Kitty motions to the server. "Put our tables together. I wish to dine with my son."

The server's face is a perfect mask of decorum, but I have a feeling we're getting some sympathy from him. "Right away, ma'am." Within seconds, our tables are cozied up to each other, and we have the world's most unwelcome dinner guests.

Not that I don't adore Kitty. I do. But dining with Elliot on my wedding day? Kill me now. But at least they don't know about today. We can have an uncomfortable dinner and let that be that. We can keep our wedding day private if I can secretly pull my rings off under the table.

But Anderson's is in full view. Shit. I casually glance down at his hand, trying to signal to him to hide it or something. When that doesn't work, I take that hand in mine as if I just need to touch him. I smile brightly at Elliot. "What a strange coincidence—"

"Not that strange," he says haughtily. "Copeland's has the best martini in Boston."

I smile and raise mine to him. "As I've recently discovered."

The look he gives me stops my heart. It's vaguely approval-like. They order theirs, and we get another round, and before I know it, things are less uncomfortable.

Kitty notes, with her eyes on our joined hands, "You two remind me of Elliot and me when we were young. Couldn't keep our hands off each other, either."

I laugh a little too hard at that. It's impossible to think of Elliot being affectionate that way. "I'm sure there are times that are like that now, too."

Anderson brings my knuckles to his lips to brush them with a kiss and stares into my eyes when he says, "We are a little more amorous today than usual, on account of we just got married."

He just had to go and bring that up.

50

ANDERSON

June's lips part in a gasp, and I know she's going to be mad that I said it, but it felt necessary. Dad's eyes bulge, and Mom stutters, "Wha ... what?"

"Today, we went to the courthouse and —"

"My son got married like some Green Card beggar?"

I try for a charming smile, but Mom hasn't fallen for those since I was a child. Still, it's my only defense. "We didn't want some big, impersonal thing like the cousins always do." I take June's hand in mine and stare into her eyes. "We wanted today to be about us."

She sighs and smiles at me, nodding as she takes my hand in hers. "I know it's not what either of you would have wanted for him, but it was perfect for us. I hope you can understand why we did it."

Dad starts to speak, but Mom cuts him off. "It is perfectly understandable. I don't like it, but I don't have to. This isn't about me. Your happiness is what matters on your wedding day."

Only then does Dad get a word in edgewise. He lifts his martini to us. "To the happy couple."

I'm almost too stunned to join in the toast, but I do. June, too, a moment later than me. We drink, and after ordering our meals, things fall into an awkward silence. I'm not sure what to say to make small talk with my parents. I've been doing it my whole life. Talking about nothing is a West art form. But now, it feels like wasted air.

What's the point exactly?

These people are my parents. There shouldn't need to be subterfuge between us. Given the last meeting we had with Dad, I'm done pretending and playing those games. Granted, we can't speak candidly in the restaurant—god only knows my father must be the target of legal investigations, and I know I am, too— but aside from pretending to be a legal angel, I am done with the hell of lying about who and what I am.

And that is why I had to tell them the truth right now.

It was eating at me the moment I saw Mom. She has every right to know her son is married. It's bad enough that we did it without her, but if she heard from someone else before she heard it from me, she might actually die of embarrassment. The courthouse is peppered with important people, many of whom belong to the same clubs as my parents. She would have heard it from someone if I hadn't been the one to tell her. I just hope June understands about all of that.

"So how—"

"A Thursday," Mom says, perplexed. "Why a Thursday for your wedding day?"

June fields that one. "Because everyone we know was at work."

That earns a smile from Mom. "Smart of you."

"Actually, it was his idea."

"You're getting nothing but coal in your stocking this year, Mister."

I laugh. "When you thought it was June's idea, she was smart. But when you learn it's mine, I'm getting coal? Not sure I like this double standard."

"I didn't give birth to June. She owes me nothing. You on the other hand—"

"Actually," June interrupts, "I owe you and Elliot everything."

"How's that?" Dad asks.

"Because you made Anderson," she says with a little shrug. "I owe you two my future happiness."

Mom softens. "I'm glad you think so highly of our son, June. And I am glad you're a part of our family now. You make him happier than I've ever seen him, and you've been a stalwart partner in his ups and downs. We could not ask for more in a daughter-in-law."

"I'm just returning the favor."

I huff a laugh and quietly tell her, "I've never had to take care of you when you were shot, and I'd appreciate it if we never, ever even that score."

She giggles. "I'll do my best to never make you have to do that."

"It's all I ask."

The conversation turns lighter—my cousin George is getting married in a few months, and Mom is heavily involved because they're having it at our country club. She doesn't even bother to make jabs about wishing that was what we'd done. She's on her best behavior, it seems.

Dad, on the other hand, is remarkably quiet. I can't tell if it's because he feels insulted to have not been at our wedding or if it is some other reason. But once Mom and June start talking about George's tablescapes, Dad quietly says, "See? You missed all this fun."

I snort a laugh. Did Dad just tell a joke? "I take it she's taken over George's—"

"Mm, hmm," he says, forking his steak. "It is a pity we didn't have the chance to witness this alleged wedding ourselves, but you were likely wise to skip the fuss."

"Alleged wedding?"

He looks down his nose at June, who is still distracted by Mom. "Am I to believe you were wed just because she's in a white dress?"

"Why would I lie about this?"

"To force me into accepting her."

"Marrying June is something I did for me. It has nothing to do with you." I smile, shaking my head at him. "Dad, I'm done lying to you about things. No more bullshit between us. That part of my life is over, as far as I'm concerned. I'm not sneaking around with her, and I'm not hiding her away. You're not going to break us up. She's my wife. You accept that fact, or you don't. That's up to you." I pause, trying to figure out how to prove it to him in a way he can't refute. "Also, feel free to look it up in the public record. I can't fake that."

He scoffs. "Anyone can fake anything."

"Okay, Dad. Whatever you say."

His gaze narrows on me. "You truly married that girl?"

"Yes. And I would have done it sooner if I thought I'd be able to talk her into it."

That narrow gaze turns to her. "She is comely."

I laugh. "That's the nicest thing you can say about her?"

"Did she sign a prenup?"

"No."

"Then yes."

I roll my eyes. "Dad—"

"Fine. She is smart and clever, and she's been a good partner to you, assuming all is as she says it is. Are you happy?"

"That would be better without the caveat, but I'll take it for now."

We get back to our food, and while it is exquisite, the company is lacking. I had so hoped to impress June with Copeland's and have a romantic supper together. Making it a family affair had not been on my radar. But it is nice to have the air cleared between us. I don't have to worry about some gossip spilling the beans to Mom, and Dad knows where he stands with me on the matter.

All in all, it could be worse.

Worse doesn't come along until dessert. June stifles her moans regarding the walnut crème brule, Mom is enjoying an after dinner drink, and Dad notes, "These are not Gretta's cookies."

"I know, right?" I tell him, having ordered the cookies myself. "It's pretty close, but not the same thing."

"Oh, he says it every time he orders them," Mom says. "But he still orders them."

"Because they are the closest I can get without sleeping with her again."

I drop my cookie at the same time June's spoon falls into her crème brule. Neither of us speaks, but I wish someone would because all I can see in my mind is my father in bed with a crone.

Mom clears her throat. Ever the diplomat, she says, "I'm sorry, Elliot. What did you say?" Her way of giving him a chance to change his choice of admissions.

But Dad doubles down. "Kitty, you knew about that. We're all adults here. What is the big deal? It was before we were official."

"So … we were dating at the time?"

"It was only a few weeks in our dating."

I'm not sure if Mom is going to scratch his eyes out at the table or wait until they get home. Etiquette would tell her to wait, but I've never seen her face turn this particular shade of blood red.

But then, she laughs. Once at first, but it's followed by more. And it's not her party laugh, either. It's a gut laugh. Has she finally snapped?

"Uh, Dad, maybe—"

"It's fine, Anderson," Mom insists. "Elliot, I did not know you slept with Gretta Copeland—wait. Her husband was still alive then. You rascal!"

Dad laughs, too, and our wedding supper is taking a turn for the outright bizarre. I'm not sure what to think of any of it, but he says, "It's not like he didn't have his fun on the side, Kitty. Don't judge."

Her flirty smirk at my father is enough to give me nightmares. "I don't throw stones at glass houses."

"What—you mean you and Dwight?"

Mom smiles and nods. "Seems we have more in common than we thought."

I did not need to know any of this. "It's a good thing you two are rich because you'll be paying a therapist for the rest of my life after this conversation."

"You're married now, dear," Mom begins. "Grow up."

51

JUNE

Today, I married the man that I love. I also discovered that his parents were sexual freaks in their youth, and I never, ever needed to know that. Okay, maybe not freaks. Maybe they were just free with their bodies, and oh God, I never, ever needed to know that. As horrified as I am to learn these things, I'm sure that Anderson feels worse. He looks a little green.

"Sweetie, are the oysters not settling for you?"

"No, the oysters are fine," he says, pinching the bridge of his nose.

Kitty smirks at him. "I thought I raised you to be less judgmental than this, young man."

He laughs once. "Then you thought wrong, Mom."

Elliott rolls his eyes. "Here, I thought you were the evolved one."

"I both need to know, and I need to never know what I'm about to ask you. How many of our family friends have you two slept with?"

They both shrug innocently enough. Kitty says, "Well, that all stopped once your father put a ring on my finger."

Elliot nods. "We've been monogamous ever since."

I wonder how true that is, but I don't voice my question. Anderson forges ahead. "But before there was a ring on your finger?"

"It was a long time ago, Anderson," his mother begins. "Truth be told, I'm not entirely certain. But not that many."

His father says, "Not that it's any of your business."

"It is my business when it's people that we actually do business with."

But his father waves his hand in the air dismissively. "It's nothing for you to concern yourself with."

He gives me such a helpless look that I have to laugh. The dinner has been uncomfortable, fun, and a little weird. If his parents had yelled at us or something, I might have felt less guilty about eloping. But they've been perfectly pleasant about it, and somehow, that makes me feel worse.

We finish with dessert, and Elliot insists on picking up the check. He tells Anderson, "I won't hear another word about it. We didn't have the chance to pay for any sort of reception, so let us cover this."

Anderson holds out his hands in a helpless gesture. "I'll consider it payment toward my therapist."

Elliott smiles, shaking his head. He looks so much like Anderson when he does that. It wouldn't bother me as much if I didn't hate the guy. "Whatever you like, son."

When we're outside at the valet, Kitty says, "We absolutely must host a reception for you. I'll take care of all the details. You don't have to do anything but show up. That'll give our friends and family a chance to celebrate the two of you. Please, you must say yes."

How can I possibly say no to that? And I try to figure out exactly how to say no for as long as I can hold out before decorum says I have to answer. I come up with nothing. "That sounds wonderful, Kitty. Thank you."

"Wonderful." She pulls me into a hug. "June, you are absolutely welcome in our family. I am so glad to have you."

It's odd, but I get choked up at the thought. The truth is, with my messed up family, it's sort of nice to join a family that's big and welcoming and warm. Elliot aside, of course. Even though his parents only have two sons, the rest of the family is big and they're quite social with one another. I've always wanted that and never thought I'd have it.

Now I do.

Their car comes first, and we say our goodbyes. Once in our car, I sort of expect conversation to erupt, but there's not a lot left to say. Or maybe today has been so emotional that we're both exhausted. But my nerves are having a go at me.

I don't mention it until we're inside of our apartment. "Should I have pushed back when your mom offered the reception?"

Anderson pops a bottle of champagne, pouring two glasses. "Why would you do that?"

"I thought we weren't doing a reception or a big wedding party or whatever. When she brought it up, I thought you might say something. When you didn't, I felt like I was sort of forced into saying yes."

He delivers the glass of champagne and I down it fast. "I didn't say anything because I wanted this to be your choice."

"Like I could tell your mom no after stealing her son away to marry him?"

"So Mom is going to get her way on everything from here on out?"

"Well, no, but I'm thinking that she gets some leeway today."

He lifts a shoulder in a casual shrug. "That seems fair. You did steal her son, after all."

I smack his chest. "I'm being serious. Your family, your

family's friends, everybody's gonna be at this thing. I won't have anyone. It's kind of intimidating."

He pulls me close. "You'll have me."

"You know what I mean."

"So invite some people. You have parents. You have friends. I'm sure Mom would love to get to know all of them."

"Oh, my hell." I slipped past him and grabbed the bottle to chug from.

"What is it?"

"The thought of my friends and family meeting your friends and family feels like two worlds colliding that were never supposed to."

He smiles, then turns me and wraps me in his arms from behind. His heat flows through me. "We're married. Of course, they were going to meet. It was just a matter of time."

"I know, I know."

"Better sooner rather than later. You know, rip the old Band-Aid off."

"Gee, you make it sound romantic."

He laughs and moves my hair over my shoulder to kiss my bare neck. It sends a shiver down my spine. "There is no mountain we cannot climb together, Mrs. West."

"Yeah, about that," I start, turning to face him. "I'm not sure I want to change my name."

"We talked about it before. I remember." His hands slide to my ass for a less-than-sneaky grab. "But I like calling you Mrs. West. Even if you don't change it, allow me that."

I loop his neck with my arms. "You don't mind?"

"You're not my property, June. You're my equal. Hell, if you want to come up with a new last name for us, I'd be down for that, too. Although, I do think it might behoove you professionally since Dad had you blackballed."

"I was thinking the same thing about my professional reputation."

He kisses the tip of my nose. "See? Great minds and all that."

I take a breath, happy to be in his arms again. "So, you think the reception will be a good thing?"

"Absolutely not."

I laugh. "What?"

"It'll be some overwrought production put on by my mother to impress her friends and our family. You heard about George's wedding at dinner—what makes you think it will be any better than that?"

"Oh god—"

"But, you will be there. I will be there. And by our powers combined, we will make things as tolerable as possible." He pulls me in tight against him. "I have faith that you and I can survive anything this world will throw at us. Including Mom's choices of canape. And what the hell is a tablescape anyway?"

I snort a laugh and lean against his shoulder. "It's how you decorate a table for an event."

"Isn't that just the decorations?"

"No—there are decorations that can go places other than the tables."

"I am the luckiest man alive."

"How's that?"

His smile is so mischievous that I feel it in my bones. "Because my wife is the smartest woman alive. She knows what a tablescape is."

"Thank god you set all your standards nice and low. That should make for a wonderful marriage."

He laughs and kisses me. It's gentle at first, but gradually, he backs me against the kitchen island. I'm trapped between it and him, and I haven't felt this good in a while. Maybe ever.

I'm kissing my husband. That realization keeps hitting me. I'm not sure if the thrill of being married to Anderson will ever go away, but for now, I'm happy to be under this spell.

He pulls back and presses his forehead to mine. At this angle, though, that's not the only part of him pressing on me. His voice is raw with need as he says, "All the reception stuff is just background noise. We can worry about it later. It is my sincere hope, Mrs. West, that you can put that aside and focus on what's important tonight."

I lick my lips, hoping this is going where I think it's going. "And what's that, Mr. West?"

"Tonight is our wedding night, and I need to make my wife come with my name on her lips."

I take another sip of the champagne bottle, trying to slow things down. I want tonight to last forever. "Your goals are agreeable upon one condition."

He grinds his erection against my hip. "Are we negotiating?"

I want to jump him right here and now. But if he can drag this out, so can I. "We are in deep negotiations. I dare say we could be at this all night."

There's a look in his eyes that tells me he is barely hanging on by a thread. "What would that condition be, councilor?"

"That you say my name when you come, too."

Lust fills his eyes as he growls, "I find your terms agreeable."

52

JUNE

Anderson brushes his lips over mine. It was almost not a kiss—it could have been a dream. But then he presses his cheek to my temple, and his voice goes thick with emotion as he says, "I can't believe we're finally married."

I breathe him in, happy and satisfied with our decision to get married today. But that's my only satisfaction at the moment. My husband is a living wall of muscle beneath his nice suit, and I want to tear every stitch of clothes from him. But he seems to need a moment for this to become real in his mind, so I stand there on the precipice of lusty madness. "Why do you sound so surprised?"

He pulls back to look me in the eyes. "Even in my wildest dreams, you wanted nothing to do with me."

My heart swells with hurt for him. I cup his handsome

face in my hands. "Then you should have dreamed bigger."

He laughs and kisses me for real this time, his arms wrapping me against him. The heat of his body pours through me, and he nibbles down from my lips to my throat as he grabs my ass over my dress. He murmurs, "I didn't know they were allowed to make wedding dresses this sexy."

"Glad you like it, husband."

He growls at that, picking me up with my legs around his waist. Thank god for the slit up the thigh, or he would have ruined my wedding dress, and I might have lost the mood over it.

No. No, I wouldn't have. Not with Anderson West kissing me.

One day, when I'm feeling particularly brave, I'll ask how it is that no one else tried to marry him. It still boggles my mind that he was ever single in his adult life. He's too handsome. Too rich. Too perfect.

Maybe every wife feels that way about her husband. At least they should get to on their wedding day.

He carries me to the bedroom and sets me on the corner of the bed before he stares into my eyes while he strips down to his skin. It's a hell of a show, and I'm tempted to make a bad joke about wishing I had some cash to throw at him. But the look on his face dissolves all humor from me. It's intense and devoted. Absolute adoration.

When he's completely naked, he's hard, too, but I don't grab for him there, no matter how much my mouth waters to taste him. Instead, I stand up and turn so he can unzip me. He kisses my neck as he does it, and I get chill bumps all over. The gown slides down my skin like a silken kiss. Anderson's lips trail down my shoulder as he unclips my bra from behind.

I'm left in my heels and wedding panties that say "Missus" on the back. Slowly, he licks down my spine as he crouches. His fingers twirl the sides of the panties for grip before he pulls them down so slowly I hardly feel it. Once they're around my ankles, I step from them and my heels. I turn and face my husband, naked for the first time with him.

Somehow, I'm nervous.

It makes no sense. We've lived together for months. I was his caretaker after he was shot, so I've fed and bathed the man. He's seen me at my worst, too. It's not like we haven't experienced each other before in every possible configuration.

Yet, I'm still nervous.

Maybe because this time, it feels like it means more. It shouldn't—marriage is just a piece of paper, or so they say. But in this moment when it's just me and him and the rings on our fingers, everything feels different. More solid. Bigger.

His lips twitch with amusement, and he softly chuckles. "I shouldn't be nervous right now, right?"

I laugh. "It's okay. So am I."

"Thank god," he says with a laugh. "It's silly, right?"

"I don't think it is. Things are different now."

He slowly nods. "I love you, wife."

"I love you, too, husband."

With that, he kisses me, and the nerves spark before frazzling away. When Anderson puts his hands on my bare lower back, it feels like being claimed. Carefully, I crawl onto the bed backward, not breaking our kiss as he follows me there. Until we lay down next to each other, every kiss is half sweet and half bite because whatever grace we've ever had before has been replaced by hunger and need. Feeling his nakedness pressed against mine makes me wild for more. I pull him on top of me, eager and wanton, and he climbs onto me for the same reasons.

This isn't our usual sexy time. This is need taking over.

I slide my legs wide around him until I belt them at his waist, and he barely has time to feel if I'm wet enough before I've flexed my legs and pulled him into me. I can only take half of him at the moment. Too tense, I guess.

He breaks our kiss and asks, "You okay?"

"Needed more of a warm-up, I think."

He smirks. "I can help with that."

"Oh, can you?" I tease.

Anderson kisses down my collarbones before settling on my breasts when he pulls out. He cups my breasts, rolling my nipples with his fingers until my back arches against him. Every touch sends a spark down low, as though I weren't already on fire for him. I can't hold still with him working me like that, and a mewling sound escapes me. He runs his tongue where his fingers had been, cooling where I'd been hot as he blows on the slick skin. I shudder, and he looks so damn proud of himself.

I'm sure he's about to come back up when he dives down lower until he's seated between my thighs, his face mere inches from my pussy. "Better make sure you're ready for me this time." His tongue swipes up over me, and my every muscle clenches, hoping for more. He doesn't disappoint.

He runs his thumbs along my folds, parting me open for him. Even though he's as eager as I am, he takes his time tasting me. My hips jerk and start—I'm too lit to hold still now. This feels so good I might die. When he sucks on my clit, I'm ready to explode, and I'm sure he'll get hurt down there from it. But then a finger enters me, and I am lost to every sensation. He drives me gasp by gasp to the edge. The tip hits my G-spot, and a lush, lazy orgasm drags through me, starting at my clit and annihilating everything in its path. Drunk with pleasure, I call out his name, and it's all the invitation he needs.

Anderson shoots up my body, an arm hooked beneath my thigh as he glides into me. I'm still coming when he does, and the sudden intrusion of his thick cock makes it all hit differently. He groans when he feels me squeeze on him, whispering, "Fuck, baby, I love you."

I want to say it back, but alas, I'm still gasping.

He drives into me, rolling himself deeper on every stroke. He hooks into my spot and works his hips at that angle to make me come again. It's like he's found the cheat code to my orgasms, and he's determined to earn them all. One after another hits me, stealing my breath. I'm lost inside my body, with pleasure ricocheting across every inch of me.

He looks into my eyes, and I know that he knows exactly what he's doing to me. I hook my hand around his neck and pull him to my lips. I need that mouth on mine the way I need air. I jut my hips up to his rhythm, meeting him on every thrust. I never want to stop. This love has taken over everything we are. The need to breathe, to think, to eat. We're just two animals chasing pleasure. Husband and wife. Woman and man. Beast and beast.

His body starts to seize, and I know he's close, but I don't want it to end. This feeling is too good. It's not even just the orgasms anymore. It's him. Keeping him inside of me where he belongs. I want us to be linked forever. But he hisses and bucks like he can't stop himself, and now, I want that, too. I want to feel him come inside of me. I need that.

I groan, "Come for me!"

He unleashes that last bit of control he'd held onto, thrashing into me like a madman as he comes, murmuring, "June," like a prayer against my lips. He pours himself into me until his body goes weak. I hold him, stroking his scalp with my fingernails to enjoy the shiver that strikes him when I do it. My fingers will smell of my husband's shampoo in the morning, and the thought makes me smile.

-

53

ANDERSON

I pant over June, "Is it possible to fetishize your own wife?"

She laughs which makes her inner walls squeeze on me, pushing me out. Odd feeling. I roll off of her, trying to catch my breath as she says, "I don't know. What makes you ask?"

"I'm not sure if I'll ever get enough of you."

"Give it time. We'll be old marrieds, tired of the way the other one breathes or chews one day."

"Nah. Not buying it." I clutch onto her thigh, enjoying the way she startles when I do it. "You could be covered in liver spots and cellulite, and I'd still want to bend you over the back of the couch."

She belly laughs. "I can't tell if that's the worst pillow talk or the best."

I grin at her, happy to see her relaxed again. After running into my folks, I wasn't sure I'd ever see her like that tonight. "Shower?"

"Ooh, yes, please."

I get the water scalding hot on her side, medium for me, then return to the bedroom. "Your fiery shower is ready, madam."

She snickers, rolling her eyes. It's the cutest when she does that because her nose crinkles and she looks almost innocent. Once in the shower, though, there is nothing innocent about June. She is the sexiest naked, wet woman who ever lived. "Why are you just standing there? I thought we were getting clean?"

"I'm distracted by the hotness that is my wife." Fuck, just saying, "my wife," is enough to give me a semi.

She giggles and turns to me. "I know what you mean, husband."

When she puts her hands on my chest, it's like all the air has been sucked out of the room. There is nothing else in existence. Just her. She traces the outlines of my muscles, and that featherlight sensation makes my balls throb for her. My cock stands at attention, still aching from what we'd just done. But I don't care. I want her again. I reach for her, but she intercepts my hand and kisses my palm. The look in her eyes is enough to drive me crazy. "What?"

"I want to know what my husband tastes like."

CHARLOTTE BYRD

I move forward to kiss her, but she drops to her knees.
She braces herself with one hand on my lower
abdomen, but with her free hand, she cups my balls as
if weighing them and testing them. The best kind of
massage. Tension builds deep inside of me, vibrating
my spine with every touch. She then runs her lips
loosely over my shaft. That sensation is an odd tease,
not enough to get me anywhere good, but all the more
delicious for drawing this out. When she gets to the tip,
though, the teasing ends.

June's tongue cradles the head of my cock before she
swallows me down. Suction is too delicate of a word to
describe what that woman does to me. She's trying to
remove my soul through my dick. It's as if her mouth
has become the place my cock longs to be. Her
excitement for the act enthralls me. The tip of her
tongue traces every vein and curve while her hot
mouth takes me deeper and deeper until I meet the
resistance of her throat.

And then, deeper still.

I have to lean on the steaming tile. "Fuck," I murmur.
There is no other word. Not to describe how I feel.
She's too good, too skilled. How can she do this to me?
How can she make me feel this way? It's beyond
wanted or lusted for. We loved each other yesterday,
but today, she told the world I belong to her.

Right now, she's proving it.

I can't stop from rolling myself into her mouth, and she
weathers every inch of me, purring as if this is the best

thing ever. She does this thing with her tongue that defies physics, and when she does it, I teeter on the brink of madness. But it's not only that she's giving me the blow job of a lifetime. It's that even now, buried in her face, I cannot wrap my head around the fact that June Devlin married me. If I died at this moment, I could die happy.

But I want more. I pull out of her mouth, and her eyes go wide. "Did I bite or—"

I grab her shoulders and help her to her feet. "You were perfect. But I need to be inside of you."

She smiles slyly. "Oh."

I turn her around and pull her hips back as she braces on the wall. Fuck, her ass at this angle is begging for it. But I reach under her for her wet pussy, and sure enough, she is more than ready for me. When I finger her there, she whimpers softly. I lean onto her back, kissing and biting her shoulder. "Need more, love?"

"Please," she begs so prettily.

I slide my fingers from her and push my cock into her until I'm fully seated against her body. There is nothing like it in the world. Penetrating June is the only thing I ever want to do. Our bodies were made for each other. Wet slaps echo on hot shower tiles as we collide together over and over. But I want more pleasure for her. I murmur in her ear, "Touch yourself while I'm inside of you."

She leans on her left forearm as her right hand vanishes in front of her. Her whimpers echo on every hard surface of the room. I bury myself deep and reach around to cover her hand with mine, stopping her hand. "What are you?..."

"Not like this." I scoop her legs out from under her as she squeals and carry her out to the bathroom countertop.

"You're going to drop me!"

"You think I'd let you fall?" There, I bend her over the countertop and take her hands to brace them on the mirror as I slide deep into her again. "This way, I get to watch you come while I'm behind you."

Her lips part in a pretty gasp, and I play with her clit while I drive into her. Slower this time. More deliberate. Staring into her eyes while I do this is enough to make me come, but I need her to come first. Nothing else matters.

June rocks herself back to meet my thrusts and wriggles against my hand at the same time. She yearns for it, and her whines send me even closer to my own climax than I care to admit. One day, we might play orgasm denial games, but not today.

Today, I need to make my wife come on my cock.

I slightly twist my hips to find her spot again, and when I feel the rough texture of it and hear her gasp, I know I'm there. She slaps the mirror, looking for some way to get the tension out. But it's her words that get me. Her voice is high-pitched when she squeaks, "So … close!"

I am determined to hold back, but the moment she comes, her body milks me, and I'm done. Every bit of pleasure shoots through me, and I come, bellowing as loud as she is. Bliss is too gentle a word for this.

Euphoria. Heaven. Something the poets haven't imagined yet.

Panting, I press my forehead to her slick shoulder. Her hair is still wet from the shower. I kiss her there and murmur, "Think we were supposed to get cleaner. Not this."

She giggles. "Shower, round two?"

"Yeah. We can try that." But the three steps to the shower are perilous on weak knees. We both make it, but it's a challenge. June's curly hair is long and straight in the shower, and she looks so different that way. I smile at her, and she gives me a funny look. "What?"

She smiles. "Why are you staring?"

"Sorry, I—no. I'm not sorry. I love staring at you."

Her cheeks go pink, and it's utterly precious. "Why are you doing it?"

"I love your hair curly, but it looks good this way, too. Perfect if you ever want a disguise because I swear you look like a whole other person with it straight."

"I used to straighten it, actually."

"Really? I don't remember that."

"It was right after college when we didn't see each other. With my hair doing whatever it feels like, I thought it was more professional to have it straightened."

The concept makes me frown. "How is that more professional?"

"Because when I straighten it, it's neat and polished looking instead of curly and wild."

"Ah."

She nods. "But after a year at my old firm, I got tired of my hair breaking from the blowouts and gave up."

I kiss her forehead and pull her close. "I know it's not up to me. I want you to look however you want to look. But if my input counts for anything, in your quest for beauty, please don't do things that damage you."

She snickers. "I'll keep that in mind."

I wash her hair, taking my time with it. June is half asleep by the time I finish, and afterward, I dry her off before myself. When I am almost done, she yawns and asks, "What are you doing?"

"Taking care of my wife."

"Why does hearing *my wife* turn me on?"

"Probably because it turns me on to say it." I finish drying myself off and take her hand to lead her back to the bed. Once there, I wrap my arm over my little spoon and bury my face in her damp hair.

"I should dry my hair or —"

"No. I want you just like this."

Her sleepy voice makes me swoon. "But the pillows —"

"They'll be fine, baby. It's time to sleep."

She smacks her lips after another yawn. "Okay." When her breathing evens out, and her body goes limp, I can finally relax. Just as I doze off, she whispers, "I love you more than anything, Anderson West."

"I love you, too, June Devlin-West."

She quietly giggles. "I'm not changing my name."

"We'll see."

"So bossy."

I chuckle. "You like me bossy."

"We're supposed to be sleeping."

"You started it."

June laughs and rolls onto her back. "Well, it seems as though my husband's body isn't ready for sleeping."

"Hmm?"

She grabs my half-hard cock in the dark. I hadn't even realized it, but being sandwiched against her ass is enough to wake the dead. She sweetly says, "Guess I'll have to do something about that."

"If you must."

She giggles as she slides underneath the blankets.

54

JUNE

"I can't believe I've never taken you here before," Anderson says as he pulls onto a private road. It's treelined and gorgeous. He drives down the road like he's done it a thousand times before, but I can't stop thinking we're trespassing.

"This is the right road?"

"June, this is where I grew up. Well, when I wasn't at the academy or at our city apartment."

Butterflies soar in my stomach. "Do I look okay?"

"You look incredible. I love that dress—but why a wedding dress? This is just a reception."

"It's our wedding reception. What else was I supposed to wear? A tux?"

Anderson growls in a way I've never heard.

"What was that?"

"Me thinking of you in a tux."

I giggle. "Really?"

He gets a wistful look in his pretty blue eyes. "You know those vintage black and white pictures of Hollywood actresses in suits because it was against studio protocol for women to wear pants, and they were tired of it?"

"I didn't know that was why they did that, but I've seen them. Greta Garbo, Marlena Dietrich, all those. What about it?"

"I have had a thing for women in tuxes since I saw those pictures. Something about the rebelliousness of it all. Thinking of you, dolled up in the retro hair and makeup … and wearing a tux … " There's that growl again.

"If you keep that up, we'll never make it to our own party."

"I'm game if you are."

I giggle at him. "No! We already ditched everyone for our wedding. If we do it again, I don't think they'll forgive us. We are not getting disinherited because we couldn't keep it in our pants."

"Oh, fine, bring that up." He huffs, smiling.

The trees part to frame something too big to be called a house. Is it a manor or a mansion, I don't know. But it's huge and gray with white trim, surrounded by more trees. The driveway loops near the front door, and it trails off to the left. Some trees divide the property there, but I can make out another building in that direction. "What's over there?"

"The stables."

"You grew up with stables? Like with horses and stuff?"

"I never told you?"

I just chuckle and let it go. I have a feeling today will be full of moments like this one. It's always that way when I'm around rich people. They are blind to the luxuries they see every day. It's not false modesty or that they're hiding things—it's just that it doesn't occur to them to bring it up. "Do you ride the horses?"

"Only the older ones. The younger ones are for racing, so they train with their jockeys, and Dad thinks they shouldn't be ridden by anyone else." He shrugs.

"Wait, so it's not just having horses for the sake of having them?"

He shakes his head. "Horses are a business until they're retired. Mom is too much of a softy to send them away or put them out to stud. When Dad is done with them, she gets to keep them. Sometimes, I wonder if he's in racing just so she has an excuse to have the horses."

"That seems like a lot of thoughtfulness. Are you sure we're talking about Elliot West?"

"The guy's an asshole, but he's her asshole."

"Ooh, save that line for when you make your toast."

He laughs and parks next to the other cars on the lot. I hadn't realized just how many people would show up to this thing. Anderson seems surprised, too. "Looks like both of them called up everyone they know. How'd they get so many people to RSVP in a week?"

I shrug. "Blackmail?"

"Let's hope not." Anderson takes my hand in his and leads us up the walkway from the parking area.

Well-manicured bushes line the stone path to the grand entrance. Half-circle steps stack to the white front doors, and before Anderson can ring the bell, a man in a uniform opens it. He's an older white gentleman with an English accent. "Mr. West, how good to see you."

"Charles, I tell you every time that's Dad's name."

He laughs politely as though they've had this conversation for years. "And is this Mrs. West?"

I smile up at him. "Yes."

"Oh, he gets to call you that in public, but I can't?"

Charles smirks. "We are fortunate for this spate of good weather. Your parents are hosting in the garden."

"Thank you, Charles," Anderson says as we walk in.

The place is immaculate, of course, but it's not just the cleanliness that makes it immaculate. It's the abundance of white everywhere. Some of the interior walls are a pale gray, but the ceilings, wide trim, and wainscoting are icy white. Thankfully, the floors are glossy pale hardwood, offsetting so much brightness, though not enough for my tastes. Wrought iron chandeliers decorate every space we walk into, as do oversized wrought iron vases with tall greenery lurching over the edges.

"The outside is exactly what I expected, but not the inside."

"How so?"

"Everything is so ... sterile."

Anderson laughs hard. "How does this surprise you?"

"I expected some of your mother's warmth to come through."

"This is the handiwork of the decorator she hired last year. I don't expect it to make it through the end of the year."

"Ah."

When we turn another corner, I'm lost. I'd never find my way out without Anderson at my side. He turns to a pair of double doors and says, "This is my mother." When he flings them open, I gasp.

I'd always seen conservatories in films but never thought I'd be in one. Glass outer walls let all the sunshine in on the exotic plants in every direction.

There's even a waterfall and a small pond with a bridge over it. Koi swim contentedly, and the moment they see us, they swim right to us, opening their mouths near the surface.

"Are they okay?"

He chuckles and opens a wooden box I hadn't noticed. There, he scoops out some pellets and tosses them to their hungry mouths. It's a feeding frenzy, and then they go back to swimming or begging. "They're greedy, that's all. What do you think of the place?"

"It's magical, but I thought we were supposed to join the party."

"We are." Anderson pulls me in for a kiss. "But I wanted one more private moment with you before everyone else steals your attention. You look extra beautiful today."

"Thank you." I sigh. "But we should go to the—"

"I know. But I love seeing you smile like this."

Heat rises in my cheeks. "Come along, Mr. West. Let's not keep our guests waiting."

He laughs. "You mean my parents."

"Them, too."

We reach the outside, thanks to the conservatory's exterior exit, and the moment we do, we are bombarded with music and people I've never met. Being early evening, amber light pours through the treetops casting everyone in a flattering glow. A few hundred feet away, several billowing white tents delineate the party from the rest of the garden, but that doesn't slow any of the guests down. I can't keep up with all the introductions as people congratulate us.

But I know a few of these people. Cole, Anderson's younger brother, beams at us. "Congratulations to the happy couple," he says as he hugs Anderson. When he hugs me, he says, "And congratulations for skipping out on the big wedding bullshit. Smart call."

"It was a mutual decision, actually."

"Well, it was smart, whoever came up with it. Our family and weddings … " He shakes his head. "You two set a good precedent. If I ever find Mrs. Right, I'm following your lead."

"Cole, where are Mom and Dad?" Anderson asks.

"Dad is at the bar over there, and Mom is corralling Mrs. Lexington away from the catering waiter she has her eye on."

"Again?"

I snort a laugh.

"Oh yeah. You know how she is about *the help*."

"Anderson West, you old son of a bitch!"

I glance up at him while he winces. "Who—"

But then I see him. Tag McAllister.

Oh balls.

He comes straight to Anderson, grappling him into a back-slapping hug. "Heard you got married, but that can't be right. You wouldn't have gotten married without your best man!"

Goody.

Anderson smiles, laying his arm around my shoulders. Anyone on the outside wouldn't see it, but his hand has hooked around my arm in a death grip. Poor guy. He tells Tag, "Actually, we got married without anyone else around. Just the judge and the court witness. It wasn't anything personal, Tag. We just wanted it to be for us."

Tag looks at me, and for a moment, I think I'm going to get away with anonymity. But I must have pissed off some deity because his eyes light with recognition. "You're the same June Devlin from Appleton, right?"

"Yep."

"Holy shit! You filled out!"

"Tag," Anderson says, sharper than expected. "Why don't you get us some wine?" It's not really a question.

"Sure, yeah. You can count on me." With that, Tag disappears into the crowd.

"We will not see him the rest of the day, mark my words."

I giggle at him. "How's that?"

"I sent him for alcohol. He is guaranteed to be distracted by something shiny at the bar."

"Nice trick." More people come to greet us, but it's one near the reception area that catches my eye.

My father is here.

55

JUNE

It's not easy to make my way through the crowd. Anderson was right about the dress—not quite the right selection for the event. My wedding dress marks me as a target, so everyone wants to stop and talk to the bride. On my way to my father, I peruse the setting.

Kitty outdid herself. The main tent is set up over a dancefloor with tables surrounding it, enough for a few hundred guests for supper. The other adjoined tents have smaller dance floors and bars, and one has an hors d'oeuvres buffet. Each table is set with pale pink peonies and lush greenery. Glass dome-covered candles somehow burn, even though they're sealed. I don't know what trickery is involved, but it's lovely.

I get distracted by guests and scenery, but eventually, I reach my dad.

He is gussied up for today. His suit is designer, like his shoes, and he has a fresh haircut. He went out of his way to make a good impression today, and I'm not sure if that's for me or because this place is crawling with rich people.

I'd like to think it's for me, but I have known the man for too long.

"Hey, Dad."

He smiles, and I don't know why, but it makes me feel like a little kid again. "Hey, Junebug." He pulls me in for a hug. "I'm so happy for you."

"Really?"

"Why wouldn't I be?"

I shrug. "I don't ... I didn't mean it like that. It's just ... I got married. After your marriages, I figured you'd be kind of sour on the whole thing."

"All I want is for you to be happy. If marrying Anderson makes you happy, then I'm all for it."

"Thanks, Dad."

He nods away from the crowd, and we end up near the outside of one of the tents. "I have to say, I was a little surprised I wasn't invited to this shindig."

"Like I said, I never expected you to be okay with this kind of thing, so I didn't want you to feel awkward."

He sighs, still smiling, but it's sad now. "Then, going forward, please know that I'm happy if you're happy.

My life, as complicated as it's been, is not the standard by which I judge everyone else's life. So, for important events like this one, I'd like to be invited. If you'll have me, that is."

It's strange to want to believe my father. Every instinct tells me he's lying. History tells me he's up to something. But the little girl in me wants to believe her father. I want to think he's being genuine, even with all the odds against it.

"Yeah, Dad. We can make that happen."

"Glad to hear it. Once I knew about this event, it made me realize just how much I want to be a part of your life. I would have hated to miss this. You're important to me, Junebug. I want you to know that."

It's no wonder he's always had a string of women after him and people to rip off. He's slick. I hate that I'm being taken in by it, but I am. Or maybe he's being real with me right now. I'll probably never know.

"You're important to me, too, Dad. I'm glad you're here."

"Really?"

"Well, yeah." I nod and smile. "You finally get to meet my husband."

"I've already met his parents. They're characters."

I chuckle. "Oh, you have no idea."

"Thankfully, they had the good grace not to bring up

the fact they didn't invite me, and I showed up at their home."

"I think special exceptions are made for parents at these things."

"Speaking of, is your mom coming?"

I shake my head. "Kitty invited her, but apparently, she's on a business trip in Des Moines and couldn't leave it."

Dad's lips tighten. "That ... that must be some important trip for her to miss this." Translation, "I am judging your mother for being absent on such an important day, but I am trying not to talk shit about her to you."

"I'm sure it is. And it's fine. Hell, I got married without either of you. I'm pretty sure she's pissed about that, and that's why she's not here."

The truth is, I had cried for an hour when I found out she wasn't coming. She told me in no uncertain terms she was hurt that we got married without her, and so she wasn't going to celebrate a marriage she had nothing to do with. Then, she hung up on me. I was glad Anderson was at work for all of that, but when he came home, it took him one look at me to know I'd been crying, and when he brought it up, I lost my shit and cried all over again. But he held me until I calmed down and then ordered me a pizza because he's the best man ever.

I'm not about to tell Dad any of that. When it comes to all things Mom, I've decided I'm not giving him any fuel against her. And vice versa. Neither of them needs to know a thing about the other. If they want to patch things up, that's between them. I refuse to be any kind of a go-between.

He tsks, shaking his head. "I'm no expert on weddings or marriages, Lord knows, but a wedding should be for the couple. Whatever they want. I hope you had the wedding you wanted, Junebug."

"I did. Thanks for not giving me shit about eloping—"

His laugh carries. "I could stand here and pretend to be the bigger man about it, but I can admit when something bothers me. There was a tiny part of me that was upset I didn't get to give my daughter away at her wedding, but I'm pretty sure that kind of honor needs to be earned, and I haven't done that yet. Maybe in ten years' time, you and Anderson can do a vow renewal, and I'll get to do it then."

"Ten years is an awful long time for you to be on your best behavior," I tease.

He chuckles. "You've got a point there. We'll play it by ear."

I'm not sure about any of this. Is he being honest with me? Or is he playing the role of the doting father to butter up anyone who might be watching? It's impossible to know. But maybe I can keep my father in my life if I keep him at a distance. Close enough to have lunches, far enough to keep him away from the Wests' friends' money.

I didn't know tightrope walking came with wedding territory, but here we are.

The band stops, and we hear Kitty's voice over a microphone. "If you will all take your seats, we will get started."

Dad leans in and asks, "How is it rich people start a sentence like it's a question but end it with them telling you what they want you to do?"

I giggle. "I can't say, but in my experience, they all seem to manage it."

He puts out his arm for me to take, and I do. From the outside of the tent, he leads me to the head table near the stage, where Anderson and his parents are already seated. He stands, smiling at my father. Dad says, "You must be the man who married my little girl."

"Mr. Devlin, how nice to finally meet you."

"And you." He gives me another hug and cheekily says, "See? I got to give you away today."

I roll my eyes. "Sneaky."

"Mr. Devlin," Kitty begins. "Won't you please join us here?" She gestures to a place setting next to mine.

To my surprise, he gives me a look as though he's checking in with me. I smile and nod, and he says, "I'd be delighted. Thank you, Mrs. West."

We take our seats, and in that moment, I am overwhelmed. There are a few hundred eyes on us, and it's like being under a microscope. If Anderson weren't next to me, I'd bolt out of here. He leans in close, "Just a few more hours."

"How'd you know?" I whisper.

"You have the same look you had when you were on stage at the auction."

I snort a laugh, thinking back to all those months ago. How had I gone from auctioning my body to a random man to then marrying said man ... it's been one hell of a ride. But with him at my side, I can handle being the center of attention. For now.

56

ANDERSON

I lean to my bride again. "This is why you never litigate, isn't it?"

She's gone pale at the thought. "Public speaking is not my forte. Please don't ask me to."

"No one is going to ask you to. I think Mom just wants to say a few words to get things started. She'll speak, we'll dance, everyone will eat, and then we'll go home. Okay?" I give her hand a supportive squeeze. "No big deal."

She gives a brave nod and forces a smile on, and I feel guilty she's so uncomfortable. But I know how much all of this means to Mom and Dad and, oddly, June's father, too. He was moved to be invited to sit at our table. But given what she's told me about the man, maybe he's working on a scheme. I'm not sure if he can fake the kind of emotion that is on his face. If so, I understand why people get taken in by him.

He looks every bit the proud father most would be on a day like today.

To my surprise, Cole is the first to take the mic. "Hello, everyone. Thank you for coming today. I'm Cole West, the youngest disappointment." He gets some good laughs out of that line, and thankfully, few in the audience know it to be true. But he grins, carrying on. "When Anderson and I were young, we didn't always get along. In fact, I can still remember the time I stole his bike, and he chased me through the house with a horsewhip." He chuckles, shaking his head, and I am glad he is starting with a mild anecdote. "When Mom caught us, Anderson lied and said we were playing Indiana Jones. I, being a genius, backed him up. I think that was the first time we ever really teamed up together. After that, Mom and Dad were up against a united force, and they didn't stand a chance." He smiles at me, raising his glass. "Now, Anderson has a new partner. Be careful with that one, brother. She's way smarter than you and far better-looking."

I smile and flip him off, and he laughs with the crowd.

Cole goes on, "May you strive to be worthy of her for the rest of your lives. Cheers."

Everyone raises their glasses and drinks. To my utter shock, my father is the next one to head to the microphone. I would have thought for sure it'd be Mom, and that would be that. We're outdoors, but there is not enough air. Is he going to be classy about this, or is he going to use today to humiliate me and June?

"I'd like to thank everyone who could make it here on such short notice. We would have liked to give more notice, but we only learned of their nuptials a week ago."

Great. He's going for humiliation.

"Love is like that, though. Sometimes, we do impulsive things. Things that perhaps we ought not do, but you know, deep down, they are exactly what you need to do." He pauses, frowning.

I have no idea where he's going with this, but I'm sweating bullets. I'm also wishing I had some actual bullets.

"My son met his bride at a charity auction."

Oh, holy shit.

"Or rather, they met when they were students at Appleton Academy, but they reconnected at the charity auction, and they have been inseparable since. I am happy to know the woman who won my son's heart is charitable and generous, qualities my son has, thanks to his mother."

Maybe he isn't trying to humiliate us?

He turns to Mom, smiling adoringly. "June thanked me and Kitty for making Anderson into the man he is because he's such a good man, and she loves him so very much. But truly, his good qualities are there thanks to Kitty. I have been lucky enough to have a partner who makes up for what I lack and who supports me and takes care of me. A wife who has made my house into a home and shown me what it truly means to love someone."

Mom softly says, "Oh, Elliot."

He looks past her to me. "It is my hope that you get to have that too, son. When I look at June, I see a woman full of possibilities, but knowing what I know about her, you are in for a lifetime of happiness. Anderson, if you're smart, you'll hold onto June with both hands and never let her go."

Wow. I knew he approved of her, but this? A knot burns in my throat, part shock, part emotions I can't pin down. I bring her hand up and kiss the back of it. "Thanks, Dad."

He smiles and nods. "To the happy couple." With that, we drink again, and Dad sits down.

After that, it's Mom's turn. "Well, for any of you who don't know me, I am Kitty West, the mother of the groom. Welcome to our home, and thank you all for coming." She smiles and sighs. "Anderson has always been headstrong, so it shouldn't have surprised me that he eloped. He's always done things on his own timetable. I think that's why he was born five weeks early—he's never been one for patience."

Leave it to Mom to start from my very beginning.

"Every mom thinks her son is special. I just happen to be right," she says slyly, earning some snickers from her friends. "When my father passed, Elliot was away overseas, and Cole was too young to understand. But

Anderson got it, and he took care of me." She pulls something out of the pocket of her dress, and when I see it, I'm stunned.

There's no way she kept that ...

She goes on, "He made me this ring out of the daisies my father had planted here. He said it was like having a piece of him with me and that my father wasn't really gone. He was right outside in our garden. Every time I miss my father, I think of this ring, though. Not the garden. I think of Anderson and how he did everything he could to cheer his mom up when she was at her lowest."

The knot in my throat grows.

Mom turns to June. "You thanked us for giving you Anderson, but the truth is, we are lucky to have you in our family, June. You are smart, kind, and patient. We could not ask for more in a daughter-in-law. Please consider this your official welcome into the family."

June sniffles as she smiles. Her eyes shine with tears, but she's keeping it together. "Thank you, Kitty."

"And as a nosy mother-in-law, I have some advice for the newlyweds." She turns to the audience. "Accept your partner's weirdness, and they will accept yours. Always make time for each other. Never assume malice when aloofness is probably the issue. And dating doesn't end with a ring on the finger. Woo each other forever, and you'll never have a bad day. To the newlyweds!"

Once again, we drink, and after not eating for a few hours, the champagne is bubbling in my head. But I don't care. We can sleep in my old room if we're too buzzed. After Dad's speech, it's hard not to think everything is going to work out. If he can get past his bullshit with June, then we can conquer mountains.

As I finish my flute of champagne, I can't help but wish to get on with things. *Just announce the first dance, and we can —*

"Anderson," Mom says, smiling. "Your turn." She holds out the mic.

Shit. "Uh, I didn't prepare anything —"

"Say something nice about your bride."

A nervous chuckle pops out of me and I find my feet, while she sits back down. I rake my fingers through my hair, smiling at the crowd. "Good evening everyone. Thank you for coming. On behalf of my wife and I, it means the world to us that you'd take time out of your busy lives to celebrate this special occasion."

Okay, what next?

"I will never forget the day I met June Devlin. We were at Appleton, and she was the new kid. She was nervous and a little shy, and all I could think was, 'There goes the most beautiful girl I have ever seen;' but I wasn't a suave preteen by any stretch of the imagination. I was your run-of-the-mill boy with a crush at first sight, so I said something smarmy, and she decked me, and I knew it was love."

That gets some laughs, thankfully. I might have dressed up the truth a little, but I didn't think she'd mind.

"After that, we were in school together a lot, but she was too good for me, and I was too bad for her. It took years before I started to become a man worthy of June. And I'm still working on that," I tease. "But tonight is for celebrating the future, not digging up the past." I raise my glass. "To my bride, June Devlin, who has shown me the meaning of love from day one. To June!"

"To June!" the audience says before we drink together.

When I look back at her, I see Mom looking right at her, too. She has expectations in her eyes. She wants June to make an impromptu speech, too, I just know it.

Nope. I am her husband, and that means I'm here to protect her.

I signal the band and mouth, "First dance." The lead singer nods, motioning to her compatriots, and they start to play. I stroll to June, hand out. "May I have this dance?"

She beams up at me. I think she knew what Mom wanted, because she looks so relieved. As she skirts past Mom and Dad, neither tries to stop her. I take her in my arms, and we have the whole dancefloor to ourselves.

In her ear, I whisper, "Better?"

"So much."

I chuckle, holding her close. "How was my speech?"

"Perfect. Thank you for not asking me to do one, too."

"You don't like public speaking, so I'm not about to do that to you. And I'm not going to let Mom do it to you, either."

"What's her deal about that? You didn't even have a choice."

I smile and nod. "I should have been prepared for it. Growing up, Mom always had this Kennedy fantasy that her children would be raised to be in politics, comfortable with public speaking, and all of that. Any chance she got, she put us on the spot." I shrug. "It's useful now, but back then, I hated it."

She lays her head on my shoulder, and I breathe her in, relishing the scent of my wife. "I know this reception was kind of thrust upon us, but I'm glad for it."

"Oh?"

"I like seeing you here. You seem more comfortable here with your family than in the city."

"That's probably because my dad gave a good speech that didn't humiliate us, and like you said, the bar is in hell for him."

She laughs, and we're blinded for a moment because the photographer gets in close for that picture. I give him a look, and he backs off. June says, "Honestly, I'm having a good time. I didn't expect to, but I am. I know we got married a week ago, but this sort of makes it feel real."

"I know exactly what you mean. It just feels like this is how things are meant to be. Like everything is going to work out. We'll have big family events here, birthdays, holidays. We can even invite your folks if you want."

"I think I'd like that. But only one of them per event. No sense in bringing the drama of the both of them together."

I nod. "Obviously, marriage doesn't always work out, but …" I sigh and smile at my wife. "When I look in your eyes, all I can think is, 'And they lived happily ever after.'"

57

JUNE

"We will live happily ever after, Anderson."

"You really think so? Even after all the crazy shit that's happened to us?"

I smile and nod. "That's exactly why we will. We got the crazy shit out of the way already."

He laughs and kisses me, and I don't even care that the photographer is capturing the moment. I'm too damn happy right now. Anderson murmurs, "That guy has to go."

"It's fine. In fifty years, when we've forgotten about today, we'll have the pictures to look at."

But then Anderson shakes his head. "I'll never forget today, June. Or our wedding day. Or the day I met you. I might forget my own name, but I'll never forget a minute I spend with you."

I swallow hard, trying not to cry again. I managed to keep it subtle when he gave his speech, but now? No. I can't do that again. Instead, I give him a peck of a kiss, and we relax into the beat of the song.

With my head on Anderson's shoulder, it's hard not to feel sublimely happy. Even with all the eyes on us, I am still relaxed. He makes me this way. Braver than I've ever known. Happier, too.

Maybe my father is calculating some scheme. Maybe Elliot said all those nice things to butter me up for some dastardly plan of his own. Our fathers can pull strings and manipulate another day. Today, they're both on their best behavior, and I'm grateful for it. Truly, they were the last two people I expected to be well-behaved today, and they're knocking it out of the park. Tag is a douche, but at least he didn't try to make a speech. Out of everyone else here, they're the only ones I worry about. Everyone else has been lovely.

Today truly is a magical day.

I lean up, smiling. "I love you, husband."

He smiles down at me. "I love you, too, wife." He kisses me just like I wanted, and like him, it's perfect. Everything about today is —

Charles dashes into the tent, coming toward us. Breathlessly, he pants, "I tried to stop them."

"Who?" Anderson asks.

But then the tent flaps are held back by uniformed police officers. Detectives Banks and Wachowski stroll in like they own the place. At first, my brain doesn't register what's happening or that I'm really seeing them. I blink a lot, trying to figure it all out. "Is that—"

"Yes," he says hoarsely. Then, louder, he asks, "What are you two doing here?"

But we know, don't we? They're here to ruin everything.

Banks says, "We have a warrant for your arrest, Mr. West, on suspicion of the murder of Neil Johnson. Turn around, please."

Anderson closes his eyes as he turns around. "Is this really necessary? Where am I going to go? We're at my wedding reception."

Wachowski puts on shiny handcuffs on my husband's wrists and sneers, "No, it's not necessary." He closes in next to Anderson's ear. "It's just fun."

Detective Banks turns to me. "Congratulations on your nuptials, Mrs. West."

"What is the meaning of this?" Elliot barks as he joins us on the dancefloor.

"Pretty sure you know all about it, West," Wachowski snaps. "Don't think your son is the only one going down for this."

Elliot is undeterred. He snarls at the detectives, "I will have your badge for this. Yours too, and anyone else who helped plan this embarrassment!"

"You're welcome to try," Detective Banks says. "But when a case is this solid, it's in your best interest to let bygones be bygones. Come along, Mr. West." He gives Anderson a nudge toward the exit. He's being taken away from me, and there's nothing I can do.

I'm speechless. What can I possibly say to make any of this better? There's nothing … except, "I love you, Anderson. We will get this figured out!"

"I love you, June!" he shouts as they take him outside.

Elliot turns to me. "We are getting him back."

All I can do is nod. I can't even see him anymore. He's blurry behind the wall of tears in my eyes.

But then I hear Kitty and Dad joining us. She has the microphone. "Thank you all for coming. As you have witnessed, we are experiencing a family emergency. We appreciate your understanding at this time. Please drive home safe." After that, she comes to me, throwing her arms around me.

I'm not even sure if I'm hugging her back. I don't feel like I'm in my body right now.

Kitty releases me, and it's Dad's turn to hug me. "Junebug, I'm so sorry."

I blink at him.

"The first arrest is always the worst."

My voice scrapes out of my throat. "First?"

He realizes what he just said and apologetically says, "Given the charges, hopefully, it'll be the *only* arrest."

I gulp, and something in me breaks. I don't know what it is exactly, but sobs burst out of me. I can't even catch my breath until Kitty rubs my back. The world presses into me from all directions, and I'm not strong enough to hold it back. My strength was just arrested and taken away from me.

The crowd isn't disbursing like Kitty told them to, either, and that does not help. Instead, their murmurs fill my head. "Did I hear that right? *Murder?*"

"Neil Johnson … wasn't that the poor boy beaten to death we heard about on the news? Surely that wasn't Anderson!"

"He's always been a hothead, but beating someone to death? I don't think he's capable of something like that."

"He was a little shit back in school. I don't know. Maybe."

"I bet he did it. The guy probably looked at him wrong, and boom."

Their words bite at me. It is like being nibbled to death by ducks. I want to scream at them to leave. If anyone has the perfect excuse to shout at a crowd of strangers, it's me. But if I do that, I don't know if I can keep my mouth shut about Neil.

Anderson is the hero who saved me from the villain, and I can't say shit about that yet.

The truth is dying to come out of me, and I'm on the brink of screaming it when Tag walks up to me. He tips his head to the side. "Wanna get out of here?"

Elliot stiffly says, "I appreciate the kindness, Tag, but June is our family now. We will take care of her."

Cole—I hadn't noticed when he joined us—tells Tag, "Thanks, man, but we've got her. Think you can find out some details from your dad?"

"I'll do what I can." Tag walks off, calling his father.

Cole puts his arm around me. "Okay, Mrs. West, how about we get you in the house?"

I know the words he said, but I can't make sense of them. "Why?"

"Because today has been one heck of a day, and you need rest."

I huff a laugh. "You think I can sleep ever again?"

"That's the spirit," he says with false cheeriness. "Come on. You're my new sister, and Anderson will kill me if I don't take care of you."

I shrug and let him guide me into the house. Thankfully, most of the guests take other paths out to their cars, so we don't see too many people inside the house. We walk upstairs, or rather, Cole helps me up the stairs because I keep shuffling for some reason, and he takes me to a bedroom.

One look around, and I know it's Anderson's childhood bedroom. Navy blue walls and a matching checked bedspread. There's a Ferrari poster over his bed. His trophies line the remaining walls, along with his pictures with his friends ... it's all so perfect and so him that I bawl uncontrollably.

Cole mutters, "Okay, bad choice. Come on." He ushers me out of that bedroom and into the one next door. "Nothing bad in here. It's just a guest room."

When I pry my eyes open, I see what he means. It's as neutral as can be—more gray and white in every direction. The bed looks big and inviting, and even though the thought of holding still right now sounds like hell, I think I need that bed. But how can I sleep without Anderson? I mumble, "Can't sleep without him."

Cole sighs. "I'm going to get you some food and a glass of water and some of those pills Mom uses to sleep when Dad isn't around, okay? And I'll check for some mood stabilizers while I'm at it. Pretty sure we could all use those right about now. I'll be right back." He runs off down the hall.

None of this feels real. My husband whisked me away to this giant estate, where people said nice things, and others arrested him. None of this makes any sense. How could they do this to us? My husband is a hero, dammit.

But they won't know that until I tell them. Maybe it's time for me to come clean. I might go to prison for hiding a body, but who fucking cares? I can't let him take the blame for this. It was self-defense. Surely a jury would see … oh god. Would they?

Cole returns with pajamas, pills, and water. "Here we go. Just … use all of this at your leisure, June. My room is just on the other side of that wall. You don't even have to call me. You can just knock. I'll come check on you, okay?"

Numbly, I nod. As he leaves, I manage to say, "Thank you, Cole."

He smiles. "You don't have to thank family, June. But you're welcome. And we're going to get him back. You'll see." He closes the door behind himself.

What the hell am I supposed to do now?

58

JUNE

Staring at my face in the bathroom mirror, I try to focus on the little things. The redness in my eyes. The puffiness. I look like a completely different person in grief. Makes it easier to pretend this is happening to someone else.

For a minute.

But then I feel it. The grief, pulling me down like undertow. Thankfully, Cole keeps bringing me water, or I might dehydrate from crying. He knocks on the bathroom door. "Hey. Sorry to bother you, but I brought some lunch."

I open the door. "Thanks."

He winces at the sight of me. "Brought more tissues, too. Is it tea bags that help with … " He gestures at my face. "… all that?"

I'm feeling only mildly insulted at the moment. "Thanks for the food and the tissues, but I need to be alone right now. I hope you understand."

"Of course. Sorry. I didn't mean anything by it—"

"I know. I'm not ... good right now."

"Understood. I know we don't know each other, but maybe calling a friend would help." When he gets to the door, he pauses. "There's a big, honking chocolate bar on the tray with your sandwich. I might not know you well, but I know women." Then, he leaves.

I head straight for the chocolate, and halfway through, it doesn't taste like anything. Nothing has since yesterday.

Cole's suggestion floats around my head. Call a friend. There's only one person who might remotely understand, and I still can't tell her everything without risking her becoming a witness. But I could stand to hear Callie's voice right about now.

Before I chicken out, I dial her up. "Hey, I—"

"Where the hell have you been?" she shouts without animosity.

"Been busy."

"Let me get somewhere I can talk."

"I'm sorry to bug you." I hear animal sounds in the background. "Are you on safari?"

She snorts a laugh. "We're at the zoo. Me and Daniel and his kids."

"Oh, hell. Callie, I'll call you later."

"Don't you dare hang up on me! I have been dying to talk to you, and I will take it when I can get it. Okay, I'm off by the ECO center, which means no one is around because no one cares about saving the planet. How depressing is that? Talk to me, girl."

"I'm guessing you haven't seen the news or social media today?"

She huffs. "You know I hate all of that."

Shit. I forgot. "Anderson was arrested at our wedding reception."

"What?" she squeaks. "You got married? Wait, arrested?"

And then the sobs start all over again. I can't help it. Hearing her incredulity is like hearing my own voiced out loud. I give her the rundown while omitting a few facts. "… since I went out with Neil right before he died, and his body was found all beat up, they think Anderson did it. I don't know what actual evidence they have."

"Well, I mean, first of all, crap. Seriously, that is messed up. But secondly, they have to have probable cause to bring charges, which means they think they have something."

"I know. I'm a lawyer, too, remember?"

She sighs. "I know, sweetie, but you don't sound like yourself. Seriously, I'm surprised you haven't been locked away in the nut house for all of this. What's the plan?"

I laugh. "Plan? What plan?"

"You're you. You always have a plan."

"Not this time, Callie."

She pauses. "Well, fuck."

It makes me laugh to hear her curse. She's no church mouse, but she's more uptight than I am about those things. At least something can still make me laugh. "Precisely."

"Okay, well, the first thing to do is talk to his lawyer. Not Pym—it sounds like that guy just wants to pin all of this on you. The other lawyer, the one you said, was like an aunt to him. Talk to her."

Slowly, I nod. "That makes sense."

"And trust her. If she's as good as he says she is, do what she says to do."

"Probably—"

"June. He trusts her. You should, too. Right?"

I sigh, unsure of what to say. How do I trust someone I don't know? "I'll try. Callie, I feel like I'm on the edge of something bad. Like one wrong step will ruin our lives forever."

She doesn't speak for a moment. "That's because it could."

Hearing that reality check is enough to send me spiraling again, and my eyes sting at the corners. "I'm not sure if that's what I needed to hear."

"Honey, I'm not going to lie to you. This is too big and important for fluffy best-friend nonsense. You deserve the cold, hard truth. Even if it's ugly."

I gulp down some of Cole's water to wash away the knot in my throat. The trouble is, it doesn't work. "Okay, tell me something good. I deserve some sugar with my medicine."

"Anderson obviously loves you."

"No shit. Something else."

"Daniel popped the question."

I want to react like a best friend should, but I can hardly muster the energy for it. "Congratulations!"

She covers the phone for a flash, but I hear a muffled, "Be there in a minute." When she comes back, her tone falls apologetic. "June, I am so sorry, but—"

"You need to go. It's fine. Thank you for taking some time for me today."

"Anytime. I mean it."

"Thanks again, Callie."

I make the call to Dana's office, and to my surprise, she's ready to see me now. Given how inconvenient that must be for her, I rush right over. Dana looks perfectly coifed, but upset. "I wish you two had told me everything when we met up before. I would be more prepared by now. You cannot keep hiding things from me, if you want my help."

"Hindsight, I guess. What do you think of his chances?"

Her brow lifts. "It's a murder trial, June. There's really only two ways this goes, and one of them isn't good."

"I'm aware, Dana. What I mean is, do you think he'll get off?"

"You're a tax attorney, right?"

I nod.

"In criminal law, Anderson looks like every guy a jury hates but usually caves to. White, tall, handsome, rich. He's well-known in the community, or rather, his family is. In most situations, all those factors confer privilege."

I gulp. "Most?"

She taps her shining fingernail on her desk before she speaks. "In criminal trials, those things often work in someone's favor, but in the past few years, juries have not been taking kindly to someone like him. You need to brace yourself for a negative outcome … " She coaches me on what to wear and how to act. Then, Dana scrolls on her laptop. "If all goes well tomorrow, you may be taking him home for the time being. Bail will be high. The Wests being the Wests, everyone knows they could jump to a non-extradition country in no time." She levels a look at me. "Do not run out on bail and make me look like a fool."

"There's no way in hell we'd do that."

"Good." She returns to her computer screen. "Our prosecutor is Tanner Walsh, and he's an asshole. Don't expect anything good of that man. He's up for re-election, so he'll be out for blood. But for now, let's focus on the bail hearing."

I don't want to. But no one asked me what I want.

The next day in the courtroom, the courtroom itself is making me nervous. All wooden interior, big windows on one side, and packed full. Everyone wants to see a West on trial.

When Anderson is brought in, he's in a suit. He sits next to me for a few minutes, and neither of us knows what to say, so we stay quiet. He looks as somber and tired as I feel, and I'm worried about what's happened to him in jail. But if I ask, I'll break down right here and now.

The judge looks like every severe authority I've ever seen in my life. A white, balding, ancient man. A true grump. Lucky us.

The clerk announces the case number I'll have imprinted on my soul for eternity, then says, "The Commonwealth versus Anderson West. Murder in the first degree. Assault—"

"Waive reading, Judge Ackerman," Dana says as she stands up. Anderson joins her in front of the table, and Tanner, the prosecutor, follows their lead, standing in front of his.

The judge nods, and the clerk sits. "So noted, Ms. Horowitz. Mr. West, how do you plead?"

"Not guilty, your honor."

"I've seen the news. The charges are shocking."

"The most shocking part is how egregious they are," she counters. "But I shouldn't be surprised by that, given Tanner's looking to run his campaign on my client's back."

He acts surprised. "You just wait a minute here, Dana, I am interested in justice for Neil Johnson. As someone who took an oath to uphold the law, I won't stop until Neil Johnson can rest in peace."

"Did you practice that line in front of the mirror this morning?"

"Your client murdered an innocent—"

"Hold it right there, Mr. Walsh," Judge Ackerman jumps in. "This isn't trial. Watch your absolutes."

Tanner gives a deep, respectful nod as though the admonishment worked. But I see it in his eyes. He's just waiting to get another soundbite out.

"Your honor," Dana begins. "If you don't limit the news presence in this trial, this case will be nothing but Tanner's campaign speeches. I'm sure you don't want to give him that kind of free press at the expense of my client's future."

"I am the judge here, Ms. Horowitz. I make the rules in my courtroom. But like you, I do not favor cameras in a courtroom, so there will be none for the trial."

"Thank you, your honor."

Tanner says, "But the people have the right to know —"

"Enough, Mr. Walsh." The judge looks down his nose through his glasses at a stack of papers in front of him. "Now, on to bail. Mr. Walsh, what say you?"

"What happened to Mr. Johnson should be taken into account. The man was beaten to death, his body dumped like garbage. The act of an animal, not a man. The murderer who did such a thing should not receive bail."

Judge Ackerman arches a brow in annoyance. "Yes, and if we had a *convicted* murderer here, I might agree with you. We do not."

"That's right, your honor," Dana says swiftly, seeing an opportunity. "Mr. West is an upstanding member of the Boston community with deep ties throughout. He has no priors and is not a flight risk —"

Tanner laughs at that. "Your honor, we are talking about a man with a strong motive to commit a heinous crime and enough money to run away."

"Fair points, both of you." He flips a paper over,

moving on to the next one. "Bail is set at one million dollars." He knocks his gavel, and that's that.

59

ANDERSON

When we walk into our apartment, it's blessedly silent. We're both quiet. But when June leans on me at the doorway, I can tell she's feeling the way I do. Worn out. Humiliated. Horrified. I hold her tight to me, memorizing the feeling just in case I don't get to feel it much in the future. "I love you. Would you hate me if I said I wanted a shower?"

She quirks a confused look at me. "Why would I hate you for that?"

"It feels like I should be spending time with you instead. Just in case."

"Go shower. I'll order some delivery."

"Anything but sandwiches, please."

"You got it."

Feels like I'll never get jail off of me, no matter how hard I scrub. I didn't sleep much there. Couldn't. The others in holding acted like animals at night, hooting and picking fights and shouting at each other. The only peace I had was when someone asked me what I was in for. Turns out, they don't like to fuck around with murderers.

The shower must have lasted longer than I thought, because the food is already here when I get out. June's in her loungewear, portioning out rice. "I thought chicken and broccoli was about as far from sandwiches as we could get."

"Smells wonderful, thank you."

"Should we talk about everything?"

"Sure. What do you want to know?"

"How was it in jail?"

"Worse than you think, but not as bad as your imagination can get. I wasn't assaulted or anything like that, but being trapped with people who clearly have mental disorders and like to be noisy all night long is a lot. It's repugnant that people who need psychiatric care are locked in jail instead of a treatment facility. Not good for them or for anyone else."

She sighs. "Well, that's better than I expected. The prosecutor is confident about the case enough that he's using it to campaign. He wouldn't do that if he didn't think it was a slam dunk. They don't have video, or we'd know about that by now, right?"

"Right. Which leaves physical evidence or witnesses."

She blows out a breath, trying to steady herself. "I cannot imagine they have much in the way of physical evidence, considering his body was in the harbor for months."

I grit my jaw, now wanting to say the words. "And that leaves witnesses."

"I know Moss has been unfailingly loyal to you, but … do you think it's him?"

"No way. He knows the stakes. Even if it were him, he knows Dad would have him taken out for squealing. He's not that naïve."

"Then maybe one of my neighbors saw something and came forward."

That's the thing I've feared the most. "I think that's most likely. Depending on what part they caught the fight at, they'll either think he was a monster or I was. Assuming they are the prosecution's witness, it's the latter."

She takes a bite, staring at the screen. It's almost like she's purposefully not looking at me. "Except, if that's the case, Moss would be up on charges, too."

"How's that?"

"If a neighbor saw the end of the fight, they saw Moss helping us clean up, which means he'd be implicated. And to my knowledge, Moss hasn't been arrested."

A cold feeling settles over me. I hadn't considered that. "Fuck."

She sets her chopsticks down and takes a deep breath. "There's another witness in all of this, and I don't even want to bring it up, but we have to cover all of our bases —"

"Just say it."

"Your father."

I blink at her. "Huh?"

"Your father knows everything. Do you think there's a chance that he —"

"No."

Her brow bunches as she huffs. "Your father is —"

"No."

"Anderson!" She faces me, frustrated. "We have to consider every possibility, and I feel like I've been facing all of them alone. I am tired of feeling alone in this."

I don't want to do this. Things between me and Dad have been … well, not good exactly, but improving. The idea that he could be the witness … it's too cruel, even for him. "Even if he were spineless enough to do that, why would he throw us that reception?"

"To keep us from suspecting him until it was too late. He knows you have Moss in your pocket, and he would be smart to worry about you ordering Moss to kill him for ratting on you. If he kept us from suspecting him until it was too late, then he could jet off to someplace afterward and stay safe from Moss."

Well, shit. That's a good plan. But still, "I don't think he'd do anything like that to me."

"He's the reason you were shot, Anderson! Can you honestly tell me a little prison time is beneath him?"

The trouble is, I can't. As much as I don't think he'd do that to me, she's not wrong about him. He has put me in life-and-death scenarios more than once, and if it weren't for Moss, I'd have been dead. But still, this hurts. My voice goes hoarse when I scratch out, "Can you blame a guy for not wanting to think the worst of his own father?"

Her face softens, and she pulls me to her for a hug. "I'm sorry, baby. I don't like this either. Forget what I said, okay?"

The trouble is, I can't.

When we go to court, her words ring in my head. Could Dad be their star witness? I shake it off when I see him, Mom, and Cole in the courtroom. Can't be him.

I keep telling myself that. Thankfully, there are no cameras in the courtroom today, so it's less of a production than the bail hearing. We have enough stress without adding to it.

Not being a trial lawyer myself, I don't know if it's normal for Neil's employer to be called to the stand, but it feels inappropriate. Late fifties, too tan, teeth too bleached, and his navy suit is stuffy. He's sworn in, and Tanner tells him, "Please state your name for the court."

"Simon Connolly." When he says his own name, it comes out haughtily, as though everyone should already know who he is.

"Mr. Connolly, first let me say I am sorry for your loss. Can you tell us what your relationship with the victim was?"

"I was fortunate enough to employ Mr. Johnson."

"Objection," Dana says firmly.

"Grounds?" Judge Ackerman asks.

"Relevance. Mr. Connolly is a founding partner at Bryce-Connolly. Mr. Johnson was a junior hedge fund manager, so I doubt they were golf buddies."

Connolly shoots a scowl at her. "I did not know him personally, but—"

The judge sighs. "Objection sustained. Mr. Connolly, please step down. Mr. Walsh, call your next witness."

The next one is a little old lady with a handbag. *Crap.* Even I want to like her. She reminds me of my grandmother.

Once she's sworn in, Tanner says, "Please state your

name for the court and why we've called you here today."

"Mrs. Linda Jackson. I was Neil Johnson's neighbor for the few months he was in Boston."

"How did Mr. Johnson seem the few weeks before his murder?"

"He was in a good mood, singing to himself in the halls. He always did that when he met someone he liked."

Tanner asks, "Did you ever see the defendant's wife with Mr. Johnson?"

She squints at June. "Yes, I believe I did."

The courtroom murmurs gut me. There's no way she ever saw June with him. She never went to his place, according to her. I whisper as much to Dana, and she nods.

Tanner smirks at us. "Your witness."

Dana puts on a kind smile as she approaches the old lady. "Mrs. Jackson, did Mr. Johnson have a type?"

She nods, blushing. "He liked brunettes with small bosoms."

Dana pauses at that, gears turning. "Women like my client's wife?"

Again, she nods. June has big tits, so I'm confused.

Dana walks back to our table, standing beside it. Then she holds up four fingers. "How many fingers am I holding up?"

"Objection!" Tanner bolts out of his seat.

"Grounds?"

"Relevance!"

"Your honor," Dana begins. "I promise you, it will become relevant in a moment."

Ackerman sighs. "It better. I'll allow it. Mrs. Jackson, answer the question."

The old woman squints at Dana. "I'll need you to hold your hand still, young lady."

But she is. "I'll do my best. Go ahead."

"Two."

The jury and those of us who can see Dana stir. She sympathetically says, "Your vision is compromised, isn't it, Mrs. Jackson?"

"I see just fine, young lady," she says, growing cross. "You held up two fingers."

Dana sighs, walking up to the witness. "Mrs. Jackson, have you ever been diagnosed with a condition that might give you impaired vision or lead to confusion?"

"I want to speak to my lawyer!"

Judge Ackerman says, "Mrs. Jackson, you have to answer the question."

Her wrinkled face tightens. "I had an aneurysm two years ago, but the doctors say I'll be fine. I just need a little help sometimes."

Tanner tries to school his expression, but a muscle tics in his jaw upon hearing that. Either he didn't know, or he didn't want her condition to come out in court.

Dana says, "I'm sorry that happened to you, Mrs. Jackson. No further questions."

The rest of the day goes that way. Tanner puts up a witness, Dana strategically takes them down. A few days pass the same way, one bleeding into the next. I'm a little out of it when we're back in session the day June is supposed to take the stand. Funny. Every day until now has felt like an eternity. But today, it feels like I blink, and she's walking on shaking knees to the stand.

Tanner starts, "Mrs. West, or should I call you Ms. Devlin?"

"Either is fine, thank you."

"Is there a reason you won't officially take your husband's name?"

Oh, for fuck's sake, you misogynistic asshole.

"I am professionally known as June Devlin. Is there a reason you haven't taken your wife's name?"

That's my girl.

"I'll ask the questions, thank you. Please state for the record your relation to the victim."

"We went out a few times."

"While you were also dating the defendant, correct?"

The jury collectively arches a judgmental brow at her.

"No, that's not correct."

He frowns. "But you were dating Mr. West before you dated Mr. Johnson, isn't that right?"

"Yes, but—"

"And then shortly after he went missing, you were dating Mr. Anderson?"

"Yes."

I'd love to beat the smug look off his face. He sneers, "Ms. Devlin, when you date multiple men at the same time, are they aware of each other? Or would you describe yourself as a cheater?"

"Objection," Dana says. "Asked and answered. She clearly stated she didn't date them at the same time, but Mr. Walsh is making it sound like she did."

The judge gives her a sharp look. "Ms. Horowitz, the objection is sustained. Mr. Walsh, find a new line of questioning, or this witness goes to the defense."

"Ms. Devlin, tell us what happened the last night you saw Mr. Johnson."

Okay, here we go.

She says, "He hung out at my bartending job, then walked me home."

"Go on."

"That's it," she lies. "He left right after. I never saw him again."

"No further questions, your honor."

60

ANDERSON

"Mr. Walsh, call your next witness."

Tanner gives me a slight smile. "The prosecution calls Yuri Kravchenko, AKA Vittorio Mastriani, AKA Pierre Cassel, to the stand."

Who?

The rear doors open, and my heart stutters in my chest as Moss walks in. He avoids eye contact, staring ahead with a determination that frightens other people. I see it on their faces. But I know what that determination means in Moss' world.

He's doing something he doesn't want to do.

Betrayal is not a familiar feeling for me. I like Moss. Though, I suppose that should be past tense. But right now, I see a man bound by duty. He's protecting someone. Or maybe he's tired of being the bloody hand of rich men. But then, my pity dies as something clicks. He's the one who told us about the video. Was that real or a trap? My gut sinks with that realization.

Turns out, when you hide a body with a friend, you should hide two bodies.

After he's sworn in, Tanner asks, "Mr. Kravchenko, what moniker do most Bostonians know you by?"

"Moss."

"That's your business name?"

"Da."

"And please state for the court what business that is."

He clears his throat and leans to the microphone. "Break bones. Stab hands. Whatever it takes to make problem go away."

Tanner paces as he speaks. "Let me remind you that you are under oath. Have you ever killed in the line of duty?"

"Da. Before I come to this country, I help many people —governments mostly—deal with their problems. I fix."

"And you worked for Anderson West in this capacity?"

"Da."

"Did you kill Neil Johnson?"

He stares down at his hands. "No."

"Do you know who did?"

Moss' face goes paler than usual. "Da."

Tanner stands up tall, readying for a coup de gras. "Who murdered Neil Johnson, Mr. Kravchenko?"

Moss looks up at him. "No one."

Gasps all around, and my gut winds tight. *What is he trying to pull?*

Tanner looks pissed. "What did you say?"

"Murder means intent. No one intended to kill Mr. Johnson. It was accident."

The prosecution asks the judge, "Permission to treat Mr. Kravchenko as a hostile witness?"

"Granted."

"Mr. Kravchenko, who *killed* Mr. Johnson?"

He rasps out, "Anderson West."

Something in me hollows out.

"Tell us what happened the night Anderson West murdered Neil Johnson—"

"Objection!" Dana shouts over the din.

Judge Ackerman slams his gavel a few times. "Order! I will have order in my court!" After people quiet down, he says, "Sustained! Mr. Walsh, one more slip like that, and you will find yourself in contempt!"

"Apologies, your honor," he lies. Tanner looks at Moss. "Tell us what happened the night in question."

"Anderson call me, says he wants to go haddock fishing—"

"Please stick to the relevant parts of the night, Mr. Kravchenko."

"This is relevant. Fishing is when you hide body."

Tanner nods. "I see. Please go on."

"I meet him to pick up the haddock—the body—at June's apartment building lobby."

There are more murmurs, but people keep it quieter this time. No one wants to be kicked out.

"What did you see when you arrived?"

Moss sits back. His voice goes quiet. "June's neck was bruised, like when you strangle someone—"

"Objection!" Dana blasts. "How does this witness know what that looks like?"

He simply says, "Because I've strangled people to death."

Without another word, she sits down.

Tanner sneers. "Go on, Mr. Kravchenko."

"It broke my heart to see her that way. Anderson ... he had been in fight. Bloodied, bruised. Clothes torn."

"And Mr. Johnson?"

"Dead on floor."

"What condition was Mr. Johnson's body in when you arrived?"

"Beaten. Bloody." He shrugs.

Tanner asks, "What happened next?"

"I gave them tasks to hide evidence ..." He details everything we did that night.

I feel sick. I can't believe he's doing this to me. Some part of me wants to hang onto the idea that he's a good guy in an impossible position. But I'm just a guy he knows. His former boss. I thought we had a bond. I took a bullet for the man. Shouldn't that buy me some kind of loyalty? I feel like an idiot for thinking we were ever anything but employer and employee.

I was nothing but a job to him. This is one hell of a resignation letter.

Worst of all, Dad won't let this go. But I can't let him hurt Moss' family. No matter how this betrayal stings, I won't let Dad punish them.

Tanner Walsh glowers at Dana. "Your witness." Then he sits, looking so pleased with himself that I half expect him to pour a congratulatory martini right here and now.

Dana's words are clipped as she speaks. "Mr. Kravchenko, why are you testifying today?"

"I have no choice."

"And why is that?"

"My van was caught on cameras that night. A man at the dock saw us carry the haddock out. Either I testify with full immunity, or I go to prison." He bows his head, his tone apologetic. "I cannot go to prison ever again."

I guess that's something. I just hope it's enough to stop Dad from retaliating against him and his family. For that matter, I wonder if Dad's already texted someone to go after them. I have to intervene.

Moss betrayed me, but I won't let his family pay the price.

"No further questions, Mr. Kravchenko."

"You're free to go," Judge Ackerman says.

As Moss climbs down from the stand, he can't bring himself to look at us. Can't say I blame him. But Dad gets in his way. He doesn't say a word. He just looks him in the eye. Then he steps aside, letting Moss pass.

I definitely have to talk to Dad. And soon.

CHAPTER SIXTY-ONE-JUNE

ONCE THE FRONT door is closed, the first words he says are, "Pizza. Extra everything, the works. Let's be bad tonight." But it turns out neither of us is that hungry. Once the pie arrives, we just pick at it. "I'm glad I got Dad under control before we left."

"Do you really think he'd do something to Moss' family?"

"Da."

I shudder, hearing that. "Don't sound like that traitor."

"I don't want to believe he's a traitor, even now."

"I know we've been married for, like, five minutes at this point, and over the decades to come, you're going to get sick of me saying this, but I blame your father."

He frowns. "For Neil?"

"No, genius, for you wanting to see the best in Moss!"

"Why, exactly?"

"I think your dad has programmed you to be too forgiving, even when someone betrays you."

"My dad has never betrayed me."

"Bullshit!" I can't keep it in. The words just flow right out of me. "The first dirty job he sent you on, he sent you off against three armed men without giving you a gun or a clue! You could have died!"

Anderson takes my hand in his. "I'm beat. Can we go over Dad's sins another time?" He asks that like we have a future ahead of us.

But I can't pretend anymore. "What if there isn't another time?"

He leaps to his feet and pulls me into his arms, but I can't let him comfort me. I can't breathe. The walls are closing in, and I push him back. He looks so hurt, but there's nothing I can do.

I can't even speak. The room is spinning. I yank my shirt over my head before jerking my pajama bottoms off and running to the bedroom. I throw myself onto the bed and breathe into my pillow to stop hyperventilating.

"June, talk to me!"

But I can't. I look up at him, tears raining down my face, before burying myself into the pillow again.

His weight dips the bed next to me. "Do I need to call an ambulance?"

I shake my head no.

"Is it okay if I just lay here?"

I nod. It's not okay, but I don't want to hurt his feelings again. I force myself to put him out of my mind and focus only on my breathing. In. Out. Long in. Longer out. Nope. Not happening. I can barely hold still. I start hyperventilating, and I can't stop.

"June, baby, we're going to figure this out."

The words shred their way out of my throat. "You can't know that!"

"You're right. But does that make you feel any better?"

"None of this makes me feel better! Moss is a piece of shit coward!"

"I won't defend him. The betrayal … " He gulps, trying to hold back his emotions. "I haven't taken the stand yet, and honestly, him forcing the truth out might end up in our favor. He laid the groundwork for me to tell the truth from our point of view. I don't think the jury will convict me."

I stare at my beautiful husband. Even now, down and out and depleted from stress, he's still the most handsome man I've ever seen. "You pretty idiot."

He snorts a laugh. "Thanks."

"Do you honestly think that a man will get away with killing someone just because he put his hands on a woman? Do you understand that happens all the fucking time with no one giving a shit?"

"I'm well aware, June. You're not the only lawyer in the room."

"Maybe not, but I don't think you get it. You killed a man who was a smart, good-looking guy who worked hard, paid his taxes, and was friendly with the little old lady next door. You killed the perfect victim, Anderson."

He shrugs. "Then, I will go to prison with a smile on my face, knowing you're safe."

My voice shatters at the words, "How can I be safe if you're in prison?"

He pulls me to him, and I let him. The feel of his lips on mine is a comfort I didn't know I needed. I hate that I must taste like tears right now. But I open to him when his tongue presses against me there. As he sweeps in, I let myself get carried away by the sensation of him. Anderson gently pushes me back onto the bed.

But everything inside of me seizes. The panic tries to come back, and if it does, I'll lose it. I push him back. "I can't do this. I don't have it in me—I don't think I've ever been this sad in my life."

Quietly, he asks, "Can I hold you instead?"

I nod, and he spoons me, pulling the blanket over us. Anderson rubs my arm up and down like he doesn't want to stop touching me.

"Do you really think there's hope?"

"There's always hope." He answered too fast for my liking.

"I mean it. Don't just say what I want to hear."

My request gives him pause. "I want to believe there's hope. I don't know if that hope will pan out. But when it comes to you and me, I will always hold out hope for the best."

"I don't think I can do that."

"How come?"

"Hope can betray you. I'd rather have luck."

He huffs a laugh, blowing into my hair. "Yeah, we could use some luck."

Out of nowhere, a memory comes to mind. In law school, one of my professors used to say that if a client is depending on luck for their outcome, then cut them as fast as possible. Luck puts people in prison.

I fall asleep, praying Professor Jenkins was wrong.

61

ANDERSON

This morning, Dana tried to get me not to take the stand. She said it was foolish at this point, but I refused. However, she did talk me out of going with the truth. She said it's a bullshit Hail Mary play that only works in movies. "... refute his claims. Make him sound like a punch-drunk thug who is making up grandiose stories to get immunity for hauling a body away."

On the long walk to the witness stand, I take stock of everything I've done in my life. I've lied and cheated — of course, I have. I'm a lawyer. It comes with the territory. I know how to talk my way into and out of trouble. That's what I've always done.

I can do it now, too.

Tanner gets his chance after I'm sworn in. "Mr. West, you face very serious charges. Brave of you to show up since you could flee the country easily enough."

Dana starts to speak, but I wave her off. "Justice wouldn't be served that way." Suddenly, everything clicks. Why my family is almost exclusively lawyers? Why men like Neil get away with things? Why has Moss been backed into a corner?

Justice is broken. Someone has to fix it.

"Do I have it right that on the night in question, you stated that you —"

"I did it."

Every person in the room has a reaction, but it's June I can't look away from. I'd thought she might cry, but she stared back at me, utterly confused. Judge Ackerman pounds the gavel until people shut up. Tanner laughs, delighted he's going to win. "Mr. West, can you say that again?"

"You're looking for a murderer, but you won't find one. You're trying to paint me as the jealous ex or say that June was cheating on me. Neither is the case. I'll tell you want you want to hear, but I will tell it my way."

He smirks. "Go ahead."

"The night in question, I went to check up on June at her new job. But I saw another man walking her home. I thought once he left, I might get a chance to talk to her, so I followed along, call that what you will. Her apartment building's lobby has glass doors, so I saw them standing at the elevator. And that's when I saw Neil get out of hand with her. She pushed him back … " My throat goes dry at the memory. "He started to choke her. She tried to fight him off ... but he was stronger. I ran in, pulled him off of her. She fell to the floor ... " The words make me sick to my stomach.

The judge says, "Please continue."

"I fought Neil Johnson. She wouldn't be safe until he was neutralized — I knew that much. He gave almost as good as he got. A couple of times, I was on the ropes. When I shoved him back, I had no idea there was a stud in the wall behind him. He whacked his head on it ... what Moss said was right. It was an accident that happened during self-defense. I never wanted to kill anyone. But I will never let anything happen to the woman I love. Not if I can help it."

Tanner clenches his jaw. "And then you hid the body."

"I shouldn't have, but at that point, all I could think of was June."

"How's that?"

"I didn't want her name to be tied to that bastard every time someone looked her up. I didn't want her to have to go through any of this because some guy tried to kill her. When he strangled her, he threatened to have sex with her body, Mr. Walsh. She should not have to be reminded of that each time she meets someone new. She deserves a clean slate." I sigh at myself. "I thought by hiding the body, I was giving that to her. It was foolish of me, but I did it for love."

Tanner glares at me. "Convenient excuse."

"No part of this trial could be described as convenient, Mr. Walsh."

"Your little story sounds romantic enough, but the problem I'm having with it is the part when you said you were stalking your ex because, to me, that sounds more like a man who lost control when he saw his ex with another man."

"Neil Johnson is the one who lost control. Moss told you about the bruises on her neck—"

"The word of an admitted murderer is what you want to hang your freedom on?"

I laugh. "You're hanging your entire case on him, so which is it? He's trustworthy or not?"

Tanner grunts, "No further questions."

June is silent when I return to the defendant table. It's a good thing because closing arguments are up next, and I should pay attention to that. But it's hard.

I told the truth. Let the chips fall where they may.

I tune out Tanner's closing. It's a bunch of lies, making me sound unhinged and June sound slutty. But when Dana speaks, I try to listen. Still, I'm in and out, too shellshocked that it's all out there. I made the choice to tell and I don't regret that, but now I have to face the judgement of the jury. I hope it wasn't too little too late. Even if it was, Dana's one of the best. If anyone can turn things around, it's her.

"... newlyweds. And so I ask you, ladies and gentlemen of the jury, to fully grasp the concept of reasonable doubt. My client is here on first-degree murder. But the facts of the case do not warrant a first-degree murder charge. In fact, they warrant no charges. Mr. West acted in self-defense of Ms. Devlin, and even if you don't want to believe that in spite of Mr. Kravchenko's testimony, you must ask yourself this, can I, beyond all reasonable doubt, say this was first-degree murder? Can I separate two people who clearly love each other for the rest of their lives on a hunch?"

My body goes sick at the thought.

"The answer should be no. The law does not operate on hunches. It operates on facts, and the fact is that even the key witness for the prosecution brought up the bruises on Ms. Devlin's neck. *He* told you what happened was not murder. *My client* told you it was not murder. The only person in this room who thinks it was murder is Mr. Walsh, a man who needs a high-profile conviction for his re-election campaign. The prosecution could not establish beyond a reasonable doubt that my client intended to murder Mr. Johnson."

She pauses and falls quiet. Somber. "There was a fight. Mr. Johnson lost that fight after he tried to strangle Ms. Devlin. The loss of life is always tragic. I won't deny that. But a loss of life does not equal a murder. Justice means Mr. West goes free. The prosecution failed to prove their case beyond a reasonable doubt. That is the standard you must uphold. The standard of the law is reasonable doubt."

With that, she sits next to us. I don't know how her words affect the jury. They're inscrutable. The judge sends them out for deliberation, and court is adjourned. But when it gets late, the judge sends everyone home for the night.

June closes the door behind us and says, "I cannot believe you did that."

"Telling the truth is the only way out after Moss."

"You're being an idealist! I never —"

"Why are we lawyers, June?"

She blinks at me. "What?"

"If not justice, then why? The world needs to know what happened! They need to know Neil was a piece of shit who should be dead! They need to know I did the right thing!"

"I perjured myself for you! I put my neck on the line for you first, and you gave that pissant DA all the ammunition he needs to come after me next! You think you were protecting me by telling the truth? You damned me!" The muscles in her neck strain. She's pissed, and I get it, but she's overreacting.

"No, I didn't —"

She grunts at me, then heads for a bottle of whiskey, swigging from the bottle. "I cannot believe you are this fucking naïve!"

"He can't prosecute you!"

"The fuck he can't!"

But I almost smile. "If he prosecutes the woman who was attacked and nearly killed, he will tank his re-election chances straight into the toilet."

She starts to speak, but stops herself.

"Besides, you lied to protect your husband after your husband killed to protect you. If anything, we seem like a couple in love."

"As much as I'd love to believe anyone cares about that, I can't. You fucked us. We're both going to prison, so thanks for throwing yourself on your sword today. You're a real hero." She saunters to the bedroom, whiskey in hand, and slams the door.

If I chase after her, this is only going to get worse. She needs to cool off, which means, I am staying out here. I'll give her an hour. She'll come out and apologize soon. No big deal.

But the thing is, she doesn't. I don't hear a peep from her before bedtime.

Ah, well. Nothing like sleeping on the couch the night before you're going to lose your freedom. When I wake up, joints crack that I didn't know could crack. But I stretch and make coffee, seeing it's four in the morning. No wonder it's still dark out.

The machine beeps when it's done—I'd forgotten it does that. I hope it didn't wake June. But as I pour my cup, I hear the bedroom door open. "Sorry, I —"

She wraps her arms around me from behind. "I'm sorry, too."

I turn around to face her. She looks like she's been up all night. "I was apologizing about the machine beeping, but I'm sorry about everything else, too. I really got it in my head that ... well, what are we fighting for, if not justice? That's the whole point, isn't it?"

"I'm fighting for our freedom. Fuck justice."

I snort a laugh. "Coffee?"

"That's not a question."

I bob my head and pour her a cup, too. We sit at the table, kind of quiet. "Justice is the only real way we'll have any freedom, June. It's a gamble, sure, but—"

She laughs under her breath in response.

"But, it's true. Think about it—if we lied and hung Moss out to dry, we'd be looking over our shoulders forever. Either because of the law or because of Moss, because you know he has scary friends. Point is, we wouldn't actually be free. We'd be waiting for everything to fall apart." I sigh. "And I need the world to make sense again."

"What do you mean?"

"I need to believe there's justice in the world. I don't want to bring kids into a world where that's a punchline."

She murmurs, "Kids ... with me?"

The odd question makes me laugh. "Who else? My other wife?"

"You're not mad at me for last night?"

"June, it's amazing we haven't been at each other's throats before all of this. I'm not happy with some of what you said, but I'm not mad, either. We're under a shit ton of pressure right now. We're going to say things we shouldn't."

She sips her coffee. "Thank you for not holding it over me."

"If I get out of this, I look forward to some groveling."

She giggles at me. Fuck, I have missed that. "Deal."

"I hate to say anything that'll take that smile off your face, but in case this goes south, I want a nice long shower. Okay?"

"Enjoy. I need more caffeine."

I kiss her cheek on my way to the shower. In case this all goes sideways, I decide to spa things up. I light a few candles, turn on some relaxing music, and keep the lights low. Once the shower is nice and steamy, I close my eyes, letting the water run over me while I try not to think I've doomed us both.

A small hand snakes around my waist, and I almost jump. "What—"

"Hey."

Again, I turn to face her. She's beautiful and naked, and I know she's too sad for fun, but it's hard not to let my body respond at the sight of her. "You're very sneaky today."

"Last chance for sneakiness. Thought I'd take advantage of it." She presses her tits against my chest. "Thought I'd take advantage of you, too."

I laugh, shaking my head. "You can take whatever you want." I press a kiss to her lips, still willing my body to remain flaccid. She might take back what she just said at any moment and—

But then she strokes me to life, and all uncertainty dies.

I take her wrists and pin her to the hot shower wall, kissing her soft lips, her determined chin, and her delicate throat. I want to devour this woman's every inch. Her moans echo through the room. I nibble across her collarbone and to her tits, those glorious things. Licking up the valley between them, I take my time and enjoy the way she shudders from my touch. I love knowing the effect I have on June.

Come what may, this is what we're fighting for. I'll never stop.

I kneel in front of her, bringing a leg over my shoulder to open her up. Her gasps kick up when my tongue hits her clit. She's already wet for me. Her sweetness is all I need, and I drink from the source as she digs her nails into my scalp. My name and curse words are on her lips as she rocks against me. I love bringing her to the precipice.

But I love sending her over it more.

Just as I feel her pulse on my fingers, I stand up, hoisting her until she's stuck between me and the wall, her legs around my waist. I thrust home, and we both shake from the sensation. But then I am trapped in her stare. That dark intensity is all mine. I pump into her, and she rolls against me until we're moving in sync, puffing breaths and gasping for more. Heat surges through me when she cries out. Her pussy milks me, crashing me into my climax as I kiss her fiercely, ravenously.

As we clumsily pry apart, I pray this isn't the last morning that starts like this.

62

JUNE

"What do you mean they're still deliberating?" I squeak at Dana. We're in her office—it's the way we've started most days since the trial began.

She sighs. "Precisely what I said."

"Is that a good sign or a bad one?" Anderson asks.

"To be honest, at this point, I'm not sure anymore. But when I hear something, I'll call you."

"What do we do until then?"

Dana smiles at me like I'm simple. "You're newlyweds. I'm sure you can figure something out."

So, we do. For two days, we make love in every way we can imagine. I tweak my neck, and Anderson does something to his back, so by the time we're due back in court, we're both walking a little funny. Considering what we're facing, I hardly care anymore. How we walk now has no bearing on what the jury has already decided.

But Anderson has this unsettling resigned look in his eyes. It makes me wonder if all that talk about hope and justice was just talk. Maybe he's been saying those things to keep me calm. I hate that for him. He should be able to tell me his feelings, but if they're scary, he tries to keep them inside. It's something he would do for me. I know he would.

The sweet liar.

I take his hand in mine as we go in, and he gives me a sad smile when he looks down at me. Today is the day. We both know it. It's all or nothing.

Once we're seated, Judge Ackerman gives a come hither gesture, saying, "Councilors, approach."

That can't be normal, right?

The three of them confer with each other, and I look at Anderson. He had more criminal law classes than I did back in school, so maybe he knows what's happening. Only he looks as confused as I am.

No one on the jury will make eye contact with me. They only look at the judge. Except for the one guy who's been ogling the clerk this whole trial.

The lawyers are sent back to the tables, and I try to get a vibe off of Dana, but she obviously can't say anything. She doesn't even doodle on her notepad.

This can't be good.

The judge begins, "Madam foreperson, I understand deliberations have come to an uneasy conclusion."

"Your honor, we have not been able to reach a verdict."

What?

"Do you think further deliberations are necessary?"

"We are deadlocked, your honor."

Oh my god.

He nods at her, then looks at Anderson. "Given the jury is deadlocked, I have no choice but to declare a mistrial."

I'm shaking. What does that mean? My law degree is failing me right now.

"The prosecution retains the option to retry this case, Mr. West. But for the time being, you are free to go." He pops the gavel one last time, and all hell breaks loose in my head.

Elliot, Kitty, and Cole head for us, but I hardly notice them. Anderson hugs me tight, murmuring, "I can't believe it."

But I need answers and shrug him off. "Dana, what—"

"It's too tight between now and election season for Tanner to use you for his campaign, so if he wants you, he'll have to win his election, and given he doesn't have this case to run on … " She smirks, then nods toward the door.

I look through the crowd and see him barging into the hall like a raging bull. A laugh escapes me, and then I'm swept up in a hug from Kitty. She clasps my shoulders in her hands and looks me in the eyes. "Thank you, June."

"What? Why are you thanking me?"

"It takes a strong woman to handle this nightmare. Thank you for standing by my son."

"It's my honor."

Next, Elliot comes at me with a handshake, but he pulls me into a hug. It's robotic, but he manages. "You've done well."

High praise from him. "Thank you, Elliot."

"Let's celebrate," he says. "We'll go to the club, have some drinks—"

"Dad, if you don't mind, I'd rather not," Anderson says. "I appreciate the gesture of it, but after this circus, all I want is some quiet time with my wife. Maybe we can do the club this weekend."

To my surprise, Elliot smiles and nods. "Splendid. We'll get in a round of golf, then meet the ladies for drinks."

But my head is going to explode. "They said Tanner could come after Anderson later. Why aren't we focusing on that right now?"

Kitty sighs. "Sometimes, June, right now is all we have. You can't stop Tanner from doing what he's going to do. But you can enjoy today. You two, go on. I need a big, stiff drink and a year's worth of sleep."

When we part ways, things feel unfinished. But Kitty's right. I'm not going to snatch future problems from current victories. I'm going to enjoy my husband.

As a treat, I take him to the Ritz. Once we're in our suite—the same one we were in last time—he asks, "So, why here?"

"Our apartment building has been swarmed by reporters for weeks now, and I'm just done dealing with them for today. They're all going to want some of your time, and well ... " I step forward and kiss him. "I want all of your time. Consider it a sort of honeymoon."

He loosens his tie. "I owe you one of those, don't I?"

"Mm, hmm."

He smirks, looking me up and down in my earth-tone suit. "Not exactly the honeymoon clothes I was expecting for my wife."

I snort a laugh. "Nor is this the destination honeymoon I've always dreamed of, but I'll take what I can get."

"I thought you said you didn't dream of a wedding when you were a little girl."

Chuckling, I admit, "I didn't. But the honeymoon always sounded like way more fun. In my mind, a wedding was a big, stuffy affair with uncomfortable clothes. But a vacation without my parents? That sounded magical."

He laughs and takes my hand, leading me from the foyer. "This way, Mrs. West."

"Where are we going, Mr. West?"

"To the bedroom, where we will order far too much room service, some clothes to be delivered, and have some peace and quiet."

"Oooh, I'll race you there."

But the second I take a step to run, he swoops me up into his arms. "No racing."

"What are you doing?"

"I didn't get to carry my wife over the threshold, so this will have to do." He carts me through the bedroom doorway and lays me on the bed. Then he winces, "Should not have done that after what we did to my back yesterday."

"Oh, honey, are you okay?"

He laughs at himself. "I'll be fine, but I'm adding in-room massages to the list of things we're ordering in here."

"Yes!" I groan at the thought.

He makes some calls for the food and massage, and then one to a delivery service I didn't know existed so we have more clothes to wear since we didn't go home and pack. He gives them our sizes and some preferences, and that's it. By the time he's off the phone with everyone, the food arrives.

I hadn't paid attention, so I'm a little surprised when three carts of food roll in. "This is excessive."

He grins. "I know."

We dive into the food, everything from abalone to a baked ziti so good I want to cry. I'm stretched out on the bed by the time we finish, and I'm convinced I'm going to give birth to a ziti baby. "This is why you ordered the massages for later, isn't it? Give us time to digest?"

He's equally beached next to me. "Yep."

Our clothing delivery comes, and I'm shocked by how well they did. But I cringe at the thought of putting on anything with a waist. Going through the pile, I sigh. "I'll stick with the robe for now, thanks."

"Yeah, I didn't think about that part of it," he says. Then he motions for me to come sit on his lap, and I'm only too happy to do so. "There are too many things on my mind right now."

"We really dodged a bullet for the time being—"

"Not that. Or rather, not only that." He brushes my curls back from my face, pinning one behind my ear. "Everything we've been through has shown me it's foolish to postpone happiness."

"I completely agree. Maybe we can look at honeymoons and book one?"

He smiles. "We can do that. But that's not what I meant."

"What did you mean?"

Anderson takes a breath, like he needs it for courage. After today, I cannot imagine what he needs courage for, so I'm a little nervous. He licks his bottom lip and looks into my eyes. "I want to have a baby with you."

"Well, yeah, I mean, we've talked about having kids—"

"Not in the future. Right now."

A nervous laugh escapes me. "I'm not pregnant, so we can't have one right now."

"Funny," he says wryly. He holds me tighter. "I want to start trying. Now."

All the blood rushes through me, unsure where to settle. "*Now*, now?"

"Yes."

"Um, maybe the most important decision of our lives shouldn't be made today—"

"On the contrary, I think it's the perfect day.

There's a nice symmetry to it, don't you think?"

My heart tugs in my chest. I've wanted this for so long. But I need to know he's not making an emotional choice that will haunt him in the future. I take his face in my hands. "You're actually sure about this? No hesitation, no questions on the inside, no—"

He kisses me, rolling me onto my back on the bed. Hovering over me, he says, "Mrs. West, I want to have your babies."

I snort a laugh at him. "If you think it works that way, we have more pressing concerns."

He grins at me, and my heart swells. "June, I want to have babies with you. As many as you want. All you have to do is say yes."

I bite my lip, not knowing what to say. It feels like a huge step. Because it is. But also because the future is so uncertain right now. We could be at trial again next year.

Maybe he is being emotional. Is that so bad? Hell, if he weren't emotional after today, I'd be worried. Still, I don't want him to regret the decision. I should say no. Or not no, but later.

Or something else could go wrong. But what if it went right?

I'm halfway between decisions, but he needs an answer. "Mr. West, I —"

Someone knocks at the door, and he grunts, "Who the hell —"

"The massages." I move to get up.

But he keeps me pinned. "Fuck them. I want an answer."

Seeing that hope in his eyes again is all I really needed. I want that quality in our kids. I'm too negative. I need his positivity to balance me out. That's what makes us such a good team.

That's what will make us such good parents. "Yes."

"Really?" he asks.

"Yes, Mr. West, I'll let you have my babies."

He laughs and kisses me within an inch of my life. The massages are wonderful and last way too long. My mind isn't on relaxation. It's on baby making. When Anderson closes the door behind the massage therapists, I can tell by the look in his eyes that's where he's at, too.

The future isn't certain. It never is. But for now, there's hope.

ABOUT CHARLOTTE BYRD

Charlotte Byrd is the bestselling author of romantic suspense novels. She has sold over 1.5 Million books and has been translated into five languages.

She lives near Palm Springs, California with her husband, son, a toy Australian Shepherd and a Ragdoll cat. Charlotte is addicted to books and Netflix and she loves hot weather and crystal blue water.

Write her here:

charlotte@charlotte-byrd.com

Check out her books here:

www.charlotte-byrd.com

Connect with her here:

www.tiktok.com/charlottebyrdbooks

www.facebook.com/charlottebyrdbooks

www.instagram.com/charlottebyrdbooks

Want to hear about new releases, free books and get exclusive giveaways?

Sign up for my newsletter!

Sign up for my newsletter: https://www.subscribepage.com/byrdVIPList

Join my Facebook Group: https://www.facebook.com/groups/276340079439433/

Bonus Points: Follow me on BookBub and Goodreads!

amazon.com/Charlotte-Byrd/e/B013MN45Q6

facebook.com/charlottebyrdbooks

tiktok.com/charlottebyrdbooks

bookbub.com/profile/charlotte-byrd

instagram.com/charlottebyrdbooks

x.com/byrdauthor

ALSO BY CHARLOTTE BYRD

All books are available at ALL major retailers! If you can't find it, please email me at charlotte@ charlotte-byrd.com

Highest Bidder Series
Highest Bidder
Bidding War
Winning Bid

Hockey Why Choose
One Pucking Night (Novella)
Kiss and Puck
Pucking Disaster
Puck Me
Puck It

Tell me Series
Tell Me to Stop
Tell Me to Go

Tell Me to Stay
Tell Me to Run
Tell Me to Fight
Tell Me to Lie

Tell Me to Stop Box Set Books 1-6

Black Series
Black Edge
Black Rules
Black Bounds
Black Contract
Black Limit

Black Edge Box Set Books 1-5

Dark Intentions Series
Dark Intentions
Dark Redemption
Dark Sins
Dark Temptations
<u>Dark Inheritance</u>

Dark Intentions Box Set Books 1-5

Tangled Series
Tangled up in Ice
Tangled up in Pain
Tangled up in Lace
Tangled up in Hate
Tangled up in Love

Tangled up in Ice Box Set Books 1-5

The Perfect Stranger Series
The Perfect Stranger
The Perfect Cover
The Perfect Lie
The Perfect Life
The Perfect Getaway

The Perfect Stranger Box Set Books 1-5

Wedlocked Trilogy
Dangerous Engagement
Lethal Wedding
Fatal Wedding

Dangerous Engagement Box Set Books 1-3

Lavish Trilogy
Lavish Lies
Lavish Betrayal
Lavish Obsession

Lavish Lies Box Set Books 1-3

Somerset Harbor
Hate Mate (Cargill Brothers 1)
Best Laid Plans (Cargill Brothers 2)
Picture Perfect (Cargill Brothers 3)
Always Never (Cargill Brothers 4)
Kiss Me Again (Macmillan Brothers 1)
Say You'll Stay (Macmillan Brothers 2)

Never Let Go (Macmillan Brothers 3)
Keep Me Close (Macmillan Brothers 4)

All the Lies Series
All the Lies
All the Secrets
All the Doubts

All the Lies Box Set Books 1-3

Not into you Duet
Not into you
Still not into you

Standalone Novels
Dressing Mr. Dalton
Debt
Offer
Unknown

Made in the USA
Monee, IL
11 February 2025

12018656R00312